A COFFEE H
CONSPIRACY

CARL RICHARDSON

North Cumbria Imprint

Published by North Cumbria Imprint
Bourne Business Centre
Milbourne Street
Carlisle
CA2 5XF

First Published in Great Britain by North Cumbria Imprint 2006

ISBN 0-9537490-1-0 (ten digit)
978-0-9537490-1-0 (thirteen digit)

Printed by Reeds Printers, Southend Road, Penrith, CA11 8JH   01768 864214

Front cover: illustration by Willy Stöwer depicting the bombardment of Whitehaven by the U24

Author's note: the main characters in this novel are fictitious. Actions and words attributed in the novel to historical characters (the Fifth Earl of Lonsdale, Kaiser Wilhelm II, Kapitänleutnant Rudolf Schneider, Superintendent Thomas Hogg, Joseph Chisham) are entirely fictitious, for the purpose of the story only.

The graceful chestnut two-year-old thundered past the post in a flowing, rhythmic surge of motion and a spatter of clods of earth, the slight figure of its rider leaning almost horizontally alongside the outstretched neck, as they came home well ahead of the rest of the field. At least, they did so in the imagination of Edward Chisam, momentarily thrilled by the sight of the world's most beautiful animal doing what it was supremely adapted to do.

As the lone horse and rider cantered to a halt by the entrance to the paddock of an almost deserted Carlisle racecourse, the horse snorting and shaking its head, the rider, a capless boy in rough working clothes easing into a sitting position in the saddle, the three men who had stood watching broke the critical silence which they had maintained during the run, with exclamations of approval and delight, as if they had all been temporarily transported, like Edward Chisam, to the winner's enclosure at Ascot.

"I believe we have a winner here, my lord," said Chisam, turning to his neighbour. "Surely you agree?"

Hugh Cecil Lowther, fifth earl of Lonsdale, was a blunt, stocky man in his early fifties, with something of the carriage of a boxer, which indeed he was, among his many sporting pursuits. But if he was also a racing man, he was equally aware of the limitations of his judgement when it came to horses, such that he now never betted on the turf. Even so, when it came to training and running a thoroughbred, he always found it difficult to resist backing his fancy. His fancy was caught now.

"It certainly looks as if you may have," he agreed with Chisam. "I like the look of him. What d'ye call him, do you say?"

"Kerry Dancer, my lord. He's from Irish bloodstock." This was from Harold Tilberthwaite, the third man present. He was part owner of the horse, and a gentleman farmer of a thousand acres of the rolling Solway plain.

"Kerry Dancer. I like that. Indeed I do," said the earl. "I'd like to see him race, though, before I decide to buy him. Not all two-year-olds have enough stamina to be really good, even this far into the season. You can't always tell."

He viewed with some amusement the concern which had clouded the faces of the other two.

"Look, I'll tell you what," he said. "You put him in for the July Stakes at Newmarket, and if he makes a fair showing, I'll buy him. You know you won't get a better price from anyone else, come what may. Now, I can't say fairer than that. What do you say, gentlemen?"

Kerry Dancer did not disappoint them. He did not win the July Stakes, but by coming a promising second, he won the earl's approval It was a new experience for Chisam, who had never had much to do with racing before, to stand in the enclosure for placed horses as one of the owners, looking down at the horse - his horse, he thought with a touch of pride: the first emotion he had felt since that numbing moment shortly before, when Kerry Dancer had just been beaten to the post by half a length by the Irish mare now standing in the winner's enclosure. Steam was rising from Kerry Dancer's flanks as a blanket was draped over him. People were milling all around the horse, perfect strangers, or so it seemed, slapping the rider, a diminutive little man in a parti-coloured silk shirt and peaked cap, encouragingly on the back; more people were wandering up and down along the platform on which he was standing next to Tilberthwaite, who presumably knew what order, if any, reigned in all this confusion. Tilberthwaite had a long experience in the racing business, and ran his racing stables as he ran the rest of his farm, as a commercial enterprise. It was because he had been momentarily short of funds in his stables account that he had suggested to Chisam, whom he knew socially, that he might like to buy a half share in a new two-year-old. Chisam, who at the time was not short of funds, and who knew nothing about racing, allowed himself to be talked round.

Here came somebody who behaved as if he had a right to be there, even if he didn't look it - a big red-faced man in a crumpled black suit and a bowler hat, which looked as incongruous on him as the bowler hats worn by South American Indians. He began bellowing in a hoarse, incoherent voice to no particular purpose as far as Chisam could make out; but Tilberthwaite beside him gave a grunt of satisfaction, and bowler hat's purpose became clearer when a green silken sash was draped around Kerry Dancer's neck. It was the prize giving - £1500 for the winner, £500 for the second, and £250 for the third placed horses. That meant £250 for himself after splitting the prize money with Tilberthwaite. Together with the winnings from the modest bet he had placed just before the race, it made a very profitable afternoon's business. Almost enough to make one have second thoughts about selling the horse.

They met the earl, not as Chisam would have preferred, in the genteel and civilised atmosphere of the Rutland Arms hotel, which would probably have disapproved of horse trading being conducted on the premises, even by an earl, but in an insalubrious tavern which was reached by steps down from the street. The place was obviously the haunt of the racing fraternity - trainers, owners, jockeys - Chisam recognised Kerry Dancer's rider in company with two or three others who, from their slightness of build looked like fellow riders - as well as punters: the successful celebrating, the unsuccessful drowning their sorrows. Only the bookies seemed to be absent. Chisam supposed that they were at the Rutland Arms. The place was packed, the rest of the saloon being only slightly less crowded than the dense crush, five or six deep, against the bar. They found the earl sharing a table in a corner with a dapper little man wearing the regulation slouch hat and tweeds of all those connected with the racing business, who turned out to be the earl's racing manager. A couple of extra stools were found, and they got down to business, shouting at each other over the litter of tankards and glasses on the table, to make themselves heard above the general din.

Chisam left most of the talking to Tilberthwaite, who knew about such things. There was a lot of talk about pedigree, sires and dams, age and handicaps and distance. The earl's racing manager, an Irishman named O'Connor, was inclined to drive a harder bargain than the earl. The difference of opinion was initially as between six thousand pounds and four thousand, with the Irishman distinctly less inclined to come up to a happy medium than the earl.

"Patrick here thinks he isn't a stayer, so he'll be no good for the big races later on," confided the earl at length. "You must admit, that would take a fair bit off his price."

Tilberthwaite was quick to retort.

"Well, you've seen him in training at Carlisle, my lord, and I can vouch that he's fast over a mile, under one minute and forty seconds. I think he's got promise. Worth every penny of six thousand."

O'Connor looked sceptical.

"Ah, but it's different when it comes to the real thing. There's something about the atmosphere at a race meeting that brings out the best in every horse, and if a horse is a good stayer, then that's where it shows. If you have doubts about that in a horse, especially in a two-year-old, then you don't want to be paying over the odds for him, because it's money you'll not recoup." This last was for the earl's benefit. If the earl wanted to throw his money away, that was the earl's business, not Patrick O'Connor's.

"Well, I'd just as soon not sell him at all," said Chisam. "I must say, I took quite a fancy to him this afternoon, in addition to which he won me nearly three hundred pounds. If you don't believe in him, then I'll show you that I do."

Tilberthwaite was uncomfortable. He needed the sale to go through, and couldn't afford the deal to be lost through excessive haggling. But the earl merely laughed.

"My word, but you've been bitten, and no mistake. Indeed you have. Horse fancying's a terrible disease when it takes hold of you, and don't I know it. Three hundred pounds every Saturday afternoon! Eh? And how about it? Every Saturday?" He was genuinely amused, and laughed out loud as Chisam reddened with embarrassment. After catching his breath, the earl went on:

3

"I like your spirit, sir, but I'm afraid fortune would prove more fickle. To spare you a fate worse than death, I'll offer you five thousand five hundred. Now then, what do you say?"

Tilberthwaite was already extending his hand over the table to shake on it, as he kicked Chisam under the table. O'Connor winced and looked away. The fact that O'Connor quite fancied the horse himself was neither here nor there.

"Done," said Chisam, and they all shook on it.

The attention of a potboy was distracted to order another round of drinks, and when these arrived, they toasted each other and Kerry Dancer with the warm and rather flat ale.

"Dammit, I ought to be jealous, you know," exclaimed the earl. "You can spend thousands on the best bloodstock - hundred percent certified first class pedigree and all that, best training facilities, exorbitant bills from horse doctors and God knows what other quacks and hangers on - present company excepted, Patrick," he said in an aside "I know how much you felt that last fifteen hundred pounds just now. You can do all that, and yet you can still find yourself buying a promising animal from one of the small stables run on a shoestring."

"Not on a shoestring, my lord," replied Tilberthwaite, "on an overdraft at the bank. At least, until now. The problem when you're a small concern is that it's always more profitable in the short term to sell your best horses than to keep them, especially when your bank manager is as unenthusiastic about the turf as mine is."

"Well, if I can make it any more profitable for you, I'll be happy to oblige, especially if Kerry Dancer fulfils his promise. You've nothing else coming up I suppose?"

"No, my lord. We were lucky with Kerry Dancer, and in a way, I was as reluctant as Edward here to sell him. Horses like that are rare enough. At least my stables account is healthy enough now for the next horse to take my fancy. Investors will always be welcome, of course." This last was an aside to Chisam, ex-investor in Kerry Dancer.

"Indeed," agreed the earl, looking at Chisam. "And how's business these days?"

"Definitely looking up, my lord, if perhaps not for the most laudable reasons."

"How's that?"

"Well, the dock strikes have pushed the prices of commodities up handsomely, but since we're not so badly affected by the strikes in Whitehaven as in many of the other ports, we're getting the benefit."

"Yes, yes, I see what you mean. All the same, it was a damnable business in Liverpool so I hear, and I know a chappie who saw it first hand. A damnable business."

"They want shooting, the lot of them," retorted Tilberthwaite with some heat

4

"Damned communists and revolutionaries. If they had their way we'd be back in the dark ages practising all manner of unspeakable barbarities - universal idleness and poverty, the prostitution of all our wives and daughters, the beggary of all that's best in England, no privacy, no decency - no! We must meet them with the bayonet and the bullet wherever they show themselves - drive the sewer rats back into the sewers where they belong." He thumped the table to emphasise his points, startling the others, even the earl, who was already acquainted with Tilberthwaite's views.

"Er, yes, I'm sure you're right, Harold," said the earl doubtfully, "although I'm not sure I'd care to be a Liverpool docker all the same. It seems a pity that there can't be a more amicable way of settling such disagreements. Violence of that sort simply can't be countenanced."

"Indeed it can't, my lord. The dockers should remember that it's businessmen like Edward here who bring the trade that gives them employment in the first place. When we see behaviour like that in Liverpool, we take our business elsewhere, and then where are they? The prosperity of business is the prosperity of the nation, and they shouldn't forget it."

"Indeed not," said the earl, anxious to change the subject. He cared little for politics, and knew that once Tilberthwaite was astride his hobby horse, he was capable of going on for hours. "Indeed not. Speaking of prosperity," he went on, with that in his voice which indicated that there was to be a change of subject, "with there being so much prosperity around this table just at present, in one way and another, I thought you might like to cap today's success with something rather special. After all, I don't part with five and a half thousand every day, or buy horses like Kerry Dancer."

He had their attention now, even Tilberthwaite's.

"As you may know, His Majesty the German Emperor is coming to Lowther for the twelfth of August, and I'm giving a reception in his honour. I'm inviting a number of local people besides my usual guests, as His Majesty has expressed an interest in meeting some of the ordinary, decent folk who make up the backbone of an English county, and I'd like you both to come along."

Actually, His Majesty had expressed no such desire; but it had occurred to the earl that something of the sort might be called for on this occasion. Most of the earl's friends were sporting types who had little interest in politics, and would care less, even if the world was collapsing around them. With the recent bloody riots still fresh in people's memories, together with the excesses of the suffragettes, Lloyd George's and Asquith's attempts to reform the House of Lords, introduce a land tax and a super tax, give home rule to Ireland, and God knew what else, the members of the German party, mostly

5

Prussian aristocrats and military officers, whose vocabularies did not include words lik 'reform' or 'democracy', getting little reassurance about the state of England from th earl's regular guests, might suspect the worst. A liberal helping of Tilberthwaite' eighteenth century bigotry might do something to reassure them that all was not lost. H knew much less about Chisam. Indeed, he only knew Chisam through Tilberthwaite, an the business of buying the horse, Kerry Dancer. Tilberthwaite knew him socially. Th earl wasn't certain whether, in the absence of anything else, he would take that as a goo recommendation for a man. It would mean, if nothing else, that he wouldn't b embarrassingly eccentric. Tilberthwaite was too narrow-minded for that.

What he did know was reassuring rather than encouraging. Chisam was businessman, deputy manager of a trading company in Whitehaven importing coco coffee and tea. His family were evidently Tory - hence the connection with Tilberthwai - although these days, that didn't mean a lot. The earl reflected that his own family wer Tory, but it was a matter of little interest to him. Also, despite the fact that he was in th import trade, or perhaps even because of that, he had evidenced no particular prejudic against Germany, a prejudice which had been growing steadily in England of lat particularly since the accession of the present emperor. Since the Kaiser was a person friend of the earl's of long standing, this was a matter of some concern. This, togeth with the fact that Chisam seemed generally intelligent and presentable, and might pro an asset if Tilberthwaite should be more than usually tactless, confirmed the earl in h decision to invite him to the function.

Chisam and Tilberthwaite were expressing their appreciation of the invitation.

"D'ye shoot, man?" the earl asked of Chisam.

"A little, my lord, although I'm afraid that if I had the field to myself, the birds wou have little to fear."

"Well, come along anyway. You can put in some practice with the clays first. Sin we'll have the cream of the German army there, I don't suppose you'll be alone on th practice range. And you never know your luck - you might make a really worthwhi bag."

"Indeed, my lord, you never know your luck."

They ordered another round of drinks.

2

As with many of England's best and most impressive mediaeval castles, Lowther castle was built in the nineteenth century. Its towers and turrets, bastions and ramparts, recalling the grandest baronial style of the fourteenth century, were, nevertheless, a product of the railway age. There was no incongruity in this. The spirit which moved the builders of the great mediaeval castles and cathedrals was the same as that which moved the great nineteenth century railway engineers; which moved, for example, Isambard Kingdom Brunel to align the Box tunnel on the Great Western Railway so that the sun shone through it on the morning of his birthday.

Unfortunately, as an example of nineteenth century architectural revival, Lowther castle was, at best, only half finished. Its interior was as much a period piece as its exterior, having a lot more in common with the fourteenth century than the nineteenth, let alone the twentieth. Even Brunel would have insisted on gas lighting for all the principal rooms; but at Lowther, his lordship was still entirely reliant on candles. Only the principal rooms were furnished with fireplaces. The tiny garret room that had been assigned to Chisam contained a simple wooden box bed with a straw mattress, and a small bedside dresser. The window looked out over a splendid view of the eastern fells of the Lake District, but was not even graced with a curtain, and Chisam observed to himself that it would be an absolute purgatory in the winter.

Another factor that made itself felt at an early stage was the matter of protocol. It was apparently expected that all guests who were not of the Kaiser's party, or serving military officers, would be accompanied by their spouses. As an unmarried man, Chisam had been advised that his partner would have to be a blood relative - a sister or cousin. A mistress would be out of the question. Chisam had therefore invited his cousin Anne, who had accepted with alacrity. To attend a reception for a foreign emperor was more than she could resist. She lived near Sedbergh, and Chisam only saw her occasionally, and could not say he knew her very well. They would have to remember that they were supposed to be partners. Anne's room was on the floor below Chisam's. Her window had curtains, but from her description, that was about the only advantage she had over him.

The earl had not been there to greet the guests who were beginning to arrive at the castle. He was in London to meet the Kaiser's party and accompany them on the journey north. Alone, as it were, in a great house which was otherwise bustling with activity as the servants and staff prepared for the arrival of the illustrious and the famous, Chisam felt at rather a loss. He knew no-one and no-one knew him. His cousin Anne had at least found an old friend in the person of the wife of one of the other guests, and they were

renewing their acquaintance in one of the drawing rooms, while watching the arrival o
some of the other guests who were being conveyed from the railway station in one o
other of the earl's fleet of motor cars. Chisam did not particularly mind. He and Anne
did not have a lot in common, as is often the case with relatives who, while not complete
strangers, having known each other through the family for many years, live in entirel
different worlds, their minds and thoughts, their very language being shaped b
circumstances entirely alien to the other party, so that they have conversation enough
between them to do little more than exchange pleasantries about the weather. Anne wa
the daughter of a parson, and still lived with her mother and father in the village
parsonage where she had been born and brought up. At thirty five, she was something o
an old maid, and her world was made up entirely of the small, often petty, but intricate
gradations of rank and status, and the equally petty rivalries and jealousies among the
genteel folk of a country parish, which had changed little in such rural districts since
Jane Austen's day. For her to attend something like this, and meet not only an earl, bu
an emperor, even if he was the Kaiser, was almost the greatest honour she could aspire
to. For Anne, the event was pure bounty. Wild horses would not have kept her away
once invited.

For Chisam, the occasion was one which evinced more mixed feelings. The splendid
surroundings of the castle and its gardens and estates, the impending presence of nobilit
and royalty, touched him only peripherally. Apart from the fact that such accumulation
of wealth and rank in one place made them seem to Chisam slightly unreal, rather than
the embodiment of right and order, he knew, as Anne did not, that the real luxury wa
not the palatial buildings, estates and gardens, the servants and staff, or the fleet of moto
cars; it was the freedom which money brought. Money allowed one to indulge one'
whims, to order one's life as one chose rather than having it ordered for one by th
routine of daily employment. It allowed one to be a philosopher rather than a winner o
in the case of most mortals, merely a survivor in the daily round of mundane existence.
allowed one not merely to possess, but the leisure to appreciate the finer things of lif
whether horses or women, motor cars or old masters. Chisam had recently had his fir
real taste of this, and having tasted it once, he knew that it was definitely for him.

Edward Grant Chisam was deputy manager of the Whitehaven Cocoa and Coffe
House Company Limited, a post which he had held for the past ten years. The compan
was principally concerned with the importing of cocoa, coffee, sugar and tea from th
colonies. Most of the tea and the coffee beans were distributed to local retailers and th
catering trade; the cocoa beans, still requiring processing, were sent to cocoa an
chocolate manufacturers. A small quantity was retained for processing locally for th

8

company's own chain of coffee houses in Whitehaven and other towns of west Cumberland. A subsidiary company ran three more in Carlisle. From small beginnings in the middle of the nineteenth century the company had grown to quite a little empire. Edward's uncle, Joseph, who had joined the company as an office boy when aged fourteen, was now the manager of both the main company and the Carlisle subsidiary. Although not large by national standards, the company was prominent locally, and both Joseph and Edward Chisam were known and respected members of the business community in Cumberland and Westmorland.

Edward Chisam's own fortunes looked bright enough. As deputy manager, he had recently assumed full responsibility for the import business, which was the mainstay of the company. A particular innovation of his was the introduction of a system of futures in the company's cocoa imports. This was now moderately successful, and was to play a role in Chisam's life unforeseen at the time it was introduced. Its introduction had been the result of a particular weakness of Chisam's - backing a somewhat chancy venture with his own money. He had noticed that since shortly before the turn of the century, prices of soft commodities had been rising continuously, if not entirely steadily, and looked set to continue rising. He had proved the point to himself, and to the company, by buying a claim on several tons of unprocessed cocoa beans, holding these investments for one, two, and three, and up to six months, and then selling them at the then current market price at steadily increased profit over the months.

But if Chisam was an entrepreneur in the world of commerce, he was only at best partly one in spirit. He got no special pleasure in dealing in such commodities, as distinct from any other type of business; it was merely that the roulette wheel of chance had slotted him into this particular business at an early age, and determined that he should stay there, at least until now. He had no sense that he was where he was ordained to be in the world. Any view of the world that did not allow for aspirations to what might be, with a bit of luck or perseverance, Chisam found oppressive. If he envied the aristocracy the kind of wealth that he could see here at Lowther, it was not just because they possessed such wealth, but also because of what they chose to do with it. Edward Chisam was very much a denizen of half worlds - never fully belonging to the world he was in, and only very peripherally part of worlds he aspired to belong to.

Staring aimlessly out of one of the front windows of the castle, Chisam was relieved to see Tilberthwaite and his wife walking up to the front entrance. Tilberthwaite's company was not necessarily the most congenial he could think of, but it was certainly better than none. Tilberthwaite had brought a spare twelve bore with him in addition to his own, for Chisam's benefit, as this was an item which Chisam did not possess. Once Tilberthwaite and his wife had settled in, Tilberthwaite suggested to Chisam that they get a bit of shooting practice in with clays. After half an hour, Chisam felt dismayed that he had not managed to hit a single clay, whereas Tilberthwaite hit most of his. It was the crows and the rabbits on his farm, Tilberthwaite explained, that kept him in practice.

"I wouldn't worry too much. There'll be a lot like you, but no-one will notice much when you're in the line."

The following day, about lunchtime, the main party arrived. The bustling activity of the servants of the household reached its peak about mid-morning. From the kitchens came tantalising aromas: the activity there might only be guessed at. At twelve o'clock all activity ceased, and first the servants, then the guests assembled in two groups on the terrace on either side of the main entrance. Even a Knight Grand Commander of the Indian Empire was not allowed to remain skulking indoors while His Majesty the German Emperor was arriving.

The first of the motor cars to arrive from Penrith station contained not the Kaiser, but his bodyguard. Two large limousines disgorged a dozen officers of the Prussian Guard, in full dress uniform. They formed up in two lines, swords drawn and held at the present with their senior, a colonel, with a blond walrus moustache and a monocle, at the head of the left hand line. They stood in dead silence after the last order had been given to draw and present swords. Chisam watched with growing curiosity. So this was the Prussian army, undefeated and feared across continental Europe since the battle of Waterloo. Each of these men would be from aristocratic families, with histories going back perhaps to the Teutonic Knights; families of great wealth, owning huge tracts of land and thousands of peasants. Chisam looked at their faces - young and fresh for the most part, if a little heavy with too much good living, but marked far more noticeably with a natural arrogance than by the duelling scars which some of them bore. It was a rather chilling sight, offset only by their archaic dress uniforms, looking for all the world like the props from a comic opera.

Presently, the sound of horses' hooves and a carriage could be heard and after a moment, it came into view on the great sweep of driveway that led up to the main entrance. It came straight through the mock-mediaeval gateway and onto the terrace where all the people were assembled waiting. The carriage was an open landau, and contained two people: the earl and the Kaiser. The earl was in formal morning dress; the emperor was in military uniform. It was a moment of drama, occasioned by the presence of one of the great. Societies set some individuals up into positions so lofty, so far above their fellows, that they come to seem superhuman, to the extent that society comes to believe its own myths and stands in awe of them. Even Chisam was affected by the atmosphere as he watched the little ceremony unfold. A footman opened the carriage door, and the earl descended first so as to formally greet his guest. There was a hushed silence in which Chisam clearly heard the earl greeting the emperor as he climbed down. "I bid Your Majesty welcome to Lowther." He then repeated the greeting in German.

The Prussian Guard crashed to attention, and the Kaiser came forward with the earl, taking it all as no more than his due. The two walked side by side between the two rows of shining swords and up to the main entrance. All the servants gave deep bows or curtseys, and Chisam, to his alarm, found that all the guests among whom he was standing were doing likewise. Caught off balance, he bowed awkwardly, almost coming up too soon and giving the impression that he was not terribly keen on the idea, which indeed, he was not. It wasn't that he was a radical or a republican: it just seemed to him so un-English, even in an age when every humble villager was expected to touch his cap to the local vicar or squire. He hoped that no-one had noticed his gaucherie. He could not see Anne - she was just behind him - but he could imagine how she had curtseyed.

With all the bowing and scraping, Chisam had missed the moment when the Kaiser had passed closest to him, and so had had only the briefest glimpse of the second most powerful man in the world.

The landau had moved away, and more motor cars were arriving. The servants remained, but Chisam's party at least could now go indoors on the heels of the latest batch of guests, which evidently included a contingent from the German navy, since some of them were in uniform. The Prussian Guard had clumped indoors on the heels of the Kaiser - apparently, their navy was not worth standing guard for.

The ball which was to be held that evening was the main event of the Kaiser's visit to Lowther. The guests were given the whole afternoon to prepare for it. For many of the women, even this was scarcely enough, such was the nature of their costume, or their vanity, or both. Chisam, not so encumbered, was able to spend time wandering around the castle grounds, which included gardens and a park. It was pleasant strolling in the warm August sunshine, with no responsibilities or deadlines to worry about for the present. He thought about Stella, and how nice it would have been to have her here. When he had told her about the invitation, she had understood about the protocol. But she would have liked to have come all the same. Life always seemed so complicated.

At length, he came upon a large ornamental fountain in the centre of a circular pond, which was shallow enough to see the goldfish swimming about in it. The fountain was done in an elaborate 18th century baroque style, adorned with nubile nymphs and fat cherubs, each apparently caught and frozen in a moment of sublime emotion, with dramatically outflung arms, lips parted in joy or surprise, and sightless eyes

11

contemplating the infinite. From the top of this edifice, from a spout held by a nymph, a fat jet of water was thrown forty or fifty feet up into the air, cascading down as soft rain onto the surface of the pond. It was restful watching the cascading water, and Chisam fell into a reverie contemplating it. Although it was entirely appropriate that a stately home should have a splendid fountain in its grounds, Lowther was more than a little primitive as stately homes went, and the fountain stood out in that respect as something exceptional. Its rococo excess made him think of Vienna, as of a place of middle European intrigue and decadence.

"Rather impressive, what?"

The unusual combination of a rather gravelly voice with a cut-glass accent startled Chisam out of his reveries. The owner of the voice was a man of about his own age or a little older. The face was fleshy and heavily marked with over-much good living. The expensively tailored and immaculate dark grey morning suit, the monocle wedged under a bushy eyebrow and the accent all warned Chisam that this must be one of the earl's aristocratic friends, which presented a problem of how he should couch his reply. Etiquette might demand certain forms of address; but on the other hand, Chisam had no idea who the man was. He had certainly spoken out of courtesy, for the path on which they stood was narrow, and Chisam had been blocking it; but rather than asking him to stand aside, the man had casually opened a conversation as a way of announcing his presence. Chisam, standing aside for him to pass, made a suitable reply; but the man seemed inclined to linger for a few moments to watch the fountain with him.

"I've got a water garden at my country place in Surrey," he said. "I keep meaning to put a fountain in - something like this, perhaps - and I always come here to have a look at Hughie's every time he invites me up. Give me some ideas."

He paused, turning to look at Chisam.

"I don't believe we've met. I'm afraid I don't know your face."

Strangely, Chisam felt rather more embarrassed than if the stranger had asked him in plain English who the devil he was, and what the devil he was doing there.

"I'm afraid his lordship only invited me here because I managed to sell him a horse," he said cautiously, and went on to explain the business of Kerry Dancer. The other laughed, a sort of gravelly guffaw, at the mention of the horse's name.

"Kerry Dancer, you don't say. The July Stakes at Newmarket. I had thirty quid on that horse, each way. Won me a nice little packet. Keep me in brandy for a bit anyway. So that was your horse, was it? Are horses your business, then?"

"It's a business I've recently taken up," Chisam said, after a moment's pause.

Chisam afterwards could never quite explain, even to himself, why he lied as he did. I

12

might be that he really did feel 'bitten by the bug' of horse fancying, as the earl had put it; or perhaps he felt that, in this aristocratic society, where an interest in racing seemed part of the way of life, to be actively involved in it, rather than being a mere dabbler would make it easier to fit in with this particular social milieu. In any event, it seemed a harmless enough lie.

However, the other, who had introduced himself as Lord Hemswell, had not intended it as merely a casual question. He was a horse fancier himself it seemed, and, despite himself, Chisam found himself being drawn into a conversation about horses at some length. His own interest was aroused. He remembered how he had felt that day when he had stood in the winners' enclosure at Newmarket, looking down on a steaming Kerry Dancer being awarded second prize. He remembered the feel of the money in his hands. It was new money - not earned, not stolen, but placed suddenly into his hands as from no-where by Fortuna, the goddess of chance. He remembered it had been a good feeling. So he listened with increasing interest to what Lord Hemswell had to say. Lord Hemswell devoted a good deal of his time to the promotion of bloodstock. He had his own stables, and he described the process of grooming a new acquisition, perhaps with famous parents, to the moment of the first big win. It was a description by a man for whom horses and racing was a way of life, and nothing could make the description sound more attractive. Although Lord Hemswell described the business in a way which did not emphasise the fact that, like any other speculative business, it was a form of gambling, there was, nevertheless, an element of that in what made the sport so attractive. After he parted from Lord Hemswell, Chisam was very thoughtful for the rest of that afternoon.

3

The ball that evening was the most splendid event that Chisam had ever attended. The main dining room of the castle had been turned into a ballroom, with tables for the guests arranged around the edge, and a central space left for a dance floor. A small band of musicians was ensconced in a minstrels gallery which projected from one of the end walls. Although the tables ran continuously around the sides of the room, there was a discreet, but strict protocol about who sat where. At the tables at the head of the hall were the earl and the Kaiser and their immediate circles; below them the most senior aristocrats, which meant, among the German party, the Prussian Guard, who were all in full dress uniform, and their wives, those who had them, and among the English, the earl's closest friends. Chisam was interested to note that Lord Hemswell was not among these. He was at one of the tables further down, where, on the German side, were lower ranking army officers, or those from less prestigious regiments, and the naval officers, all of whom were in uniform, and some accompanied by their wives. Not many wives however, much to the pleasure of the women among the English party. At the bottom end of the room were those guests, like Chisam, invited from the local community. Not all those who sat at the top table were aristocrats, at least among the earl's circle. Chisam felt sure he recognised one or two of them from the Newmarket tavern where they had sold Kerry Dancer. There were hardly any Germans down at the bottom tables; and the Germans evidently segregated themselves by degree much more rigidly than the English.

After all the guests had entered the hall, everyone turned to watch the entrance of the earl and the Kaiser. The doors were thrown open, and the major-domo made the announcement.

"His Imperial Majesty the German Emperor; His Grace and Her Ladyship." The earl was accompanied by his wife; beside them walked the Kaiser, alone, since the Kaiserin had not come to Lowther on this occasion. The earl and his wife were in evening dress; the Kaiser was in military uniform. As they walked slowly towards the far end of the hall, the band broke into the national anthems, first the British, then the German. The Germans stood, if a little stiffly, for 'God Save The King', and the British remained standing, if a little stiffly, for 'Deutschland Über Alles'. Chisam's table was on the left hand side of the room, and as the Kaiser was walking to the left of the earl and his wife, he passed within a few feet of where Chisam stood, and for a few moments Chisam had a clear view of the emperor's face. He had seen pictures of the Kaiser in newspapers, and he recognised the same, rather disdainful aristocratic face. But now, in the flesh, Chisam was startled to notice what he took to be signs of weakness. The impression he had from ten seconds or so of gazing at the face of the emperor was that it was a weak face; the face of a man who lacked something one would expect in the leader of a great power. Perhaps the rather foppish moustache had something to do with it; but the pale blue eyes and the set of the mouth beneath the moustache spoke of fickle indecision. The thought that on the mere word of this man, the heir of Blücher and Bismarck, the whole of Europe could be plunged into war, Chisam found disquieting.

The evening's entertainment was divided between the main hall or ballroom, and an adjoining room which was doing service as a buffet lounge. After giving the first dance to Anne, then taking the second with Mary, Tilberthwaite's wife, while Tilberthwaite danced with Anne, Chisam and Tilberthwaite found themselves at a loose end, since there were more men than women at the ball, and both Anne and Mary went off in search of more illustrious partners. As with many of the women from among the invited guests, they were determined to have danced with an aristocrat of either nationality before the evening was out. Together, they reviewed what scraps of German they had between them, which was not a great deal. Although nothing had been said about the matter, there was a sort of tacit understanding that class distinctions would operate on the dance floor. The earl danced with his wife, the wives of some of his close friends, and the wives of one or two of the most senior of the German party. The Kaiser did likewise. None of the hoi polloi attempted to ask Lady Lonsdale for a dance, and the fact that each group tended to keep to its section of the floor helped to minimise the risk of such unfortunate mistakes. On the other hand, it was not considered unacceptable for unattached aristocrats of either nationality to approach a pretty woman for a dance whatever her social class, and it was on this that Anne and Mary and other women from their group mainly based their hopes.

Chisam and Tilberthwaite, thus abandoned, returned to the buffet lounge, where they were agreeably surprised to find how freely expensive champagne and wines flowed to help wash down the cold salmon salad. It was here that Lord Hemswell found them. Their conversation turned naturally to horses.

"You know, it's a very satisfying feeling," Tilberthwaite munched through a mouthful of salmon, "when your judgement about a horse has paid off, and you've got money in the bank to prove it. You see a horse, and you like the look of him - he's got good points, carries himself well, good pedigree, promising form ; and you grab him - and it pays off." He proceeded to tell the stories of his recent successes, including his most recent, Kerry Dancer, which Lord Hemswell had already heard about from Chisam. Tilberthwaite had had rather more to drink than was good for him. Chisam was embarrassed, but Lord Hemswell evidently was not.

15

"But surely," said Lord Hemswell "is it not just as much a pleasure to nurture an animal which does not do well on the field, at least in terms of prize money, and yet which you can see has got character and qualities which you cannot but admire. You know that the animal is first class, but for one reason or another has had bad luck. But you persist with him because you know that, given time and fortune, he will be able to repay your patience."

Tilberthwaite admitted that he couldn't see it. Either a horse paid or it didn't. You had to look at it strictly as a business proposition. Lord Hemswell persisted, however.

"The principle applies more widely, I think. For example, supposing you had a son who, although you knew him to have good qualities, did not do well through ill fortune or naivety about the ways of the world. You would not, surely, cut him off without a penny when you knew he was not a bad sort, and was at least trying his best. You would at least give him time and encouragement."

Tilberthwaite shook his head. "I cannot agree with you at all. I would certainly not be so indulgent towards any son of mine. A father has a right to expect his son to follow in his footsteps, and with the example of his father before him, a son has no excuse for not doing at least as well. A son must prove his manhood by the time he reaches the age of manhood; otherwise, you know he's going to be no good. Such offspring bring shame on their fathers and their family, and there is no choice but to disown them. This is entirely different from what we were speaking about just now. This is a family matter, a matter of family pride. Horses are about business, and while there's no room for emotion in business in my view, it's on a different level. If a horse doesn't pay, you get rid of it in exactly the same way as you would any other part of your business which didn't pay. That's not pride, it's just business sense."

"I can't comment from experience about sons," said Chisam, "not having any of my own. But I can't accept that there aren't at least some businesses in which an emotional involvement is the only way of truly understanding the nature of the business."

"You sound like a man after my own heart, sir," said Lord Hemswell. He continued, looking at Tilberthwaite "I am not sure if I would be able to measure up to being a son of yours, sir, meaning no disrespect; but in the matter of business, I have long felt that there are two approaches to the turf - the strictly business approach, and what one might call the romantic approach. The business approach is, at its best, sound commercial practice, and someone who runs a stable that way is to be admired." This for Tilberthwaite's benefit.

"At its worst, it becomes mere grasping avarice - beneath the dignity of a gentleman. You see it in bookies, for example," he added reflectively, as if the thought had just occurred to him.

"The romantic approach is subtly different. You approach the matter, not from the point of view of simply making a profit in the short term, transaction by transaction, but of having an eye, a sort of sixth sense, or intuition if you will, for quality, even if that quality has not yet demonstrated itself in terms of performance. It's more of a risk than a straightforward commercial transaction because your emotion or your intuition is involved. It's more than just a question of assessing past form and measuring the points and dimensions of a beast - it's something intangible and immeasurable, and it's exciting because it's something only you know about - it's your hunch, and the risk is in backing your hunch. You only have to remember that quality pays in the end."

Tilberthwaite made noises of disagreement, muffled to inaudibility behind salmon salad. Chisam was about to respond, when there was a small commotion in the entranceway to the buffet lounge which communicated with the ballroom. A number of people were coming in from the ballroom, bringing with them an atmosphere of tension or expectancy from something which was happening in the ballroom. Most of the newcomers were German officers, from both services, but there were also some English, including two or three women. The women seemed to be scandalised by something - one could tell from their manner without hearing their words. Their men, on the other hand, seemed more amused than scandalised. One of the German naval officers, catching sight of Chisam, called out to the others and pointed. They made their way over and gathered round Chisam's group, and Chisam was embarrassed when he realised that it was he himself who was evidently the centre of attention. The newcomers were all naval officers, and they continued their conversation as they surrounded Chisam's group. One of them, seeing Chisam's evident bewilderment, helpfully explained.

"Ihre Frau hat viel Glück am Tanz, nicht wahr?" which provoked a chorus of guffaws.

Chisam had little or no German, but he had an uncomfortable suspicion that he knew what the man was talking about.

"I'd better go and see what this is all about," he said to Tilberthwaite and Lord Hemswell. Tilberthwaite followed him into the ballroom. It was immediately clear what the commotion was about. Anne had scored. Of that there was no doubt whatsoever. She was at the wrong end of the room - most of those at the bottom end of the hall, where she ought to have been had stopped dancing and were gazing at her with emotions that seemed to range from admiration to horror; those at the top end of the hall were continuing to dance as though nothing were amiss. Anne herself appeared somewhat dazed and pale faced as she whirled round in the arms of her partner, who was - Chisam had to blink and look twice to confirm what he saw - the Kaiser. Chisam and

Tilberthwaite could only stare, speechless with dismay. They could get thrown out for this. There could hardly be a greater social gaffe, a larger enormity which could be committed by such lowly guests as themselves. There was no sign of the earl, when Chisam permitted himself to glance away from the enthralling spectacle of Anne and the Kaiser dancing together. Perhaps the earl was organising servants to have them dismissed from the hall and driven at once to the station, or perhaps even escorted unceremoniously to the front gate.

They were joined by Lord Hemswell (which, Chisam realised later, must have been a good indication that they were not likely to be unceremoniously evicted), and by some of the German officers, and they all stood watching. The orchestra played the last few bars of the waltz, ending with a flourish, and the ill-matched couple brought their pirouetting to an end with a deep curtsey from Anne; the Kaiser, whose ears had gone distinctly pink, either from anger or embarrassment, inclined stiffly forward from the waist ever so slightly, in the bare minimum of acknowledgement. They parted, and returned to their rightful ends of the room, Anne being escorted by Mary Tilberthwaite, whose envy was plain to see on her face. Chisam had no immediate opportunity to ask Anne how she had managed to achieve such a violation of what was right and proper, because on reaching them, she collapsed into a chair and passed out. Mary Tilberthwaite, still envious, fanned at her ineffectually. Mary was not much more forthcoming at first about what had happened, but by degrees they got the story from her. They had been bolder than most of their class in edging their way up the hall to where the most eligible catches were dancing.

Quite unexpectedly, according to Mary, the Kaiser had appeared. Anne had been standing next to a titled lady from the earl's immediate circle, and when the Kaiser had said, apparently to this lady: "Wurden Sie mögen tanzen?" the lady, who evidently knew no German at all, seemed either not to understand, or not to realise that the Kaiser was addressing her. She had made the mistake of looking at Anne next to her, perhaps thinking that the Kaiser was admonishing this upstart commoner for being so far up the ballroom. To her and everyone else's astonishment, including the Kaiser's, Anne, who had understood the emperor's words, and evidently deciding to seize her chance, gave the deep curtsey which was the customary way of accepting an offer to dance, and stepped forward. The Kaiser, completely nonplussed for the moment, could not then refuse her without displaying very bad manners, even though Anne was a commoner. A bolder man might have done it, but not, apparently, at that moment, His Imperial Majesty the Emperor of Germany. Stiffly accepting what seemed inevitable, he had accepted Anne's hand.

18

Chisam was still looking round apprehensively for the first signs of disapproval from his host. Would there be a painful interview with the earl first, or would some supercilious butler merely come to inform them that they were *personae non gratae*, and that a motor car was waiting to take them away? However, the minutes passed with no sign either of a summons or of a supercilious butler, and the dancing had meanwhile resumed. Chisam only gradually became aware of the rather strange atmosphere which now surrounded him as a result of Anne's exploit, although he had had no part in it himself. Some of the German navy was still standing in a little group nearby, occasionally casting him glances of quizzical amusement. The penny began to drop when Lord Hemswell, who had rejoined them again remarked:

"You two seem to have become the event of the evening. Everyone's talking about you, even the stuffier ones who disapproved with every fibre in their bodies."

It seemed to be true, especially when some of the German navy eventually came over and offered to buy all of Chisam's party drinks, including one for Anne, who was finally coming round again. And the earl had re-appeared at the top of the ballroom; while he could not, for obvious reasons, come down to Chisam's table to join in the growing sense of bonhomie there, it seemed at least that they were not going to be thrown out.

4

The following day, the twelfth, was a Saturday. The shooting party started out early afte a large breakfast which, Tilberthwaite assured Chisam, they would be grateful for by th time they came to eat the equally large packed lunch they would take with them in grea wickerwork hampers. Chisam was impressed by what could be done if you had enough servants - they must have been up half the night, although he supposed that the Kaise didn't stay every weekend. The fact that Chisam had not been excluded from th shooting party confirmed that he had not yet fallen from grace. He had not spoken to th earl, but the shooting party was a large one, including some of the ladies who were t come as spectators, generally of someone in particular, and he would not have expected to have done so anyway. Last night's incident was in the past - over and done with. Onl some of the notoriety remained - there were undoubtedly a few with a coarser sense o humour who were a little disappointed that Anne was not coming to ogle the Kaiser as h loosed off heroically at the grouse.

They started off a little after nine in a long convoy of motor cars. Apart from th members of the party, and a number of servants, the cars carried a large quantity o baggage. As well as the guns and shooting equipment, there were the hamper containing lunch, a marquee and a collection of parasols in case it became excessivel hot, or alternatively, started to rain, a croquet set and a lawn tennis set in case any of th party got tired of the main business of the day, a paraffin stove, iceboxes for th champagne, and a camera, complete with photographer to record the victoriou sportsmen with their day's bag.

It took the convoy more than an hour to reach Wemmergill Moor, where the shoot wa to take place. It was the first big shoot Chisam had ever been on, and he was struck b the complexity of the business, dictated in part by the sheer size of the area to be sho over. As they reached the moor, beaters and gamekeepers were dropped off at strategi intervals, to be in the right places when the shoot started. It was a bit like a militar operation, with the earl as general directing the battle order. Finally, the party split int two main groups: the earl and the Kaiser, with most of the senior guests, taking up wha the keepers had vouchsafed would be the best positions for the game; while the lesse guests were allotted rather less favourable positions a little farther down the moor.

They stood in a long line about ten yards apart. Tilberthwaite was on Chisam's righ and on his left was a German naval officer. It took a while to assemble the lines, with senior gamekeeper walking along the line to make sure everyone was in place before th signal was given for the beaters to begin. The shooting started slowly with a singl report from up the line among the earl's group, followed by a spatter of further shots. Chisam, craning his neck to see where the action was, missed the first birds over their section and was recalled with a start by the sound of a gun going off seemingly right in his ear. In fact it was Tilberthwaite, ten yards off, opening the honours for their section. The birds would appear suddenly, with most of them falling equally suddenly to the fire from the most skilled shooters along the line. Only the odd one or two made it to safety, flying over the heads of the shooters. It was two or three minutes before Chisam felt he had got the timing of it well enough to risk squeezing the trigger for the first time. The practice session of the previous day was only the second time he had ever used a shotgun, and for the first half hour or so, he was just getting used to the way the thing handled. After that, he still had problems with the timing of the shots: most of the birds which appeared had fallen to the fire of experienced shooters by the time Chisam pulled the trigger, which was embarrassing. If he fired too soon, it tended to make the birds scatter, much to the annoyance of the experienced shooters, which was also embarrassing. Eventually he got the hang of the timing sufficiently to be able to fire when the rest of the line did, in order to minimise embarrassment. It took most of his concentration to do this, so he didn't have much left to spare for anything else, like taking aim; but it meant that he managed to get through the morning without looking too much like a complete bungling amateur. As it happened, he wasn't the only amateur on the line; but by the time they broke for lunch, which Chisam found as welcome as Tilberthwaite had predicted, he thought it unlikely that he had brought down a single bird. But the lunch was excellent, washed down with crisp, fruity Rhine wines which had been brought by the German party, and kept cool in iceboxes.

It was shortly after they had resumed after lunch, having taken up new positions, that the incident occurred which started a chain of events that was to change Chisam's life. They had all just moved forward, and the line had become rather straggly. Chisam was a little farther forward than most of the rest, and the gamekeeper on that part of the line had evidently not noticed this to correct the irregularity. A covey of birds shot out of cover ahead and flew at the line a little to the right of Chisam, who was slow to fire. Not so slow, however, was the young man just beyond Tilberthwaite: missing with the first of his two barrels, he committed the cardinal sin on a shoot of swinging round towards the line to follow the birds in flight. They were flying very low, and Chisam, out in front, was suddenly in imminent danger. The German naval officer on his left had seen the danger coming and was quick-witted enough to act on it. Letting out a great shout, he bounded to his right and pulled Chisam to the ground. His shout had startled the young man as he was in the act of firing, and almost too late had caused him to pull the barrel

21

up an inch or two. Chisam felt the wind of the blast of shot passing inches over his head

The young man came hurrying over, profuse with apologies, with Tilberthwaite an some of the others on his heels. Chisam got up slowly, still feeling rather shocked. Th angry outburst at the young man, which was his first impulse, was left unsaid. Chisan was generally slow to anger, and the poor fellow was so obviously distressed at what ha happened, and full of apologies and remorse. It was his first shoot, and in the excitemer he had forgotten the rules. Chisam at length contented himself with the observation:

"Well, just think how you'd feel if you'd killed me, and let that be a reminder of th rules from now on. We'll say no more about it, as no harm's done."

The young man retired, crestfallen. It would be appreciated, and not just by him, tha Chisam would 'say no more about it'. Nevertheless, the incident would quickly becom generally known, and the young man might well not be invited to a shoot again as result, and he knew it.

The incident had caused a general pause in the shooting on their section of the line, bu when it was established that no-one had been hurt, people drifted back to their place again. Chisam, however, turned to thank the German naval officer, who had certainl saved his life. He felt a little awkward, as well as grateful.

"I hardly know what to say. How do you thank someone who has just saved your life And indeed, put his own life in danger in the process. I shall be ever in your debt, sir He stuck out a hand and introduced himself.

"Chisam. Edward Chisam. I am most grateful indeed, sir."

The German shook his hand, but as he remained silent, a thought struck Chisam.

"You do speak English, do you? I'm afraid I've no German."

The other laughed.

"Yes, Herr Chisam, I speak English quite well, even if I say so myself. In fact, I hav been using it to good effect of late. Your lady wife's conquest at the ball last night ha been the most interesting topic of conversation ever since. There are some mo extraordinary versions of what happened already being spoken of."

"Indeed," said Chisam with a smile, "then you must have heard one of them, for Ann is my cousin, not my wife."

"Ah, then you will not have been so jealous of our emperor as some have been sayin But - my apologies." He corrected himself, and completed the introductions.

"Seebohm. Fritz Seebohm. Kapitänleutnant."

He clicked his heels together and inclined forward from the waist in approved Germa manner as they shook hands.

"Perhaps we can adjourn until the next stand is made for a new drive, and drink to n very lucky escape with some of that excellent German wine," Chisam suggested. He felt a little dry in the throat, a reaction to the recent shock. It would be a little while before he would be able to hold a gun steady, and given his already poor aim, to carry on shooting just now would simply be a waste of cartridges.

"I was about to say so myself," replied Seebohm.

Leaving their guns with one of the bearers, they tramped over the springy heather to the small marquee that had been put up to house the refreshments. They were offered prawn cocktails and blue stilton, which went very well with the cool wine. There was also an assortment of sweet muffins. They stood at the entrance to the marquee, watching the progress of the shoot. Privately, Chisam was in any case glad of the break. He had already started to find the shoot somewhat tedious. Blasting away at the poor wretched birds as they were driven from cover was not really his idea of an enjoyable pastime, even if he was able to hit any of them.

Chisam asked Seebohm what the equivalent of a Kapitänleutnant was in the Royal Navy, and when Seebohm told him a Lieutenant-Commander, asked him if he had a command of his own. When Chisam expressed surprise when Seebohm said he had not (given that he was clearly not without influence in high places, to be included in the Kaiser's party), Seebohm laughed.

"I'm afraid I have not told you the whole story. I am of the naval reserve: my full rank is Kapitänleutnant der Reserve, and reserve officers, even favoured ones, are only rarely given commands, at least in peace time. However, if one is, as you put it, of the emperor's party, which I am more or less permanently, it is almost obligatory to be an officer in the armed forces; and since the army is still rather too much a Prussian institution for my liking - I am from the south myself, which is the only really civilised part of Germany - I chose the navy, and in particular, the naval reserve, so that the military side of my life is reduced to a minimum. You see, in real life, I am a businessman."

"Really," said Chisam, his interest aroused. "What line of business are you in?"

"Well, I suppose basically you would say it was confectionary, especially high quality chocolate - we even export to Switzerland - but also patisserie - I can't think of the English word - but fancy bread like lebkuche, gingerbread, you know, and also sugar, which I deal in wholesale. I have factories in Freiburg, where I live, and also Amsterdam and Emden."

"Well, if that isn't a coincidence. I am also a businessman, and in a not dissimilar line of business." Chisam described his interests in the Whitehaven Cocoa and Coffee House Company, and in particular, his interest in the import business. This seemed to interest

23

Seebohm particularly; but their conversation was interrupted by signs that the shoot wa coming to an end, and the party was starting to make preparations for the journey back to Lowther.

Chisam re-joined Tilberthwaite for the journey back. The chief topic of conversation not surprisingly, was the progress of the shoot. Tilberthwaite's personal score, verified b the gamekeepers, was forty-five, with another nine probables. Chisam was questioned with interest about the shooting incident; but he tried to deflect the questions by makin a joke of the matter.

"There seems to be some doubt about whether I was a shooter or a grouse on thi shoot," he said. "I'm certain I didn't hit any grouse, despite my best efforts."

There were further questions over the dinner table at the banquet that evening; but i was a formal occasion with much ceremonial centred around the earl and the Kaiser a the head of the dining hall, and Chisam found it easy to drop into the background of an conversations that were going. He did have to go through the whole thing at least onc more for the benefit of Anne, and Mary Tilberthwaite, who had spent the day in charabanc on a trip to Keswick and Derwentwater, organised for wives and others no involved in the shooting party. Earlier, however, Chisam had been intercepted for moment by the earl who said that he had heard that Chisam had had an unpleasant shoc during the shoot, and he hoped that all was now well.

"It is, my Lord, and I hope no more need be said about it," replied Chisam. He added after a pause, "I also hope that it won't go hard with the young man concerned. It was a accident, and I'm quite sure he will have learned that lesson so he'll not forget it again."

"I think you're probably right. You know, you've proved to be quite a diversion thi last day or so, you and your cousin. Not everyone approved last night, of course. Some c the Prussian officers thought it was final proof that England's going to the dogs; but kept the conversation off politics, and that's something to be thankful for, eh?"

"Indeed, my Lord. Did . . . His Majesty make any comment?"

The earl looked at him seriously, frowning slightly.

"No," he said shortly. And indeed, there could be no other answer.

After dinner, Chisam again found himself talking to Lord Hemswell. Flattered by th interest of this man of the turf in one such as himself who really knew little about th matter, Chisam was even more flattered when, at length, Lord Hemswell invited hir down to his country place in Surrey where he kept his stables. The invitation wa casually made, but there was no doubt that Lord Hemswell expected him to come, an Chisam, missing the subtlety of the moment, accepted. From Chisam's point of view, was an evening as well spent on deliberate business as the previous twenty-four hour had been spent on happy accidents. He assumed that it was Lord Hemswell's intention to interest him in the purchase of a racehorse; but he knew that there would be no obligation on himself, and nor could any be expected. Besides, he might well become interested . . .

Later still, while the port and cigars were being served in the lounge, he renewed his acquaintance with Kapitänleutnant Seebohm.

"You know," said Seebohm, as they lit up their cigars, " I think an excessive fondness for sweet things is one of the national characteristics of the English. Take this wine, which you like to call port wine, for example." He held his glass up to the light, to examine the rich colour of the vintage ruby they had been served. "It's much too sweet for my taste. And the sweetness is strengthened by increasing the alcohol. All these wines are produced especially for the English market. Strong, sweet wines for a cold, damp, northern land. To me, this is about as Portuguese as . . . as . . ." he floundered for a moment before continuing, "as Yorkshire pudding."

"I know that a lot of port and sherry is made for the English market," said Chisam, "but are they the best representation of English taste? Surely you have something in Germany just as sweet. And there are some Spanish wines I have tasted - ordinary wine, not sherry - which are far too sweet even for my taste."

"Well, perhaps you are right, wine is not the best example. You are not great wine drinkers in England, I think." He puffed at his cigar. "You may remember I told you that I was in the confectionary business, and that we export a lot. England is one of our best export markets. We have a big market in Germany and Holland, of course, and also Austria and Italy; and we even export to Switzerland, and you have to be good to be able to do that. That is like exporting wine to France. So! We export also a good deal to England, and the kind of chocolate you English like is the sweet kind with milk fat. The dark, bitter chocolate, with not much sugar, which is the kind we like best in Germany does not sell well in England. Most of our exports there - here - are of the light chocolate with lots of fat and lots of sugar. There is even a market for a kind of white chocolate, if you can call it that, which is almost all made of fat and sugar, which to me tastes foul, but some people here in England like it. I would say that nearly a quarter of the sugar we use is for the goods we make for the English market. In fact, I will tell you that our sugar account is now so large that I have not long since started to sell speculative bills - futures, I think you call them - which are re-payable after a certain time - one month, three months, six months, und so weiter. It's very profitable at the moment."

Chisam was immediately interested.

"Do you do that on your firm's account, or on your own?"

Seebohm did not quite follow, and said so. Chisam explained about his own futures scheme with his own firm, and how it had started out as a private venture with his own money.

"Ah, yes, I see," Seebohm said at length. "That is an interesting question." He considered it for a few moments, savouring a sip of port. "Perhaps I should start answering your question by telling you a little about my own situation. I have told you that I live in Freiburg, which is in the grand-duchy of Baden, in the south-west of Germany. My wife, Sophia, is of the Hochbergs, the ruling family of Baden. To be precise, she is a cousin of the present grand-duke. She is also related by marriage, through her sister, to our emperor, which is one of the reasons why I am of the emperor's party here, although Sophia is unfortunately not well at present, which is why she could not come herself. I am therefore, in a sense, of the ruling family of Baden. I don't know how much you know about Germany, but, let me say that although we are now an empire, under one emperor, some of the old German states, such as Baden and Bayern have kept a certain measure of independence. The ruling families of these states have a good deal of power and influence. My company is a family business, and so, with connections to the Hochbergs, we are in a favoured position, more so than other companies. Also, our laws are rather different from your English laws. This means that especially as we are a family business, we can legally do certain things which you might take exception to in England."

He paused for a moment, and took another sip of port before going on.

"You know, when you asked me about the sugar futures I sell, I was not sure if you were approving of it or not. You English can be very priggish about all the wrong things. Perhaps it is your Protestant religion, your Church of England, that has something to do with it. Speaking as a - how shall I say - an easy-going Catholic, I must admit that there is something about Protestantism and Protestant society which I have never quite been able to understand. It's not so easy to put into words, but it has sometimes struck me as kind of difficulty in coming to terms with the fullness of human life. I sometimes think that the devout Protestant is haunted by guilt as if by a ghost. The spirits of Johann Calvin and Martin Luther are telling him that he must not allow himself to enjoy the worldly goods and chattels which he must nevertheless spend his life piling up if he is to be assured for his immortal soul. You are excessively priggish about money and sex because, although you secretly enjoy them, your religion tells you that you are sinful if you do enjoy them, so you feel guilty about them. They can only be taken honestly if it is without enjoyment, as if it were a duty."

Chisam laughed. It was so far from being in any way an accurate description of himself.

26

that he couldn't help laughing.

"Guilt!" he exclaimed. "Guilt - well, I must say that's rich coming from a Catholic, even an easy-going one. How you can tax us with being guilt-ridden when you have your confessionals and penances, your rosaries and your celibate priests, I don't know. You know, it's a funny thing, but I've always thought of the average Catholic as being haunted by guilt, or if he's too hard-faced for that, then at least being haunted by a guilt-ridden priest pestering him to come to mass and confess his sins."

Seebohm gave a guffaw of laughter which sounded above the general murmur of conversation in the room.

"Well, my guiltless Protestant friend, let me tell you one or two things. First, you only go to confession if you have something to confess. Of course, if you are guilt-ridden by nature, you will be there every week; but if, like me, you have an easy-going conscience which is not too hard on you, you don't see the need to go at all. Oh, you go a couple of times in a year, to keep your hand in as it were, but that doesn't mean you feel guilty about anything in particular; and as you can see, I don't have a rosary. As for celibate priests, I am not familiar with the theological arguments behind that, but then, no-one is forced to become a priest. And, in general, most people get on with their lives without worrying very much about such things. But I do have the impression that there is a different attitude to such things in Protestant countries such as England; but whether that is from religion or from the temperament of the people I am not sure. I always think of the word 'Puritan' in this connection - a most English word, but it sums up something very spartan in the Protestant mentality, which means that there are things which Protestants are not so easily capable of accepting."

"Such as what?"

"Well, let me see. Have you seen the gardens here?"

"Yes, I have. They're most impressive aren't they? Grand, but beautiful. It makes you see the point of being rich."

"I wonder if they do. However, what did you think of the great fountain?"

"Ah, yes, all those naked ladies - nymphs, or whatever. I must say, for someone who has only known me for a day or two, you seem to be able to read my mind remarkably well. But I should say that such statues are not that uncommon even in England, particularly if you go to London, to the British Museum and the big art galleries. And, I suppose it's not unpleasant to see a pleasing female form, although . ."

"Although you felt it was just a bit naughty, eh? And what are your art galleries and your British Museum but places where you English go to see foreign art. All very fine, of course, but where it is a bit much for your reserved English taste, you can remind

27

yourselves that, after all, it was done by a foreigner, probably a Catholic, whose taste must have been suspect."

"Now you are exaggerating," protested Chisam.

"Oh, no, I'm not. And I shall prove it. You have not been to my part of the world?"

Chisam confirmed that he had not.

"Well, that fountain in the gardens here is only a small example of the kind of bad taste that is taken for granted in south Germany and Austria, and even more so in Italy. If you were to go into almost any village church in Baden or Bayern, or Austria, I am sure that, having seen some of your churches here, you would find them quite alien. All those statues and madonnas and rich ornaments and painting - those were the things that drove the original Puritans to smash all the churches here in the time of Oliver Cromwell, and although, hopefully, we live in more civilised times now, something of that feeling still exists today. That is why your churches are so spartan compared with ours, because you feel that that is proper. But even when you set out to be magnificent and opulent, you are far behind us in what you do, or rather, what your Protestant sense of taste allows you to do."

Chisam wanted the point explained, and Seebohm went on, after reflecting for a moment.

"As one of the emperor's party, I have visited a number of the richest country palaces in England, including the royal palaces at Windsor and Balmoral. You will not have been to these places?"

"No, I haven't, although I have seen pictures of the interiors at Windsor; and I have visited the palace of Holyrood in Edinburgh."

"And do these places have an excess of bad taste?"

"I think the bad taste, if you want to call it that, was about what you might expect from people who had unlimited amounts of money to spend on such things."

"And the bad taste?"

"Well, the spending of large amounts of money on frivolous ornamentation, which no one can derive either pleasure or benefit from."

"Ah, but that is where you are wrong, or rather, where you are limited by your imagination. Large and grand as Windsor is, it is, on the inside especially, plain and bare compared with what we have in Germany. Even compared with our ordinary country mansions, yours are as plain on the inside as a country cottage; but compared with our best . . . Perhaps you have heard of the last King Ludwig of Bayern? He built three palaces for himself in the last century. The interiors of those palaces are the greatest display of wealth that I have ever seen. Even the emperor has nothing to match them - or course, he is a Lutheran. But at Linderhof, in the state bedroom, the bed is surrounded by a balustrade in solid gold, and all the walls are covered in carvings in the rococo style, like the fountain here, but all in gold. There is a kiosk in the Turkish style also at Linderhof, where there is such an amount of gold and silver inlay, and marble and precious gems in the walls and the ceiling and the furniture and even in the floor, as even the most decadent Turkish Sultan ever dreamed of. At Herrenchiemsee there is a great hall of mirrors which puts the one at Versailles to shame. And again at Linderhof, the king had a great cavern dug out of the cliffs above the palace, and water pumped in to make a lake, and a large quantity of electric lighting put in so that the whole cavern, including the very water, was made to glow with light, pure blue, or green, or pink, depending on which colour they made the light. There was a great gilded gondola on the lake, in which the king was rowed over the water at these times. They used to stage scenes from the operas of Richard Wagner there - the king was slavishly devoted to Wagner. You see, you have nothing to compare with that here.

"But the greatest thing the king built was the castle at Neuschwanstein. The throne room at Neuschwanstein has to be seen to be believed. I have never seen the inside of a room like it anywhere. The other rooms are almost as amazing. Everything down to the smallest detail is of the most expensive - no cost was spared. As for the outside - it is the most beautiful in the world. It is built on top of a great crag of rock, like your Edinburgh, but it has towers and turrets that stand tall to a great height above the top of the mountain on which it is built, and all in white stone, or painted white, and richly decorated in the Bayrisches style. It is surrounded by hills covered in pine trees, with a lake in the valley bottom, and the high Alps in the background. It would take your breath away to see it. It is now so famous in Germany that we make models of the castle in coloured sugar, which people will keep for looking at rather than for eating."

The mention of this stirred a memory in Chisam.

"Tell me," he asked, "did you ever send one of those to the firm of Rowntree in York?"

"Why, yes, we did send one, as a present. You see, I am distantly related to the Rowntree family on my father's side, and since we are not much in competition, we maintain friendly relationships."

"Then I have seen it, this sugar castle. We - that is, my firm - also have business dealings with Rowntree. They have a standing order for some of our cocoa, and I go to York on occasion in connection with this. On one such visit they showed me this model. They didn't tell me it was of a real castle. Frankly, I wouldn't have believed them if they had."

"Well then, have I made my point?"

"Yes, yes, you have convinced me that there are people of great wealth who are prepared to spend even more of their money on pure decoration than I would have thought possible. What I don't understand is why they do it. A certain degree of public display is obviously necessary to establish one's prominence, but beyond that it is surely a waste. After all, if money is power, there must come a point where one's money could be more effectively spent than on more gold leaf and stucco."

Seebohm was thoughtful for a moment, his face serious for a change.

"You have not had much to do with those who have great power or great wealth," he said slowly. "And from what you have said I don't think you really understand what possession of them does to people. I have seen it first hand, in Germany, and in England, and elsewhere. We have been speaking rather in jest about the spartan tastes of Protestants, even wealthy Protestants; and I think, the humour of it apart, that there is truth in what I have said. But you must understand that what I meant by it was a difference in style only - it is as ephemeral as that. What is more real is the consequence, not so much of wealth in itself, but of belonging to a society, a *Gesellschaft* of the wealthy and powerful. What matters to such people is rank and status, and above all, prestige; and it very often requires a certain flamboyance to maintain one's prestige. Sometimes it is easy for such a one to maintain his prestige. Sometimes it is not so easy, and especially in such cases, the prestige and the great amount of money needed to maintain it become like a kind of addiction. They are craved as much as the opium pipe is craved by the opium addict. It can be dangerous to be in the company of such men at such times, dangerous not least because quite often one doesn't know that they are suffering from this particular affliction until it is too late. If you expect to move in these circles more than occasionally, then, even if you are not dazzled by all this," he waved his hand to indicate the splendour of the assembled company , "or even greater splendours, or you profess not to be, then don't be fooled by it either."

Chisam was in a sufficiently good mood not to be put out by the sudden seriousness of Seebohm's little speech in what had been an evening of entertaining conversation. Nevertheless, he did not forget it, and indeed, was to have cause to remember it later.

For the rest of the evening, they swapped amusing anecdotes about their respective businesses. They finally parted - it was the last day as a guest at Lowther for Chisam and others of his non-aristocratic rank - the best of friends, and agreed to correspond to keep in contact. It was to be a correspondence which would have much consequence for them both.

30

5

The offices of the Whitehaven Cocoa and Coffee House Company Ltd occupied a rather dingy suite of rooms in an upper storey of a drab sandstone warehouse of a building overlooking the town's market place. At the best of times it was not a cheerful scene. Although Whitehaven had been laid out for Sir James Lowther by Robert Adam with the same enthusiasm for town planning that had created the fashionable cities of Edinburgh and Bath, the result was disappointingly unimpressive, alloyed as it was with that certain air of sleazy drabness that always accompanies industry. When it was pouring with rain, as it frequently is in Whitehaven, even in August, the most sanguine of temperaments could not fail to be affected.

Edward Chisam was not particularly sanguine when he returned there on the first morning after his departure from Lowther. It was not that he had time to brood over what had happened during the previous few days, or about what might have been. He was occupied immediately with the familiar and the not so familiar - with all the problems of running an import business. A cocoa boat had been damaged by bad weather, and had had to put into Brest for repairs. It being an English ship in a French yard, these were expected to take some time, perhaps as long as three weeks. Chisam had to sort the matter out with Merlyn Thomas, the shipping company's agent, and then see about supplies to their customers, who were expecting their orders as usual. He would have to draw on the stocks in the company's warehouse. These would eventually be made good, when the Brest shipyard workers finally deigned to give the 'Cardigan Bay' their attention.

In the meantime, there would be an effect on the price of cocoa in the local markets. Whitehaven was not the principal port of entry for cocoa into Britain, but it was one of the more important, particularly in the north. The effect on the price of the firm's cocoa futures, caused by speculative buying in the wake of the news about the 'Cardigan Bay', was most gratifying to Chisam in particular, who by this time had his own portfolio. All these expectations were fulfilled when the 'Cardigan Bay' finally reached Whitehaven nearly a month late. Beneath all this surface excitement, however, Chisam was unable to suppress a certain feeling of restlessness. He could not readily have articulated why he felt this. When he had gone to Lowther, it had not been with any specific ambition or intent, other than to make the most of what opportunity might provide. On the face of it, opportunity had not been unkind. He had made the acquaintance, in Lord Hemswell, of one who was well known in the racing world, and also, presumably, had useful social connections. He had even had an invite to go and look over his stables. He had also made the acquaintance of a member of the Kaiser's entourage; although what might come out of that given that it was highly unlikely that he would ever see Seebohm again, only time would tell.

He could not expect to be invited to Lowther again merely on the strength of having been invited once, and then under unusual circumstances. In any event, perhaps once would be enough. The main point of going to Lowther was surely to observe, to see what was possible, and especially, to see what was different from what he knew. What he knew was trade, and the dull narrow-mindedness, the meretricious vulgarity that he found so depressingly universal among his own class. Being in trade meant that he met only that class of person, and he felt irritated and confined by their society. At Lowther, he might not have found anything specific, but he had been given some idea of where to look. One thing had been clear - he had been confirmed in his attraction to the world of the turf. It was glamorous, risky, but with the potential for high rewards, not just financially, but in terms of prestige.

He was, therefore, disappointed when his visit to Lord Hemswell's stables in Surrey did not fulfil the expectations that he might have entertained of it at Lowther. It had been a most pleasant weekend in Lord Hemswell's big country house in the lush Surrey countryside; but the expected business which Chisam had looked forward to had not materialised. Lord Hemswell, for his part, had been equally disappointed. The promising two-year-old from another stable that he had had in mind when he had invited Chisam down to Surrey, had been sold by private deal, instead of by public auction as he had expected, and so the main point of the visit had been lost. They made the best of their time with a hastily organised shoot on the Saturday afternoon, followed by a trip to the West End to see a show. A hint by Lord Hemswell that they might afterwards visit a high-class brothel was studiously ignored by Chisam, and Lord Hemswell did not press the point. He noted that Chisam, relatively prosperous and in his forties was still a bachelor, drew certain conclusions, and mentally shrugged his shoulders. As it happened, Chisam's reason for turning down the brothel would probably have been even harder for Lord Hemswell to understand than the reason he erroneously assumed. On the Sunday they went shooting again, and they parted on friendly terms the following morning, but with only a vague commitment to re-establish contact should a suitable horse materialise in the future.

His rather sombre mood communicated itself to Stella when he next visited her. Stella Robertson was the widow of a bank manager, and she lived in the house that she had shared with her husband for some eleven years, a modest but roomy terrace on the outskirts of Whitehaven. She and her husband Frank had been friends of the Chisam

32

family for years, and Frank had been banker to the Whitehaven Cocoa and Coffee House Company. He had been much older than his wife, and when he had died, some seven years earlier, he had left her a widow in her early thirties; not too old by any means to marry again. She had chosen not to do so, however. In the first instance, Frank had left her very comfortably off, and she had been able to keep up the house, and the style of living to which she had become very appreciatively accustomed. Frank had, however, tied much of their finances up in a family trust, and not only Stella, but also their daughter would be denied access to it if she married again. In addition to this, seven years of living on her own had allowed her own personality to re-assert itself, after having been subordinated, quite properly of course, and without any rancour on her part - it had been a happy marriage - to that of her husband. But now, she had come to like the luxury of being mistress in her own house too much to be able to contemplate the bondage of marriage without apprehension. There was no financial incentive for her to marry again, and so she had not done so. She was, nevertheless, at thirty-nine, still a relatively young woman. Her relationship with Chisam had developed slowly, and it had the advantage of beginning from the familiarity of a long friendship. She knew a lot about Edward Chisam and what kind of man he was. In contrast to her husband, he was just two years her senior, and quite different in character. Frank had been dependable, unimaginative, very correct in his manner - everything a bank manager should be. Edward was temperamental, sometimes a dreamer, sometimes hard, sometimes amazingly perceptive, at other times blindly naïve; and he was, well, unconventional. It was this last that had allowed their relationship to develop in the way it had. He fulfilled an emotional need in her in a way she did not really understand, and in a way which Frank had not - something she found very difficult to admit even to herself. But it also had the additional interest of being an illicit relationship, as all such relationships were of necessity in Edwardian England.

For Chisam, Stella was, if not the centre of his life, then the brightest light by far in his firmament. The fact that their relationship was unconventional and illicit, in addition to their friendship, meant that he felt unrestrained by her presence - he could confide in her and seek her advice or opinion, tell her about his failures and misgivings as well as his successes and ambitions. He could talk to her in a way he could not with any other human being. She was a silly woman sometimes: she had been married too long to old Frank for some of that not to have rubbed off on her; but otherwise, she was a lively and intelligent companion and he knew he was lucky to have her. And she was also a good-looking woman in a big boned, maternal sort of way which he found deeply attractive, so that Stella, after an hour's blissful ecstasy on the big four poster bed she had once shared

33

so prosaically with Frank, would sometimes feel almost as much like a mother cuddling her child, as a lover, in a way which left her feeling strangely moved.

And thus it was on this sultry September evening; and Chisam was glad that he had borne his embarrassment at turning down Lord Hemswell's suggested visit to a brothel - he had guessed what had been passing through his lordship's mind. He had seen what the pox did to people, and he was afraid not only for himself, but also for Stella. The fact that she had no hold or claim on him meant that whenever they came together it was because it was what they wanted most at that particular moment; and that such feelings rested on unspoken assumptions as a form of trust between them, which made the idea of loyalty quite natural, even to one such as Chisam, who was not especially highly principled.

Stella could not understand Chisam's moroseness on this occasion. He had been the guest of aristocracy twice within a month, and might expect to be so again before very long. Up to a point, she was impressed by what he had done. But it was a point which troubled her. One thing about Chisam which she did not like, or at least, could not come to terms with, was his overweening ambition, which he was at best only half aware of himself, she was sure. She admired ambition in a man, but it was so like Edward to take it to excess, following some will o' the wisp of a dream, which she felt was bound to bring him disappointment in the end. Success which would have pleased almost any other ordinary mortal was no comfort to Chisam.

He was not to be comforted on the subject now, either, and it was a relief to both of them to drop it and turn to pleasanter things. And even Chisam could forget his ambitions when he felt his passion being aroused once more by the broad, round spread of Stella's breasts, so soft and yielding against his skin, enveloping his mouth, his eyes, his consciousness.

6

Autumn was merging into a cold and rainy winter, and Chisam's hopes of Lord Hemswell were fading with the year, when his existence was momentarily brightened by the arrival of a letter for him, not bearing a London or Surrey postmark which he had been keeping an eye open for, but with an exotic stamp, which proved to be German. Chisam was genuinely surprised. He had not thought that Seebohm would have had the time or the inclination to maintain a correspondence, even though they had parted at Lowther with vague promises to keep in touch.

Seebohm had recently returned from a trip to the Cameroons territory, as German west Africa was called. It was partly an official visit - Seebohm was one of a party from the German colonial office - but he had managed to combine it with a business visit on behalf of his family's firm, which got a lot of its cocoa and some of its sugar from the Cameroons. The letter was full of Africa - the heat and the flies, the primitive conditions, the great size of the country. Most of the business part of the trip, including a visit to a cocoa plantation, the description of which greatly interested Chisam, was in the coastal area, which, according to Seebohm, was the worst sort of country for white men. The oppressive heat and humidity, the mosquito-ridden mangrove swamps full of snakes, leeches and foul stenches had given it the well-earned names of 'malaria coast' and 'the white man's grave'. Seebohm himself had had a mild dose of malaria which had shaken him a good deal and laid him low for a week. After that, however, the party had gone up country to the northern plains, where the climate was drier and more bearable, for a few days' hunting.

"If you have only shot grouse in England," Seebohm wrote, "or perhaps chased a harmless little fox with a great pack of hounds, you can scarcely imagine the thrill of stalking a lion or a rhinoceros which has at least a sporting chance of getting you before you get him." He enthusiastically recommended a trip to Africa as an experience not to be missed if the opportunity arose, and even suggested that Chisam might consider taking a trip on one of the Whitehaven cocoa boats. It was something which had not occurred to Chisam before, and the idea intrigued him rather more than it attracted him.

Stella said, when he showed her the letter: "It sounds very romantic. Would you take me if you do go? It's called the Gold Coast where the ships go, isn't it? What an exotic name! We would be the talk of the town if I came back wearing a lionskin coat." The hint of a smile told him that she was not serious.

"I don't think you'd enjoy it really," he said gravely, and pointed out the part of Seebohm's letter describing the mangrove swamps and the malaria. "Besides, women

who go out to Africa are generally considered to be not quite respectable. You wouldn'
want there to be any cause for that, would you?"

They were in bed together, and she kicked him.

It was towards the end of January that a letter arrived from Lord Hemswell. In it, hi
Lordship began by noting that it had been some time since they had last spoken, and h
was presuming on Chisam's still being interested in the business they had discussed a
that time. He regretted that the expected opportunity had not arisen during Chisam'
visit, and hoped that the visit had nevertheless been remembered as a pleasant one
Chisam wondered if he still remembered the brothel incident. Obviously it was of n
consequence, since his Lordship was now writing to Chisam with something in particula
on his mind. This was a three year old mare called Glaramara which had don
particularly well in the last season - and here he referred Chisam to the variou
newspaper cuttings he had enclosed with the letter, and which had mystified Chisam
when they had fallen out of the envelope when he opened it. They turned out to b
cuttings from the racing pages of various newspapers, all concerning Glaramara. Most o
them showed the horse either winning, or at least being placed, and, as Lord Hemswel
was careful to point out, as time progressed (the articles were all dated), at graduall
lower odds as the horse became noticed, and latterly with some well-known jockey
aboard. It went without saying that the horse had taken his Lordship's fancy, and th
point of his writing to Chisam at that particular moment was that he had informatio
that Glaramara was to be sold. It was expected to fetch a good price, and as Lor
Hemswell did not have enough liquid capital to enable him comfortably to afford to pa
out the whole of the expected cost, would Chisam be interested in buying a share of th
animal? Chisam would, he knew, wish to make his own enquiries about the horse befor
deciding whether or not to commit himself, and if so, by how much. However, if he wa
interested, could he write back within a week, as the sale was expected in about ten days

Chisam was uncomfortably aware of the fact that, although he had become intereste
in racing, and had been attempting in the last few months to educate himself about th
racing world - he had even come across Glaramara in his perambulations through th
racing columns - he was still very much of an uninformed amateur in the business. H
had no idea, for example, that Glaramara was about to be sold, let alone for what kind c
sum - Lord Hemswell had quoted a figure - or that it was such a good buy. The idea c
committing several thousand pounds on the strength of his relatively small knowledg
gave him pause for thought.   On the other hand, this might be just the opportunity h
had been waiting for.

He consulted Tilberthwaite. Tilberthwaite, however, was unhelpfully non-committal. It occurred to Chisam that he might be feeling a little piqued by the fact that he had not been approached first with an offer to go into partnership in a bid for Glaramara. If that was the case, then it was entirely unreasonable. It had been Lord Hemswell who had drawn his attention to Glaramara and had first made an offer. He could hardly be expected to have acted differently. That didn't help him much now, however.

"Aye, I heard about Glaramara," said Tilberthwaite ruminatively, in answer to Chisam's question. "The owner was an old lady, widow of Lord Knaith, who died late last year I think, and the trustees of the estate have had to sell off some parts of it to keep it solvent. They had a small stable, and it looks as if that's had to go. So, I shouldn't think there's necessarily anything wrong with the horse because it's being sold."

"Would it be a good investment, though?" persisted Chisam. But Tilberthwaite would not be drawn.

"I daresay it might be, I cannot really say, as I don't know too much about the animal myself. If Lord Hemswell's putting his money into it, then it should be alright." And that was as far as he was prepared to go.

What made up his mind in the end was the conviction that Tilberthwaite's reticence was due in part to a touch of envy, and that, given the chance, Tilberthwaite would have invested in the horse himself. He therefore wrote back to Lord Hemswell and agreed to buy into the new ownership of Glaramara to the amount of half the value, or four thousand pounds, whichever was the smaller sum. He could not attend the auction himself due to his business commitments, but Lord Hemswell would see to that, and the horse would become part of his Lordship's stable. Glaramara eventually went for £7500, and so Chisam became once again a paid up half owner of a racehorse. He could not take the same amount of interest in it as he had with Kerry Dancer, since Glaramara was stabled at the other end of the country, and business commitments did not permit Chisam to go racing every other weekend, as Lord Hemswell evidently did. Also, unlike Kerry Dancer, Glaramara did not make a good showing initially, and while there was no prize money coming in, he had as per agreement to pay his share of stabling costs and all the other expenses of maintaining and running a racehorse.

Stella observed wryly that it might be as well for him to build up some goodwill in this way, even if it did cost him some money. After all, if he was going to make his mark in the business, he might one day want to establish a stable of his own, and might equally want to ask Lord Hemswell to invest in it in the way his Lordship was asking him to do at the moment; a reversal of roles which his Lordship might not particularly appreciate. Her comment took Chisam somewhat aback. Even he had not yet given any consideration to the idea of establishing his own stable, and his respect for her increase accordingly. Privately, Stella hoped that a disappointing experience with Glaramar would cause him to lose interest in the racing business altogether. She felt it was foolish aberration on his part, and would do him no good in the long run.

Chisam was not so pessimistic; and indeed, as Stella had suggested, was prepared t accept a certain measure of disappointment for the sake of possible future benefits. An then, quite unexpectedly, Glaramara won a big race. Chisam's half of the prize mone paid off most of what he had spent on the horse so far. Within a few weeks, the horse ha repeated the feat three times, and come second on a number of other occasions. It seeme at last to have justified the faith which Lord Hemswell, and Chisam even more so, ha put in it. As it turned out, this winning streak was due more to a run of good luck than t any outstanding ability in the horse. In the long run, Glaramara was to comfortably pa its way with a modest margin of profit, rather than making the fortune of its owners.

But this favourable start with the first jointly owned horse was to cement the busines relationship between the two men, to the extent of Chisam's being prepared to consid further such ventures. Lord Hemswell did not rush matters, however. As Chisam ha sensed on his first visit there, Lord Hemswell had not yet sized him up, and was still n sufficiently sure of him to venture immediately something financially much bolder an riskier, thereby risking losing the goose that was so far proving willing to lay golde eggs. His Lordship therefore proposed that, before Glaramara's record started to becom mediocre, the mare be put to a stud, and the offspring be sold at auction on the streng of Glaramara's and the sire's record. It meant Glaramara's being withdrawn from racin for a while, but Chisam was agreeable. The foal, when it was old enough, fetched satisfactory price.

In this way, over the succeeding months, Chisam's confidence in his own judgement these matters, and in Lord Hemswell, was built up. It was not that he actually knew great deal more than in the beginning - there was no substitute for experience, Tilberthwaite might have told him - but everything seemed to be going mo satisfactorily; and so he was not unduly alarmed at the first sign of difficulty. By t autumn of 1912 it had become customary for Chisam to have a fifty percent interest in aspects of the partnership with Lord Hemswell - purchase price of horses, the cost maintaining and racing them, and of profits. At this stage, there was no obligation on h part to continue this arrangement; but he felt that if he were to reduce his commitment would diminish his standing in the eyes of Lord Hemswell, and in the circles in which was beginning to move. A weakness in this arrangement, for Chisam at least, was th some of the horses they bought were sold at auction rather than by private deal. It was such an auction that autumn that Lord Hemswell allowed his vanity to rule over his wallet, and followed the bidding for a particular horse up to far above what it was really worth. For Chisam, when he learned what he would have to pay as a half share, it was an unpleasant surprise. On this occasion, it turned out that the horse did not do too badly, and was not a liability. In addition, the cocoa futures due the following month paid an unusually large dividend, which got him out of his immediate difficulty. Nevertheless, for the first time he had had to borrow money to tide him over, which was not something he was used to doing, at least in his personal life. Had that been all, he would not have been too alarmed; but worse was to follow.

During the winter and spring of 1913, Lord Hemswell, seemingly without any sense of propriety, bought a series of horses at auction at prices well over what they were worth. Most of the horses had been bid up by people who knew little about horse racing, but who had taken it up as a fashionable interest - people from high society who were a great deal wealthier than Lord Hemswell. Some of the horses were of very good pedigree; others weren't. In any event, the rate at which Lord Hemswell was buying them was far too much for someone of his financial means, or for his small stable to cope with. For Chisam, what was most alarming was the fact that he had no control over what Lord Hemswell was doing. In order to honour his side of the agreement, Chisam again had to go into debt for each of the succeeding transactions. Sometimes, the horse acquired would do well, so that some of the losses were recovered in prize money; but overall Chisam was going further and further into debt. When he eventually demanded to see Lord Hemswell to ask him what he thought he was doing, his Lordship suddenly became very elusive and could not be contacted.

One result of Chisam's going into debt was to strain his relations with Stella. He had not said much to her about his racing connection with Lord Hemswell, since he realised that Stella did not approve, and he had said even less since things had started going wrong. However, he knew that she was aware of what was going on, and when he had to cancel a trip to London they had planned together, which had been worked out in careful detail because of the need for discretion, Stella's feelings were such that she felt moved to speak.

"You have lost your sense of proportion," she said to him sharply when he told her about the cancelled London trip. "It is quite senseless to go on in this way. Not only is it not worth it, but if you do go on you will become a laughing stock among those very people you are trying to impress. You already know what I think, so I won't tax you with it again; but I must ask you what you intend to do. If you wish to be made a laughing stock, then that's your business, but I should tell you that I do not."

She hoped that she was not sounding shrewish; on the other hand, she meant what she said. She felt that if she could jolt him out of this evil fascination which seemed to have gripped him, she would be doing him a great benefit. If she could not, then at least she would know where she stood with him.

Chisam however, did not need convincing in the matter. Quite apart from the value he put on his standing in Stella's eyes, he simply could not afford to go on in this way. It was a matter of considerable regret to him that it had to end like this. It had seemed at one point that the arrangement with Lord Hemswell would be a successful way into the world of racing. The fact that Lord Hemswell had turned out to be a business liability was simply bad luck. Chisam's ambitions had been dampened, but not quelled; but faced with the alternative, he was resigned to regretting the passing of an opportunity which had turned out not to be one after all. He trusted he could learn from the experience, and put the matter behind him.

He wrote to Lord Hemswell to this effect, regretting that he was no longer able to continue their arrangement for financial reasons, and hoping that his decision would no inconvenience his Lordship too much. He was sure that his Lordship would be able to find someone more suitable for such a partnership. He informed him that he was instructing his solicitor to arrange the sale of his half of the horses that he had already bought into, and which he could now no longer afford to maintain, given his current financial position, and said that, of course, his Lordship would have first refusal of these. He rounded the letter off with suitable pleasantries, and there, he expected, would be the end of the business.

The letter which he received in reply from Lord Hemswell a week later was, therefore, a very rude shock.

7

Chisam stared in disbelief at the letter. It was blackmail. He read it through again, but there was no doubting Lord Hemswell's purpose. He had couched the letter in such a way as to make the justifications for what he was doing seem almost reasonable; but the fact remained that it was blackmail. It was a shock to realise that a member of the aristocracy - from Chisam's point of view, part of the Establishment - would be capable of such a thing. Beyond that it made him feel sick to realise that it was at least partly his own fault that he was in this predicament.

The lever which Lord Hemswell was using to exert pressure on him was his relationship with Stella. In order to dispel any lingering misgivings his Lordship might have had about him following the brothel incident, Chisam, on his next visit to Surrey, had given a broad hint that he had a mistress who was otherwise a respectable woman. Lord Hemswell had been appreciatively amused, but had not appeared to show any special interest in the matter. In fact, anticipating what was to come, his Lordship had seized on this snippet of information as he would a gift from the gods. He had gone to particular trouble to find out who Chisam's mistress was, and what her position in life was, with such discretion as not to alarm either Stella or Chisam that they were being spied on. Lord Hemswell, as Chisam was to find out, was an experienced blackmailer, and he knew how to be discreet. On the other hand, he knew how to sound a high moral tone when it was least justified.

It was a matter of great disappointment to him, Lord Hemswell wrote, that Chisam had turned out to be a man of such mean principles. Their arrangement may not have been legally binding, but it had been, as he had seen it, an understanding between gentlemen, which was something not lightly to be cast aside simply because it was not legally binding. Quite apart from the embarrassment caused to himself, Lord Hemswell wrote, if it became known that his business associate was less than a gentleman, it was a matter of principle which ought to be upheld. He felt it would be in the interests of Chisam's moral education at least, if he were to insist that their arrangement should continue, legally binding or not. If Chisam failed to honour the agreement, his Lordship foresaw that Chisam's reputation as a gentleman would be ruined, not only in this way, but in other ways as well. He felt sure, for example, that as a result of the initial scandal, it would come out sooner or later that Chisam was having a fornicatory relationship with a Mrs Stella Robertson, widow of a Whitehaven bank manager, now living at her former husband's residence in Whitehaven. Quite apart from a consideration of Chisam's own position, it would be a grave weight of responsibility to risk destroying the reputation of an 'otherwise respectable widow' - Chisam ground his teeth as he recognised his own words to Lord Hemswell being cast mockingly back in his face - and his Lordship hoped therefore, that in due consideration of all these things, Chisam would be prepared to reconsider the rash decision announced in his last letter.

What was he to do? If he continued paying as Lord Hemswell demanded, he would soon get into serious financial trouble. Things were bad enough already, but once he agreed to continue the arrangement, he would be completely at Lord Hemswell's mercy. It was not as if he would have to pay a fixed amount at regular intervals like other blackmail victims. He would simply have to wait on what Lord Hemswell demanded, and then somehow try and find the money, since the demands were still ostensibly related to racehorses purchased at auction. Chisam was under little illusion, however, that by now this was a piece of fiction, and that what he was faced with was straightforward blackmail. On the other hand, he could hardly countenance compromising Stella, which meant, as far as he was concerned, that he dared not say anything to her about the fact that he was being blackmailed about their relationship. Still less could he face breaking off their relationship, even though it was already under strain. Stella would know that some external factor was involved and would demand to know what it was. He suspected that Lord Hemswell would continue to try and blackmail them both regardless. In any event, Stella was the most important person in his life, and he was damned if he was going to end his relationship with her just because of Lord Hemswell.

But who else could he turn to? It had always seemed to him that he had not been short of friends, but now that he came to consider the matter in the light of his present troubles, he knew that there was no-one else he could trust with any certainty if he confided in them. His sense of depression was increased by this realisation. There was only Stella, and while he would have done almost anything not to have to involve Stella in this sordid business, the more he thought about it, the more he realised that it was inevitable that she would have to be told. He knew that, while Stella might be broadminded enough to sin in private, albeit with a friend and confidant, she certainly would not be prepared to sin in public, or even be suspected of so sinning, and with the threat of exposure hanging over her, he felt he could be in little doubt of her reaction. The ending of their relationship might only be temporary, until he found the resource to end his connection with Lord Hemswell, or it might not be. On the other hand, if he did not tell her of the threat, and Lord Hemswell exposed her, he was sure that she would never forgive him.

It was his apprehension on this last point which eventually decided him to throw himself on Stella's mercy and confide in her. He felt so angry and confused that he could

42

not for the life of him make up his mind what he was going to do, and there was no-one else he could confide in. All his fears about Stella's reaction were justified, however.

"I simply cannot understand why you persisted with this business even after I warned you against it," she said. "It was rash and irresponsible, even without this other . . . But this . . . this threat. Surely you can see that it puts me in an impossible dilemma?"

She turned away from him, to walk over to the window and look out over the panorama of the town lying below in its hollow, a jumble of dark grey buildings, with jutting pit stacks on the headland to the south rising above the tangle of masts in the harbour, and the dull grey band of the sea just visible beyond. Her turning away from him was more than symbolic.

"I don't want to hurt you, Edward," she went on, still standing with her back to him at the window, "but you must know that we cannot carry on as we have been. That must end from today. You must see that I have no choice in the matter. I could not face what would happen to me if I were exposed. And I'm sure you wouldn't want it either. And even if you were to give in to Lord Hemswell's demands, or find some way of discharging your obligation to him, he would always be in a position to expose me so long as what he accused me of was true. If you can accept that without bitterness then we can still be friends, as long as it doesn't go any farther than that. And then you will also have your answer to Lord Hemswell. You must trust that this is the wisest counsel."

She turned to face him, and for a few moments he was silent.

"It seems that I have found out that I mean a lot less to you than I had thought," he said.

"What do you mean?"

"I mean that the first thing you sacrifice is our relationship, as if that's the least important part of this, or of your life."

"I've already explained that I have no alternative."

"You haven't even thought about it. If it meant anything like as much to you as it does to me, you wouldn't be so immediately sure that there is no alternative to simply ending it all."

"I will not risk exposure, so I have no choice but to end it. What other alternative is there?"

He was again silent for a moment before speaking.

"I would have preferred it to have been a happier occasion to ask you this, but since it seems my hand is forced . . . If we were to get married, then there would no longer be any basis on which Lord Hemswell could threaten us."

She frowned, and shook her head.

"You already know my mind on that. I have chosen not to marry again because I prefer the freedom of being single. And I could not marry you because that would not be accepted here."

"I have long hoped that you might relent on that point, Stella. It seems unfair and unreasonable that we should be bound by old-fashioned conventions . . ."

"There are other reasons as well, which I'm not going into here. But on that point alone, I cannot relent. This is Cumberland, not London, and society here is very small - too small to risk offending, unless one is prepared to go into exile, which I have no wish to do. That applies as much to you as to me. If we were to marry, you would be seen as trying to better yourself at my expense, and you would be frozen out, as would I. This is too small a place for that."

"You give me nothing to hope for, then. We cannot marry, and our relationship is at an end. In one moment, you have taken the heart out of my life, Stella."

"We can still be friends, at least."

"Friends! What does that mean? Nothing, and you know it. We would hardly ever be able to see each other, and the occasions when we did would to me simply be a mocking reminder of what we once had. Having been lovers, such a thing is meaningless, at least to me."

"I'm sorry Edward, but there can be no other way."

"And am I then to keep paying Lord Hemswell to buy his silence about something which no longer exists? That seems very hard."

"That is exactly why we must end our relationship, for both our sakes. With nothing between us, it will no longer matter if Lord Hemswell carries out his threat, and makes his allegations public."

"I fear it won't be as simple as that. It may be some while before it will be safe to allow Lord Hemswell to carry out his threat. In the meantime, his silence will have to be bought, as you say, for both our sakes. I still have my own position to consider. But with no hope of anything for the future, that will be very hard."

"I didn't ask you to get us into this predicament. It's your own recklessness that has done that. As a woman, I am more vulnerable to the consequences of it than you, so there's no alternative for me if I am to protect myself."

They lapsed into silence, as if neither knew what else to say.

"I think you had better go," said Stella at last. "There is nothing more for you here now."

"Must it end like this? Might we kiss just once more, for the sake of what we once had?"

44

She shook her head.

"We must start as we mean to go on. The relationship is ended, because that is how it must be. It would not be right to kiss now. Not now. Will you take my hand in friendship before you go?"

If she had thought that he might not, she was wrong. He reached out and took her hand for a few moments, holding her gaze. Then, without another word, he turned and left.

When he had gone, she sat down suddenly on the sofa, buried her face in her hands and burst into tears. She knew that she had done the right thing, for Chisam as well as for herself. She knew how imprudent it would be for her to continue to associate intimately with someone who had shown himself to be as foolish and naïve as Chisam had been, quite apart from the blackmail threat. That innate sense of caution which every woman feels when assessing a member of the opposite sex was telling her to exercise caution now, and she, being a sensible woman, had heeded it. But she was not a hard woman, and the effect of the sudden and abrupt severing, evidently for good, of the only intimate relationship in her life since she lost her husband, left her in a state of shock and distress, however prudent and sensible her decision might have been. Her distress was increased by the thought that Chisam would hold her responsible for his predicament, and that his love for her, which she still cherished, would turn to bitterness.

In truth, had she but known it, Chisam felt little anger against Stella. He was as distressed as she was, even though, as he had had time to prepare himself, it had not been as much of a shock for him; but he could at least understand how she had felt that she could not have acted in any other way. It had been his fault rather than hers. And yet, he felt, he had done nothing which was in itself wrong, or even reprehensible. He had not actively and knowingly engaged in anything which might be thought of as misconduct in any sense. He had been gullible, certainly, and it rankled him whenever he thought of it; but it had taken the active malice of Lord Hemswell taking advantage of his gullibility to bring this predicament upon him.

Lord Hemswell. Chisam's thoughts began to follow a predictable pattern. Lord Hemswell had not only failed to help him realise his ambition to extend his life in a new venture into the world of racing, in a way which had left him feeling humiliated, but he had also effectively destroyed his old life as well. His position at the firm had not been affected so far, but the extent of his debt was now such that, should it become known about, he must certainly fear for his position. Fortunately, Lord Hemswell appeared to be ignorant of this.

But the ending of his relationship with Stella had taken all meaning and all pleasure out of his life. As the days and weeks passed, and summer merged into autumn, and the emptiness of his life oppressed him more and more, the strength of his feelings against Lord Hemswell grew. Not long after the ending of his relationship with Stella, he had written to Lord Hemswell indicating what had happened, and suggesting that, under the new circumstances, to proceed with his threat would now be fruitless.

He received no reply; a silence which was ominous rather than encouraging. However, when his solicitor, as instructed, attempted to sell his share in the horses already bought, this provoked a response. Lord Hemswell's letter, curt and brief, informed him that if Chisam persisted in his attempt to sell, he would break the scandal about him and Mrs. Robertson. Even if he had broken off all connection with the lady, so that nothing could be proved, it would damage her reputation and social standing. Chisam knew when he was beaten. He could not afford to sue, and even if Stella could, he knew she would not wish to. He had to accept in silence what was, in effect, the theft of many thousands of his own money for Stella's sake. Almost as bad as the loss of the money was the humiliation of being treated in this way. It made him hot with rage every time he allowed his mind to dwell on it. It was a continuing humiliation, because he had no redress - he could not get back at Lord Hemswell in any way. His only consolation was that his humiliation had not been made public: his Lordship's conduct over the attempt to sell the horses at least would probably be a police matter, and he was evidently not so reckless as to be unmindful of that.

But Chisam was left with his life in shreds. It was a setback so unexpected, and one which had affected him in such a personal way, that he did not seem able to ride over it and put it behind him, as he might have done with a more conventional business deal that had gone wrong. He could not seem to pull himself together. Not only his confidence in himself, and in life in general had gone, but his judgement seemed to have deserted him also. He started making errors which cost his company money, and this was noticed. Not only did this mean that all prospects of advancement within the company, or indeed anywhere else, were gone, but also he had continually to fear for his existing position.

The one source of relief to him at this time was his cocoa futures scheme. Even though through a certain amount of mismanagement due to his declining judgement, this produced less money than it might have done, it was still a welcome, and at times a substantial source of income. It enabled him to cover up some of his mistakes with discreet transfers of money, and also to begin to repair his own shattered finances. It meant that the prospect of bankruptcy, dismissal and disgrace began gradually to recede from him.

He was, however, too close to Stella for him to have that peace of mind which might have enabled him to adjust to his new circumstances philosophically. Physical proximity alone would have been bad enough, but occasionally he would chance to see her. Only occasionally, as she knew his routine, and took care to avoid meeting him as far as she could without serious inconvenience or it being too obvious. Between intervals, long intervals of many weeks spent thinking about her, he would see her or glimpse her.

In the early spring, at a Saturday afternoon function for the Conservative Party which he was attending on behalf of his firm, he came across her quite by chance.

"Stella . . ." he had begun irresolutely, but before he could gather his wits to go on, she had given him a very cool "Good afternoon, Mr Chisam" and passed on. He had scarcely remembered the rest of that day, such had been the impact of this rebuff. Twice more during that spring and early summer she had thus denied him in public, and yet each time it failed entirely to destroy the hope that she might one day relent towards him. It took a fourth occasion to drive home finally what Lord Hemswell had done to him.

It was the evening of a hot day at the end of July. He was in Carlisle where he had been consulting with the manager of the firm's Carlisle subsidiary on that company's wholesale orders. It had been a full day. He had begun it in Whitehaven, and travelled up to Carlisle on the early train. He was staying the night in the city, and therefore he decided that that evening he would go and see a variety performance at the Palace theatre. It was a typical variety evening. There was the inevitable comic, and a woman who performed a miniature play about the life of Bonnie Prince Charlie, performing all the parts herself, evidently being a quick-change artist. There was an Indian musician with the unlikely name of Doraswami, who performed amazing and outlandish music on the violin. For those with more conventional musical tastes, a Signor Torti, an Italian tenor, sang selections from Verdi and Puccini operas, including the ever popular 'Your tiny hand is frozen', which, while not bringing the house down - this was, after all, Carlisle and not Milan - had tears in many an eye.

Chisam's enjoyment was abruptly and rudely ended when suddenly he saw Stella in one of the boxes. She was with a man, and it was obvious from the way they sat together that he was more than just her escort for the evening. Chisam recognised the man. He was Robert Harrison, a prominent Carlisle banker. He did not know if Harrison was married - presumably not if he was able to be seen thus with Stella. It was a shock to know that Stella was now with another man. It was the end of any remaining hopes he had of her. A more slowly developing and deeper hurt followed from the reflection that, since Harrison was a banker, Stella must have known him from Frank Robertson's time, and had possibly been intimate with him during the period when she had also been intimate with Chisam.

He left the theatre at once. The sweet tones of Signor Torti had suddenly become an irritation. He had to be alone and in silence with his thoughts. He could no longer keep his despair at bay, and in his hotel room it overwhelmed him as he paced up and down, his thoughts not focusing on anything in particular, his mind in that state of hyperactivity which follows shock. He could not think coherently about his predicament, or what he was going to do. He had been very much in love, and for the first time he felt anger, and even hatred, for Stella, at betraying him when he needed her. Now, there was only hatred, of Stella, of Harrison, her new partner, of Lord Hemswell, and increasingly, of himself, for his own stupidity and weakness. When he finally went to bed, his emotions had exhausted him and he slept heavily, his dreams untroubled by Stella, or Lord Hemswell, as if his mind could take no more of them.

He awoke early. It was a Saturday, and he had no commitments until Monday, a space of two days in which he might have the freedom of privacy. Instinctively, he knew what he was going to do with those two days. He could not stay in the hotel room. Nor could he go home, as his privacy was likely to be disturbed there also. There was a farm in upper Ennerdale, above the lake, where he had sometimes gone on walking holidays in earlier years. He had not been for the last couple of years, but he knew the farmer would have a welcome and a room for him even if he arrived unannounced. Hill sheep farming was a hard and precarious existence: any extra money would be welcome, and Chisam always paid well. He would find a refuge from people in the forest, or on the bare fell tops above.

He rose, dressed, and checked out of the hotel without breakfast, and made his way through the still empty streets to the railway station. By train and carrier he made his way to Ennerdale Bridge, from where he walked the remaining four miles to the farm. It was mid-morning when he arrived, and the sun was already making him sweat. Hartley the farmer was up on the fell side somewhere with his son, but Dorothy, his wife, made him welcome as he had expected. She revived him with cold roast mutton and hot sweet tea while he explained what he wanted. He would pay for full board and the rent for the room for both nights, Saturday and Sunday, but she was not to be concerned if he did not return in the evening and spent the night on the fells. It was fine weather, and he had done it before, so there was no reason for her to be alarmed.

Dorothy packed up some food for him, and by mid-day he was walking up the valley among the trees of the forest. Ennerdale is a narrow valley and the forest spread part way up the fell side on either side. From a vantage point on the lower slopes of High Stile Chisam could see a glint of the blue of the lake through the trees below and to the right of him, and the steady rushing of the stream in the valley bottom still reached him. He stayed in that spot for a long time, sitting on a fallen tree and letting his mind wander

48

without settling on the problem which had driven him there. He watched a succession of brightly coloured beetles making a laborious and steady progress over the carpet of pine needles among the undergrowth. He watched expectantly as a rather small spider cautiously approached a rather large bluebottle that had blundered into its web, and felt a certain satisfaction when the spider finally made a rush at the thrashing insect and fastened it in a deadly embrace, the bluebottle's vain buzzing becoming intermittent and weaker until it was quiescent, and the spider went about its gruesome business. Chisam felt cocooned by the trees and enjoyed the solitude they gave - it was a pine forest, the underbrush of deadwood dense and the trees closely spaced, with few signs of active life apart from insects. Even birdsong was only heard occasionally.

Eventually, however, there grew upon him a feeling akin to guilt, that he was wasting time, letting precious hours slip away in daydreaming and refusing to face the main issue. He had to make decisions, and in order to think, he had to walk. He found his way back to the path and continued up the valley. He started climbing as he did so, finally leaving the trees, moving diagonally up the fell side as he neared the head of the valley. He doubled back as he reached the saddle, and began walking up the ridge to High Crag. As he reached the summit, the sun was going out in a spectacular blaze of light behind silvery banks of cloud which lined the edge of the western sea, itself a bar of pure silver light beyond the darkening lowlands spread out, foreshortened, at the distant mouth of the valley. The darkness came upon him as he continued on up the ridge towards High Stile; the darkness of the night, and the darkness of his mind. The night, however, was not dark: soon after nightfall the moon rose in a near cloudless sky and transformed the darkness with a light so bright that it might almost have been a dull afternoon in winter, and Chisam, from his vantage point, could see for miles. Shortly before midnight he reached the summit of High Stile, at 2600 feet the highest point on the ridge. It was indeed a high place; and now the land was laid out before him, a jumble of anonymous-looking peaks with familiar names: Gable, Pillar, Red Pike, Grassmoor; looking not alien and lunar as might be expected, for the moonlight was gentle, but eerie and mysterious. The light glistened softly on black waters, on Buttermere immediately below him, on Crummock Water beyond it, on Ennerdale Water on this side of the ridge, and in the distance, on the sea.

In that high place, the High Stile, that stepping stone to nowhere, Chisam faced his despair, the darkness of his mind which no moonlight could dispel. He had sensed for a long time that this ordeal was coming. His despair was a slow unremitting disease. It was not the sharp, frenzied agony of the rejected lover. He had not come to the remote eyries of these empty hills because of Stella. He had loved Stella, and loved her still if he were

49

to admit it, and she had hurt him deeply by her rejection of him. His mind would carry the scars, the bitterness of the destruction of that love, to the end of his days, so much had it meant to him. But the true nature of his malaise was more general. He had lost his way, and he did not know how to go on. His past had been nullified, and he had lost all prospects for the future. More than that, he had lost all confidence in himself; he had lost his ability to cope with life, or what he saw was left to him of life: he had lost the will to carry on. It was true that he might, in time, be able to repair his finances sufficiently to come out of debt, to cease having constantly to worry about demotion or dismissal. He might, one day, find another woman who would be prepared to countenance an arrangement as unorthodox as Stella had done, although it was not a likely prospect in view of his altered circumstances. Anything more than that was as elusive as ever. Such limited prospects as these, and the price he would have to pay for them - years of cheerless self-sacrifice, left him feeling utterly daunted. He felt he could not see it through, that he did not have the courage to face such a penance. But for the same reason, he did not have any other future. A younger man might seek a new position, or even go out to the colonies; but Chisam felt that he was too old for that. He did not yet know what he wanted, but it was not this. It had taken the failure of his attempt to become involved in the world of horseracing to bring to the surface the realisation of how much, subconsciously, he had been counting on it as a means of escape from an existence which had become a confinement, almost a prison. It was now worse than that because of what had happened.

From the summit of High Stile he had continued to wend his way along the ridge following the path in the bright moonlight over outcrops of rock, tussocks of coarse grass and springy heather. He passed the summits of Red Pike and Starling Dod; the short summer night came to an end as he approached Great Borne at the western end of the ridge, and silhouetted the tops of the central fells on the skyline behind him as he stood on this, the lowest and westernmost of the summits along the ridge. From there, the path led down a little way onto the long flat shoulder which flanked the twin limestone callosities of the summit on the northern and western side.

This was the end of the road, or so it seemed. This was where his reluctant feet had all along been bringing him, the place which his memory had inexorably and insistently been urging into his consciousness. He came to the place. In the clear morning light, its soft greenness was like a soporific, alluring, inviting him into its enveloping embrace. There was Floutern Tarn, a long, narrow, boat-shaped pool framed between two green mounds, its vivid cold blue providing the contrast which made the green around him even more gentle. It looked, indeed it was, the easiest thing in the world to walk forward

50

so as to dip one's fingers in its cold, quiet water. He did not know how far away it was - the sheep he could see grazing, almost motionless, around its shores appeared as white mites on a leaf - it was perhaps a thousand feet down to where the fine brown runnels of watercourses criss-crossed the bright green of the boggy hollow in which the tarn lay. He knew that, hidden beneath the edge on which he stood, the green mountainside was broken by an outcrop of rock, and that he would die when his body hit that, before coming to rest, lifeless, in the green embrace of the moss of the bog, its soft promise fulfilled.

Gazing down at the treacherously peaceful valley below, Chisam gazed at his ordeal - the courage to face life, or the courage to face death. In a moment, unbidden, the madness of impulse came upon him, and he moved forward to jump quickly, now, while the blinding rush of impulse had cleared all thought from his mind. Thought, however, is quicker than action, and even as he went forward, he was betrayed by his imagination. He saw as in a dream, the green valley swim and move, the outline of the tarn blur and shake before him as his eyes filled with tears of shame and mortification and he experienced one brief moment of terror.

He was alive, he was dead; he was alive again. Was the courage, the impulse which failed him in the last second while he still had control of his destiny before unrelenting gravity took over, a mark of his weakness, of cowardice? Was a coward a man in whom the imagination is quicker than the mindless impulse? Was it a lesser courage which turned him away from that green edge to face the prospect of life that had driven him up there? Chisam did not know. All he knew was that at the end, it was not fear of the pain of death which had defeated the impulse - had he not chosen that deceptively gentle place with just that in mind? - but simply of death itself, that nameless fear of oblivion which is with us always. Perhaps the truth was that the nature of his courage had been tested, and his imagination had not yet been sufficiently blunted by despair to make death utterly desirable, for the impulse to carry him to oblivion. He was not a coward, any more than any of us are, even if, for the moment, he thought himself one. He simply knew exactly where he stood in relation to life and death. The reserves of life which he had discovered up there on the ledge might still one day desert him, and death might then become utterly desirable. But he knew that, having once tried and failed, he could not jump now. He would not try again - he was safe from that, at least for the moment. He was shaken, not just by the imminence of death, but by the knowledge that just for a moment, a half second, he had been fully committed to death. The fact that the madness had been drawn, and exorcised, as it were, and he was still alive, left him with a certain inner calm. But there was no elation in still being alive. He knew that his trek through the night over the ridge had been in preparation for this moment, and his drawing back at the last second now made him feel a coward. And there was the thought of what he now had to face, down there in the world of men.

Slowly, he made his way down off the mountain, reached the lane, and made his way up the valley back to the farm. It was late morning when he arrived, and again he found Dorothy alone. She gave him food and drink, but could get little out of him in return, beyond the admission that he was tired, and his unshaven face and air of exhaustion told her that already. He asked Dorothy if she would show him to a bed, since he hadn't slept for the best part of two days, and he felt he could sleep the clock round. However, he wanted to be called for dinner, which he would eat with them, and pay his respects to his host, whom he had not seen yet.

Dinner was a strained affair. Hartley, the farmer, and his son Harold, a lad of about twenty, were both there as well as Dorothy, and something of Chisam's sombre mood must have communicated itself to them. There was much loud silence, punctuated by the clinking of cutlery and unnecessary clearing of throats, and a reluctance of anyone to meet the eyes of anyone else, especially Chisam's. However, the meal wasn't to end that way. It was Hartley who, with a certain boldness, given the difference in rank between them, broached the subject which was in different ways, on all their minds.

"I hope you'll forgive me speaking out of turn, Mr Chisam, but you've clearly got something pretty serious on your mind, and I . . that's to say, we . ." He glanced at Dorothy, and Chisam found that a small corner of his mind could still be amused by the discovery of the true origin of this question.

"We was wondering if there was any way we could help."

"Well, it's kind of you to ask, but in fact you've done the most helpful thing you could by agreeing to have me here at such short notice. I know you've been kind enough to put me up before, but I did just turn up on your doorstep unannounced."

"Oh, you've been no trouble, Mr Chisam, no trouble at all," Dorothy interposed. "Indeed, you've hardly been here at all," she went on with a suggestion of embarrassment.

"I . . had a difficult decision to make, and no-one could help me make it. I needed to be by myself to think about it, which is why I'm grateful for being able to come up here," Chisam explained a little stiffly. "Well, now I've made my decision, and everything's all settled. I can only thank you once again for your hospitality, and assure you there's nothing more you could do to help."

He hoped he had cleared the air, and so it seemed he had; but he noticed Hartley looking at him curiously for a moment before turning away. Later, as he was preparing to

52

retire to bed for the night, he exchanged a few words with Hartley, and expressed regret at not having seen him or had a chance to speak with him before that evening, given that he had to be away early on the morrow.

"That's alright, Mr Chisam," said Hartley slowly. "I did see you though, early this morning, out on Great Borne."

Their eyes met for a moment, and Chisam could not speak. Hartley let his eyes wander away, as if he was seeing again what he had seen of Chisam that morning. Finally he looked down at his boots.

"Aye, well, I'll be saying goodnight, Mr Chisam. Perhaps you'll come again when things is a bit better with you."

They shook hands, and retired to their respective rooms, Chisam very thoughtful. He never did find out if Hartley had been a witness to those long moments on the edge above Floutern Tarn, or whether his imagination had read things into Hartley's words and behaviour which weren't really there.

He left early the following morning, walking to Ennerdale Bridge, where he caught the carrier to the railway station, and the first train into Whitehaven. He was due at the company offices at nine. This was the other side of the ordeal, the side he had turned away from death on Great Borne to face. He was dreading the coming day, dreading the very arrival at the big, grim building in Whitehaven's tawdry market place, the dingy offices with their impersonal bustle, the constant apprehension about the power and possible malevolence of the presence behind the heavy panelled door marked 'Manager', and the periodic apprehension at the quarterly visits of the company auditor. The auditor had just paid the company a visit, and his report was expected that week.

And yet, he had no more particular reason to feel dread than he had done on Friday. Today would be exactly the same as Friday - nothing would have changed, and nor would anything change. Tomorrow morning, and for every succeeding morning until the end of his days, he would have to rise from his bed, and journey to face the same wearisome, grim monotony, without respite. It was the psychological barrier of that first morning after he had decided to turn and face it that was making it such a daunting prospect. As the train rumbled slowly into Whitehaven, past the wheels and chimneys of the pitheads up on the hill, and the lines of grimy coal trucks standing on sidings, Chisam remembered the famous lines spoken by Macbeth; his emotions were stirred, and by the time the train stopped in the station, he was feeling very sorry for himself.

Such was his state of mind, that there impinged on his consciousness only very gradually an awareness that something was different. It was nothing he could put his finger on at first; more of an instinct, an intuition that something had changed, or rather,

53

something had happened. He looked about him as he walked towards the statio
concourse, but he could see nothing that was obviously wrong or out of place. Th
station was its usual bustle of activity at that hour of the morning, with people coming i
to work from surrounding towns and villages; trains hissed and steamed, carriage door
slammed, uniformed porters lounged or waved and gesticulated at each other or helpe
old ladies negotiate the precarious step from carriage to platform, and people like himse
hurried by, not quite late for work, groping for their tickets to show at the barrie
However, he also noticed that the people who were waiting for trains, who normall
stood aloof from each other, each trying to pretend that they were the only one on th
platform, in the best British tradition, were actually engaging in conversation, and one
two groups were huddled round a newspaper; others were looking across at the opposit
platform, where a group of bored-looking soldiers were sitting or standing. Chisam ha
seen them there before - they were from the local battalion of territorials, obviously o
their way up to Carlisle to join the regiment for manoeuvres. The only unusual thing wa
that he had always previously seen them going up on a Friday evening: if he saw them o
a Monday morning, they were arriving in Whitehaven, not departing. He was mystifie
Had the prime minister been assassinated? Had there been trouble in Ireland, perhap
even a rebellion? The press had been predicting something of the sort for a while no
especially in relation to the Home Rule Bill. There had been reports of gun-running, an
illegal armies, but it was hard to know what was really going on. He passed through th
barrier and out into the station approach, intending to press on to the office in th
market place - someone there would know, presumably. But there was a newsboy on th
other side of the station yard, not a normal feature of the station approach, and itself a
indication of something unusual, and he was doing a brisk trade, too. Well, he wou
find out sooner rather than later. He crossed over to buy a paper, and as he did so, he fe
the shock jolt his mind, indeed his whole body, as he caught the words of the boy's cr
repeated endlessly as he mechanically handed out papers and took money.

"War . . . War . . . War in Europe. War . . . War in Europe."

Chisam bought his paper and quickly turned to the foreign news pages. He stood
silence as he took in the meaning and import of the news; the office, the newsbo
everything forgotten in that moment. Something was happening to him. As his ey
hastily scanned the columns of print, the close-typed words seemed to blur and run in
each other, like the faces of people seen from the window of a train which is gatherir
speed. Something to do with that trouble in the Balkans - he vaguely remembered fro
the previous week. It hadn't seemed very important. But the headlines stood out, and t
sense of shock was re-doubled. "Germany and Russia at war." "France invaded

54

German troops." "War between France and Germany certain." "Luxemburg and Belgium invaded by Germany." "British ultimatum to Germany." "War with Germany unavoidable."

War with Germany. Germany . . . Germany . . . The name resounded through his mind, and all his thoughts were eclipsed by the effect it had on him. He did not experience the feelings of patriotic hatred which were shared by most of those around him, standing with their newspapers as he was. The name seemed like the incantation of a spell that had caught him in its thrall. He remembered the cold, aristocratic Prussians at Lowther, and their arrogant air of assumption of the invincibility and the divine right of themselves and their country. He also thought about the genial, quick thinking German naval officer with the booming guffaw and enough after-dinner conversation for four men, who had saved his life, and left him with the feeling that he had known him for two years instead of two days. Germany . . . Germany . . . He was filled with a strange, fey emotion - neither hatred nor its opposite, but simply an awareness of the strength and power of the country, some of whose people he had come, so briefly and dramatically, to know, which for a moment was of such intensity that it left him physically almost shaking; but inwardly it blessed him with a sense of tranquillity such as he had not known for a long time. He could not at that moment see any greater tangible hope for the future than he could before, but for reasons that he could not have explained even to himself, he no longer felt afraid.

8

Seven months of war had produced changes that were subtle rather than dramatic, on lif
in the backwater of west Cumberland. In Kent, it was said, when the wind was from th
east, you could hear the guns rumbling on the front in France. There had been rumour
of a threatened invasion launched from the captured Belgian ports; and more substantiv
reports of bombardments of some of the east coast towns by airships, or 'Zeppelins'
which were of doubtful efficacy to judge from the British reports of them.

In Cumberland, the war had a more indirect effect. Many of the younger men had le
to join the colours; not a few in direct response to Lord Lonsdale's advertisemen
published in the local press not long after the outbreak of the war, for volunteers for th
Cumberland and Westmorland Yeomanry, which had challenged its readers to conside
'Are you a mouse, or are you a Man?' Chisam had thought it in rather bad taste, but i
had had an enthusiastic response from the county's young men. Now, six months late
some of the names of those who had been so proudly publicised by the local press a
having volunteered, 'as a patriot' or 'for king and country', were starting to appea
again, in the casualty lists. These were largely private tragedies among a people nc
given to public expressions of grief outside the staid and formal conventions of the tim
The postman and the telegram boy became objects of fear among families who ha
fathers, husbands or sons away at the war. The newspapers were full of the wa
recruitment posters began to appear on billboards, and the local gentlewomen organise
whist drives, raffles and jumble sales 'in aid of our brave soldiers at the Front'.

The war had gradually ceased to be something new, and had started to assume a kin
of grim permanency in people's minds, so that the days of peace as recently as th
previous summer now seemed absurdly naïve and unreal. And yet, in a contrast that wa
slightly eerie, there was much continuity from those peacetime days: the continuity c
routine, of work and business. For the many like Edward Chisam, whose lives were on
peripherally affected by the war, their existence continued to be dominated by th
circumstances and vicissitudes which had dominated them before the war. In Chisam
case, the war had proved to be a mixed blessing. A number of younger men from th
company had left to join the army, and although their places and their prospects wer
kept open for when they returned, as month followed month and the war appeared t
become increasingly intractable as well as expensive in human life, that seemed less an
less likely. To the extent that Chisam had seen some of them as possible rivals an
successors to himself if he failed to maintain his precarious balance on the tightrope wa
between bankruptcy and public disclosure, he felt his own position was a little easie

Only a little easier, however: his main cause for anxiety, the company's auditor, while far too old for military service, was, with the relentlessly unimaginative mind of the accountant, regrettably far from senile.

On the other hand, the war also made life more difficult in another way. The company, depending as it did on ships for its overseas trade, became vulnerable to the threat from German commerce-raiders, whether real or perceived. These had made little impact as yet, and no ship carrying any of the company's goods had been attacked, but this had not prevented the insurance companies from pushing up their premiums, cutting the profit margin on every shipload. The company, as a response, had started to take a greater interest in the cocoa futures scheme managed by Chisam, and Chisam, who by that time was milking the futures stock for all he could get out of them, found these attentions unwelcome. Since Chisam was also still principally responsible for the import side of the company's business, and therefore had to deal with the insurance companies as well as negotiate with the ship owners, this made his position doubly delicate. It also allowed him scope to obscure some of his more embarrassing financial transactions. His personal finances had certainly improved over the previous twelve months, although he was still heavily in debt; and his speculations on the local cocoa market were such as to significantly affect the market price. Often he had to be cautious in order to be discreet, a restriction he often bore ill when a large profit had to be foregone. The insurance agents and the ship owners, whose unreasonableness, and, he felt at times, downright avarice, caused him so much trouble, were often particularly intransigent.

With the constant anxiety about being so much in debt, it was all very depressing. Other developments served only to increase his depression, and the growing feelings of cynicism which were part of the air of world-weariness which he cultivated as a kind of defence against despair. Not long after the outbreak of the war, Chisam read in the London newspapers of the appointment of Lord Hemswell to a senior post in the War Office.

"This well known and popular 'man of the turf'," the newspaper informed its readers, "moved by a deep sense of patriotism and having humbly offered his services to his king and country, has taken up the burden of high office in the Military Procurement Department of the War Office. Lord Hemswell's great organising ability, and his wide knowledge of military life, means that the country is assured of another capable hand on the helm of the nation's affairs in these troubled times of war . . ."

Even Chisam, who was not unused to seeing such prose in the press of late, was taken aback by the cloying sycophancy of the unknown hack writer in London about this particular item. He had looked Lord Hemswell up in the local library's copy of Debrett's, and learned among other things that his lordship's only formal connection with the military had been a brief commission in the Guards back in the '80s. He had started as a lieutenant and finished as a major, an achievement which, in so short a time, spoke much for the power of wealth and privilege. In peacetime it would certainly have been though unusual for someone like Lord Hemswell, this 'man of the turf', to have been appointed to a position in the War Office. Now, however, with everything military being expanded it would be a different matter. Lord Hemswell was apparently now largely responsible for the procurement of much of the equipment for the British army. The idea that this would most probably take second place to the personal avarice of one man, Chisam felt was disturbing: more than that, it was demoralising. The amount of money now available for tenders by private contractors would be vast, and the potential benefits to the post-holder were obvious. Chisam wondered if Lord Hemswell had used private knowledge of the embarrassing secrets of certain individuals in high places to get himself appointed to the post. The job itself probably didn't pay a great deal compared to the private incomes of most of the people who tended to fill such positions; but the potential size of all the various 'gratuities' would be enough to make anyone who was adept at engineering such transactions impressively wealthy.   And indeed, in the subsequent months, Lord Hemswell certainly seemed to be moving up in the world, to judge by the reports in the London newspapers. He bought a new town house in the most fashionable residential district of London. Just before Christmas, his name was mentioned in the 'Court Circular' column in the London 'Times' , as one of the guests at a private Royal function at Windsor. His name started to appear in the Society gossip columns; and of course there were more expensive racehorses, and Lord Hemswell's colours became fashionable at the big race meetings.

Chisam found that what affected him most was not so much the example of Lord Hemswell himself, in isolation, as it were, but the idea that there were others in high places who had 'a hand on the helm of the nation's affairs', who were similarly motivated. He had no means of knowing if it was so, but the suspicion was there. All around him, people allowed themselves, quite uncritically, to be guided in their view of the war, by the newspapers, which seemed to have become little more than purveyors of official propaganda as far as the war was concerned, and shared in the growing general hatred of the Kaiser and the German nation at large. Even after several months of war all this left Chisam largely unmoved. Even though Germany had started the war, this produced in him none of the jingoism which was echoing all around him, so profound had become his disillusionment, and his cynicism about the other side of the story. He was not naïve: he knew all about corrupt business practices - indeed, he was hardly in position to moralise about them himself - but the realisation that when it came to human greed there were no taboos, that there was no level of society above which morality might be expected in even the most immoral, affected him more than he realised at the time.

Other events followed which were to deepen his sense of disillusionment. Although his personal finances had been improving steadily, he had been in serious debt for over two years. His main creditor was a local syndicate of bankers who, from requiring from him a detailed account of all his financial business, probably knew more about him than anyone else. For the most part, he had dealt only with the senior partner, Vincent Morgan. Morgan was elderly, and very correct in his manner, and while Chisam always found the monthly meetings, where he had to account for his every action in the previous thirty days, deeply humiliating, he at the same time recognised that Morgan dealt with him as courteously as the situation allowed, and was probably not a little embarrassed himself by the sordid nature of their business. This was in spite of the fact that, as far as Morgan knew, Chisam's debt was due to his irresponsible extravagance: the idea of blackmail could not be even hinted at.

On this occasion, however, when he attended the bank chambers, Chisam was informed by a secretary that Mr Morgan was ill and unable to attend, and that he would be seen by another partner in the syndicate instead. The other partner turned out to be none other than Robert Harrison, Stella's new lover. Harrison was neither courteous nor embarrassed by the situation: indeed, he seemed to relish the detailed humiliation of Chisam. His questioning probed the most intimate details of Chisam's life, to an extent that was patently more than was necessary for the establishment of the financial position, and seemed to be intended to satisfy some personal whim of Harrison's. Chisam concealed with difficulty some of the murkier of his dealings on the cocoa exchange, which strictly would have been the business of his employer and not his creditors. But Harrison's manner became increasingly provocative.

"You know, if banking has an adverse reputation, it's precisely because of people like you," he said, in a lightly conversational tone which carried an edge of superciliousness that made it vastly arrogant. "You think you can take money from other people, the hard-earned money which honest and decent citizens have saved, in pounds, or even shillings, every week at the bank, just so that you can indulge your profligate weakness for gambling. You're a wastrel, Chisam, an idle, profligate wastrel. It's only because of the generosity and tolerance of some of my colleagues, generosity which you haven't been slow to take advantage of, that you've managed to get away with it for so long. If I had my way, you would be locked up."

"My God, I'm not having that from you, Harrison, or from anyone . . ." Chisam had half risen from his seat, the humiliating questioning, and now this, having goaded him into a response. Unconsciously, his fist had clenched ready to strike; but Harrison was still master of the situation, and seemed quite unperturbed by the possibility of violence.

"And what would you prefer?" he said silkily. "To be reminded of what you are, by me, or that we should foreclose on you, with all that that would involve. You'd better bear that in mind before making too much of your injured pride and conceit. And you can sit down again, too. Don't think I'm in the least impressed by your histrionics."

Chisam was about to give effect to his half-formed intention to punch Harrison in the face, when it suddenly occurred to him, like a revelation, that that was almost certainly what Harrison was hoping he would do. Harrison was looking for an excuse, an opportunity, to bring about Chisam's public humiliation and destruction. Chisam immediately came to the obvious conclusion: Harrison knew about his former relationship with Stella, and his jealousy was such that he wanted revenge. He could not do so in any direct way for fear of injuring Stella, so he needed to provoke Chisam into some action that would be sufficient justification for the syndicate to foreclose on him.

Slowly, Chisam let his fist drop, and he sat down again, a curious expression on his face. His manner was very transparent; but the moment was lost on Harrison, who, swept along by the tide of his own self-righteous wrath, was imposing further conditions and restrictions on Chisam. Moments earlier, these would have been sufficient to bring Chisam's anger to the surface, especially the stipulation that Chisam should report to the syndicate not monthly, but weekly, with an even more detailed account of his affairs than before. Now, Chisam controlled his anger, and reflected that he probably stood a good chance of persuading Vincent Morgan to reverse Harrison's unreasonable stipulations. Chisam also had to control the desire to taunt Harrison about his jealousy. For one thing, he could not be certain that Harrison knew about his relationship with Stella, and there were still considerations of discretion involved therefore. Also, as he hardly needed reminding, it was Harrison who now had Stella, whatever had happened in the past, and whatever Harrison's knowledge or suspicions about it might be. He was unable, however, to resist a frosty response to Harrison's rudeness.

"Be careful you don't go too far, Harrison, or you may find that I have a case against you for professional misconduct."

It was a mistaken intervention, designed to salve his vanity, and it was his vanity, in the end, that suffered.

"Don't you threaten me, Chisam, because I'm not having it, not from the likes of you, especially not from the likes of you, a feckless wastrel who's in debt up to his ears. Let me warn you for the last time: one false step on your part, and we'll ruin you. That's a

60

promise."

Chisam left the interview feeling shattered, his morale drained. The feeling of depression and hopelessness that he had managed to keep at bay for some time was starting to return, stealing upon him like the influence of a drug. As events seemed inexorably to take a turn for the worse, it was an influence that was difficult to resist. Matters were not improved when he had to go through a similar ordeal for the next three weeks, before Vincent Morgan recovered from his inconvenient illness, and brought him, as he had hoped, some relief from Harrison's vendetta. But other developments were to follow.

After the first shock of seeing them together in the theatre box that evening in July, Chisam had gradually come to regard Stella's relationship with Harrison with a resigned and sullen acceptance. There was nothing he could do about it - he knew where he stood with Stella - and for the most part, the pressures of his day to day existence tended to push the matter to the back of his mind, where it remained in abeyance, although never forgotten. He was reminded of it when, occasionally, he would see them together at some formal event or function; but it had not occurred to him that Harrison desired more from his relationship with Stella than he had, even though it would be the only proper interpretation that might be put on their association in public. Seeing the announcement in the local press therefore came as a renewed shock to Chisam.

HARRISON : ROBERTSON. The engagement is announced of Mr Robert Harrison, J.P. of Stanwix, Carlisle, partner in Morgan, Semple, Brown and Associates (Bankers), to Mrs Stella Robertson of Hensingham, Whitehaven, widow of the late Mr Frank Robertson, and daughter of Mrs and the late Major R. G. Fenwick of Appleby.

Why should it have such an effect on him? The officiousness of seeing it in print perhaps. The fact that it underlined once and for all that he had lost Stella for good. Surely he had not been in any doubt about that since that evening in the theatre the previous July. The fact that he had never sought marriage with Stella, nor she with him, had led him to expect that she would treat any other man in the same way. The fact that she was now marrying Harrison when she had never sought marriage with him made him feel somehow belittled. But above all else, there was a sense of loss. They had been together and he had felt such happiness because of her. And beyond that, there was something darker - that she who had loved him, and received his love, could also be capable of loving, indeed of preferring, a man he found so completely loathsome. It was as though Harrison had not only taken Stella from him physically, even if that was not strictly the case, but also even the image of her that he had held in his affections and his memory, by showing it to have been a false image.

The wedding, when it took place, was a very splendid affair, with the marriage ceremony taking place in St James' church. There was a large guest list, and most of Whitehaven society seemed to be on it, to judge from the report in the local newspaper. There was the inevitable photograph of the couple taken outside the church door, Harrison looking relaxed and handsome in formal morning attire, top hat in hand, and white carnation buttonhole, and Stella looking - well, happy. Serenely happy. One could not doubt it. Even if one of Harrison's attractions was his wealth and position, there was no doubt that Stella was also very happy to be marrying Harrison the man. Chisam, looking at her in the picture, at her radiant smile, and the elaborate white bridal gown, and wondering if, during the ceremony or the subsequent celebrations, she had thought of him, or their time together, even once, briefly, decided that she had not, not even briefly. With the single-mindedness of her sex, she had cut him out of her life, and now, on her wedding day, her thoughts would have been wholly absorbed by her new husband. For her, he was dead and buried in the past. For Chisam, it seemed as if his degradation was complete. He had lived without hope for more than two years, and whatever had sustained him during that time was now also gone.

Exactly a week to the day after Stella's wedding, he received the letter.

9

The letter was addressed to Chisam at the company offices. The foreign stamp and postmark immediately distinguished the letter from the rest of his mail, as did the fact that the address was typewritten. The stamp was Dutch, and was franked with an Amsterdam postmark. Despite his curiosity, some instinct decided Chisam not to open it in the office, and he put it in his pocket to open later at home. It was a long day, and from time to time his thoughts returned to the letter. When he eventually opened it, it still nevertheless took him completely by surprise.

The letter was from Fritz Seebohm. There was no doubt of that, even though Seebohm had not signed the letter, but only typed his initials 'F. S.' at the end, and had made no explicit reference to who he was. A few words at the beginning of the letter about their conversation at Lowther were enough to establish his identity to Chisam beyond any doubt.

"I hope that the war has not produced feelings of bitterness between us," Seebohm had written. "It is the fault of neither of us that Englishmen and Frenchmen and Germans are fighting each other. Even those who are fighting are fighting anonymous men in different uniforms - they are not motivated by personal hatred. Surely, therefore, it would be wholly inappropriate for us to feel such personal animosity because of the war, especially when, apart from the war, we have discovered we have many interests in common. Therefore, there is no reason why we, who have known each other for four years should not meet, on neutral ground, as individual men, to discuss a matter of mutual interest. I am writing this in Amsterdam. I shall again be in this city on Thursday, Friday and Saturday of the week after next. If you will make the journey, I should like very much to see you again, Chisam. It seems a long time now since I tried to convince you of the superiority of Catholic bad taste over Protestant prudery, and there is much to show you here in Amsterdam to convince you further of that. And there is the particular matter I wish to discuss with you. I shall not take it hard if you do not come. These are difficult times, and it may be that I am asking too much. But if you do come, I shall be very pleased to see you again."

If Seebohm was acting on his own, he was taking a considerable risk in sending such a letter. Such an attempt to open a clandestine line of communication across the front line of the trenches could cost him his life. Even if he was acting on behalf of German Naval Intelligence, it was still a highly risky venture, assuming he had no idea of what Chisam's circumstances might be. The demi-monde of espionage was barbed with mistrust and betrayal, and was the last thing that Chisam needed in his present position.

But although these thoughts occurred to Chisam so that he was not unaware of what the risks might be, they carried no great force with them. In the position he was in, such risks could no longer carry the alarm that they would have done otherwise. He had already been betrayed, and now, there was nothing else. Betrayal was now double-edged, and he could contemplate it with a kind of equanimity. And in any event, there was another aspect to it. His eyes kept going back to, and re-reading the last sentence of the letter: " . . . if you do come, I shall be very pleased to see you again."

Why should he feel such emotion on reading a trite platitude like that? Because, perhaps, it wasn't written as a trite platitude. He knew somehow that Seebohm really would be pleased to see him again. How long had it been since anyone had wanted to see him, as distinct from requiring to see him? True, Seebohm evidently had something he wanted to talk about in particular, but this was different. To be able to talk to someone who was interested, to exchange news, anecdotes, jokes, opinions; to be able to communicate with another human being. He remembered the long conversation in the smoking room at Lowther, and he immediately felt that he would be very glad to see Seebohm again; someone who would not judge him for his mistakes, but accept him as an equal, without prejudice. The intensity of the feeling was such that for a moment his eyes were moist with the emotion it produced. It would be good to see Seebohm again. How strange that the only human being in the world who might still regard him as a friend should be counted as one of the enemy, because he was a German.

Thoughtfully, Chisam began to consider the implications of the letter. Even before he had weighed up the pros and cons of the matter, he sensed instinctively that this was going to prove a watershed in his life. Nevertheless, the fact of the war made it a serious matter. It meant that Seehbohm was an enemy, especially as he was presumably still a serving officer, and any attempt to communicate with him would be regarded by the authorities as a treasonable offence if it was discovered. Even to hang on to Seebohm's letter without reporting it would presumably also be a serious offence. Indeed, Seebohm was surely taking a risk that he would report the matter to the authorities, and perhaps even go to Amsterdam acting as their agent. In the same way, Seebohm himself might be acting as an agent of his Government for purposes of their own.

With some impatience, Chisam dismissed these ideas from his mind. Quite apart from the fact that he could see no conceivable reason why the German Government should be interested in him, he felt that the sense of friendship between himself and Seebohm would preclude duplicity of that sort: or perhaps he believed in that so strongly that he was prepared to allow his judgement to be influenced by it. Either way, he was not in the mood to care.

In fact, it was more than a passing mood. It was the harvest of four years of bitterness and disillusionment, four years of the insidious corrosion of those bonds which tie a man's loyalty and identity to his own community and his country. Chisam was not, even in normal times, a particularly patriotic man. He was a loner, and had a certain streak of selfishness that many such men have who have not formed the habit of communal living which a family usually brings. He did not form personal relationships easily, but those he did form he valued very much, and without them was conscious of his isolation. Beyond that, his experience was limited, and those wider communal ties were already rather weaker than normal when the acid of disaffection began to eat away at them.

It was a strong acid. He had been tricked, cheated and ruined by a prominent member of society who, apparently because he belonged to the social establishment, was rewarded for his conduct with honours and high office, while he, Chisam, was punished and ostracised for something which, gullibility apart, he was not responsible for. And once society had decided to victimise him, it would not leave him alone, but behaved like a cat with a mouse it had caught. Those responsible, not content with effectively bankrupting him with blackmail, or charging usurious rates of interest on the resulting enforced debts, had destroyed the only enduring personal relationship in his life, and would even, if they were able to have their way, like to see him reduced to the gutter, or prison, or worse. These were only individuals, but they were individuals representative of society, and society smiled on them because they were successful in what they did; and because they were its own, and Chisam was not. And these were the people who would now expect him to show loyalty to them by turning away from, and even betraying, a man whom he regarded as a friend. Chisam did not need to give the matter much thought.

If the same unquestioning loyalty and obedience was expected of him as was expected of the thousands, many of whom had been more unjustly treated by their country than Chisam, who were dying in the trenches, who, then, was the betrayer? If it took a self-centred, selfish loner, perhaps even a coward in his own estimation, to resist such a betrayal with a counter-betrayal, then so be it. From his embittered frame of reference, such loyalty made little sense to Chisam, as the war itself was making increasingly little sense. What occupied his mind on that long, lonely, extraordinary evening was not whether he should go to Amsterdam, but only whether he would be able to make the journey.

The main problem would be how to account for the time involved, probably a period of three or four days. He would have to pay for the journey out of his emergency reserve, a store of cash which he had not declared to his creditors. A journey to Amsterdam and back would make a significant inroad into this; but if it was sufficiently important, then it would have to be done. He considered the matter. As far as he knew, the packet boats were still plying between Hull and the Hook of Holland, despite the recent naval blockades. Hull was not far from York, where the company had regular business with the Rowntree company. It would not be in any way unusual for him to arrange to deal with outstanding business in York the week after next, and once there he was a good hundred miles nearer his objective. From York, he could telegraph the packet boat company, book a ticket at short notice, and be on the boat the same morning.

And in the event, it proved to be almost as simple as that. York was more sombre than he had ever remembered it, with a great many of those walking through the narrow streets in military uniform. Union flags flapped from many flagpoles, as if to remind those not in uniform of their patriotism. They slapped and fluttered, standing out stiffly in the high March wind that whistled through the streets whirling dust in people's faces and causing women to clutch at their skirts, as if trying to wake the city up to the alarums of war after it had slept the slumber of peace for centuries past. Hull, which Chisam did not know as well, was different. The bustle there was more purposeful, the sombre atmosphere more in keeping with the nature of the place, a drab, east coast seaport. Among the shipping on the windswept, white capped expanse of the Humber were the grey shapes of warships - on the move and belching black smoke from tall stacks, or swinging at anchor in the roads, while others were tied up along the quay with stevedores pounding up and down their gangplanks. There was even a submarine in the dock, the first time Chisam had seen such a vessel, a curiously tubby thing, lying so low in the water that no part of it reached as high as the top of the quay. The uniformed presence here was naval rather than military. Sailors thronged the bars and public houses near the waterfront. One of Chisam's first impressions of Hull that morning was seeing a large party of sailors forming up at the railway station, each man laden with his dunnage before setting off down to the docks under the supervision of a petty officer with a thick Ulster accent. There were also re-assuring reminders of more normal times, such as the trawlers unloading fish in the fish dock. And the packet boats were still sailing to Holland. Although trade was beginning to fall off now that both sides had imposed naval blockades, as long as there was trade, businessmen would still need to travel back and forth between the two countries. There were no curious looks or suspicious enquiries when Chisam collected his ticket from the steamship company's office.

The packet boat was Dutch, and flew a huge Dutch tricolour above its taffrail, no doubt in the hope that it would afford protection from the warships of either side. More perhaps than the sight of the warships themselves, or all the other flags and uniforms, the sight of this flag made Chisam uncomfortably aware that he was entering a war zone. But he did not spend much time worrying about it - there was much else to occupy his thoughts. At just after eleven, the ship slipped its moorings and edged out into the Humber. Soon the North Sea rollers, whipped up by the gale that was blowing out over the Dogger Bank, caused the ship to plunge and heave, and Chisam had a more immediate and physical cause for preoccupation. It was a long time since he had made a sea voyage, and the first time in rough weather, and he was horribly sick. The voyage seemed interminable. In fact, it lasted eleven hours, and it was dark when they finally edged into the shelter of the Hook of Holland, where lights twinkled invitingly across the gulf of blackness that still separated them from the ship. By this time, Chisam had almost forgotten the reason he had crossed the sea, forgotten Seebohm and the war, or the fact that he was about to land in a strange country whose language he did not know, and among whose people he would be an alien, and perhaps an unwelcome one at that. All he wanted was to get off the ship, to get off the rolling, heaving ocean, onto dry land, any land, as long as it was solid and unmoving under his feet and gave him relief from the scourge of seasickness. If the Dutch police had arrested him and taxed him with being a spy, he would have confessed to anything for the privilege of a room and a bed and some quiet where he could be alone with his misery.

In the event, he finally found these things, after the landing formalities had been completed, at an inn a little way out of the port on the road to Rotterdam, for the price of two guilders. His phrasebook Dutch proved to be largely unnecessary. His hosts, the middle-aged couple who ran the inn, not only spoke passable English, but the grins on their faces, which they took no trouble to conceal, suggested that they were not unused to having seasick English travellers turning up on their doorstep on the point of collapse, and prepared to pay anything for relief.

The following morning, feeling much recovered, he took a train into Rotterdam, and from there went by train to Amsterdam. He booked into an hotel, partly because he did not know how long his business with Seebohm was going to take, and partly because the idea of going back to the Hook for the night, preparatory to a return voyage to Hull the following day, was more than he could bring himself to face at that moment. He had to bear in mind, however, that the longer he stayed in Holland, the greater the likelihood that questions would be asked at the firm about what he had been up to all this time in York, which was where he was supposed to be.

By one o'clock, he was outside again, making his way to the hotel where Seebohm was staying, according to his letter. It looked quite an expensive hotel; the sort of place Chisam himself might on occasion stay at when he was on legitimate business. Seebohm had said that he would be posing as a Dutchman from Groningen - having some

acquaintance with that district, he could manage the Frisian dialect, providing he didn'
have to say too much. Chisam hesitated for a minute on the street, looking across at th
hotel entrance. Once he made the move and contacted Seebohm, he would be committe
in the eyes of the authorities, and presumably beyond redemption. And supposin
Seebohm himself was different from the Seebohm he had been four years earlier a
Lowther - supposing the war had changed him, despite his assertions to the contrary? A
the expectations he had built up in anticipation of this meeting might prove quit
unjustified. But surely Seebohm would not have brought him all this way for nothing. H
could not believe it. Seebohm had something specific he wanted to talk about. An
Chisam had not come all this way, and suffered that appalling voyage to turn back now
He hesitated no longer, and crossed the street to the hotel entrance.

It was an anticlimax after all.

"Mr van Dijl is not in at present - he is out to lunch," the hotel clerk told him i
response to his question. "Do you wish to leave a message?"

"No, I'll call back again in half an hour."

Damn! It was almost as if fate was trying to act as a sort of surrogate conscience b
making things difficult for him. Perhaps he would get cold feet in the next half hou
perhaps he would realise that what he was doing was wrong, and come to his senses. Bu
it wasn't that which troubled him. He no longer had any sense of conscience in th
matter. For the egoistic Chisam, loyalty had to be earned; it could not be expected, as
was obviously expected of millions of a lesser breed of men. What troubled Chisam wa
equally a product of his egoism, but at a much more personal level: was this meetin
whatever it would be about, the prelude to another betrayal? By the time he returned t
the hotel, he was in a despondent mood.

There was a different clerk on the desk this time, and ja, Mr van Dijl had not lon
returned from lunch. If mijnheer would care to leave his name . . . Chisam climbed th
stairs and made his way along the corridor to room 109. He knocked, hesitantly.

"Binnen," said a muffled voice from within.

He pushed the door open and stood on the threshold. Seebohm was standing near th
window looking down into the side street it overlooked, with the air of a man with a lo
of time to kill, and inadequate resources of spirit for such tedium. Chisam recognise
him at once, and when Seebohm turned to see who it was, recognition was mutual. H
face split into a broad grin, and he strode over and clapped both hands onto Chisam'
shoulders.

"Chisam!" he exclaimed, and stood for a moment, looking at him at arms length.

"Seebohm." Chisam was overcome by the emotion of the moment, and for a minu could not say any more. Seebohm, with theatrical exaggeration, was motioning him to silence.

"Come in, come in," he said, and closed the door quickly. "It is best if you do not use the name of Seebohm here," he said, by way of explanation. "Since I am booked into this place as Pieter van Dijl, it would be best, for appearance's sake, if I were to remain Pieter van Dijl, even to you."

Chisam noticed the humour in Seebohm's face as he went on.

"It is only to save embarrassment with the hotel staff, you understand. After all, I might just as well be a German Seebohm as a Dutch van Dijl; it makes no difference to them. But if I start off as a van Dijl, and switch to being a Seebohm in mid stream, especially after meeting a slightly disreputable looking Englishman, they might think I was up to no good, and demand higher tips for their silence, like the parasites that they are."

He paused, and regarded Chisam, still staring at him, mute.

"I don't think, you know, that you would ever make a very good secret agent - indeed, please God that you don't ! But . . .But . . ." - he gestured expansively, and motioned Chisam further into the room - "you came! After all the hours and days I have spent , increasingly convincing myself that I was wasting my time in this wretched place, you have come! My dear Chisam, it's good to see you again."

"And it's good to see you again my friend, truly it is." Whatever else happened, it felt good to be given such a warm welcome. Seebohm motioned him towards a chair.

"Do the staff here really demand tips?"

"They don't demand in so many words, but there are certain channels through which an assessment of one's tipworthiness is communicated. If it is sensed that one requires discretion, for whatever reason, then a certain tip is required. If you don't pay, then it would be wise for you not to visit the same place again. You obviously don't know as much about living in hotels as I do."

"I suppose not. But am I not a slightly disreputable Englishman? This place is much grander than the hotel I am booked into."

Seebohm drew up a chair.

"Well, I was hoping that you would tell me what kind of an Englishman you have been over these last four years."

Chisam was not sure how to proceed. He was pulled between two inclinations. On the one hand he wanted to describe all that had gone wrong with his life over the previous four years to Seebohm, to canvass his sympathy. He had bottled it all up for so long that he badly wanted to talk to someone about it. Indeed, this was one of the motives that had

69

impelled him to come to this meeting. Against that was an innate sense of caution, tha
he should not be offering hostages to fortune in such a situation. He temporised.

"Well, I'm afraid you'll find my personal reminiscences rather tedious, and ver
depressing. The man you saw at Lowther was very different from the man you see befor
you now. But tell me, in remembrance of that time, tell me that we can still spea
honestly together; that you are still just Fritz Seebohm, the man who saved my life, as
am just Edward Chisam."

For a moment, Chisam regretted having pushed the matter so far so abruptly, as he sa
Seebohm's mood change and become more sombre, almost as if he had donned it like
heavy overcoat. Seebohm rubbed his hands over his face, and was thoughtful for
moment before answering. At length he said:

"I know why you have come here, my friend. I mean, I don't know the details - perhap
you will tell me presently - but I know in general terms why you have come. You say yc
are different from the man I knew at Lowther, but you are not. People don't usual
change that much. What changes is their awareness of what they are. Some people don
ever learn much in this way, but others learn a great deal; and one of the things the
learn is that, in the end, we are all alone. That realisation can be heightened, and it ca
be obscured, by circumstances, but it is never entirely forgotten once learned. And it is
a time such as this, when every man is submerging his own troubles in the great upsur
of patriotism and the general coming together of society in the excitement of war, th
you have left your country and come here alone. So you see, I know, before you have to
me anything of yourself or what your reasons are for coming here, that you are alon
with yourself, and probably were so long before you set out on this journey. Without an
doubt, it is an extraordinary thing to do at such a time as this. As soon as I saw y
standing there in that doorway, I knew . . ."

But he did not know! How could he know how much more to it there was than that?
proved to be the certain sense of irritation produced by these thoughts, rather than h
earlier emotions, that loosened his tongue. He did not, however, abandon caution. Apa
from anything else, he did not want to diminish himself in Seebohm's eyes
misrepresenting himself through haste.

"Indeed, you are right, and I shall tell you just how right you were in your gue
Perhaps you speak for yourself also in that respect - you too are here alone."

"Touche! But before we become embroiled in all that, can I offer you something to e
and drink? I don't know if you have eaten or not."

Chisam had not, and coffee and sandwiches were ordered and gratefully received.

At length, Chisam cautiously pushed the boat out with a question.

70

"Tell me, what do you think of the war?"

"The war . . ." Seebohm sighed reflectively. "The war. Well, in some ways, my views about the war have not changed, while in other ways I have had to change them. I should say that I am not by temperament a man of war, and when the war started, I was very sad that it meant that I was to be cut off from my friends in England and France. It was a total intrusion into my private life. But that is the way with war. Many have lost a good deal more than I have.

"At first, I must tell you, that I had little doubt about the outcome of the war, whatever other feelings I might have had about it. After all, we started the war. If the war party in the Government hadn't been in the ascendant - von Moltke and the Prussian General Staff - the Austrians would not have dared to go as far as war with Serbia; and once there was war, von Moltke had poor old Emperor Wilhelm over a barrel, as they say, and he had to agree to bring Germany in with Austria. So - I assumed that the Prussians, having started the war, knew what they were about - and not without justification. Whatever else might be said about the Prussians, they are the finest army in the world. They beat the great Bonaparte at Waterloo, thus saving the skin of a certain Duke of Wellington; they beat Napoleon III in 1870; they beat the Danes; they beat the Austrians: so why should they not be victorious again? It seemed a most reasonable assumption that von Moltke's confidence in the ability of his army was well founded. We would quickly roll up France in the west, as we had done before, and then turn east to deal with Russia.

"But then came the battle of the Marne, and we were stopped - the invincible Prussians were stopped, short of any strategic objective. Well, these things happen in war. We would regroup, attack again, and break through, to Paris, to the coast, and to victory. After all, we were only opposed by the French, and a motley assortment of British and colonial troops. But - it has not happened. We are still stopped, much as we were after the battle of the Marne all that time ago. Neither side can break through, and it looks as if that is the way the war is to go on for the foreseeable future. Perhaps we will make a breakthrough when we have defeated the Russians, and we can concentrate all our forces in the west; but somehow I rather doubt it - and in any case, when will this be? And now, we have imposed a blockade against Great Britain, and the British have imposed a counter-blockade against us. A blockade! And this is the war which was going to be over by Christmas.

"Well, as I have said, I am not a man of war. The prospect of a short war, with victory at the end of it, is something we can all look forward to. The prospect of a long war, with no end in sight, is a different matter, and with sea blockades it could be a disaster. I am a businessman, and in our business we are especially dependent on overseas trade. So

71

- what was I to do? You understand that I cannot easily face impoverishment. Apart from anything else, I have a certain position in society to keep up, and for that I require the income from my business. So you see how it is. I think perhaps you do, as your company is in rather much the same position, is it not? I should be interested to know. Tell me what you think of the war."

Chisam, although his sense of caution did not leave him, felt that he was beginning to see the light. However, what had not come across, even vaguely, was any sense of deep disillusionment with what was going on, and therein lay his caution. If Seebohm was not so disillusioned, would he understand such disillusionment? All the memories and impressions from the previous months crowded into his mind, and he hardly knew how to start. But Seebohm had asked him about the war, and that was easier to answer.

"The war hasn't affected me personally very much, at least, not so far," he admitted. "I have a cousin, whom I haven't seen for years, in the army somewhere in France. But I haven't been touched in a personal way by the loss of close relatives and loved ones, as an increasing number of people around me have been. I haven't been stirred by the war as most other people seem to have been. Indeed, from the beginning, I've felt a certain detachment from it - a detachment which you were astute enough to diagnose as soon as I came into this room, and which stems from . . . a feeling of malaise about the motives of some of our leaders, and others in positions of influence."

"Ahem," Seebohm interrupted. "You may find it strange to hear me say this, but I would rather we didn't bring politics into this more than can be helped. Indeed, I hope that, even if your motives for coming here are mainly political, my taking this view reassures you about my role in this. I say this as one who has just made some uncomplimentary remarks about the Prussians and some of our politicians, and while they may have been responsible for starting the war, they aren't the main reason why I am here. I think I know what you mean - this war is mostly about the very kind of politics that I think you were referring to; but unless it is unavoidable, I thought we could simply take such matters for granted. After all, politicians will be politicians; and if you do have a particular axe to grind, then there may be several means to the same end, as one might say."

"Yes . . ." Chisam ruefully reviewed all his good intentions before he had begun to speak. "What I was trying to say perhaps was that my motives for coming here are personal, to do with particular individuals, including some politicians, rather than with the war in general. The war is, if you like, a means to a personal end. I don't know what sort of detail you'd be interested to hear in my story. As I think I said before, it's rather sordid and rather boring. But not knowing what it was you had in mind when you wrote your letter, I had no idea, when I set out, whether it would have any bearing on my own problems. My motives for coming here are partly personal, partly political. They are also partly financial, which is what I think you were hinting at. If you like, we could proceed on that basis."

"A means to an end!" Seebohm got up and paced about reflectively. "Indeed, a means to an end. I want very much to hear your story, my friend, sordid details and all. However, I think it would be better for both of us if we were to begin with something concrete and specific. If after that, you want to tell me your story in more detail, you will feel freer to do so."

Chisam indicated his acceptance of so proceeding.

"And so, a question for you. How is the market for cocoa these days? Four years ago it was looking hopefully prosperous, if I remember. Has it lived up to its promise?"

It wasn't a question Chisam was expecting, and he considered for a moment before replying.

"Well, not especially so, no. There haven't been any dramatic improvements. I suppose it's not really in the nature of the business that there would be. I mean, you don't get wildly fluctuating demand for cocoa, or tea or coffee. It's more a case of the firm maintaining its share of the market, which we . . ."

"Ah, no, I think you misunderstand. When we spoke at Lowther, if you remember, you told me about a cocoa futures scheme you had set up. I was particularly interested because I had started a similar scheme myself, only in sugar, and I will tell you about that presently. But I should like first to hear how your scheme has progressed."

Chisam was still not sure what this was leading up to. However, it didn't sound as if Seebohm was merely making polite conversation - his interest was more specific - and there could be no objection to talking about the cocoa futures scheme. He briefly outlined the scheme, indicating the main factors involved, and ended by saying that it had been a consistently profitable venture - not massively profitable, but providing a steady and much needed source of income.

"You see, it has been my misfortune to fall into debt, largely through bad judgement - bad judgement of people, mainly, but I've been made to suffer for it. Without the money from the cocoa futures scheme, I wouldn't have been able to carry on."

Seebohm reflected for a moment. He didn't want to appear unsympathetic, which he was not; but it was a relief to him that his task had been made a great deal easier by what Chisam had just told him.

"The scheme is proving invaluable at the moment in keeping you afloat financially," he said thoughtfully. "Suppose its profitability was to be doubled, or trebled overnight: that

73

would perhaps see you in the clear financially within a fairly short time, and thereafter it would be all profit, is that not so?"

"Yes, that's true, it would," said Chisam slowly. "Although I can't see how that could be done."

"Suppose I could arrange that for you. How would you feel about that?"

"I should be very grateful, of course, but . . ."

"Grateful enough to do the same for me?"

"Well, I should say so, yes. But I'm afraid you've lost me. I think you'd better explain."

Seebohm nodded.

"Indeed, I shall. Let me begin my explanation by going through the mechanics of the business. As you know, the price of a commodity, especially something like cocoa, varies largely according to its availability, and also equally importantly, to its expected availability. Futures are speculations in the price of a commodity at fixed periods of time ahead. If one expects the price of a commodity to rise, it is profitable to buy futures. In time of uncertainty as at present, the price may fluctuate, but on the whole shows a general tendency to rise over time. This has been the case with sugar, as I know from my own business, and with cocoa also I think?"

Chisam nodded in confirmation. Seebohm continued.

"This means that futures are more or less continuously profitable, as you have said yourself, but also that profitability varies because of uncertainty of supply. It is this uncertainty," - he emphasised the point with his finger - "which is the difference between a futures scheme which is of modest profitability, and one which is of considerable profitability. Now, at the moment, the uncertainty is due to the war, to the possibility that the ships carrying the cocoa might be attacked by warships of the German navy. The uncertainty is general and diffuse, and I suspect is not very large at present, as few ships which carry cocoa have been attacked so far. However, suppose the nature of the threat were to change."

He looked at Chisam and said, "I have not lost you yet?"

Chisam, slightly puzzled, shook his head.

"Well," said Seebohm, "before I go further, perhaps you can clarify something for me. The cocoa which is traded by your company is imported into Whitehaven, is it so?"

"Occasionally we will get a load through Liverpool, but apart from that, yes, all our imports come to Whitehaven."

"Which other ports are the main entry ports for cocoa?"

"Liverpool and London are the main ports, followed by Whitehaven, then I think Bristol and Glasgow and one or two others."

"But Liverpool and London are the main ports for cocoa?"

"Yes."

"Now, do you know the names of the ships which usually bring cocoa into Liverpool and London?"

Chisam was once again somewhat taken aback by the curiousness of the question, and paused before answering.

"I think I know the names of most of the Liverpool ships, given that it's a fairly steady trade. I'm less familiar with the London side of the trade."

"Could you find out if you had to?"

"Yes, I'm sure I could."

"It is something I want you to do. The names of all the ships which bring cocoa into Liverpool and London, as far as you can find them out. Now, one further question. Does your firm have a preferential trading position in Whitehaven?"

"Yes, we do, if I follow your meaning. If there was an increase in trade in those commodities which we deal in, we would benefit the most from it."

"You do indeed follow my meaning. And so! Now I have laid almost all my cards on the table. You can see, I trust, what it is I have been leading up to."

"I've got a fair suspicion, I suppose, but I still can't see how it can be done."

Seebohm stood up, to pace up and down in front of the fireplace. He wagged his finger again, to emphasise his point.

"Consider the implications," he said, "of what I am suggesting. At the moment, there is a diffuse fear among English traders and shipowners about the threat posed by German warships, especially submarines. The fear is diffuse because, as I said before, not many ships have actually been attacked, and those only randomly. If a succession of ships carrying cocoa and similar goods into Liverpool and London were attacked, causing a marked reduction in the supply of cocoa into those ports, the inevitable result would be a rise in the price of cocoa. And it would be a rise in the price of your firm's cocoa, given that the trade into Whitehaven was, for some reason, not affected by the activities of German warships."

Chisam was feeling distinctly unhappy at this, however.

"If," he said, " I give you the names of the ships which carry cocoa into Liverpool and London, you can arrange for the German navy to sink them. That's what you're saying."

"That's what I am saying. You are wondering, perhaps, how I may ordain what the German navy does. After all, when you last saw me, I was a mere Kapitänleutnant der Reserve, without even a command of my own. That was in peacetime. In war, things are different. Since then I have transferred to the active list, and have been promoted, such are the fortunes of war. I now command a flotilla of submarines which are operational in the waters around Great Britain. It is an irony of fate that I who am dismayed by the prospect of a prolonged war, and especially by the blockades that have recently been declared, am among those most responsible for enforcing this same blockade. However, you English have a saying - it's an ill wind that doesn't blow some good. That is why I am here, and why you are here."

"But," said Chisam slowly, "if I give you the names of these ships, I will have the blood of their crews on my hands. That is what it would amount to."

Seebohm, in his pacing, had come to a stop in front of the window, and he continued gazing out of it down into the street below for a few moments before answering.

"From an operational point of view, such information is of little consequence. A ship is a ship is a ship, and if it's an enemy ship, we will endeavour to sink it."

He looked at Chisam.

"Contrary to what you may have heard, it is not our policy to sink ships without warning. Whenever it is operationally possible, without endangering our own vessel, we will stop a ship and allow the crew to take to the boats before sinking it. Cases which you may have heard of to the contrary are either lies, or other factors have been involved such as the submarine being fired on from the ship. I tell you this not as a representative of the German navy, but as Fritz Seebohm, who, I hope you can believe, is not a cold-blooded killer."

Chisam could not indeed believe such a thing of Seebohm. He was, nevertheless, far from happy about the idea of naming the ships. Even if what Seebohm said was true, i still felt somehow like a betrayal; and while it was one thing to betray a cynical ruling class, it was another thing to betray ordinary seamen who were, in general, worse of than he was.

His thoughts were transparent to Seebohm, who was standing regarding him quietly.

"Would it make any difference," he said, "if I were to tell you that all the ships that pass in and out of Liverpool will be subject to attack, and subject to the fortunes of war we will sink many, if not most of them. The information which I am suggesting you give me will only affect the order in which they are sunk, not whether they are sunk. The British authorities know that the submarines are already in position - witness the sinking of the battleship 'Formidable' recently."

Still Chisam didn't speak.

"You still want confirmation that what I have told you is true," said Seebohm. It was statement rather than a question. "Very well."

He went across to his travelling case and withdrew a paper, which he dropped int

Chisam's lap.

"That is a list of ships which have visited Liverpool between the beginning of October last year, and last week. We may not have got them all there, but I think we have most of them. A number of them are obviously regular visitors. The list comes from information supplied by the commanders of submarines that have been covering the approaches to Liverpool, and monitoring the traffic."

Chisam gazed at the list, too surprised to speak. It was not a fake. Among the involved pattern of names, dates, times and map references, he recognised the names of the ships which he knew carried on the cocoa trade with the port of Liverpool.

As if anticipating his thoughts, Seebohm added:

"We don't, of course, know what these ships are carrying in the majority of cases, only their names and movements. If we were to sink these ships in the usual way, then the ships carrying cocoa would only be sunk in a random way, although I don't doubt that we would get most of them eventually. If, however, you tell me which are the ships carrying cocoa, then I will make sure that the efforts of our submarines will be concentrated on those ships. This would have the consequence for you personally which we have already discussed."

Chisam was clearly wavering. Pushing his advantage home, Seebohm added:

"There would, of course, also be a benefit to your country's war effort. If we were to concentrate our efforts on ships which we knew were carrying cocoa and similar commodities, then attacks would be reduced on ships carrying all other kinds of cargo, including munitions ships."

Curiously, unknown to Seebohm, this last point almost had the opposite effect to the one intended, just momentarily. The reference to helping his country's war effort made Chisam think suddenly of Lord Hemswell, waxing fat on the proceeds of corruption in his honey pot in the War Office. The idea of helping him in any way, as this presumably would indirectly, filled him with revulsion. But it was only for a moment. Seebohm's point seemed to provide him with a moral justification of sorts for going along with the scheme, which the other points, however telling, had lacked. As far as the arguments about the matter went, Chisam was won over. He had come to Amsterdam in the hope that Seebohm would be able to offer him some way out of his predicament, and Seebohm had not disappointed him. It was not what he had expected, but he felt that his doubts had been cleverly anticipated and fairly met.

"Enough," he said, raising his hand as he did so, as if to stem Seebohm's persuasive eloquence. "You have won. I will tell you which ships carry cocoa. But first, you must tell me what it is you wish me to do for you in return. You have said more than once that

77

this is a matter of mutual interest, although I'm not sure how I can help you."

"I wish you to help me," said Seebohm, "by doing exactly the same for me as I am doing for you."

Chisam looked mystified.

"But I don't have any submarines to command. I don't follow."

"Well, our cases are slightly different, I agree," said Seebohm. "But what I meant amounts to the same thing in the end. Putting it simply, what I am proposing would make your business, and in particular your futures scheme, more profitable by, ah, making life more difficult for your business rivals and creating an artificial shortage in cocoa. What I should like is for something similar to be done for me. I know that the Royal Navy would be most interested in information about the details of movements of German or other ships trying to beat their blockade. I want you to supply them with that information about certain ships in particular which import sugar and other commodities for my business rivals. I would send the information to you from here in Amsterdam, and you would pass it on anonymously to the British Admiralty. There would be no need for this to involve you in any danger of discovery. I would send you the information in a disguised form using a kind of code which we can agree on here today, so that if any of my letters were intercepted, their real meaning would not be evident. Once you had deciphered the information, you would post it to the British Admiralty from somewhere in central London, having taken certain precautions to maintain anonymity."

He was in deep waters now: but that was the case anyway, regardless of the details of what Seebohm had to say. He wished he didn't feel so tired, tired in body and spirit, tired of finding himself always in a position of weakness, where he had no choice . . . But this was surely different - this was a way out, an escape route.

"Well then, if you wish it," he said at length. "Although it intrigues me to know why it would not be simpler for you to post your letter in Amsterdam directly to the Admiralty instead of doing it through me."

"No, it must be done by you. The main reason is that the British authorities would be less inclined to act on information that came from Holland, which has a border with Germany, than if it came from somewhere in London, where the embassies of half a dozen or so neutral countries, some with axes to grind against Germany, would be the likely source. I insist that you must be prepared to do this for me, as I am prepared to act on your behalf, otherwise the whole deal is off."

Before he answered, Chisam wondered how much the German navy was privy to this side of the deal, and how much Seebohm was acting in his own interests without their knowledge. The idea of this possibility, and its implications, intrigued him; but it was this, as much as anything else, which enabled him to accept Seebohm's proposition. However much or little Seebohm might tell him about his own problems, this hint that such there were, was enough to satisfy Chisam at that point. It was a pleasure which warmed him, to discover that Seebohm, even Seebohm, could be weak and devious and human, and that he could reach out a hand to him, not just as a friend, but as a kindred spirit.

10

The house martins were back, confirming beyond any doubt that spring really had come. All the gardens and embankments of the town were painted yellow with a brightness of daffodils and a shy hint of purple crocus, sudden glimpses of cascading colour bringing moments of perfection even to grimy old Whitehaven. But it was the exuberant whistling of the house martins, and the sight of them diving and swooping around the eaves and gable ends of the neighbouring houses which seemed most confidently to proclaim the fullness of spring to all who had a heart to listen.

For once, Edward Chisam had the heart to listen. His trip to Amsterdam had brought a new purpose to his life. It was extraordinary how good it had been to be able to talk to someone about the things that mattered to him most, something he had not been able to do since he had lost Stella. Seebohm was as good a listener as he was a talker, and the fact that they were engaged in similar businesses made him an understanding listener. Chisam now found it much more congenial to think of Seebohm as a fellow businessman than as a German naval officer. The bond between them had been cemented by their shared business interest, a new business venture, however unorthodox.

It was extraordinary, too, how this new window of opportunity had helped lift the load of oppression that had weighed down on his mind. At times he was almost made light headed by a feeling that he could thumb his nose at his creditors, his employer, the authorities, and society in general.

He would forget at his peril, however, that until there were specific developments in relation to it, that it was still a precarious satisfaction. He had not been back in Whitehaven a week, and no further developments had taken place, when he was suddenly called to the manager's office one afternoon.

"I've heard rumours," said the manager, when he came to the point of the interview "that your personal finances are in an extremely parlous state, and that you have been engaged in some very dubious financial transactions. Now, you know the very great importance we set by our staff maintaining the strictest financial probity. It's in view of this, and of the nature of the rumours, that I felt that the matter had to be clarified to my own satisfaction."

Chisam remained silent for long seconds before answering. He did not lose his head second thoughts were beginning to give him ideas about the nature of the rumour.

"May I ask what dubious financial transactions I am supposed to have indulged in according to these rumours?"

"I'm not sure I can say," said the manager, now slightly defensive perhaps, but with certain blankness in his eyes. "I believe horses were mentioned."

"Horses. I see. And may I ask the source of this rumour, sir?"

"No, you may not."

Chisam was surer about the defensiveness, now. "Bloody Freemasons," he thought to himself. You could never be sure who they were or who they were in league with. Under other circumstances, he might have expected to have been invited to join the Masons: his evident exclusion had left him with an enduring suspicion of the organisation and its members. He didn't know if Lord Hemswell was a Mason, but he was much surer about Robert Harrison, and the more he thought about it, the more it sounded as if Harrison was the source of the rumour.

He stood up. He was breathing rather heavily, the result of strong emotion. For a moment, he was reminded of the madness that had almost sent him to his death on Great Borne, for what he was about to do would have seemed to him in a more normal frame of mind almost as suicidal in terms of his position. But at that moment an idea had occurred to him which gave him such a sense of exhilaration that for the moment he felt he had the courage, or at least the bravado, to do almost anything.

"Then, sir," he said, "I will treat this rumour, as all rumours should be treated, with the contempt it deserves. If I were charged by an accuser, who had the courage to face me not only with accusations, but with evidence, then it might be a different case. Finally, may I say that if ever I came to regard my personal finances as being such as to jeopardise my position with the firm, or the firm itself, then sir, I should make a point of being sure that you were the first to know."

He walked out of the room, unbidden. Once outside, he was amazed at his own audacity. He returned to his own office, and was further surprised when he was not summoned again by the manager. Harrison had evidently been too cautious to supply facts - dark hints over the port after dinner, or whatever these Freemasons got up to, were apparently as far as he had gone. However, in the more sober frame of mind that now came to him, he began to see flaws in the exhilarating idea which had given him such audacity. He wasn't sure what he was going to do with it, but the only immediate course of action required by the idea could still be followed without any immediate consequences.

In the meantime, he had to reckon with the fact that his position now looked very precarious. He couldn't think of any particular reason why Harrison would want to put pressure on him at this moment, so he had to assume merely that Harrison was now ready to expose him, and was trying to engineer an exposure of the situation without compromising his own professional reputation. Chisam supposed, as before, that the man was motivated by the malevolence of an unquenchable jealousy, and was probably no entirely rational in the matter. It was a malevolence which made him feel cold. He wondered briefly what it boded for Stella, but he no longer had the sense of sympathy with her that he had still had even after she had ended their relationship. It was as though they were now separated by a great gulf.

It was a gulf which was as much of his making as of hers. A year ago, six months ago, he would have collapsed under the strain of this moment. He was now nearer to ruin than he had been when he had looked death in the face on Great Borne. He needed, now a then, time to think, to decide what to do. He may have nonplussed the manager by his brazenness on this occasion, but he knew he had gained little respite by that. Next time i would be different, and the next time would be soon.

But unlike six months ago, he was not completely alone and isolated. His meeting with Seebohm had given him a new status. The secret knowledge of another dimension to his life, one with incalculable possibilities, he hugged to himself, as a shaman might his talisman. The new dimension had a momentum of its own, however. The power behind the talisman lay in Germany, and if that brought to Chisam a sense if independent strength, it also restricted his freedom of action. Events would now go forward whether he willed them or not. Ships would be sunk, or at least attacked, whether he willed it or not, and therefore, he might as well be a beneficiary of the consequences. But he knew, as a result of the interview with the manager, that he did not have much time left. It seemed that, short of professional misconduct, Harrison was now actively trying t expose him. He had to get out of Harrison's clutches, and only Seebohm could help him do that now. Unless Seebohm delivered on his side of the bargain very soon, it would be of no use to him - and nor would Chisam then be in a position to fulfil his side of the bargain. His dilemma took a very practical form, however. In order to take full advantage of Seebohm's bounty when it came, he needed to buy as many of the cocoa futures as he possibly could - in fact he needed to throw in every last penny he could lay his hands on if he was going to make it worthwhile. But if disclosure came first, he would need cash as much as possible, to smooth the way of escape, from the law, and from the country if necessary. If he delayed buying futures until after events started to happen, the rising price of the futures would reduce the amount he would be able to buy, and also the resultant benefits. Any money he retained as cash would result in the same effect. But he had to decide very soon, or all might be lost.

He found himself, a day or two later, walking out along the south mole of the harbour past the old spiked cannon still guarding the harbour entrance against the return of the notorious Paul-Jones, who never did return, down to the lighthouse and the sea. It was

82

clear, blustery, cold day in April, gulls raucous in the wind, the sea empty and tireless, its rolling energy crashing against the grey ashlar bastion beneath his feet. It was extraordinary that he had still not made up his mind what to do. How little faith he had in himself! Was it mere indecisiveness, or a lack of courage? He had already had cause to doubt his courage; but now the thought irritated him. And yet, there was more to it than just a calculating financial transaction. To have to grab his cash and run would be most humiliating: degradingly so, for there could be no turning back once he had started to run. The alternative prospect of success was alluringly close, but he still wanted time to make the decision, and the move, at his own pace. Whether that was cowardice or indecisiveness, it was the way he liked to make decisions even if he didn't always get the opportunity to do so.

It was nearly high tide, and there were two or three fishermen on the mole with lines out over the parapet. They were all middle-aged or elderly men, as was to be expected of course; but then it seemed to Chisam that it would be so anyway, in war or peace. Fishing, at least under those conditions, was a pastime for those with patience, and the sedateness of age. He watched them for perhaps twenty minutes, perhaps longer, and during that time, none of them caught a fish. Occasionally, one or other of them would reel in his line and cast again, the line shooting out from the rod over the sea before disappearing into the waves, its owner settling back into his patient vigil. It was almost as if they would have been surprised had a fish taken the so patiently proffered bait. Chisam found it absorbing to watch them. Identifying with their unhurried purposefulness focussed his attention, and seemed to bring order to his mind in a way which, had the mole been deserted, the restless sea on its own would not have done. He felt that he could have stayed there until the sun went down, watching expectantly each time a line was reeled in to see if there was anything on the end of it - still only the bait? - well, there was no hurry - until the departure of the fishermen drove him away also, suddenly unwilling to face the emptiness of the sea. Here, where time was measured by the tides and the sun, he found the space for the emotional part of his mind to catch up with the rational part, in his sub consciousness. His reason had told him that he had little choice left in the matter; but now, whether the substance of his thoughts was instinct, choice or reason, it amounted to much the same thing in the end.

Two days later, he was due to attend at the bank chambers in the town to give the usual monthly statement of his accounts. It was something he had to steel himself for beforehand, especially now that things were reaching such a delicate stage. And as luck would have it, Vincent Morgan, the senior partner, was not available on this day, and his place was taken, once again, by Robert Harrison. The interview was conducted in

Harrison's office. On this occasion, Harrison did not go out of his way to be unpleasant and was merely cold and distant. The technique he adopted was one of clinical probing, rather than mere browbeating, which Chisam found even more disturbing. Possibl Harrison had been warned by Morgan not to go too far, a danger which he was in an case presumably well aware of. Scenting victory over his quarry, in the expectation c his covert rumour mongering having the desired effect, he could, or so Chisam reasonec substitute the pleasure of expectation for that of emotional self-gratification. With victor so close, it was best to be careful.

As he sat speaking to Harrison, Chisam thought about the half-formed idea that ha come to him during his interview with the manager a few days earlier. It was still onl half-formed: he had got no further forward with it since then, and the objections to it tha had occurred to him at the time seemed just as valid now. The idea still would not g away, however, and just as it seemed quite impractical, equally, it remained curiousl alluring. In any case, it did not require much from him at that moment. Casuall therefore, he steered the conversation with Harrison so that he was referring back t events and transactions that had taken place some time ago. As expected, the ledge which Harrison was using did not go that far back, so he had to go through to Vincer Morgan's office to get the relevant ledger, leaving Chisam alone for a few minutes i Harrison's office. As Chisam remembered from the last interview with Harrison, th latter had a supply of his special notepaper on his desk beside the blotter. There were tw piles, for headed and plain sheets, in an attractive and very distinctive light pearly gre bond paper, an idiosyncrasy which, to Chisam, seemed somewhat effeminate. It was th work of a moment to take a few sheets from each pile and slip them into his pocket. H experienced a twinge of apprehension, lest Harrison was in the habit of keeping tally the number of sheets of his notepaper. Such parsimony was beneath even Harrison however, and when Chisam eventually emerged onto the street, and a grey, rainy day, h mood was, for once, not quite as grey as the weather.

The decision which had slowly been maturing in his mind, Chisam was now ready act on. A major limitation on his actions was that he could not, under his presen circumstances, borrow money, as this would immediately come to the attention of h creditors, such was the nature of the small financial community in west Cumberland. meant that he was limited to his own resources, or else, to what he could acquire by oth means. Over a period of several weeks, therefore, he managed discreetly to se everything and anything which he could turn into cash. He pawned a number of fami heirlooms which did not belong to him, including some silverware, which he had to tak

84

to London, since they were beyond the resources of Whitehaven pawnbrokers, not to speak of the danger of tongues wagging. Old Harry Elliot on Tangier Street was a good enough fellow, Chisam supposed, for a pawnbroker, but even Harry was human. Acquisition of cocoa futures was easier, since the futures business was in his hands already, and he soon had a satisfactory stock of them in his name, a fact which was conveniently unknown to anyone else.

His trip to London had not been occasioned by his need to visit the better class of London pawnbrokers, however, but by the arrival of a letter from Amsterdam. It was long overdue. Having taken the drastic step of sinking everything he had into cocoa futures, he was now anxiously awaiting action from Seebohm. Indeed, he had reached the stage where he had begun to doubt the veracity of his mind, and to wonder whether the whole business had taken place at all. It was curious how insubstantial life could seem at times. His memories of the visit to Holland were still detailed and vivid. Recalling the sea voyage to Holland still made him feel ill, and he now had a distinct aversion to the prospect of crossing the sea. And his memories of Seebohm himself, of the imperative power of that voice and personality, which had seemed to fill the room with its energy. Such memories could not be merely the product of his imagination; but the tangible evidence of his trip was very little - a sailing timetable from the steamship company, a bill of fare from an Amsterdam restaurant, a receipt from the little guest house on the Rotterdam road. Each held a memory, and yet they might just as well have belonged to someone else. Memories that had carried him with confidence back across the North Sea had now begun to need something more substantial to re-assure him.

He was waiting for news from the sea, news from his contacts in the maritime communities of Whitehaven and other ports, news that would give him the re-assurance he needed and confirm that Seebohm would fulfil his side of their agreement. It was the letter which came first, however. He had been so pre-occupied with his own affairs that his side of the agreement had tended to slip to the back of his mind, and he had come, subconsciously, to assume that his interests would have priority. Perhaps Seebohm didn't trust him and wanted to commit Chisam to the agreement before he acted himself. More than likely, however, Seebohm simply saw his own interests as being more pressing than Chisam's.

Carefully, Chisam opened the letter. It did not appear to have been tampered with, and the contents seemed completely innocuous, much as he had expected. He set to work diligently, using the codes and procedures he had prepared from what Seebohm had told him. At length, he sat back, and took in what he had written. Even after translation it still looked cryptic, the information being kept to a minimum. There was a list of names

85

of ships, names such as 'Helgoland', 'Königen Margrethe', 'Nordstern 'Rheinmädchen', each name followed by a map reference and a date. Chisam gazed a them with mixed feelings. In an illogical way, it was a slight salve to his conscience. A least he had not had to do this. This, surely, was the stuff of betrayal. He at least, had no divulged the locations of ships whose whereabouts were not already known. Th distinction might be seen as academic, but at that moment, it was something Chisar wanted to hang on to. There was, despite the alien appearance of the German name something rather pathetic about the list. He had never seen the 'Königen Margrethe' c the 'Nordstern', but he could see them clearly in his mind's eye - very little differe from the grimy, weatherbeaten ships he knew at Whitehaven. It was not difficult t imagine the terror of the simple, rough men who sailed in them, if an enemy warshi was to loom on the horizon raining shells down upon them. The image disturbed him. he could believe such things of the Royal Navy, how much less faith could he have in th German navy? He thought again of Seebohm. To be beset by doubts made it so difficu to judge. At best, it was a matter of judgement, even if that was based on faith; but a worst . . . They were saying now in the press, that the Germans were beasts, and by som it was meant literally. Thinking of Seebohm, Chisam could dismiss such things as wa hysteria - an insidious poison that seeped into one's way of thinking without volition. H had to have some faith, faith that his judgement was right, faith that there was more humanity than the worst of it, the meanest, the most bestial. It was surely his only hop that he still had such faith.

The following weekend therefore, he made a brief trip to London, and carried o Seebohm's instructions exactly as required. Despite all the precautions he had taken, ar the knowledge that there was no possibility of the letter being traced back to him, h heart was in his mouth as the letter dropped irrevocably into the darkness of the pill box. He had well and truly taken hold of the lion by the tail. It was now up to Seebohm make sure that he saw no more of the lion than its tail. With a curious reluctance, turned away from the pillar box, and set off in search of a pawnshop.

11

It was not often that Chisam saw Harold Tilberthwaite these days. Before the war, their acquaintance mainly related to horses, but they also met socially, especially at functions for the local Conservative party. Chisam had long since been cured of any hankering after horses he had once had. His social life had become, of necessity, very limited in the last three years, but he still attended Conservative functions as representative of his firm, which was a prominent supporter of the local party. Chisam had never had much interest in politics: his attendance at such functions now he saw very much as a duty, not an interest. It was a duty which he tried to avoid when he could, mainly to avoid meeting former acquaintances who had withdrawn from him, as his financial circumstances had become more straitened.

Tilberthwaite was one of those who had withdrawn from him - not in any overt or unpleasant way, but simply in the way that one seems to see less of people whose lives have followed a different path. As they could not avoid meeting now at such a small function - a reception given by the local MP - Tilberthwaite made a point of coming over and greeting Chisam. So much had happened since they had last met, that at first, Chisam felt ill at ease by the jarring of memories of the past with those of the present. It was not until they had made polite conversation for two or three minutes that Chisam came to himself sufficiently to become aware of Tilberthwaite's curiosity. It was not a hostile curiosity. It was entirely natural for someone in Tilberthwaite's position to be curious about the fortunes of a former partner who has, according to rumour, fallen on lean times. It was equally natural for Chisam, already reserved about the matter, to be even more so, and to tell Tilberthwaite no more than he probably knew already.

The conversation progressed more easily when it turned to the subject of Tilberthwaite's fortunes, if only because there was nothing of any great moment to discuss. Tilberthwaite had acquired more land, and with the extra income from this, he had expanded his racing stable, which was now doing very nicely indeed.

"Still on a strictly business-only basis mind - none of your fancy ideas and sentimentalities."

Chisam refused to be drawn, however, so Tilberthwaite nodded sagely, and with an 'Aye, well," lapsed into a momentary silence.

The conversation evidently was not over, though, and Chisam asked Tilberthwaite if he saw much of Lord Hemswell these days.

"Aye, at race meetings now and again. Don't usually get to talk to him, though. Of course, as a member of the aristocracy, he'll have his own crowd to be with; but there's some, like Lord Lonsdale, who will talk to a man and not mind who he is. Lord Hemswell, well, he seems to have taken high living to heart so much. It's always th very best part of the first-class stand for him - no expense spared, all the stewards bowin and scraping. He's always in with a certain crowd: I know he's something important i the Government; but all those hangers-on who follow him round remind me of nothin so much as crows that hang around an injured lamb, waiting for it to die."

Chisam was about to comment on the incongruity of the analogy, but Tilberthwai went on.

"Y'see, it doesn't do for folk to get above their station and become too familiar wit those who are their superiors and betters in society - especially if their betters don always set the example that's expected of them."

"Oh? What makes you say that?"

"It's nothing definite, mark you; but there was a young man, one of the crowd tha goes about with Lord Hemswell, who shot himself in London a few weeks ago. Officiall it was the usual thing - took his own life while the balance of his mind was disturbed but there were rumours that he was in debt from gambling, and some of the rumou were saying it was Lord Hemswell he was in debt to."

"You say these are rumours - and no more than that was said?"

"Nay, and no more will be if you ask me. Even if the rumours are entirely untrue, fo will do well to take heed. It's as I said before, a matter of knowing who and what you ar and what you're fit for."

They both lapsed into silence. Chisam could imagine how it might have been for th young man - the persistent letters, the ever more thinly disguised threats, the insiste demands for money, more and more money. The 'gambling debts' had very likely bec the cover for some more personal secret, as it had been with Chisam. At least Chisa had had rather better luck, even if it didn't seem so sometimes. The unknown you man's luck must have run out very quickly, with his money.

"I was wondering . . ." Tilberthwaite's voice interrupted his thoughts "if you saw mu of Stella Robertson these days - although I suppose we should call her Stella Harris now that she's married again."

The mention of Stella's name was sufficient to bring Chisam out of his reverie. gave himself time to answer, to adjust to the sudden change of subject, and to think ba furiously to remember how long he had known Tilberthwaite. Yes . . .yes . . .he w fairly sure . . .

"Stella . . ." he said vaguely. "You, ah, knew Frank Robertson, of course?"

"Oh, indeed I knew Frank. A fine man - one of the finest. Salt of the earth. It's alwa

88

a great loss when someone like Frank dies, but I felt it was especially tragic for Stella. They were so well matched."

"Indeed, yes," said Chisam agreeably.

"You were a friend of theirs as well weren't you? I seem to remember . . ."

"That's right. My family and Frank's family were friends for many years. I'm afraid I myself have rather lost touch with Stella since Frank died. And of course, as you say, she's married again since."

"Yes . . ." Tilberthwaite paused, but there was clearly more to come. "Y'know, she'd have made you a fine wife if you'd been minded to propose to her. Maybe I'm speaking out of turn here, as I don't know either of you as well as I might, but I can't help feeling that she'd have been more suited to you than to Robert Harrison."

Chisam expressed surprise, which was genuine in so far as it related to Tilberthwaite raising the subject at all.

"Stella is an attractive woman, I agree; but I'm not sure that such a match would have been thought entirely suitable. It's as you said just now - a matter of knowing who and what you are, and what you're fit for."

"Oh, I didn't mean that in any personal way, you understand - it's just that, well . . ."

"But surely," said Chisam gently, "when Stella married Robert Harrison, as I remember it, everyone agreed that they were perfectly matched. It was the wedding of the year in Whitehaven. What has prompted you to make such a comment?"

Tilberthwaite went through various motions indicating embarrassment and reserve, before speaking.

"I'm telling you this as a friend of the family, you understand," he said at length. "I always understood your family and Frank Robertson's to have been close, closer than I ever was. I had thought that you'd kept in closer touch with Stella than you evidently have, and . . . I suppose I was rather disappointed to hear that you hadn't. And of course, she has now married again . . ."

"Yes?" said Chisam encouragingly. They were on very thin ice, and he was mentally holding his breath.

"Well, it's not exactly a secret. I mean, I think it's fairly well known in London, and as far as I know, Stella also knows - which is why I thought of turning to a friend of the family to see if you might be able to suggest a way to help. I suppose it's as much out of respect for the memory of Frank Robertson as anything else; but the shame and humiliation Stella must be feeling does stick in my craw. Y'see, Robert Harrison has a mistress in London. Whenever Harrison's in London, apparently she's very much in evidence on social occasions, and she's accepted more or less as if she was his wife. I've only recently found out about it, but apparently he's known this woman since before he married Stella. Evidently it's part of a lifestyle to which he was accustomed, and which he hasn't been prepared to give up just because he's got married. I don't think Stella knew when she first married him, but she knows now. That sort of thing may be acceptable in London, but it's not acceptable in more respectable communities, and the idea of Frank Robertson's widow being treated like that just sticks in my craw. Trouble is, I'm not so close to her as gives me the right to approach her about it. If you're not the right person then such an approach would be grossly improper. So, as I said, I was wondering if you, as an old friend of the family . . ."

It was strange indeed to see Tilberthwaite, the ebullient Tilberthwaite of old, so hesitant and unsure of himself. Quite naturally, Chisam's loathing of Harrison was intensified by this revelation. A repulsiveness was now seen to be even more repulsive on closer inspection, and Chisam was at first inclined to anger. But equally naturally, caution prevailed, and he permitted himself only a muted expression of his anger. He was still on thin ice, and ostensibly, Harrison meant little or nothing to him. He also began to take on some of Tilberthwaite's hesitancy when he realised, as Tilberthwaite had done, that the problem related, not to Harrison, but to Stella, and it was a problem that mattered so much more to him than it did to Tilberthwaite.

"Do you know the woman's name?" he asked at length.

"I believe she's a Mrs Fitzpatrick. I don't know her first name."

"A widow?"

"Apparently, yes."

"A regular little widows' benevolent society is our Mr Harrison," remarked Chisam. After a pause, he went on: "You'd better tell me what you know, and I'll see what I can do. But I can't guarantee anything, as I haven't really had any contact with Stella for quite a while."

"Well, if you can do anything, I won't be the only one who will be grateful. There's one or two old friends of Frank's who feel that Stella's moved away from them since she married Harrison. He moves in a different circle, you see."

Chisam did see. But he did not know if there was any prospect of his being able to help any more than the other contacts Tilberthwaite had cautiously sounded out.

Later, at home, turning the matter over in his mind, he was visited by that debilitating sense of powerlessness which afflicted him with depression at his worst moments. He was in possession of information which in almost any other circumstance would be extremely damaging to Harrison - and yet, it was of no use to him. Harrison still held all the cards. The existence of Mrs Fitzpatrick was evidently public knowledge, so Harrison

90

had no fear of disclosure in that regard; beyond that, he obviously didn't care what social conventions he violated, or what others thought of him. He was wealthy enough to buy whatever he wanted, and had no interest in anything else.

And Stella? What of her? Was the idea of approaching her realistic? The passage of time had not dimmed the recollection of the feelings he had had for her, when he allowed them to come to the surface; nor had it dimmed his recollection of the nature of her rejection of him. But he thought he had come to terms with that now. It was an episode in his life that had become, like a rock stratum, overlaid by layers of more recent times and events. It took an incident of this kind to fault and shear the strata and bring these memories to the surface again, and to suggest to him that his acceptance of Stella's actions was based more on habit of mind over time, and the soporific of routine, than that he had emotionally come to terms with the situation. It was disturbing to have to go again over things which had long since been buried; even more so to contemplate the effect of seeing Stella again under such circumstances. It would be very easy not to. He could make his excuses to Tilberthwaite if necessary.

But he wanted to see Stella. He had promised Tilberthwaite that he would do what he could, but that was more of a justification than a reason. Having been intrigued by what Tilberthwaite had told him, and especially by the possibilities it implied, he had looked into his heart, and found that his feelings for Stella had not changed. Partly, it was simple carnal desire - the memory of their physical relationship, and her way with him, which no other woman had had. What he had had with Stella had been unique - it would not be possible with any other woman. But there was also something else. He had reached an age when he was starting to have certain regrets about never having married or had children. He had never been the marrying kind, and still less a family man, and he would have found the impositions of either intolerable; and yet - an ancient instinct made him experience a special sadness sometimes when he saw children; the thought that none of them would ever be his, that his seed would die with him, wasted, useless. In the lives of his contemporaries, wives were loved, neglected, hated or cheated; children were adored, tolerated, ignored, or beaten, and were causes of joy, irritation, apprehension or disappointment; but for them all, it was a way of life, a life that filled the other half of their existence, outside the world of work. To the extent that they were conscious of having these things in common, Chisam was excluded, an outsider. When their conversation turned to their marriages, or the achievements or shortcomings of their children, Chisam felt his exclusion, and a certain wistful regret. Now, these thoughts related to Stella. He knew it was the height of foolishness. He was a middle-aged bachelor who, for the best part of twenty years, had valued his independence as a bachelor, and had enjoyed all the pleasures without responsibility which bachelors traditionally enjoy, to the envy of their married contemporaries; and now he was having regrets. It was laughable, he told himself. But few middle-aged men can laugh at themselves, and certainly not in relation to this matter. Part of the reason he was a bachelor was because he formed relationships only with difficulty. His relationship with Stella had been the main relationship of his life; the only one that might have progressed to marriage had circumstances been different. The ending of the relationship meant for Chisam not only the loss of Stella herself, but also of his main life-chance in this world. He had put it behind him - one has to in order to survive and carry on. But now, the matter had been raised again, unwittingly, by Tilberthwaite, and he experienced it once more in all its rawness. He felt he had to see Stella again, whether that would resolve the thing for him or not. It was not a decision lightly taken. To attempt to see Stella when he was so much at the mercy of Harrison was clearly dangerous. Indeed, it was foolhardy but evidently his sudden compulsion would not now be satisfied with anything less.

Harrison lived in Carlisle, and conducted much of his business there; but the partnership of which he was a member were bankers in a number of towns in the area including Whitehaven. It was possible, therefore, for Chisam to arrange to go up to Carlisle on a day when he knew that Harrison would be out of the city. There were still risks, however. He was known in Carlisle, as his company had a subsidiary there which he visited fairly regularly in the course of his work. Even though Harrison's house was in a relatively quiet square, he might be recognised there. For that matter, he might be recognised by the maid who opened the door. Well, he decided, the risks were small enough to take. He would not be put off now.

A few days later, Chisam arranged to visit the firm's Carlisle subsidiary, to cover his real reason for being in Carlisle. He had allowed himself plenty of time, and from the city centre made his way, by a circuitous route, to Harrison's address. For the benefit of the maid, he gave his name at the door as 'Mr Edwards'. He was shown into a drawing room and asked to wait. It was a distinctly unpleasant couple of minutes, alone in the expensively appointed room. Although he knew that Harrison was out of town, and that there was no danger of his being surprised there, this was Harrison's house, his property his private domain. He was oppressed by a sense of guilt, as one who trespasses; the schoolboy illegally in the headmaster's study to sneak a preview of the exam questions the violator of a man's private life. It was so easy to see Harrison in the room - there was much that was reminiscent of pearly grey bond notepaper, and all that went with that More powerful still was a mental image of Harrison himself; a Harrison whose animal anger could break through the steely, sneering sarcasm of his external manner.

He had still not properly recovered himself when the door opened again, and Stella came into the room. She stopped dead when she saw him.

"Edward!"

She seemed initially more surprised than angry. He stood for a moment, silent, gazing at her. Even before he spoke, he wondered if, after all, he had done the right thing in coming here. He had not realised how much it might affect him seeing Stella here in this room, in this place; part of Harrison's private realm. He had not allowed his thoughts to dwell on images of the details of Stella's domestic life with Harrison as being unhealthy and fruitless, and this had helped him to get over his loss. It was unsettling therefore, suddenly to be confronted with the reality of Stella's domesticity.

And with Stella herself. It was a long time since he had seen her, and it felt strange for him to recall how familiar they had once been. That was gone now - now, he had no sense of it. He noted too, how time had marked her since they had parted - were those streaks of grey in her hair?

"Stella -" he began. "Whatever you might think of my coming to see you here . . ." He had rehearsed his little speech, but not very well, and he stumbled over it. "At least, will you accept that I have come here in good faith?"

"Well, until I know what you've come for . . ." She was not going to make it easy for him.

"Please close the door," he said. She did so, then turned back to face him, waiting expectantly.

"May I ask how you are?" he went on.

"I'm very well, thank you," she answered formally. "And you? I trust that all is well with you?"

The question took him slightly aback. Perhaps she thought the servants could overhear them still, and was therefore speaking formally - she had known of his difficulties all that time ago. Perhaps she had just forgotten - after all, he meant nothing to her now. But he hadn't come here to discuss his own troubles.

"Oh, much as usual I suppose. Stella, I don't want to beat about the bush - I know that I'm no longer a worthy subject for your confidences; but at least tell me if there is any way I can help. I understand that one or two old friends of Frank's have also been concerned enough to want to help, but haven't been able to make contact with you. You've . . . avoided them, or made contact difficult for them. I admit it was something of a subterfuge that gained me entry here, but now that I am here, will you tell me if there is any way I can help?"

A look of puzzlement, tinged with annoyance, had clouded her face as he spoke.

"Help? What makes you think I need help? What kind of help?"

"Any kind of help - legal help, financial help, even just moral support. I know it's none of our business really, but if you've rather cut yourself off from your circle of acquaintances of Frank's day, you may be feeling a certain difficulty about re-establishing contact, if you feel you'd like advice or help . ."

"I'm sorry Edward, but I'm afraid you are beating about the bush. Will you please tell me what you're talking about?"

Chisam cautiously drew breath before speaking.

"I'm talking about Mrs Fitzpatrick."

"Mrs Fitzpatrick. What about Mrs Fitzpatrick?" Her face, and her voice, were menacingly calm.

"Harold Tilberthwaite told me that Harrison - your husband - is having an illicit relationship with a Mrs Fitzpatrick in London, a situation which is humiliating to you, but which you are unwilling, or unable to do anything about. I came here on behalf of one or two of Frank's old friends to see if there was any way we could be of help to you."

"I see." She walked slowly over to the window, and stood gazing out of it. "So the tittle-tattle has reached here at last. Is that it, or did Harold Tilberthwaite provide you with any more details while he was about it - lurid descriptions of how the monstrous rakehell whores his way round London while the poor little widow woman he married pines away at home, perhaps? Well, did he?"

She turned to look at him, her eyes flashing; but she went straight on without giving him a chance to answer.

"I suppose you know that Mrs Fitzpatrick isn't generally known about up here. Only in London. Are you proposing to change that - you and Harold Tilberthwaite and the others? Wanted to know if I would be anxious to stop you - to buy you off? Is that it?"

"Stella, upon my soul, such a thing never entered my head. Never! It shocks me that you should say such things - that you could believe me capable of such a thing Especially after . . ." But seemingly, she had forgotten. It was so long ago, after all Perhaps it was self-centred of him to think it could be otherwise. He went on more quietly.

"I came because . . . I had to know if you needed my help. Because this is Harrison's house, I had a strong aversion to coming here for . . other reasons - but I couldn't let the opportunity pass by - I had to know if you needed my help. You see, you married Harrison after several years of independence. Things are different now. It may be that you felt that, for financial or social reasons, you weren't able to divorce Harrison, his conduct notwithstanding. So, I wondered if, given our former acquaintance, indeed, our

94

former intimacy, you might feel that I could offer you practical assistance, even perhaps a way out of your difficulty."

Quite unexpectedly, she laughed - a silvery peal of genuine merriment.

"Edward, you are priceless. I do believe you really mean it. You're quite right, of course, it is none of your business, and not only have I no reason to discuss it with you, but it was an intolerable liberty for you to come here at all. I ought to have you thrown out now. But perhaps I do understand you, even if you don't understand me."

She turned to gaze, unseeing, out of the window, before speaking again.

"Yes, I know about Mrs Fitzpatrick. She's not unlike me in many ways - a widow, of a Guards officer, I think, killed in a train crash a good few years ago. She's still fairly young, and good-looking, and also comfortably off. Robert's known her since before I married him, and they've been intimate with each other, on and off, for many years. I've met her, and I have to say that she's a charming woman - I'm sure that, under other circumstances, we could have been great friends. For many women, the discovery, after their marriage, of such a relationship, would be enough to end the marriage. Notwithstanding the financial hardship, and the social ostracism that face a woman who divorces her husband, even when he is the guilty party; for such women, the humiliation of a husband's infidelity outweighs all that. Such women are either so fortunate that they can afford to be intolerant of infidelity in their men, or so unfortunate that the only man they have been able to get is not worth the humiliation of his infidelity. For me, it is different."

She turned to look at him for a moment, before continuing.

"I don't know whether this will be something you will understand - there are certain things which women see differently from men, and this is one of them. Some women are fortunate enough to attract men who stand above the ordinary run of men; men of extraordinary vitality, ability and talent, men of natural social superiority; men of extraordinary attractiveness therefore. Such men are naturally dominant, and women cannot help finding them attractive. To know such a man is a privilege. To know that such a man finds you attractive - indeed, to be wooed by such a man is, for almost any woman I would think, one of the supreme fulfilments of her womanhood. It's because of that that you don't hesitate to accept if the opportunity of having such a man comes to you - even though you know that you are letting yourself in for heartache as well as joy. For that great mass of women who are neither blessed with great beauty, and therefore have a similar command over men, nor so ugly that they can scarcely get an eligible man, for that great mass of women, such men, while possible, are rare because they are so few. A woman is lucky if she attracts him, while he can have the pick of many ladies,

95

and if he is a man, he does have many. So a woman in such a position will almost always know the pain of jealousy, because she has to share her man with others."

She turned to him at last, and went on.

"So you see, Edward, your purpose in coming here is quite misguided and quite fruitless. I know that we had much happiness together you and I, and I haven't forgotten those times. But you must understand that now that I have Robert, those times, and indeed, you yourself, are nothing to me. However happy I may have seemed at the time, I know now that you simply don't compare with a man like Robert. He is superior to you. I would be prepared to put up with a whole harem of Mrs Fitzpatricks, however much heartache it caused me, if I could still have him, even just a part of him. If he humiliated me to my face with his other women, I would accept it if it meant that I could still have a place in his affection, his love. His merest caress is sweeter and means more to me than anything you could give me, or any woman."

She caught her breath slightly.

"I see from your face - does what I say appal you?"

Chisam looked at his boots. He could not speak, and continued with bowed head in silence for long moments.

"I suppose it does, yes," he said at length, almost to himself, inaudibly. He was not sure whether he was more disgusted with Stella or with himself. Despite everything that had happened, he had not expected anything quite like this. He had expected reserve, pride even stubbornness on Stella's part; but such a complete abandonment of pride, such a willing acceptance of a base and abject humiliation, it seemed to him, was a denial of the human spirit, both for Stella and for himself. For all his years of bachelorhood it came as a revelation to him that, what was surely a mere physical craving could bring Stella to have such contempt for another man, as a man, and for herself as a woman.

His distress must have been evident, because Stella quickly brought the interview to an end. She walked over to the door and rang for the maid.

"You had better go," she said.

Confused, he prepared to leave, but made one last effort before the maid should arrive, mindful of what turmoil might be ahead.

"If you should change your mind, or if your situation changes for the worse, please remember . . ."

But the maid had opened the door, and Stella made no response to his appeal. It had become a distasteful embarrassment to continue the interview, and she was anxious to see Chisam go. Her position was such that she did not even bother to admonish him not to repeat what had been said. She knew it wasn't necessary. He had come expecting to fin

96

her suppliant, ready to accept his guidance and help, given what he evidently perceived as her moral plight. She understood him enough to know that she was stronger than he was, and she only needed to show him this to make him realise how things stood. She had dismissed him once, and now she dismissed him again. She could not waste any more of her time with him.

It was Chisam who left the interview in moral submission and humiliation. What he did in the hour after he left the house he scarcely remembered. He found himself seated on a park bench somewhere, his head in his hands, not caring who saw him or where he was. Things had gone so disastrously wrong that he could scarcely believe what had happened. Stella . . .Stella . . . surely that was not his Stella. His Stella? How could he have been such a fool? How *could* he have been such a fool? Not even feckless love-sick adolescents made such ridiculous spectacles of themselves. He could already writhe at the memory of it. But in the longer term, it was not so much the memory of the details of what had happened that affected him the most, as the fact that Stella's words had revealed a chasm of darkness that he could scarcely comprehend.

12

The days following the visit to Stella, Chisam passed in a kind of emotional limbo neither able to dwell in his mind on what had happened, nor able to drive it out of hi. thoughts. He did not contact Tilberthwaite again; indeed it was only after a day or tw(had passed that he remembered that it was Tilberthwaite who had been the instigator o the meeting with Stella, and in consequence he could only think of Tilberthwaite wit! irritation. How long he might have continued thus, he did not know, even thoug! nothing practically had been changed by what had taken place: it was a state of mind tha had him in its thrall.

It was something as prosaic as the morning paper which brought him back to reality. I was such a small item that he almost missed it. His eye was caught by just one word because it was printed in italics - *Rheinmädchen*. Even before he read the item, he knev what it was about, what it meant. 'Prize ship brought to Hull' was the headline. He rea. on. 'Two Royal Navy torpedo boat destroyers, the *Swift* and the *Speedwell* intercepte(two German merchant ships in the North Sea on Sunday. The German ships wer ordered to heave to. One of them, the *Rheinmädchen*, did so, and a prize crew was pu aboard from *Speedwell* under the command of Lieutenant Atkinson, the second office! The other ship, whose name was not discovered, refused to stop and made off at spee(Both British ships fired warning shots, and the German ship was seen to be hit; howeve! it managed to make its escape despite being damaged. *Swift* and *Speedwell* then escorte the *Rheinmädchen* to Hull, where it was discovered to be carrying a cargo of suga! coffee, and timber from Brazil, bound for Bremen.'

"If you had asked me," Chisam thought to himself musingly, as if in answer to th newspaper, "I could have told you that the other ship's name was 'Nordstern'."

The information in the letter which Seebohm had sent him he now only had in code form, having destroyed his first translation of it; but the names of the ships had stayed i his mind, and he could remember most of them. The identity of that other German shi was known to only a very few men in England, and he wondered what efforts were no* being made by the Admiralty to find out the source of the letter they had received, whic had ultimately brought them the 'Rheinmädchen' as a prize.

The news conveyed by the newspaper article was also a cause of a certain amount c irritation for Chisam. The arrangement between himself and Seebohm seemed t working well so far, for Seebohm, even though that side of it was the more difficult an uncertain. It would be much easier, Chisam imagined, for Seebohm to direct one of h submarines to intercept a British merchant ship, than it was to tempt the Royal Navy 1 intercept a German merchant ship in the way it had just done. The latter was a remarkable achievement, and aroused in Chisam a good deal of admiration for Seebohm for such ingenuity, and not a little pride in himself for having had a part in it. But Seebohm's continued inaction on his side of the arrangement was causing mounting irritation in Chisam. He knew enough of the sea to realise that, at sea, things rarely go exactly according to plan, that the uncertainties of weather as well as of wartime could well result in delays or opportunities missed; but Seebohm had not indicated that he expected this to be a major difficulty for his submarines, and nor did Chisam believe that this was the reason for the delay. Everything now depended on Seebohm; but he could think of no reason for Seebohm's continued inaction, other than the suspicion that he had merely been used as a messenger by Seebohm, who had no intention of carrying out his side of the bargain. And Seebohm was effectively uncontactable.

At this stage, however, Chisam did not seriously believe that Seebohm was simply using him as a messenger. It seemed quite evident that Seebohm would need Chisam's continuing co-operation to achieve his purpose, and that would require Seebohm to carry out his side of the agreement. Nevertheless, while he was still in a sombre mood following his visit to Stella, Chisham decided to give serious consideration to what he would do if the arrangement with Seebohm fell through, and his position became untenable. In consequence, he spent some time in the local public library, consulting certain directories.

As it turned out, Chisam did not have to wait very much longer to learn that his pessimism was unfounded. He heard the news first on the grapevine a few days later. He had not long arrived at the office that morning, and he could tell that Mr Graham, one of the under-managers, was excited about something. Chisam rather liked Graham. He was older than Chisam - about fifty as far as Chisam could judge - of thin, slight build, balding, with greying hair, and of very nervous, almost timid disposition. He had fallen on hard times before the war through unemployment, and had been taken on as an under-manager on a temporary basis to cover for Mr Nicholson, the previous under-manager. Mr Nicholson was one of the volunteers of 1914, who had gone to the front with the local regiment, and was generally regarded by all in the firm as a hero. Chisam had privately been rather glad to see him go, for personal reasons, but of course, could say nothing in public. Early in 1915, Mr Nicholson had been reported as 'missing'. In practice, this usually meant 'killed'; but because a few men reported as 'missing' sometimes later turned up alive, the firm officially refused to accept that he was dead until this was positively confirmed by the army. Anyone who even hinted otherwise was liable to receive a severe reprimand. Poor Mr Graham, who was so desperately anxious about his job, was continually being reminded that it was only temporary pending Mr Nicholson's return, a return he was expected to hope for as publicly as everyone else. Chisam would have told him not to worry - from what he had heard about the war in France, Nicholson was almost certainly dead - but Graham was so excessively eager to please the firm, as well as being painfully honest, that Chisam regretfully could not confide in him, however much he sympathised with the little man. His plight was indicative of the atmosphere at the firm, an atmosphere that had also become part of Chisam's daily life. It was a relief therefore, when some interesting or unusual news helped to break the atmosphere.

He had come in a little earlier than usual, and Graham was the only other person about, apart from the clerks in the outer office. Graham, having perceived Chisam as being generally sympathetic, confided his information to him.

"Have you heard the news, Mr Chisam?"

Chisam confessed he had not.

"It came over the wires last thing yesterday. I don't think many people know yet. Jameson's have lost a cargo."

Jameson's were the principal importer of cocoa into Liverpool, and one of the largest in the country. They were therefore a rival enterprise, and Graham looked pleased at the news, as well he might.

"We don't have all the details, but apparently the ship, the 'Corfe Castle', was sunk by an enemy submarine yesterday somewhere in the Irish Sea. The survivors must have reached Ireland, because the news was on the telegraph from Dublin."

"How much of her cargo was cocoa for Jameson's?" Chisam asked as casually as he could.

"I'm afraid I don't know that yet," admitted Graham. "But I'm sure we'll get the news before long. It is exciting to be one of the first to know. It must be good news for our firm, even though it is a tragedy for the poor seamen and their families."

The last point made Chisam thoughtful. The event seemed so remote from him that it was difficult to feel involved personally. He could not even be sure that it had anything to do with Seebohm, even if it sounded as though Seebohm had finally made his first move.

"What else did the wires say?" asked Chisam.

"Only the bare facts, really - that the 'Corfe Castle', bound for Liverpool from Accra on the Gold Coast had been sunk by a submarine yesterday in the Irish Sea. We know that the 'Corfe Castle' is a Green Funnel line ship which regularly carries cargoes for Jameson's. And we know that Jameson's have been reducing the number of their sailings by increasing the amount each ship carries."

Their own company had been doing the same thing, and it was not hard to guess what the loss would mean to Jameson's. Fewer ships meant, in theory, less risk of a ship receiving the attentions of an enemy warship. But when a ship was lost, the blow would be proportionately greater. The details about the 'Corfe Castle' started to come in during the day. She had been sunk about 10am the previous morning by a German submarine. The submarine had surfaced and stopped the ship with a warning shot from its deck gun. The crew were told to take to the boats, which they had done with alacrity, and the submarine had then torpedoed the ship, waiting on the surface until it had sunk. It then submerged itself, although its periscope had been seen for a little while afterwards, apparently observing the lifeboats. The ship had been sunk about midway between St David's Head and the Irish coast; about seven hours later the first of the lifeboats reached the coast of County Wexford, and the news of the sinking was made known to the outside world. Almost the entire cargo of the 'Corfe Castle' was reported to be cocoa, bound for the warehouses of William Jameson and Son, merchants, of Liverpool.

The response was gratifying. The 'bunching' of the supply of cocoa into fewer and larger shipments meant that a temporary shortage was created by the loss of the 'Corfe Castle'. During the course of the next few days, Chisam, as part of his daily routine, kept in regular touch with the price of cocoa in the various markets. Within a day or two, the price on the 'softs' market in London rose by nearly £100 per ton initially, before it fell back again. In some of the local markets, particularly Liverpool, price rises were even steeper. London merchants were able to make up most of the shortfall to customers who needed supplies of cocoa without delay, and on this occasion it was London merchants who scooped the largest part of the windfall profits. But Chisam did not need any urging from the manager to make the company known to Jameson's customers, many of whom were only too pleased to avail themselves of the offer.

"It's a golden opportunity for us Chisam, and I expect you to make the most of it. Naturally, one is sad when a British ship is sunk by the enemy, but I'm sure that no-one would blame us for taking advantage of good fortune."

Chisam assured him that the matter was already well in hand.

"And has it had the same effect on the prices of our futures in cocoa?"

"Well sir," said Chisam, after considering the matter thoughtfully, "I'm afraid that the effect on the futures is much less than on the price on the quayside - in fact, there's hardly been any reaction so far. I'm not sure why this should be - perhaps it's the uncertainty of supply in the future due to the war. I must admit, it is rather disappointing."

"Hmm, I see. I had rather hoped . . . Ah, well, it's just one of those things, I suppose. You know more about it than I do, I expect, and we can't be too greedy."

He was thus dismissed.

One of the problems Chisam had not been able to think of a solution to in advance, w
how to avoid such unwelcome attention to the futures scheme. In the end, he had bee
saved from plain mendacity by being able to tell the truth. The absence of any response
the sinking of the 'Corfe Castle' in the futures market had left him despondent a
completely at a loss. He didn't know why it should be so, and the reason he had given
the manager was his best guess, and not merely an attempt to dissemble.

For a day or two his despondency deepened, as the prices on the quayside ro
gratifyingly, while the futures market remained flat. He certainly hadn't foreseen th
and it occurred to him to wonder if Seebohm had. Their cases were very much the sam
and as it was a German ship which had been 'lost' first, presumably Seebohm alrea
knew what Chisam had just discovered about the effect on the markets. If he had priva
sources of information from London, through a neutral embassy perhaps, Seebohm mig
have sunk the 'Corfe Castle' to see if the effect he had seen in Germany was repeated
Britain. That might well mean that the whole business was finished. Hope seemed
centre around the fact that it now wanted only a week or so to the next date and m
reference he had sent to the Admiralty. Yet if the Admiralty took the bait again, and
came off, it might confirm the trend. If so . . . .

There was a lot of war news from France that week. The Allies had launched a l
offensive, and at that stage in the war there was still a general belief that the next l
push would be the decisive one that would win the war, and the newspapers were full
this one. There were glowing accounts of German positions overrun, of this village a
that ridge taken, accounts of acts of heroism, the confusion of war. But a day or two lat
the casualty lists started to appear, and they told their own story. Chisam had beco
numbed to the news of the fighting in France and generally took little interest in it; l
when, on this occasion, he looked at his atlas to see what had been won in exchange
all those casualties, running into scores of thousands to judge from the newspapers.
was in truth pitifully little. He could not imagine how the war could go on in that w
The supplies of manpower were not unlimited, and yet the generals on both sides w
behaving as if they were. Perhaps the war would be lost by the side which ran out of m
first. It was surely the most barbaric war that had ever been fought. He wondered
Seebohm had any relatives or friends in the army, and how he felt when he read the v
news from France. Perhaps he would read it as Chisam did, while scanning
newspapers for news of that other, less public war, being fought at sea. But perhaps
didn't read newspapers at all, being a naval officer with access to official information
was still hard for Chisam to think of Seebohm as being one of those directly involved

producing the casualties he read about.

Chisam was still in this depressing state of limbo when, a couple of days later, he went down to the harbour to meet the 'Benin Trader', which was carrying a load of the company's cocoa as cargo. It was a perfectly calm, still day, with a high, light grey overcast of cloud, more like autumn than spring; but it suited his mood. He walked along the quayside, picking his way between long lines of stationary railway trucks laden with coal, behind the ugly grey boxes of the steam cranes, and past one of the Whitehaven colliers in the loading berth, to a vantage point where he could watch the 'Benin Trader' as it nosed its way cautiously through the narrow entrance to the Queen's Dock. The intermittent roar of coal being poured through the chute into the collier echoed flatly round the harbour, emphasising its stillness, as all eyes watched the 'Benin Trader' as it glided almost silently in. A rope was thrown from the bows by a little man in filthy overalls. He missed, and the rope splashed loudly into the still water of the dock, among the floating driftwood and other rubbish. As the little man scrambled to pull the rope in, the ship's engine went into reverse to take the way off the vessel. A stream of abuse shouted at the little man from somewhere aft was drowned by the next load of coal going into the collier. Conscious by now that everyone in the harbour was watching him, the little man didn't miss the second time, and the 'Benin Trader' was slowly pulled over to the side of the dock.

By this time, Chisam had been joined by Merlyn Thomas, the shipping company's agent, and Reed, from the customs office. They waited while the ship was made fast and a gangplank run out. Thomas was a Liverpool man, but he had been so long away from his native city that he only had a trace of the accent. Reed was a local man, large, heavy and florid, with coarse red hands like those of a butcher. In fact both his father and grandfather had been customs men at Whitehaven. He had sometimes entertained Chisam and Thomas, as they had waited for a ship to berth, with accounts told to him by his grandfather, who had hunted smugglers running cargoes of rum onto remote beaches on the coast of west Cumberland on skiffs that made discreet night crossings from the Isle of Man.

On this occasion, the 'Benin Trader' was not scheduled to be carrying anything for the bonded warehouse, so it was expected to be a routine visit for Reed. "Although," as Reed was fond of saying, "it's often on the routine visits that the most interesting things happen."

As they ascended the gangplank, Chisam was momentarily fascinated by a glimpse through an open porthole into the domesticity of some crew member. On a shelf just inside the porthole he could see an earthenware drinking beaker with a razor and a

103

teaspoon in it, a half-finished wooden model of a sailing ship, a packet of washing soda and dimly visible inside the cabin, some garments hanging up to dry on a string. The porthole itself was furnished with gaily coloured chintz curtains. For the men who crewed this ship, these cramped little cabins were 'home' for most of the time. The 'Benin Trader' and her sister ships, the 'Benin Venturer' and 'Benin Enterprise' plied monotonous trade between Whitehaven and west Africa, and apart from the limited time spent in port, the lives of the crew were spent at sea on the six week voyages. The 'Benin Trader' was about two hundred feet long, grey painted steel with the rust showing through in patches and jarring with the red lead paint along the waterline. A single stack stood high amidships, immediately abaft the bridge and superstructure. Fore and aft of this, most of the space between the blunt bows and the high poop was occupied by the cargo holds. A spartan, battered, shabby little ship, which that strange, hard, rootless breed of men who go to sea in the merchant service, a service more unforgiving than almost any other, made their own. It seemed to Chisam pathetically little to call home. Was it penury or rootlessness which drove some men to endure such an existence; and were these men therefore the fittest and ablest survivors in a savage world? But the image came again into his mind of other ships like this one, from Liverpool and London: an image of the beaker and the model ship smashing to the deck as the ship heeled over with its hull ripped open by a torpedo, the sea bursting into the little cabin drowning in an instant the small tokens of domesticity that had turned a cramped steel box into home.

He shook his head, as if to clear it. He had no reason to feel guilty or repentant, he told himself. He was not responsible for the war, and he was doing no more than those who were responsible for it. He reached the top of the gangplank and paused, like a naval captain about to be piped on board his ship. No-one piped them on board the 'Benin Trader', however, and they had to make their own way to the captain's quarters.

The 'Benin Trader' was carrying timber and cocoa from the Gold Coast. The timber, mostly teak and other tropical hardwoods, had been loaded first, swung up into the hold by means of the ship's own derricks, due to the absence of any proper port facilities along that coast. The cocoa, great hessian sacks of beans, was loaded directly on top of the timber. The captain of the 'Benin Trader', James Baker, had described how the cocoa was brought out to the ship from the beach by the local natives in great open canoes fifty or sixty feet long, which had to negotiate several hundred yards of tremendous Atlantic surf before reaching open water where the ship was at anchor. Captain Baker was not one of life's optimists. He had gone to sea as a boy, and served in the merchant navy all his life. At one stage he had been a deckhand on an Argentine ship whose captain, apart from being a drunkard, had been such a malevolent tyrant that Baker had eventually deserted. That had been in Callao, Peru, from where he had had to make his own way home. Despite this, he had won promotion, gaining first his mate's certificate, and eventually his master's certificate. But he could not for a long time get a ship of his own. His fortunes seemed at this stage to have been dogged by ill luck, and he spent a long period serving as first mate on a series of different ships in various parts of the world. One of these had been a timber ship, taking a cargo from Quebec to Liverpool. On its way down the St Lawrence River, it had been rammed by an American ship travelling in the opposite direction, bound for Quebec. Baker's ship had been very badly damaged, and had eventually foundered, and although the crew had managed to take to the boats, three men had been killed in the collision. The collision had taken place at night, and Baker had been officer of the watch at the time. In the court of inquiry which followed, Baker had been exonerated of any blame - it emerged that the captain of the American ship had been intoxicated with drink and was entirely to blame for what had happened.

But the fact that the ship had been lost while he had been the officer on watch had seemed to taint him with guilt or ill luck for long afterwards.

"Baker? Weren't you in the middle of that St Lawrence business recently? Officer of the watch weren't you? Well, I'm sure you can appreciate my position, Mr Baker. I know you weren't to blame for what happened, but our firm has its customers' views to consider as well, and if they weren't happy . . . You understand, of course. We'll be in touch if we want you . . ."

Baker had gone through a very rough patch, during which it had required a lot of strength on his part to keep going. It was a strength which had eventually been recognised by the Whitehaven and Colonial Shipping Company, which had taken him on as first mate in the 'Benin Venturer', and finally promoted him master of the 'Benin Trader'. In return they received a strong and undivided loyalty from Baker, who also ensured, as far as was humanly possible in the merchant navy, that at least one of the company's ships was 'dry'. As a result of his experiences, Baker had become a staunch supporter of the Temperance movement, and a tyrant towards anyone who sought to bring drink onto his ship.

And so, when Chisam, Thomas and Reed were ushered into the captain's cabin, to be greeted by a somewhat philosophical Captain Baker, they were served not with something in a glass, but with mugs of cocoa, creamy with the first fresh milk to have been brought onto the ship for several weeks.

"One of life's little pleasures, gentlemen," he said when they had all been handed a steaming mug. "No doubt it seems a small thing to you, but it's one of the things I look forward to at the end of each voyage, after drinking watery cocoa for weeks."

105

They commiserated with him good humouredly.

"But has it been a good voyage, all in all, apart from the cocoa being watery?" asked Merlyn Thomas in the same vein.

"In these days Mr Thomas, any voyage is a good voyage when both ship and cargo arrive on time - give or take a day or two - and in one piece. We lost thirty six hours hove to off Corunna when the propeller shaft started running rough in bad weather, but we managed to put that right ourselves. Although I must say, there were times when I despaired of ever seeing England again. Good engineers seem as hard to come by as good seamen these days. You all saw that performance when we were docking, I suppose? I've had to put up with that kind of thing all through this voyage, in different ways. Landlubbers! You can always tell them on the first voyage out. The first big sea and the rush below, or to the side, or to the heads, or sometimes they just do it on the deck. I don't know which is worse, being under complement, or watching their damn' fumbling incompetence. It's the war that's done it - the navy's taking the best men and we don't seem to be able to replace them."

But Captain Baker had probably always complained about landlubbers, and probably always would. It helped him to keep his spirits up in trying circumstances. His audience was sympathetic, but shared his pessimism.

"Well, if the navy is responsible, then things are likely to get worse before they get better," Reed observed. "It looks as if we're settled in for a long war."

The others agreed. Chisam was not happy about the idea of a ship carrying one of his cargoes, crewed by landlubbers and hove to for thirty six hours, presenting a sitting target for a German submarine - he suspected that the submarines under Seebohm's command would not operate as far south as Corunna. The moment passed, however. Captain Baker was, after all, sanguine enough about the matter, and he had had a rather more personal interest in it than the others. Indeed, the captain was now reminding them of the cargo which, landlubbers notwithstanding, he had brought safely into port. He led them over to where they could see the forward cargo deck, where unloading had already begun. The battens were off and the hatch covers being removed. A steam crane on the dock alongside was already dangling a sling to be filled with the big brown sacks of cocoa beans that filled the hold to the top. Soon, the company's warehouse would be full - a guaranteed supply to its customers, and an equally solid guarantee for anyone who wanted to invest speculative money in the future supply of cocoa from the Whitehaven Cocoa and Coffee House Company, especially if supplies from other sources were interrupted by the war. If only the markets would respond in the way in which common sense suggested that they ought to.

The first sling full of sacks touched down on the quayside, and its contents were manhandled by the dockers into the waiting wagon, the first sack making a rattling thump as it was dropped in. To Chisam, watching from the ship, it was a deeply satisfying sound. This cargo was a reassuring reality, to set against so much that was uncertain elsewhere.

The newspapers were still dominated by reports of the recent big offensive in France, but a couple of days later, Chisam came across the item he had been looking for. It was a small paragraph, when he found it, at the bottom of the second page of the foreign news. It was almost exactly the same as before: one ship this time, the 'Königen Margrethe', with a cargo of coffee and sugar from Porto Alegre in Brazil, bound for Hamburg, where the ship was registered. The interception had taken place further north than before, off the coast of Norway, although the report was careful to point out that it had taken place on the high seas. The German version would doubtless have it differently. The 'Königen Margrethe' was taken to Aberdeen where its cargo was examined and unloaded. Once again, Chisam experienced a feeling of frustration at not being able to know whether Seebohm was now beginning to see those benefits of their arrangement which were still eluding him. He was going to have to wait for a while longer before he would be able to find out.

13

Stella Harrison turned the pages of the ledger which she held in her hands, with growing disquiet. She had come up to her husband's study to fetch a book he had asked for, and not being able to see it at once, she had begun to look round the room for it. Opening a drawer, she discovered a number of odd-looking books which turned out to be account ledgers. Each one bore a name. She would not have examined them any more closely if she had not noticed that one of them bore the name of Edward Chisam. Curious, she picked it up and opened it. She had not thought about Chisam for a long time. Even after his recent ill-starred visit, she had forgotten him at once, so completely had she become involved in her new life. But the past cannot be erased so completely, and Chisam was an important part of her past, however little she regarded him now. Once, she had taken pleasure in his company and his affections, and even considered herself fortunate in having them. But even then she had known about the weaknesses in Chisam's character without yet understanding their import: weaknesses that had eventually destroyed him and made it necessary for her to sever her relationship with him. She had felt that the long years of marriage to Frank Robertson had left her naïve; that the end of her relationship with Chisam had left her more worldly, and more confident in her judgements.

Now, here in Robert's study, that confidence was disturbed. When she had married Robert, she had already known that, for an older woman who married a younger man especially a man as attractive and desirable as Robert, there was always the risk of heartbreak caused by younger rivals; and when this had happened, she had not been completely unprepared for it. She was diminished in her own eyes, but then it was possible to recognise this as part of what often happens when falling in love. It was the price she had paid for her own resolution of the conflict of emotions. But when Robert was diminished in her eyes, this she was not prepared for.

The ledger she held was evidently an account of Chisam's personal finances going back over several years. It was written in her husband's handwriting. The amount of detail increased as the entries became more recent: the early pages were confined to large transactions only; but there in black and white was the chronicle of the financial disaster that had befallen Chisam. Stella had not known of the details before now - she had never been interested at the time - but now, seeing it like this caught her imagination. It was not possible to know what all the figures meant, but the overall picture was abundantly clear. Chisam had, over a fairly short period, gone massively into debt. Memories of that time came crowding back into her mind, and although it did not exonerate or excuse

Chisam, what she held in her hands explained some of his behaviour at that time, which she had thought strange and eccentric. The idea of being in debt to anything like this amount was quite terrifying, as she allowed herself, for a moment, to imagine it to be her debts catalogued in the sparse, eloquent figures on the pages of the ledger. The memory of the note of pleading, of near desperation in Chisam's voice and in his eyes on the last occasion they were together in the house in Whitehaven suddenly no longer produced in her the same sense of revulsion that she had felt at the time. She did not, even now, feel that she had made a mistake in cutting off the relationship with Chisam - that was something any sensible woman would have done - but now the matter involved Robert, in a way that was not at all to her liking.

As she turned the pages the amount of detail on them became greater as the entries became more recent. It was clear that, as a client of her husband's partnership, Chisam was having to accept the supervision of his finances by Robert Harrison, as representative of the partnership. The detail, the smallness, even pettiness of many of the recent entries made it equally clear that Harrison was using his position to impose the maximum possible humiliation on Chisam, who, as a result of his situation, was more or less bound to accept it. It was this that caused her disquiet. She knew that such arrangements were made when someone fell into very bad debt, but she also knew that, it being such a delicate subject, there was a right way and a wrong way of handling such cases, and that it took considerable professional skill to handle them properly. She could not believe that Robert lacked such skill; which suggested very much that his attitude was deliberate, and therefore presumably malicious. She felt she needed to know why. Was it on her account? Did Robert know about her former relationship with Chisam, and was this the result? What was Chisam to Robert?

She bit her lip as she stood staring unseeing at the study wall, the ledger still in her hands. What was she to do? It would be easiest just to forget it. Chisam was nothing to her, and it was not a matter of great moment what happened to him. But Robert . . . Robert was demeaning himself by such conduct, and worse: he was very likely risking his professional reputation, and therefore, his career. It wasn't worth it, not for Chisam. If she could do anything to stop it, it must be stopped. She looked down at the ledger again. On the last page, after several blank pages, was written a date: 31st August; and below that, the word 'Finis', underlined. It almost looked as if Robert planned to foreclose on Chisam on that date, come what may. What blind malevolence could lead to such folly? It was easy to understand the need to dissociate oneself from failures, lest one's life became encumbered by them, or tainted by their failure. But once cast off, they could safely be forgotten. What was incomprehensible to her was the need to pursue such people to the bitter end. She could not see, any more than Harrison, had he thought about it, that in the end there is no difference between the two attitudes. Indifference can be as effective a form of malevolence as any other.

Stella put the ledger back into the drawer with the others. She had still not decided what to do. What if all this was on her account, and Robert knew about what had been between her and Chisam? Should she feel apprehensive, or grateful, in view of Robert's own liaison with Mrs Fitzpatrick? She desperately did not want to have a row with Robert about that - she knew the weakness of her position, and how easily it could be destroyed by rashness on her part. But if Robert was taking foolish risks, especially when there was absolutely no need . . .

She could not remain there any longer. Robert would be coming up to see what had become of her. She resumed her search for his book, quickly found it, and descended the stairs once more to the drawing room. She had made her decision. Whatever she did, she suspected, this matter was not going to go away; and it had the potential of becoming worse if she kept silent, than if she did not. After handing Harrison his book, she remained standing for a moment before speaking.

"Robert, will you tell me what Edward Chisam is to you? I have a reason for asking."

Harrison looked at her sharply.

"Edward Chisam? Why do you ask about him?"

"You sent me to your study to search for a book. In searching, I came across some ledgers in a drawer, giving, as far as I could tell, details of the accounts of debtors. One of them was Edward Chisam. It seemed to me that you were going beyond what would be deemed as acceptable in your dealings with him - almost tyrannical to judge from some of the entries in the ledger. I was not only surprised, but apprehensive. I don't know whether Edward Chisam is the kind of man who would protest against such treatment to the point of contesting it, but if he were - well, could it not damage your reputation?"

Harrison looked at her coldly.

"I'm sure I don't know what you mean," he retorted. "Edward Chisam is a contemptible worm who is getting his just deserts for his past profligacy. It seems to me perfectly in order that he should be made to account for it, as all such debtors are."

"But he is not being treated as all such debtors are. He . . ."

"I do not wish to speak of Edward Chisam. It is a subject distasteful to me, particularly here in my own house. I wish the matter to be dropped."

He spoke with all the authority of one who is used to being obeyed, and Stella had to swallow down the fear which tightened her throat. Was it bravery or foolishness which made her go on.

110

"But . . . if he should bring against you charges of professional misconduct, think how that would damage your reputation. What is Edward Chisam to you that you should take such a risk?" Her voice faltered a little as she spoke.

Harrison had risen to his feet in anger.

"Stella, I will not be crossed by you. You will not tax me about Edward Chisam, or about anything else, when I have expressly forbidden it."

"I was only concerned . . ."

"I will be the judge of what is worthy of concern in such matters. I surely have the right to expect the support of such confidence in my judgement from my wife."

She did not answer, and her silence seemed to provoke him.

"You ask me what Edward Chisam is to me. He is nothing to me - a worthless scoundrel. So worthless that I cannot imagine why you have made such an issue of him. Perhaps I should ask what Edward Chisam is to you. You used to know him, I understand, when he was a client of Frank Robertson. For such a tenuous link, your concern for him now seems strange indeed. I should like to know whether Chisam was ever anything more to you than a client of Frank Robertson."

Stella felt as if her cheeks were flaming scarlet. She had not properly thought through what she was doing, and now, as the result of her own rashness, she was confronted with the awfulness of her situation. Her flaming cheeks were due to anger as well as to shame. How unfair that, while she had had an illicit past, Robert, who had an illicit present, should be the one to make her feel guilty and tax her with it. But she could not afford the luxury of indulging her anger. The price would be too high for her to pay. She knew that she would have to lie to keep the peace, and she hesitated now because to lie, especially to her husband, went so much against all her moral instincts that she had to steel herself to do it. But she did not have to lie. Harrison interpreted her reddened cheeks and continued silence as signs of guilt.

"I see," he said stiffly. His anger was now cold and deliberate. "You may as well spare your blushes, for me at least. They betray no modesty in you, or none that I know of."

He stalked out while he still had control of his temper. Stella remained standing quite still, surprised and shaken by his departure. No row, no display of temper, only an icy coldness, which was far worse. It would have been so easy to have had an argument about her side of things - about Mrs Fitzpatrick. Perhaps that was partly why he had left so abruptly - because in an instant he had seen as clearly as she had done how much their relationship was balanced on a knife edge. But he had been angry and she was afraid of his anger. She did not know what it presaged. Slowly, she sat down on one of the high-backed chairs, and gazed unseeing at the flames dancing above the coals in the fireplace.

111

14

The S.S. 'Truro' was torpedoed in the western approaches at ten minutes past eleven on the 21st of April, on a brilliantly sunny spring morning, with a fresh south-westerly painting winking white caps on the wave crests of a coldly dark blue sea. Rolling heavily in the swell and hove to a couple of cable lengths off were the ship's boats containing the crew, who had been allowed to abandon ship beforehand by the submarine's captain. The men watched grim-faced and in silence as the submarine manoeuvred, with evident awkwardness, for position, as the 'Truro', no longer under command and with propellers stopped, slowly broached to under the influence of wind and waves. Half an hour earlier they had been the crew of a ship, standing watches, checking navigation, tending engines, stoking boilers, chopping vegetables in the galley, sleeping off watch - all the mundane routine of a ship at sea and the encompassing monotony of its enclosed community. It was a primitive existence, but a man could feel cocooned from the world within the steel walls of the ship.

Suddenly that was gone, and in the space of time it took for a submarine to surface and fire a couple of warning shots from its deck gun, they had become refugees. In the tense minutes when the boats were being lowered there had been little time to think of personal possessions, and most had nothing but the clothes they wore. Others had taken advantage of the need to go below and rouse the crew off watch, and had snatched what they could conveniently carry - a duffle bag, a life preserver, a bottle of gin surreptitiously concealed under a coat, a fiddle minus its bow ("I could maybe use it as a paddle if needs be," the man had assured the bosun, knowing he would rather die first); another man clutched a book which he said was a bible, although it didn't look like one: no-one had very much. The few minutes allowed by the submarine's captain hardly gave time to see whether each boat had its emergency stores laid in, let alone to check whether it was seaworthy, and now it was too late for recriminations. The last boat had pulled away from the ship, its oars occasionally clashing or catching crabs as the oarsmen got used to the unwieldy boat and the heavy swell.

With a suddenness that was startling, a tall plume of white water rose against the side of the ship and hung in the air motionless for several seconds before falling back. The men in the boats felt the visceral shock of the explosion through the water before hearing its rumbling roar shake the air. Their sullen silence was finally broken - after a moment of awe, fists were shaken in the direction of the submarine, and rough voices were raised in anger or derision. However hard shipboard life may have been; however impersonal the war, or the motives of the unseen crew of the submarine, this was a personal attack on them, which left them shocked and angry. Even the little that they had had been taken away from them, and their ship had been destroyed in front of their eyes. No-one felt grateful for being allowed to take to the boats first - human gratitude is rarely so philosophical. What they knew was that, had they been left alone, they would have been docked in Liverpool within twenty-four hours, with pay in their pockets and able to sample the delights or otherwise of the taverns, brothels and other entertainments of the waterfront: the familiar end of another voyage. Instead, they had been singled out as victims of this senseless act of malevolence, part of a war which had hitherto seemed remote.

The sinking of the 'Truro' was ungainly and swift. Within ten minutes she was gone, the sun glinting briefly on her stationary propellers before they disappeared under the water, the surface of which continued to be disturbed from below by the release of air and gases from internal explosions as the sea extinguished the still hot boiler furnaces. The submarine had already gone, submerging quietly and unnoticed. Only flotsam and debris were left - pieces of wood, a lifebelt, part of a tea chest, a distress flare, a sack of cocoa beans from the cargo in the hold, a spreading film of oil; and a little way off, a group of boats with an equally forlorn cargo of human flotsam. The boats eventually started to move off together, steering a ragged and uncertain course north-eastwards towards the nearest land.

By the end of that week, four more ships carrying cocoa to Liverpool or London had been sunk, and additionally, by chance, two others bound for Bristol, in a rising tide of destruction wrought by submarines operating from Wilhelmshaven in the western approaches to the English Channel and the southern Irish Sea. The ensuing shortage of cocoa was not immediately perceived by the markets as being due to anything other than chance. They were having to adjust day by day, and week by week, to the increasing problems caused by the German blockade; but as the shortage in cocoa persisted in the major ports as further ships were sunk, the apparently charmed life led by ships bringing cocoa into Whitehaven was noticed at last. The manufacturers and the dealers were not slow to respond, and as before, the price on the quayside rose most satisfactorily, and it soon became more than worthwhile for the Whitehaven Cocoa and Coffee House Company to increase the quantity of cocoa it imported. Extra cargoes meant extra risk; but as long as the luck held, it would be worth it. Even if the luck didn't hold in the long term, the killing made whilst it had would still make it worthwhile. But this time, the speculators also noticed, and more discreet killings were made on other markets. It became possible for those who dealt in the cocoa futures of the Whitehaven company to feel that, at last, life was good. This happy band now included Edward Chisam, who had been lucky in another way. As before when quayside prices had risen, the manager had enquired of Chisam how the futures scheme was responding to the improvement in the company's fortunes. He had asked too soon - there was a delay between the rise in price on the quayside and the rise in prices in the futures market, and Chisam was once again able to report in all truthfulness that the futures market was flat.

"It must be due to the general uncertainty of the war," he assured the manager sagely. "We may have been lucky so far, but that can only be by chance, and the markets must know that our turn will come sooner or later . . ."

The manager had agreed, but said that he still intended to go ahead with bringing in larger cargoes.

"We might as well make the most of it while it lasts," he said.

The futures market in the company's cocoa did not remain flat for long, however. Indeed, it was almost alarming just how fast the market did move once it had started. Clearly, some speculators had little faith in the company's long term immunity from the misfortunes of war. Prices could be expected to fall back somewhat, therefore, with early profit taking, but then Chisam was expecting to do some of that himself; so in general he had cause to feel well pleased.

One other person noticed the apparent good fortune of Whitehaven bound ships. A naval intelligence officer in the Admiralty, whose job it was to plot the details of the casualties of the German blockade, noted the absence of such casualties among the Whitehaven ships. It was not a cause for any suspicion, for there was nothing definite to be suspicious of at this stage. Seen from London, it was not remarkable that the Germans should not have bothered much with the trade into a minor port in the north of England. The anomaly was merely noted as a curiosity. But it was noted.

On the same day as the futures market in the Company's cocoa reached its initial peak, Chisam received a further letter from Amsterdam. It was in code, and so had to be translated, or rather, extracted, from the innocuous missive in which it was contained. Again, there was no evidence that the letter had been tampered with, giving reassurance that their security had still not been breached. This was the first direct contact Chisam had had with Seebohm for some time, and he examined it long and with interest. The substance of the letter was further information about the movements of certain German merchant ships, to be passed on to the Admiralty in London. As before, it was a simple list of names, times, dates and positions, and Chisam could only guess at how it would be received by the Admiralty. Had he been able to know, it would certainly have given him pause for thought; but at that moment, the most interesting part of the letter was personal message from Seebohm. It was only brief, due to the limitations of the method of coding used, but it was none the less welcome.

"I trust you are prospering as the result of my endeavours," it read, " which I hope to continue. As I am not the only player in the field, you may suffer an occasional mishap. I will use my influence to avoid this as far as is possible. Your own efforts have brought considerable prosperity on this side of the water, after some initial disappointment - perhaps you found this also? I look forward to further prosperity as a result of this letter. If you need to contact me, use the *poste restante* address. F.S."

This was indeed good news. It was as he suspected - the delay in the market's reaction to events was temporary only, and thereafter - well, Seebohm was looking forward to 'further prosperity'. Chisam reflected that it must have taken a certain amount of courage to have continued to give special orders to his submarines when there was no sign of any particular benefit accruing from them. He had no idea exactly what risk Seebohm was running in doing such a thing, but he suspected that it was not inconsiderable if any of his superiors found out. Perhaps he had had to buy one or two of them off. It was something which had occurred to him at the time of their conversation in Amsterdam, and he had borne it in mind ever since. He supposed that, as with many things, as long as it was going well, there wouldn't be many problems; it was when things started going badly that awkward questions would be asked.

But at the moment, it was going well, both for Seebohm and for Chisam. Indeed, so well had Chisam been doing recently that he was now within sight of clearing all his debts. It still seemed almost too much to hope for, but he was feeling more lighthearted than he had done for a long time. It would surely not be long now before he could cock a snook at Harrison, and indeed, at all his persecutors. It was something he was starting to daydream about.

One consequence of Seebohm's letter was that it necessitated a further journey to London in the near future. This was required by Seebohm for his purposes, and also helped maintain Chisam's anonymity. Accordingly, he arranged to travel down the following weekend, and stayed overnight in an hotel.

The train journey was long and tiring and uncomfortable. When he arrived at his hotel, therefore, he went straight to bed and slept for several hours, leaving an order that he was not to be disturbed. Waking in the early evening, he ordered some food and coffee; but when it came, he found he had little appetite for it. He drank the coffee, but left most of the food; for he found that suddenly he was troubled by another hunger. It had been a long time since his relationship with Stella had ended, and since that time he had been virtually celibate. As a lifelong bachelor he was used to periods of celibacy, but occasionally the desire became greater than normal, and almost compelled satiation. On one such occasion he had had a liaison with a Whitehaven shopgirl, who, while she would not normally have attracted him, compensated for that by making herself more than readily available. It was because she had made herself available when he had wanted her that he had succumbed to the temptation. But she had not satisfied him as he had wanted - the girl was obviously used to a man or men who wanted physical gratification only and never anything else, and he had felt disturbed by the fact that he had not been able to evoke anything more than that in her. Occasionally he would see the girl in the town, but she did not acknowledge him - perhaps she sensed his wish to forget the matter, and he was grateful for that at least.

Now, the desire was on him again, and he could not suppress it. At length, he donned his coat and left his room, and sought out the head porter, who was usually an authority in these matters, and for a small consideration, learned from him the best place to go.

Outside, the light was starting to fade and the lamps were being lit as he walked through the streets in the direction of the city centre. In the fashionable residential street of Knightsbridge, carriages could be seen waiting to take people to social gatherings or to an evening's entertainment. On his rare visits to the capital, Chisam was always struck by how much more in evidence this class of society was in London than almost anywhere else he knew. Even as he passed the front of an elegant Georgian town house, the front door opened, and four young people emerged, two boys and two girls, all perhaps in their early twenties, and all dressed in formal evening wear, and descended the steps to where a footman in eighteenth-century costume stood by the open door of a carriage. They talked animatedly amongst themselves as they walked to the waiting carriage, and from the snatches of conversation Chisam caught as he walked past, it sounded as if they were on their way to a dinner party. Although the two young men were almost certainly serving officers on leave, all four of them looked as if they hadn't a care in the world. They were in their element, and all was as it should be. Chisam did not think that any of them noticed him as he walked past on the other side of the street. They would be his superiors socially - people of his station did not live in houses like these - but the gap was not so wide that had circumstances been different, he might not sometimes have been one of their company, perhaps attending the same dinner party. As he walked on, his mind was suddenly flooded with the inner imperative of this train of thought, so that even as he walked, his very consciousness was seized by the image which again took possession of his mind, of a man, cold and alone, stumbling towards the only light visible on a vast desolate moor, the lighted window of a house. Within, in the warmth and mellow light, well dressed people could be seen taking their ease with food and drink, and laughing

116

and talking together. He could see them so clearly through the glass, that it seemed that they must be able to hear his knocking, weak though it was - but they gave no indication of being aware of his presence; and as they talked on, it seemed as if the light blurred and faded, so that at last there was only the moor and the cold splendour of the winter stars, each frail and bitter point of light like a needle in the wind, piercing the warmth of his body and the strength of his spirit.

It was only slowly that he freed his mind from the spell of this waking dream, which for long moments made him virtually blind and deaf to his physical surroundings, such was its fascination, and he walked forward heedlessly, as a man possessed. So it sometimes came upon him; and yet he felt, as a mystic does, that such moments, unlike the dreams of sleep, were moments of profound revelation because they brought into focus more sharply than is ordinarily possible, something of the essence of reality, however daunting the revelation might be.

It was with some difficulty that he located where his straying feet had taken him, as he stood, gathering his wits in the growing gloom which darkened the streets on the edge of Soho. He had overshot his destination and had to walk back some of the way. The streets here were meaner and less imposing; many of the buildings were shabby or of indeterminate purpose. His destination, when he came to it, was such a building. It might have been built at any time in the last hundred years, as a house, an office, or an hotel, and might still be any one of those - a drab Victorian brick building, with modernised windows which did little to improve its appearance. Most of the windows were blank with drawn curtains or blinds, although a chink of light showed here and there.

Having never been to this place before, he was not 'known', and so he had to establish his credentials with the doorkeeper, a large, unsympathetic man, whose job was to ensure that only those whose credentials were sufficiently good were allowed in. Having satisfied this judge of sinners, he was then introduced to Madame. Without having met her 'on the job', Chisam would otherwise never have guessed her profession. She was fiftyish, sensibly dressed in respectable tweeds, had an upper middle class air of calm authoritative efficiency, and might easily have been a spinster schoolmistress in a village school. The impression was by no means entirely misplaced. She was, after all, a businesswoman, and needed to know all the aspects of her business, including the ability to assess her customers and their requirements.

She hesitated a little, however, as she looked at Chisam.

"And now, sir, what would we like?"

Even her voice could have been that of a schoolmistress, one who did not expect her children to be wayward or disobedient. She was clearly a little uncertain about Chisam, however, and she went on encouragingly. "Do you like a lady to be small and petite, large and well built, and a little boisterous, perhaps?"

When Chisam rather diffidently indicated a preference for the latter, she thought for moment, and then said, "I think Janet will be the one for you." She pulled on a bell rop and in a moment a girl appeared from the back somewhere. Madame turned to her a murmured something, whereupon the girl disappeared into the back again. Turning Chisam, Madame said, "If you will come this way, sir."

She led him up the stairs to a room on the first floor. She lit the lamp, then said, "Jar will be up in a few moments." Then she went out, leaving Chisam alone to wait. T room was distinctly shabby, with very old flock wallpaper that was peeling a little places, a threadbare square of carpet, a bed, a chair and a small table. It seemed ve functional for a place which evidently had something of a reputation. He was st standing in the middle of the room, taking it all in, when the door opened again, and young woman came in. She was a big girl, not fat, but simply of large build, and b boned. Her hips were broad and beamy, her arms and shoulders were strong looking, a she was very full bosomed. Her face was broad and open, with a narrow, slightly hook nose, and prominent cheekbones. But it was not an unattractive face, with a wide, f lipped mouth and a mass of dark blond hair to match her very blue eyes. She was dress in a loose blouse and skirt with no petticoat - with no undergarments at all, as he four and she was barefoot.

He had only a few moments to take all this in, as she took only a moment to size h up.

"Haven't you taken your clothes off yet?" she asked in surprised amusement. "He let me help you." She was clearly an expert at undressing gentlemen, and almost befc he knew it, Chisam found himself naked but for his socks. While he was taking these c Janet unbuttoned her blouse and slid it from her shoulders to reveal her breasts, hea and deeply rounded, their softness evident in the way they quivered at her every mo She unfastened her skirt and let it drop to the floor, and she stood before him as naked he. Her tummy was a joy to behold, her broad hips adding to its shapely beauty. I thighs were full and round, and rubbed together excitingly as she walked towards hi She kissed him gently on the mouth: he noticed that her lips were warm, but her no which touched his cheek, was cold and bony.

"Do you want me to be a bit rough with you?" she asked, smiling. She tickled his pe with her fingertips. He smiled and nodded, too overcome to speak. She pushed him o the bed and clambered on top of him, the pressure of her soft warm flesh overcoming residual fear and coldness. First, she gave him her breasts, which had wide bro

118

nipples, and their infinitely yielding pliable softness and elusive musky scent aroused him still further. At length, he sought her mouth, and he clung to her fiercely, wanting her to know how much he needed her, and it seemed to him that she responded and understood. Whether it was indeed empathy, or simply the talent of her profession, he didn't care. When their mouths parted, she climbed off him to reposition herself, and as she did so she presented her bottom to him. Of all the parts of a girl's body, her bottom is the most arousing. The broadness of Janet's hips gave her a bottom which was the sweetest expanse of rounded softness he had ever dreamed of. Her cleft was wide and deep, and each half of her bottom was underlined with a soft crease which curved round in a wide, broad smile. Overcome with desire, he held her by the hips and pushed her forward onto her tummy so he could sate himself, first on the softness of each cheek, and then on to the almost taboo area of her cleft. As each cheek curved down to meet the other with taunting eroticism, her skin became even softer, more sensitive and moist, each little pore standing out as if in anticipation. The rich warm scent of her cleft drew him down and down and he lost himself finally in a sensual ecstasy. He still held her by the hips, and her broad female softness seemed to permeate and envelope his whole consciousness.

Janet, however, soon grew bored with this, and after a little while she pushed him off. She forced him down onto his back, and straddling him with her knees, she gently sat on him. He kissed and explored her softness with his tongue before giving way to sucking her as she was now sucking him. When they were ready, she quickly and adroitly turned round, sliding herself down his tummy and enveloping him. In the last few moments they clung together in a sweating embrace, each spurred on by the exertions of the other. He climaxed first, but as she was on top, she made him keep going until at last, they both stopped moving, exhausted.

Janet was a good girl. She did not despise all men, as many of her profession did, and in the case of Chisam, she sensed that she was the first woman he had had for a long time. Indeed, she had quite enjoyed him herself; his amateurishness amused her, and his lack of any unpleasant vice, apart perhaps from his rather childish interest in her anus, was a refreshing change from some of the clients she had had to deal with. She sensed that, for Chisam, the aftermath of sex was as important as the sex itself, and so she allowed him the illusion of love, feeling that it was quite safe to do so. He cuddled her like a teddy bear and she allowed herself to be cuddled, returning his kisses on her cheeks and forehead. At length, they lay still together, each held in the stillness of the other.

The spell was broken unexpectedly. Through the closed door came the sound of voices

119

from the passage outside, the voices of a man and a woman. Their words were nc distinct, and they were audible only for a few seconds as they walked past, but Chisai recognised the man's voice - it was that of Robert Harrison. He lay still for some time taking in the implications of this discovery. For Chisam, any contact with Harrison wa unpleasant: the very sight of him made him feel physically sick, such was his loathing c the man, and both consciously and unconsciously he tried to avoid situations where h knew he was likely to meet him. Although this was in a sense a public place, Chisam' being there was a part of the most private and personal part of his life, however sordi others may have seen it as being. Harrison had already intruded brutally into that part c his life with Stella. Coming across Harrison here of all places gave him a feeling almo. of paranoia - that he had nowhere left to hide from the prying eyes of a malevolei hostility. He knew that this was irrational because this encounter of sorts was purely matter of chance. Harrison was there for exactly the same reason that he was, of tha there was little doubt. But this only fuelled the anger that was his inevitable reaction. H anger was not far below the surface, and grew as his mind dwelt on the matter. One the reasons why he had never visited a brothel when he was with Stella was his fear getting the pox and passing it on to her. Fear of the pox was one of the things he had he to face before he had come to this place now: the urgency of his desire had enabled hii to push the fear to the back of his mind. He also no longer had responsibility for anyoi else. Harrison had - he was still with Stella.

He had not moved in the long minutes since the sound of the voices outside had fade away again, and had given no particular indication of his inner turmoil. Janet, to who the voices had meant nothing, sensed that something had happened, however. The lii between them, however tenuous, seemed to have been broken. She stirred, as preliminary to indicating that the session was over.

"Janet," he said, a little diffidently - it was the first time he had addressed her by h name - "did you hear those voices outside just now - in particular, the man's voice?"

"Yes, I heard them."

"Have you ever heard the man's voice before - heard it here, I mean?"

Janet hesitated before replying. It was not unknown for clients to hear the voices people they knew in this place, so she was not sure what was coming.

"I . . . may have done," she hedged cautiously. She was immediately apprehensive she felt Chisam stiffen with anger beside her. Obviously, it mattered to him. It d matter, and for a moment, Chisam felt like shaking the girl to get an answer out of he but he knew that he could not, and that it would do no good. After what they had ju done together, he could not raise his hand against her. That kind of violence was not

120

him. Instead, he lay still, looking up at the ceiling without speaking for several moments. At length, he said quietly, "It's important that I know. It doesn't matter where or how I find out, so there's no need for your name to come into it at all. I know who he is, and I have the evidence of my own ears that he's been here once. I just wondered if you'd heard him here before."

"Yes . . . he has come here before. I don't know how often, but I've heard his voice two or three times, and I saw him too, one time." She gave a description which fitted Harrison fairly well.

Chisam smiled inwardly. How little he knew about women, he was only too ready to admit to himself; and yet, in this brief illusion of love, for one more moment, he felt an intense affection for this unknown girl who lay beside him. He gave her a sudden hug, and kissed her.

"Now, now," she said admonishingly, "Time's up - you've had your money's worth."

She stood up and stretched with her arms above her head, the muscles of her magnificent bottom tightening momentarily. Chisam forced himself to look away lest he become hopelessly excited again. He could not afford another session with Janet that night.

Ten minutes later, he stepped out into the street again to begin his journey back to the hotel. The walk would be a trying one - he was not familiar with the way back, and he had much to preoccupy his mind. It should have been a pleasant stroll, reliving the experiences of the evening; but Harrison had spoilt that for him. The question of what to do about Harrison presented itself to him once again, even more forcefully. Harrison had been too near the centre of his troubles for too long for it not to seem increasingly the case that Harrison was the problem, and that to deal with Harrison would be to solve his problems. Even if he fully realised that this view unrealistically over-simplified matters, it was an over-simplification that at once made the whole business easier to grasp, and emotionally more satisfying to do so. The idea which he had held in the back of his mind about striking a blow against Harrison once more came into his thoughts, and on this occasion he felt more than equal to facing the difficulties and obstacles involved. With the discovery he had made that night, some kind of turning point had been reached.

He had been walking for some time in the general direction of his hotel before he noticed the fact that the streets, while no longer mean and dingy, were still dark. All the street lamps were extinguished and there was no light showing in any window he could see - or rather, only an occasional chink of light from behind tightly drawn blinds or curtains. Nor were there any people about. Even when he turned into Knightsbridge, there was no-one in sight, as far as he could see in the gloom. The deserted streets, the

121

black shadows of buildings merging into the night on either side, were so different from the familiar face of these same streets by day that it was difficult to reconcile the image in the memory with this dark reality.

The feeling grew upon him that the whole district, perhaps all of London had been abandoned suddenly by the entire populace, leaving himself as a lone straggler who had failed to heed the warning of some impending catastrophe. The feeling, and the apprehension were real - the streets were dark and deserted - it was not his imagination. Something was happening, or was about to happen, only he could not imagine what. The feeling of danger was enhanced by the fact that he could see occasional chinks of light from behind the curtains or blinds that masked most windows. It looked as if the people were still there, but were afraid to leave their houses and come into the street. As this idea took hold of him, he was tempted to knock on the door of a likely looking house and ask the people within what it was that they had so fearfully fastened their windows and doors against; but his innate reserve discouraged him from being so bold, and he walked on hoping to discover the reason for himself. There were only more dark streets, however, each as deserted as the last, yet each with sufficient hints of a human presence behind the blacked out facades to increase the impression of some impending disaster. There was stillness as well as darkness - the almost subconsciously heard murmur of noise that permeates the air of every major city even at night, was absent. If he closed his eyes, he might have been in the main street of a Cumbrian village in the small hours rather than in central London. If he looked up, he could see the stars, and lighter patches representing clouds moving across the darkness, as he might see them from a village street, unobscured by bright street lights. Only the width of the streets and the scale and grandeur of the silhouettes of buildings that towered above him on either side undermined this illusion. His sense of reality was stretched to the extent that he wondered if he had not in fact fallen asleep in Janet's warm, breathy embrace in the dingy bedroom in Soho; that the exquisite peace following their ecstasy had for him lapsed into this dark dream of menacing streets. He was now in that other world inside his head, that was sometimes more real than the physical world in which his body walked. But there had been no occasion for him to retreat from the physical world. Indeed, he had not felt so good for some while. He was as a man who has suddenly been blessed with good news, and is momentarily oblivious of care.

Here at last was somebody. In fact, it was three people, and when he drew close enough to see them clearly, they turned out to be a policeman and two soldiers, one an officer. When they saw him, the policeman challenged him and demanded to know his business. Chisam, who had approached them with only one thought in his head, to ask them what they knew of this curious blackout, was somewhat taken aback. He was not accustomed to being challenged in this way, not by policemen at least. He certainly did not want to tell them that he had just visited a brothel, and for a moment, he could think of nothing to say.

"I'm . . . visiting London on business. I'm just taking an evening stroll before returning to my hotel. I seem to have walked into something very strange here. Why have all the lights been put out, and all the people gone from the streets?"

"I'm surprised you didn't hear the warnings, sir. All the streets were covered as far as I know. Perhaps you were indoors at the time - a theatre, perhaps?" Chisam was slightly disconcerted by the policeman's shrewdness.

"It's an airship raid, that's what it is," the policeman continued evenly. "The military people," he cocked his head slightly in the direction of his two companions, "say there's a German airship heading up the Thames towards London. Seen off the Essex coast heading up river. I'd never have thought they'd dare attack London, but that's what they say. I must say, I've never seen anything like this before, in all my years in the force."

There was the slightest hint of condescension in the policeman's voice towards the military, which was evidently not lost on his two companions, one of whom, the officer, now spoke.

"These airships can be quite dangerous, which is why various precautions have been taken, including this blackout of lights, and requiring people to take shelter, preferably in basements and cellars, and not wander about the streets."

He sounded as if he was reciting official instructions. But, as if to even the score with the policeman, he continued: "May I ask your name, sir, and which hotel you are staying at?"

Chisam told him

"I would suggest that you get back to your hotel without delay. We happen to be going in that direction ourselves. If necessary, we'll find somewhere where you can take shelter on the way there, just in case there is an attack, although I doubt myself if they'll get through to London."

"How will you stop them?" asked Chisam, interested. Not knowing much about airships, he genuinely could not imagine how it might be done.

"Well, ah, hmm, I'm not sure of the details - not my unit's responsibility. Besides, it'll be restricted information."

"If you'll fall in with us, sir," interjected the policeman, now in a more genial tone. He had evidently appreciated Chisam's last question.

They proceeded in silence, and their perambulation was only interrupted when they noticed a light showing in any window they passed, even if this was only a chink between curtains. The soldier, a corporal, would knock on the door of the offending premises which appeared to be the only reason he had been brought along, and the policeman would then inform the offending householder of the error of his ways.

In this way, at length they came into Kensington. They had just turned into Kensington High Street, when Chisam became aware of lights in the sky behind them, to the east, in the direction of the city centre. They all turned to look. The searchlights of the batteries in Hyde Park had been switched on. Great beams of light, spreading fanwise from an area behind the trees of the park, which were thrown into sharp silhouette as a tangled mass of branches, obscured half the sky to the east. The light was brilliant white, and caught wisps of smoke or mist passing through the beams near the ground. Chisam had never seen such a sight before. Even the great beams of light from the lighthouses on St Bees Head, and at Whitehaven, were not to be compared with this. The light from the searchlights was much more intense, while retaining an ethereal, insubstantial quality. In the sky above, the searchlights picked out great luminous patches in the cloud base, which seemed to race through the light at prodigious speed. The almost total darkness around them completed a sense of unreality, so that the scene might have been part of an enormous stage set for some theatrical extravaganza - one of Wagner's operas perhaps, the lights representing celestial ways down which the valkyries would descend to claim the fallen in the stillness of the night. It was a sight whose drama commanded all attention, and yet the reality of it was never forgotten. Chisam was suddenly made aware of the other side of war - its excitement, adventure, even beauty.

Equally suddenly, he was made aware of the temerity of such thoughts. There was a loud bang of an explosion from somewhere near at hand, followed many seconds later by what sounded like its echo from a great distance. The first explosion had made him jump; it was followed by another, and then another, in increasingly rapid succession, so that the echoes which followed each one were lost in the general cacophony. Chisam found that he was not frightened - he just felt a general apprehension that this was not a good place to be at the present time. He looked round for the others, to find them still gazing back in the direction of Hyde Park. It dawned on Chisam at that moment that the explosions were the sound of gunfire, not airship bombs, and that the echoes were presumably the sound of the shells bursting up in the air. This was dramatically confirmed when a piece of spent shell casing hit a nearby roof with a crash, showering the street below with slates and other debris. The searchlights were waving about ever more wildly, trying to illuminate the target being shot at by the guns, which, ironically

124

must have made things much more difficult for the gunners. The quiet night was turned to bedlam, and when the policeman gave a shout, barely heard above the noise, and began walking very briskly back along the way they had just come, Chisam and the two soldiers followed without hesitation. Within a few minutes they had sought refuge in the relative calm and safety of Notting Hill Gate underground station.

A number of other people had already had the same idea, and before long there was quite a crowd spilling along the platform. When a train pulled in - the tube trains were evidently still running, even if everything on the surface had stopped - very few people got on, apparently taking the view that they were safe enough where they were without incurring the extra risk of being caught in a tunnel by a power failure or worse. The sound of the gunfire could still be heard faintly, and occasionally a heavier explosion would make the ground shake slightly, although whether this was due to bombs or to two or three guns firing together it was impossible to tell. This went on for about twenty minutes, although it seemed longer to the tense and largely silent group of people on the station platform.

Chisam, standing alone among the crowd, experienced a strong feeling of unreality. This was London, England: and yet this was also war, the war he had read about in the newspapers for so long. Not since he had sailed across the North Sea in the Dutch ferry had he felt so close to it. As he stood there in the underground station, he tried to see the thing in perspective; but he knew that however tempting it might be on such an occasion as this to allow himself to become caught up in the superficial excitement of the war, so that temporarily it blotted out the unsavouriness of what had been before, he would always find himself, so to speak, as Gulliver in Lilliput: he could not, in the end, become a Lilliputian. Wars were made by politicians, generals and bankers, who were often on more familiar terms with their opposite numbers in the enemy camp than with many of the people on their own side. Within the confines of their own circle, where one's obligations and duties were as clearly laid out as one's privileges, going to war was as natural and normal a thing to do as going to make one's fortune overseas, or assuming responsibility for some great office of state: whatever the occasion demanded, one should be ready for it. Even beyond this, however, the interlocking of all the social circles in Lilliput ensured that however much of a surprise it was for the others, they too would recognise the necessity of an imperative that was part of themselves. Only the non-Lilliputians would still feel bewildered, and most of those would fall in with the rest, because it was the easiest and most acceptable thing to do. To keep a clear perspective of the matter amid the thunder of the guns was no small achievement.

When the noise of the guns eventually died down over London, and the policeman,

125

who had ventured up to street level, came down again to say that all was now clear and the danger had passed, Chisam ascended into the freedom of the cool night with a clear head and a light heart. In the streets, some lights had come on again, and the way the light glistened wetly on the road surface indicated that there had been a shower of rain, which had perhaps cooled the combatants' ardour. There was now a keen breeze, such as usually comes with the crisp, clean masses of cumulus which could be seen towering overhead even in the darkness of the night, set in a clear sky in which the stars could still be seen. It was a night of primeval spring, pregnant with the forces of nature; and already, the tense, feverish claustrophobia of the airship raid had the unreality of a dream. For his part, Chisam, at all seasons now a Gulliver among Lilliputians, striding briskly back to his hotel, was carefully turning over in his mind the wording of a particular communication he was going to write on a certain distinctive brand of pearly grey bond notepaper. The fogs of war, at least for the time being, had vanished.

15

Korvettenkapitän Fritz Seebohm tore off the top sheet on his desk calendar to reveal the new day's date. It was the 28th of June. This was one of the little rituals with which he started the day, before he turned to the work which awaited him. Usually it was a ritual that he performed as a matter of course, to satisfy himself, as it were, that the new day had begun, so that he was in the right frame of mind for the day's business.

This morning, however, he was pensive as he allowed his gaze to wander over the view from his office window, of the wide expanse of Wilhelmshaven harbour. Along the quaysides on both sides of the river, as far as the eye could see downstream towards the North Sea, lay the great ships of the Grand Fleet, one behind the other, merging into a skyline of masts, funnels and superstructures, so that one ship could hardly be distinguished from the next. They were an impressive sight - a picture of naval might; but Seebohm had a certain contempt for them. Nearer at hand, and partly obscured by the quaysides and the endless rows of long, low, single storey buildings that seemed to characterise military establishments everywhere, lay the dark, narrow shapes of his submarines, each one quite distinct with its single conning tower breaking the line of the deck amidships. Only four submarines lay there, tethered together in a row - the rest of the submarine dock was empty. Too many of the big battleships had swung at their moorings for weeks or months, Seebohm felt, while his boats were out on patrol in the eastern Atlantic and the North Sea, as they had been since the day the war began. It was a continual source of pride that it should be so, but the captains of the battleships, all of them senior to him, had almost forgotten what it was to have the worry of operational problems.

This morning, Seebohm knew that he was faced with an operational problem - one of his submarines was overdue. It still might mean nothing - submarines were overdue sometimes, but would turn up nevertheless, having been delayed for any of a host of reasons. But the longer the vessel remained missing, the more likely it was that it was not going to come back. If it wasn't coming back, it would be his first loss, for so far in this war he had been very lucky. Several of his boats had had near misses, including one that had run aground within sight of a British shore battery; but the British were such bad shots that the submarine had managed to kedge off before the gunners got their range. But now, it looked as if he was facing his first loss. Operationally, it would not be a major problem. In the short term it would be a matter of re-deploying his forces to cover the schedule of patrols; and then the missing submarine would be replaced by a new boat with a new crew. In the end, the problem was not an operational one. Seebohm knew the missing vessel's captain and officers, some as personal friends, and also many of the crew. These would be his loss. His also would be the task of writing the letters of condolence to wives, mothers, fiancées - words that would begin the devastation of so many lives scattered across the country. To the grimy, squalid back streets of Duisburg, Essen and Düsseldorf, where the spectre of war was already adding his account to the tolls levied by more established landlords of misery, of disease, and of useless wastage in factory and mine; to isolated farmsteads huddled on the vast plains of East Prussia, where the scattered families, separated by great forests and barren heath, blinding summer light and bitter winter cold, were united by a common identity and heritage, as are all frontiersmen, and a unity of purpose in the eternal struggle with the Polish enemy; to the little fishing villages, each piled higgledy-piggledy on the banks of its creek or river mouth, its pathway to the North Sea across the endless bleak tidal flats, where the loss would be mourned of one more of the village menfolk to the ancient enemy, the sea; to mountain villages of wide, steeply pitched roofs and low eaves, clustered round the onion dome of a little white baroque church below the steep meadows of the summer pasture, where cow bells tinkled rudely in the green and white silence of the celestial peaks, as fresh as time's beginning, and where death at sea, and the sea itself, were things alien and incomprehensible; to families of every degree and condition, from industrial hovels to country houses, across the length and breadth of Germany his letters would go - another thirty-five among the increasing flood of such letters, bringing news of the tide of blood which was staining Europe.

Seebohm looked at his calendar again. The 28th of June - a year since the murder of the Austrian archduke which had precipitated this war. It was a war he had not wanted, and would have opposed if his position had allowed him to do so. But having accepted the inevitable, he had done what he could to make the best of it. He had sought and got promotion, been transferred to active service, and now had command of a flotilla of submarines, and a freedom of discretion in his command which was the envy of many of the same rank serving in one or other of the idle battleships. It was a discretion that placed him in a position better than he had imagined possible when he first realised with dismay what the war would do to his firm and its trade. It was an expression of confidence in his capabilities, in his ability to use the resources at his disposal to the advantage of his country. He hoped that over the months that he had had this responsibility, that he had discharged it well. But beyond that, given what he considered to be the unusual way in which he had arrived at this position, he was justified in allowing some of the benefits of his newly-won powers of discretion to offset some of the disadvantages he had met with as a result of the war.

The benefits had recently proved to be such a cornucopia of wealth as to be something of an embarrassment. It was as much as Seebohm could do to remain nonchalant in the face of such good fortune, so as not to draw the attention of others, especially his superiors. As well as being lucrative, however, it was also attended by some uncertainties. There was financial uncertainty - Seebohm found, as Chisam was to do, that futures in sugar remained flat for some time after the shortages began, and the only profits were the relatively modest ones from the rise in the quayside price of sugar. Seebohm had almost given up on the business when the private speculators got wind of it and the enterprise took off. There were in addition, political uncertainties. Not long after the outbreak of the war, severe limitations were placed on the Berlin stock exchange, and most dealing by central institutions was suspended. If you weren't careful you could find yourself in serious trouble. However, as Chisam had also found when similar restrictions were introduced in Britain, such restrictions sounded rather more impressive than they were. For dealing at a local level, restrictions were much more patchy, and of course, if you knew the right people, there was no need for officialdom to be involved at all. Naturally there was a price to pay for this - it was necessary to ensure that the right people had financial incentives to maintain discretion, and there was always the risk that one of them might unreasonably increase the price of discretion. But that was also a business matter.

Another uncertainty was operational - his orders to submarine captains relating to specific British ships, with particular times and places were unorthodox and curious, and although they were based on information collected by the submarines, there was an ever present danger of questions being asked by someone higher up. And finally, of course, there was Chisam.

June 28th 1915 - he could not have foreseen such times as this a year ago, in the far off, easy-going days before the war, when he was a peripheral member of the Imperial court. It was strange to remember the things that mattered then: the social round, the engagements, the embarrassments as a result of etiquette or differences of rank, the attraction of desirable appointments; the perpetual background of cynicism and bitchiness which are endemic in every court. It was a good life, and it had been his whole world; and yet he had never been satisfied in it. Because Sophia, his wife, had married beneath her, it had always irked him that his position was dependent on that of his wife. It was the bane of his life to feel apprehension whenever his position was questioned by some Prussian aristocrat whose ancestors were of impeccable breeding, or at least, had had the foresight to remove any embarrassingly unaristocratic names from the record. How often had he disgusted himself by going out of his way to sneer in public at the

129

middle class of his origins, at the bourgeois trade and business which was the only wa; his self respect was preserved from the humiliation of being dependent on his wife. Ther were some at court who endured such humiliation apparently with an easy mind Seebohm's middle class morality would not permit himself to be so base.

Then the war had come, and his world had collapsed. He had been banished t Wilhelmshaven - not in the retinue of a flag officer on one of the prestigious command in the Grand Fleet, but to the command staff for these new-fangled submarines. Howeve foolishly, he had at first taken it as a slight, as confirmation of his inferior status. The his income was threatened by the blockades, and at last he had been shaken out of hi lethargy. The war was the best thing that had happened to him, and yet enough remaine of the old Seebohm to enable him to approach it from his own personal viewpoint. H threw himself wholeheartedly into the war - both the war with England, and his ow personal war, the war of Seebohm u. Sohn GmbH. He found that he was made for such war: it enthralled him; it became his whole life. Being consigned to the unfashionabl submarines meant that he was a bourgeois once again - such things would be beneath an self respecting Junkers - and so he could fight his own kind of war, with people h understood, or who at least were on his own level. The possibilities turned out to b dazzling - and intriguing. And of these, Edward Chisam turned out to be the mos intriguing. This dull, dour, conventional bourgeois Englishman, snobbish, clas conscious and ambitious, yet precariously insecure and in deep financial trouble - how had this man come to be the key, in more ways than one, to his war?

The conception of the scheme had been maturing in the back of his mind for severa months. The spark that had given it life, the stroke of genius almost, was the idea c trying to contact Chisam, to see if he would become the instrument to give the schem effect. It was a hunch, a guess, that it might work. What made it akin to genius was tha it was a guess based on so many complex uncertainties that it would be impossible to b sure of anything beforehand; and also that it was based essentially on his memory c those few days at Lowther before the war. Apart from the shooting incident, they ha been drawn together by the discovery - and it was indeed a rare discovery - that they wer in the same business: a lucrative, precarious, sometimes not quite legal business, whos interest would have increased enormously with the coming of war. The guess lay i Seebohm's expectations about how the war might have affected Chisam, and in Chisam reaction to it. They were very different in personality. Chisam was ambitious, but he wa too much of a dreamer, had too much imagination to give him the cutting edge c successful ambition, or the ability to cope with its essential loneliness. Seebohm was a extrovert, an optimist, and used to having his own way, so much so that to be baulked c

130

thwarted was intolerable to him. He was not an aristocrat, but enough of that way of life had rubbed off on him for it to be unacceptable that he should allow himself to be put upon in the way that Chisam evidently allowed himself to be. Seebohm was sure that he would never have allowed himself to have got into the mess that Chisam had fallen into; but even he, Seebohm, could not have guessed at that circumstance. That was the great discovery he had made in Amsterdam. The meeting in Amsterdam had succeeded beyond even his most optimistic expectations. If Chisam turned up in Amsterdam in response to Seebohm's letter, Seebohm would have to assess whether Chisam had come of his own accord, or whether he had gone to the authorities with the letter, even though, in the first instance, there would have been little enough that the authorities would have been able to do with such a situation. But, in the event, Seebohm had decided that this was not what he faced. During their long conversation in Amsterdam, Seebohm had formed a strong impression of the depth of Chisam's disillusionment and disaffection. Despite all the reservations which Chisam had taken to Amsterdam, he had made no attempt to conceal his disaffection, which remained as deep as ever. Seebohm was as sure as he could be that Chisam had come to Amsterdam of his own accord; and from that certainty, the success of the scheme was assured.

But nothing could be taken for granted, especially in matters of this sort. One who is disaffected, but who has not gone into exile, who has remained amongst those from whom he is estranged, is subject to pressures beyond his reckoning: pressures from without, and from within, which sap the will and confuse steadfastness of purpose; the pressure of isolation which waits, ever present, to haunt those who stand aloof from the crowd; and that atavistic emotion of the herd, whose power must be experienced to be understood, of blind patriotic nationalism, hatred of pompous emperors and their acolytes, of continental foreigners, of the members of the neighbouring tribe, of the unknown savages in the darkness on the other side of the hill - something from within answers the pagan shout, as it has for a hundred centuries, and will do for as long as injustice breeds violence.

So it was with Chisam. His contempt for the cheap patriotism which surrounded him was secure as long as nothing seriously disturbed his belief that most of the propaganda was fabrication, which on the whole it was. There is nothing so revoltingly base and vile as the British press in a jingoistic mood, and the British press had been excelling itself in that regard for many months. The extent to which this tirade of calumny and shallow bombast, particularly in the gutter press, was having its desired effect was depressing; but as long as the transparency of its distortions and fabrications remained manifest, it was not too difficult to remain unmoved by it, other than in regretting the loss of a free

131

press. But the war itself had become nastier than anything that had gone before; th
slaughter in France was far worse than in any previous conflict, with virtually nothin
being gained as a result, so that military commanders on both sides were beginning t
countenance anything which would give them an advantage over the other side.

Much was made of the matter in the press when the Germans started using chlorin
gas against the Allies at Ypres in Belgium, causing heavy casualties. Even the sceptica
Chisam had been disturbed by the news of this new and even more barbarous way o
killing; although in the overall scale of things, it did not make much difference to th
general barbarity of the war on the western front. Much more disturbing, particularly fo
Chisam, had been the sinking of the Cunard liner 'Lusitania', which was torpedoed by a
German submarine off the coast of County Cork when the ship was six days out from
New York, bound for Liverpool. No warning had been given by the submarine, whicl
had surfaced briefly immediately after the 'Lusitania' had sunk, and for a few moment
some of the crew had appeared, and were seen standing silently surveying the floatin,
wreckage and the boats filled with survivors, pitifully few of whom reached Ireland
According to the newspaper Chisam read, 1254 lives were lost, including women an
children.

The submarine did not have a number. In many of the accounts of submarine attack
published in the newspapers, the submarine's number, as seen by survivors, wa
reported. From these reports, Chisam had been able to make a provisional list of thos
submarines that operated under Seebohm's command. The list was incomplete, and n
number could be assigned to the 'Lusitania''s attacker; but the attack had taken place i
an area where several of the Liverpool cocoa boats had been sunk, presumably b
Seebohm's submarines, and the 'Lusitania' had been bound for Liverpool. All hi
cynicism and disillusionment notwithstanding, Chisam was severely shaken. The pres
of course, had gone to town. The 'Huns' were called beasts and murderers, and it wa
described how there was rejoicing in Germany and Austria over the numbers killec
Chisam's first reaction had been near panic - that this must be his doing; that th
responsibility for it could be laid at his door as surely as if he had himself given th
order, or pulled the very lever which had sent the torpedo on its way. Was it not he wh
had been instrumental in luring German submarines onto Liverpool-bound ships? And i
the submarine commanders had become bolder, more reckless of human life, mor
callous, more brutal, could he wash his hands of it and say it was nothing to do wit
him? He knew he could not. He who had gone to Amsterdam to see the controller c
these submarines, and written out a list of ships. The fact that the 'Lusitania' had nc
been mentioned in Amsterdam did not carry any significance at this stage.

The letter that Chisam wrote to Seebohm had been written during this period of panic, and Seebohm had at least recognised this. In it, Chisam had accused him of abusing grossly even the spirit of their understanding, for the sake, he assumed, of cheap vainglory.

"Whatever the glory, whatever the financial reward, the taking of so many innocent lives can never be justified. It may be that what they say in the press here say about the German people is true, and that there is in that race a streak of barbarism which in the end cannot distinguish the line which delineates the boundary of civilised behaviour. I have to tell you that, as an Englishman, I will not partake in such barbarism, and I dissociate myself entirely from this monstrous act, and refuse to accept any responsibility for it. If this is how you mean to go on, then you must consider our understanding to be at an end . . ."

It was an hysterical letter, a fact that even Chisam recognised when shortly afterwards, he re-read the copy he had unwisely kept. He had not yet reached the stage where he would become embarrassed by it; he was still in a state bordering on shock, and was very uncertain as to what to do. But he realised with regret almost as soon as it was sent that the letter was ill judged and ill written, and he was even more uncertain about what Seebohm's response would be.

Seebohm had in fact been uncertain himself at first. He had, not unnaturally, been offended by the grosser generalisations of the letter, but was too urbane to allow such things to ruffle him. What had concerned him more was the way Chisam apparently perceived his own personal conduct in the carrying out of their agreement, and what the future of that agreement now was. It had become too important to Seebohm, too lucrative source of revenue to be dismissed merely because of Chisam's exaggerated sensibilities.

He was sufficiently disturbed to make sure that the letter which he at length sent in reply was as unpleasant a surprise for Chisam as Chisam's letter had been for him. He had started by justifying his position, both in general, and in relation to the 'Lusitania'. He quoted facts.

"I deny that I had any responsibility for the sinking of the 'Lusitania', an event which was as much a shock to me as it was to you. The ship was sunk by Kapitänleutnant Schweiger of the U20, a vessel which does not belong to the flotilla under my command. I do not know whether Kapitänleutnant Schweiger was acting specifically under the orders of his own flotilla commander when he sank the 'Lusitania', and even if he was, I do not know what those orders were. I cannot, therefore, be held responsible for everything done by Germany, any more than you can be held responsible for everything done by England, and under the circumstances, it would be foolish and naïve to proceed

133

under any other assumption. We have assurances from each other as to our ow particular conduct, and that is enough.

"Those assurances also carry with them obligations and sanctions. I have acted in goo faith, as I believe you have done, and our enterprise has grown out of that. But havi begun, it has now acquired its own momentum, and is not now lightly to be cast asid We are also in each other's power, given the irregularity of these undertakings - if it w all thrown up now for no good reason, then the obligations of secrecy and trust on bo sides would be thrown up with it, and your position is still much more precarious tha mine . . ."

Alas for Seebohm! What he had written was still only too true, and for that reason, the moment it had the desired effect. No rash or hasty decisions were taken under t goad of outraged sensibilities - nothing, indeed, was done. But at the same time, it w the worst thing he could have written, for although its first effect had been to che Chisam in the full surge of his panic over the 'Lusitania', its more considered effect w not what Seebohm would have wanted or intended. For Chisam, it was as if Seeboh was threatening the only thing in the world that was left to him, by making unacceptable for him to go on with it. In an instant, with the news of the sinking of o ship, it had turned to ashes in his mouth, and now Seebohm's letter told him, as seemed to him when he read it, that he must eat the ashes. He saw more clearly than ev how much this venture had come to mean to him. It had been possible, after so ma grim months and years, for him to re-discover a fascination and an excitement in l which he had abandoned hope of seeing again. It seemed, so painfully it seemed, t Seebohm was repeating the betrayal by Lord Hemswell, but in a way more subtle th even that artist in blackmail was capable of.

Seebohm had only been dimly aware of all this, on the basis of what he knew abo Chisam. He was not another Lord Hemswell, for all that he saw the matter just as mu from the point of view of self interest, and that the instrument he chose to use on t occasion was suspiciously close to blackmail. Their enterprise had indeed acquired own momentum, and had become something greater than either of them, and Seeboh in his concern to keep it going, as well as for more purely self-interested reasons, used the most appropriate means of doing so, or so it seemed at the time.

Events did not repeat themselves. Chisam's response had been silence, a trucul silence which, as the days and weeks passed, only increased the uncertainty and expectation of an imminent change. It was in fact an entirely unsatisfactory outcom his letter, which Seebohm began to have some regrets about having written, althou unlike Chisam, he did not nurture his regrets for long. Rather, it seemed that, with

134

either of them having done anything to warrant it, their enterprise had turned sour simply because of a change in the climate of feeling; that they had become infected with the emotions that charged the war, and now suffered from the same sickness.

Not knowing whether Chisam would continue to cooperate in releasing the information Seebohm sent to him to the British Admiralty made Seebohm consider whether to continue sinking Liverpool and London bound cocoa ships. It would hardly be consistent with what he had written in his letter, that their enterprise was 'not now lightly to be cast aside', but it might have the effect of bringing Chisam back to his senses. The more he thought about it, and the longer Chisam's silence continued, the more he returned to the conclusion that something had to be done to jolt Chisam out of the moral sulk he appeared to have lapsed into, and make him see where his interests lay. It was unlike him to be so indecisive, but he had first arrived at this conclusion over a week before, and had still not acted on it.

The knock on the door seemed to come from a million miles away. His reverie had been so profound that he had temporarily forgotten where he was. He shook himself and stood up to clear his head. His eye fell on the clock, and he stifled an exclamation of annoyance. Surely he had not daydreamed for so long - he must be getting soft. Curse the man Chisam. He would have to settle this nonsense quickly before he lost his grip. He glanced out of the window at the river and the sky, and saw that after all it was going to be a lovely day. The surliness of the North Sea had given way to something sweeter and gentler from the south as he had dreamed, making the day seem propitious. There was really no excuse for him to have wasted his time so - he self consciously squared his shoulders and straightened his jacket so that no-one might suspect him of having just been slumped over his desk, as it might have been one of the loafers down on the quayside. Having resumed his dignity, he sat down again and faced the door.

"Come in."

It was only a midshipman with the morning's signals - a very small midshipman, a boy of perhaps fourteen, smartly turned out, insofar as it was possible for a midshipman to be smartly turned out, and wide-eyed with curiosity, having been detailed this morning to take messages to one of the very parlours of power. He carried it off well, giving a perfectly executed salute as Seebohm dismissed him with a curt nod. When the door closed again, Seebohm permitted himself to relax again before turning to the signals, and the business of the day.

135

16

Lieutenant-Commander David Maxwell strode into his office on the second floor of th
Admiralty building just as Big Ben was striking the half hour for eight thirty, dim
heard across the noise of traffic in Whitehall.

"Morning, Sedgeford."

"Morning, sir."

Lieutenant Sedgeford, his deputy, was already seated at his desk, as a good assista
always is first thing in the morning. Maxwell dumped his briefcase down by his desk an
struggled out of his coat. The weight of Maxwell's briefcase made the floor shake as
dropped; it bulged, not with papers, but with packets of sandwiches of thick brown brea
made for him every evening by his wife, concerned to make sure that he did not g
hungry during the day, as she knew that he became so absorbed in his work that l
would otherwise neglect himself. Lieutenant Sedgeford, who was unmarried, was n
sure whether to pity or envy his superior, who steadily munched his way through tl
sandwiches from morning till evening. Sedgeford was sure, however, that the sandwich
would be missed if they were not provided.

"What's new?" asked Maxwell as he hung his coat up. It was a question with which l
started every day, almost as a form of greeting than as a question. In the Nav
Intelligence Division, particularly this section of it, for every event that was really ne
there was a lot of very routine work to be gone through. In time of war, German nav
signals traffic might be thought a source of great fascination; but in fact it was
anything even more mundane and trivial than British naval signals traffic. Piecii
together pictures of what was going on was no less essential a task for all that, and it v
this task which occupied most of Lieutenant Sedgeford's time. The more interesting b
were for Maxwell's attention, but by arriving at the office first, Sedgeford sometimes g
a first look at them.

"I've sorted the priority signals that have come in so far - nothing very much there,"
said. "One or two interesting ones from Dover about German airship movemen
otherwise it's all pretty routine. However, the Diplomatic stuff has just come in."

"Ah!" Maxwell rubbed his hands together. This was definitely his preserve. T
intelligence material that came in with the diplomatic bags from the various embassi
around the world was much the most interesting, not to say reliable source of informati
they received. It had already been sorted before any of it reached Maxwell's office,
course - some of the information in the diplomatic bags was too sensitive for the likes
Maxwell and Sedgeford to see. A section within the Foreign Office allocated t

information that came into their hands as they saw fit. If someone like Maxwell in naval or military intelligence suspected that he was being denied information which he needed to know, it was an extremely hard job to get any cooperation from the Foreign Office, which jealously guarded its own. Such information as did come Maxwell's way from this source was therefore all the more interesting for what might not have been revealed. What was revealed was often interesting even when it wasn't relevant to the work in hand - one filed it away for when it might become relevant.

This morning, however, brought news of more particular interest, which Maxwell greeted with a triumphant "Ah-ha!" Sedgeford sat up expectantly.

"Something definite at last about the 'Wrathful'," continued Maxwell.

"The 'Wrathful'!"

It was one of the main cases they were working on at that moment.

"Information from the embassy in Norway," went on Maxwell. "This confirms that the boatload of survivors which fetched up on the Norwegian coast south of Bergen was from the 'Wrathful'. The information from the embassy is that the survivors say that it was definitely a submarine that sank the 'Wrathful', and also that they're convinced it was an ambush."

Sedgeford gave a soft whistle.

"Nasty!"

"Nasty indeed," echoed Maxwell. "This business takes on a very different complexion."

He opened a filing cabinet beside his desk and pulled out a file marked only with a number.

"Will we be able to keep this one, do you think?" Sedgeford asked as Maxwell opened the file.

Maxwell regarded him for a moment.

"I don't know. Technically, I suppose, it's now a security matter, or at least, one which the security people will now have to be involved in. We might catch it for having kept it to ourselves for so long, even if the line between intelligence and security is indistinct sometimes. But ultimately, we were responsible for sending the 'Wrathful' out to catch that German ship, and therefore in a way, for her loss, and so we have a natural and considerable interest in finding out what's behind it all. In any case, we shall need the assistance of the security branch to find out who in particular was responsible for sending us this."

He picked up a piece of paper from the now open file - the last fateful missive from the unknown source that had sent the 'Wrathful' on its last voyage. It was written on an attractive and very distinctive light pearly grey bond notepaper.

137

17

Chisam could not decide whether this was bad luck, or perhaps good luck after all. It was a trivial, inconsequential thought in the back of his mind, which kept intruding it triviality into the forefront of his thoughts. What quirk of his psyche allowed him such distraction at this moment? The day of judgement was at hand, and he had been give advance notice of it by an angel, who had found him deep in sin. Was he fortunate t have foreknowledge of his doom?

What foolishness was he capable of! The angel, if such it be, was a very tarnished on from Fleet Street, and the day was likely to be that of his own judgement. He perused th newspapers every day for just such news as this - by chance, had he missed it, this sma paragraph, who knew what danger he would unknowingly have walked into? Such wa the limit of his fortune on this misbegotten day.

The important thing was that he did know. That small paragraph which warned him of his danger, also told him of his fate. For anyone else, it was just another item of wa news. Another large Allied offensive had been under way for some time in France, s this item was tucked away towards the bottom of the page. It had a headline, however, a it was undoubtedly the most important naval news of the moment.

'British Cruiser Lost', ran the headline. 'In a statement issued by the War Press Burea yesterday, it was admitted that the light cruiser *Wrathful* was sunk on Tuesday last by a enemy submarine. The tragic loss took place between Shetland and Norway, where th *Wrathful* was patrolling to intercept any German blockade runners. It was reported that German ship had been sighted when the *Wrathful* was struck by a torpedo from submerged German submarine. It is thought that part of the cruiser's magazine explode Only one lifeboat got away from the ship, and this reached Bergen with 39 survivors . .

It had taken a few moments for the significance of it to sink in. It was the phras 'patrolling to intercept blockade runners' that made him look again, and he wonder later if its inclusion in the report had been deliberate, or an error on the part of t authorities. For him, it was enough, and he suspected it was an error - and if so, it wou probably be the last. He checked the date, but he knew in advance what he would fin The ship that got away was without doubt the 'Heidelberg' - the date and place talli with the newspaper report, confirming it was the last ship on the list he had sent to t Admiralty. He knew nothing else about the ship. He suspected it had sailed from a Sou American port, and had presumably carried a cargo of sugar for one of Seebohm's riva - rivals who would now, whether they knew it yet or not, enjoy a respite from t predations of the Royal Navy.

Why? Why had this happened? Why had it all ended like this, for he knew without a doubt that this was the end, not just of his curious arrangement with Seebohm, and their even more curious relationship over four years, but the end of everything. It was hard, hard to face up to the fact that he had been duped yet again, when he ought to have learned that lesson from the first time. It was much harder to believe that he had been duped by Seebohm. At first, he could not believe it. Of all the men in the world, he would have trusted Seebohm. What made it harder to believe, was that Seebohm could have written as he did about the 'Lusitania' knowing that he was planning this. The thought came to him that this was Seebohm's response to Chisam's ill-judged letter; but he knew he could not now believe that. A British capital ship must have been the objective all along - the sugar futures were presumably just a blind, or at most a sideline. It was the hardest conclusion to draw, but the only one he could allow himself to accept. Anything else would be folly. It left a niggling thought in the back of his mind, however.

One by one, the implications of the catastrophe presented themselves to him, at first fleetingly and incoherently, accompanied by as many wild and fearful speculations, which denied him stability of thought. He realised that he was now horribly exposed. Seebohm, presumably having no further use for him, might spill the beans at any time to the British authorities in order to divert attention from his other source of information in London - he evidently had one. By his own action, by his own stupidity, out of hatred of Harrison, Chisam had already laid a trail for the authorities up to Cumberland. To complete the last link in the chain from Carlisle to Whitehaven would not take them very long. This thought gradually came to dominate the rest, but he could still not think coherently about it.

Oh God! What a mess. What an appalling mess. He bowed his head until his brow touched the opened newspaper spread on the desk before him, and he closed his eyes, trying to quell the panic inside him, and straining to see the faintest light in the darkness, as if he might thereby see his deliverance.

Ten minutes later he was walking briskly out along the long south mole of the harbour. He needed the sea, needed its boundless freedom and restless energy to renew his spirit and invigorate the sagging life force in him, and to restore his confidence in himself and give him space to think. Nature is impartial with her bounty: the sun shines equally on all men, the winds blow as sweetly, and the sea . . . the sea would be his haven, his solace, his escape. He walked along the top of the parapet with nothing but the wind between him and the sheer drop of gnarled, sea worn ashlar to the water below. It was a fine evening, and the tide was coming in, surging vigorously and menacingly into the harbour to cover the green slime and evil mud of low tide, and to liberate the grounded

139

fishing boats. One or two anglers had their lines out over the wall, but their presence did not trouble him. At the mole's elbow, where it bends to sweep north to the lighthouse on its tip, he stood at last with the sea before him and the wind in his face. He felt nearer to heaven than he had done for a long time. All the works of men were behind him, and the prospect was of nature alone, unsullied, as it seemed, by the mark of Cain.

At least he could think more clearly now, and his stomach was no longer taut with panic. What remained was a dull, depressing pessimism about himself and his capabilities which seemed to stand like a barrier between himself and the future. He needed something to give him the strength to leap the barrier.

But what was he going to do? Indeed, what choices were left to him? When he had gone to Amsterdam for that fateful meeting with Seebohm, it had been a new beginning, an escape from the sordid trap in which he found himself. It was a fresh start, which he had not dared to hope for before; and it was so easy to see how it might have been so indeed, so nearly was. But after six short, turbulent months, he had apparently come to the end of his rope, for the second time.

But to address this pessimism was also surely to answer the question of what he was to do. Was he really to blame for what had happened this time? Was he really responsible for the sinking of the 'Wrathful'? Uppermost in his mind had been the idea of contacting Seebohm, perhaps even by going to Amsterdam again, in order to discover the truth, and to save their arrangement and prevent the catastrophe that now loomed from overwhelming them both. The misunderstanding between them might be so small as to need no more than five minutes of discussion to dispel it completely - what folly it would be not to at least make the attempt. He had turned to Seebohm once before, and found, for the first time in his life, a man he could understand, and who understood and respected him. In his solitary existence, Seebohm was perhaps the nearest Chisam had had to a friend, although the admission of that much would be wrung from him with the greatest reluctance. A friend will not desert you at a time of crisis, and nor do you abandon a friend. Therefore, he must go to Amsterdam again to see Seebohm, to discover what had gone wrong.

Before him, sunlight sparkled softly on a gentle evening sea, a sea of that indefinable colour which is the colour of tranquillity, touched in a myriad places by the silver of heaven. It lay as a barrier before him, another existence, like the barrier in his mind. To leap the barrier . . .

He knew that he would not go to Amsterdam. He would not see Seebohm again. All that was in the past; and the knowledge of that, the realisation of it, was like a great burden being taken from him. The knowledge in his heart was the knowledge certainty, the knowledge of reality, and now that his mind was calmer, it came to the surface and was as clear as the sunlight that sparkled on the water. He had learned the lesson of betrayal, and he found that in it, at the end, there was no bitterness. A man is what he is - he may be hated for it, but it is an error to blame him for it, or even to hold him culpable. For that to be possible, he would have to be capable of being other than himself.

There was no longer time for bitterness. He only wanted to know what the truth held for him, to drink it eagerly in great draughts, so that he might know the extent of his realm, both without and within himself. The last tie with the rest of humanity had parted, finally eaten through by the acid of betrayal. But, its purpose done, the acid had drained away and left no residue. It was only good to know the truth, a truth which his heart had long known - now he had accepted it, and its light fell upon him. For some men, at the last, there is no society, no contract, no bond, no commonality, no trust; because they are vulnerable, because they are made of a different metal.

Chisam did not know whether he had the constitutional strength to stand alone: completely alone without the comfort of society in the smallest degree - where every man's indifference might become hostility given the least opportunity. For nine tenths of humanity, it was something he had already accepted. To close the door on the last tenth would be the hardest thing to do. But only when he had done that would he be free.

He took a deep breath, savouring the smell of the sea and the feel of the wind on his face. For the moment, it was enough to stand high over the sea's edge and watch the sun decline imperceptibly towards the peaceful water, as if its course to the point where it would touch the sea measured the compass of a brief oasis of tranquillity, inviolable by man or God. He watched until the sun was gone, until the orange-red disc, its edge ragged and uncertain, had melted away, the last fragment of its arc evaporating into the evening sky.

As he walked back along the mole, it seemed, as he walked, that what had changed was that he now faced a different set of problems from the ones he had faced when he had walked out there. The reality was that he had changed. He had adjusted to circumstances, in the way that a geological fault, subjected to increasing pressure from the earth, will suddenly move and adjust to resolve the tension. He had understood that he could no longer hang on as he had been trying to, helplessly reacting to events, totally dependent and totally vulnerable to others for every change of fortune. Out there on the mole, he had finally repossessed his destiny back into his own hands. He would only have the one opportunity to take it, but this time he knew what he must do to see that it was not lost.

And perhaps . . . perhaps - his stride quickened as he thought about it - perhaps the acid that had eaten away at him for so long had not entirely drained away. Perhaps there was still a small residue left, with work still to do.

18

A year of war had been sufficient to touch most aspects of English life, usually adversely; and this included, not least, the sport of kings. No kings were present at the York racecourse, however, to witness the 2.30 race on a fine early August afternoon. Indeed, there were very few people there at all, in comparison with pre-war race days - a few members of the County Set still clinging to old routines - a summer ball, a garden party, the local hunt, the races, an occasional spell of duty in the local magistrates' court, although even that had been falling off lately. One supposed that most of the criminals were now in the army, and those who were left lacked the enterprise of their peers. The art of magistracy had suffered an unexpected decline, and gently diminished the importance of those who practised it, who had not also joined the great throng that marched along the broad highway of war, but who were left, too old, or too young, or too rich, to ensure that the Midhursts, the Oakhams, the Beverleys, and the countless small country towns in little local backwaters remained forever England.

But what was left to them in their diminished importance was also diminished. Summer balls were strained and lacklustre affairs now that most of the young men were gone; garden parties were now all in aid of this or that aspect of the war effort, lest guilt should sour the strawberries and cream; and there had been such a decline in racing that now only the enthusiasts kept it up, fearful, perhaps, for the future of expensive breeding stock. It was a most depressing decline, and there were some who wondered whether the very things the war was being fought to defend were not being destroyed in the process.

But at least on this day at the York races, someone was keeping up one of the traditions of the place. Neither Edward Chisam nor William James Earl would have thought of themselves in that capacity, any more than the others who went to the races, or to the theatre or the opera, to conduct a little business in the shade of the main interest. If it were not so, then such places could scarcely exist, for only a fanatic goes to the races only for the horses, and they are a rare breed, as was now only too evident.

Edward Chisam was in York that day on official business, which meant that his expenses were paid and his time was accounted for. He chafed under such restrictions, but knew that they must be kept up, right to the very end. His purpose in being in York, his real purpose, was, after all, to finish with that once and for all. Whether William James Earl suffered under any similar restraints, Chisam did not know. He had first met Earl rather more than a year before, at a meeting in York of representatives of various interests in the cocoa and chocolate trade. William James Earl represented his own interest, as he generally did. He was a middleman, a fixer, an arranger, a man who bought and sold things and took a commission; whose business was to leave the people who mattered with the conviction that he was indispensable. He had thus made himself indispensable to part of the cocoa trade, including some of the country's principal chocolate manufacturers. He was therefore an indispensable participant in such meetings as Chisam also attended from time to time. He was not only in cocoa: he had interests in other fields which evidently took up much of his time. But he was careful to keep his business affairs satisfactorily compartmentalised, so as to avoid unnecessary complications. Chisam therefore only knew that part of him which was in cocoa.

One might have supposed that Chisam had had enough experience of double dealers to be warned off any further involvement with them; but this time, at least, things were different. Chisam was dealing with Earl on equal terms, even if it did not immediately appear so. If the truth were known, it would not have been possible to say who was the greater double dealer on this occasion.

At that moment however, the general impression was that it was very much Earl who was doing Chisam a favour. They were in the members' pavilion - Chisam was Earl's guest, his own membership having lapsed long since - ostensibly watching the 2.30 which had started ten minutes late owing to an over-frisky horse which had had to be brought under control before the race could start. Earl was genuinely watching the race in fact, having placed a bet on it. He sat hunched over the back of his chair, his eye glued to a pair of binoculars. He was a young man, in his early thirties, with a tendency to dress rather foppishly. His face had the freshness of youth, and he had an easy manner born of the enormous confidence that had carried him thus far through life with much to show for it. He was a man in his element, doing what he was good at, however that might be judged by others not graced with such a measure of audacity, or shamelessness and good luck. Only his eyes, with their deadpan hardness when at rest, gave a window for all their opaqueness to the outside world, onto the man within.

The five horses in the 2.30 swept round the far side of the course, strung out in a line and half hidden by the fencing, so that from where Chisam was sitting, the jockeys seemed almost to be gliding along, a series of humped backs and peaked caps, the furious pounding of legs and hooves invisible underneath. Then they were round and into the straight, legs flying, whip arms flailing rhythmically, streaming past the pavilion and the post. Earl lowered his binoculars and turned to Chisam with a rueful expression.

"Well, I suppose you can't expect to win them all," he said. "They ought not to have allowed that kerfuffle at the start - the horse should have been disqualified - but then, seems to be the way of things these days, don't you agree?"

It was Chisam's turn to smile ruefully.

144

"Believe me, Mr Earl," he said, " there are stories I could tell you about horseracing which would reassure you that nothing very much has changed. Not in horseracing, at least."

"I expect you may be right."

Earl's eyes were opaque again. He liked to be surrounded by charm and wit, but he had discovered that Chisam had little charm, and not much more in the way of conversation, at least of the sort that amused him. Chisam, in short, was a bore, and it was only the fact that he had something to sell that made him of any interest. Why, the man didn't even bet on the horses, which was the ostensible reason why they were at the races.

Chisam, for his part, kept his life as tightly compartmentalised as Earl did his. These occasional sojourns at the races brought back many memories. It was fortunate that at least he never went down to the winners' enclosure on these visits, to see the victorious jockeys riding in triumph, the horses standing patient and proud, steaming after their exertions; to remember the feelings of proprietorial excitement or disappointment . . . and the bitterness . . . It was fortunate, too, that the atmosphere was gone now, or was only a shadow of what it once was, with nearly empty pavilions, and the despondency of war, even here. Perhaps it would never be the same again.

Earl was fiddling with his binoculars, a distraction which recalled Chisam to the present.

"A drink, Mr Earl?"

"Thought you'd never ask. Make mine a brandy and soda, will you?"

Chisam regretted the expense, but it would be worth it. They sat and waited while the drinks were fixed and the waiter brought them over. Earl took an appreciative swig from his. He savoured it for a moment, while regarding Chisam speculatively.

"So, what have you got for me?" he asked at length.

"Cocoa futures in the Whitehaven Cocoa and Coffee House Company. One month, three months, and even six months, if you want to be that bold."

"I am a bold man, Mr Chisam, but we shall see. What else have you brought me? Presumably you haven't come to York just to sell me a few more futures."

Chisam was nervous. Everything depended on this meeting with Earl. None of his other clients had the capacity to take so much stock off his hands at such short notice. He chose his words carefully.

"Well, look at what I'm offering you before you become too sniffy about it. I haven't brought you all the way to York just to deal in small change. Futures are risky and profitable, and under present circumstances they are very risky, but also highly profitable. It's for you to judge how much risk you want, and how much profit you want."

145

"How much are we talking about first of all, in round numbers?"

Chisam remained cautious.

"In percentage terms, returns have varied from three hundred to eight hundred percent depending on circumstances. Six hundred percent is typical. Therefore, I'm offering them at five fifty."

"How much?"

Chisam told him. Earl was thoughtful. Even he had not expected such a large sum to be involved.

"That must be a substantial part of the entire stock," he said at length. "The Whitehaven Cocoa and Coffee House Company isn't all that big by all accounts." H paused, the question hanging in the air, unspoken.

Chisam looked embarrassed.

"I need the money," he admitted. "I've been heavily in debt for some time, and m creditors are due to foreclose on me within the next fortnight. If I can meet them in ful when they do, they will have no cause to enquire where I got the money from."

"Meaning?" Earl's eyebrows were raised slightly.

"Well, meaning, as you must be aware, that these transactions," he indicated the coco futures, "are not quite - official."

"I see." The dubious nature of the transaction did not interest Earl nearly as much a Chisam's reason for selling.

"How did you come to be in debt?"

"Well, it was because of . . . horses."

A moment of amused surprise, and then Earl laughed aloud immoderately, a grea guffaw of laughter, followed by irrepressible chuckles as he regarded Chisam' discomfiture.

"That explains much about your behaviour here, my word it does."

Chisam gave a wan smile. "Put like that it may sound funny, I'm sure; but let me als assure you that being in debt in the way I have been is far from funny. If you lear anything from your association with me, the most valuable would be not to get into deb My life has been blighted by it in ways you could scarcely imagine."

The amusement which had creased Earl's face was replaced by the opaque stare agai as he regarded Chisam unsympathetically.

"Who are you in debt to?"

The question shocked Chisam. It was as if Earl had slapped him in the face. Howeve much he had had to endure such humiliation from his creditors, it was not acceptab from anyone else. All the grinding down of his spirit in the last few years had not le him that demoralised, however much he needed Earl's cooperation now.

"I can't see how that's of any interest," he said coldly, returning Earl's stare.

Earl shrugged. It was not of great consequence whether Chisam told him or not. Offhandedly he said, "I just thought it would add authenticity to your story. To say it was horses . . ."

Chisam blinked at such effrontery. It seemed pointlessly provoking, over and above the most circumspect business caution. And yet, such effrontery would explain how Earl had got where he had. In any event, the conversation was suddenly turning sour, and he needed to finish this quickly. It would be unwise to indulge his temper now - too much was at stake. The mention of horses . . . Again, he chose his words carefully.

"I . . . got into debt to a Lord Hemswell. He was . . . is . . . a big name in the racing world."

"Lord Hemswell? I seem to have heard the name somewhere, although I'm sure it wasn't in connection with horseracing."

"I believe he has a junior post in the Government. I remember seeing the announcement in the papers last year."

"Yes . . yes . . . Well! I expect it'll come to me. Can't just seem to place it. It's probably not relevant anyway. So!" He peered at Chisam, his eyes screwed up quizzically. "You're selling the stuff 'cause you need the money in a hurry. That does put a rather different complexion on the matter, as I think you must agree. It depends on how much you need the money, of course, but you're the judge of that. However - what did you name your price as? Five hundred and fifty percent? I think we can do better than that. After all, if you really do need the money in a hurry . . . I'll take them off you for a hundred and fifty percent."

Chisam shook his head.

"The only thing you'd be saving me, Mr Earl, is time, and although I'm short of time, I'm not that short yet. I could still get a much better deal from other clients."

Earl scratched his chin thoughtfully for a few moments.

"Why are the margins so high?" he asked. "You've no need to prove it, because I already know from the earnings on the futures I own now. But I've hardly ever come across anything with such enormous mark-ups on the nominal price. I have the feeling that there's something I don't know."

"Oh, I don't think there's any great mystery about that. It's supply and demand in the market adjusting to the circumstances. Circumstances in this case meaning the war."

"I'm afraid I still can't see it. Why the war? I've not noticed the war having such a dramatic effect on other businesses I deal in."

"Well, I don't know what other businesses you have, but import businesses have a particular vulnerability in wartime. The ships which carry their cargoes are at risk of being attacked and sunk by enemy warships and commerce raiders, especially submarines, and this has been happening increasingly in recent months. The main cocoa and coffee importers in London and Liverpool have suffered badly in this way. They've lost a lot of cargo, and quayside prices have risen sharply as a result. We've benefited from the general rise in prices, and because we haven't lost any cargoes so far, that seems to have created an extraordinary buoyancy in futures for Whitehaven Cocoa and Coffee House Company stock."

"Extraordinary indeed. You say you haven't lost any cargoes so far, but that's no reason to suppose you won't in the future; and if you do, you'll be in the same fix as the others."

"And yet, the market seems sanguine, extraordinarily sanguine."

Earl frowned down at his drink for a moment. They were going round in circles, and he felt slightly irritated.

"I expect you have a theory about it," he suggested.

Chisam's smirk was irrepressible.

"I expect I do. Wouldn't anyone blessed with a large and, how shall I say, potentially uncertain source of revenue. You spend a lot of time thinking about it, and yet in the end it doesn't really do you any good. There's nothing you can do about it, other than making sure you're not over extended financially. The bubble may burst eventually, but unless the Germans start doing something different, there's no reason why it shouldn't go on as it is for some while yet."

"And why shouldn't the Germans start doing something different?"

"Well, if they are to, why haven't they done it already? It's not much of a theory for what it's worth, but the impression one gets is that it isn't worth the while of the Germans to attack Whitehaven or Whitehaven shipping. It's only a small port compared with London or Liverpool, and it isn't likely that the Germans have the resources to attack every small port around the coast. Whitehaven can't take the very big ships that sail out of London and Liverpool, so it wouldn't ever become an alternative to those ports. If the Germans concentrate their attention on the main ports, then it's likely that Whitehaven shipping will come off lightly, because our ships take different routes to Liverpool bound vessels."

"The Germans attacked Whitby in December," objected Earl, after a moment's thought.

It was the moment when Chisam knew he had won. He had sensed that Earl had taken he bait, unable to resist the sums of money involved, and now he saw the last of Earl's esistance crumbling away.

"But that only confirms the point I'm making," he said. "The attack on Whitby was an solated attack which hasn't been repeated. Also, it was the town itself that was shelled, not the town's shipping. There's no evidence that the Germans have the resources or the ntention of attacking every small port, still less its shipping. They're concentrating on he major ports, and I believe that that is what they will continue to do."

Within ten minutes the deal had been struck, signed and sealed. It was a good deal, in hat both men felt that they had obtained a bargain. Indeed, if the truth be told, both felt hat they had pulled a fast one on the other. Earl had felt considerably more interest in he Whitehaven company's cocoa futures than he had shown. This opportunity to acquire the majority of the stock, even if the price was a little higher than he would have iked, was a gift. He felt fairly sure that, in the not too distant future, Chisam would be icking himself for having let all his holdings go. Well, it would be hard luck. He ntended to keep this particular gift horse to himself.

As for Chisam, such was the ensuing bonhomie, that he was even persuaded to place a et on a horse in the next race. It came in last.

149

19

The police seemed to be everywhere at once. They tramped in and out of the open fro door with a familiarity that was contemptuous; in every room they poked and peered a examined, emptying drawers onto the floor and rifling through the contents, pulli books off the bookcase shelves and flipping through them one by one; dusting wal doors, door handles, furniture, for fingerprints; rifling through papers, ledgers and fi from the bureau; they tramped up and down the stairs, and called to each other in lo voices: it was a veritable invasion. The police were masters of the house, and it was wi that arrogance that they walked through its rooms.

The former master stood by one wall of his study, watching helplessly while thr plain-clothed policemen systematically rifled its contents. Robert Harrison was wh with anger. What was happening was a violation of the rights he held most sacred - t rights of property. But it was more than that: the leisured examination of the small details of personal papers and effects was a violation of privacy. Such privacy was one the privileges of property, and this violation, this leisured, contemptuous violation wa rape of that privacy. It was as if he himself was being raped, being forced passively watch it, compelled even to cooperate with it, cowed, impotent.

Harrison was shaken as well as angry. His impotence was not simply because the pol had a justice's warrant for what they were doing. Had it been a local matter, he wou have contacted the chief constable and the justice, both of whom he knew personally - a town such as Carlisle, society was small enough for that to be inevitable - and problem, whatever it was, would have been sorted out in a much more civilised mann This gross intrusion need not have taken place at all.

But these were not the local police. They spoke with London accents, and the warra although signed by a local JP, was for Scotland Yard's Special Branch. Scotland Y was only a name, but he had a good idea of what it represented. He reviewed again in mind all the recent business deals where he had sailed close to the wind, to put it more bluntly than that. The police had so far not deigned to tell him exactly what tl were looking for; merely that they were investigating a 'serious criminal offence'. himself had been officially cautioned, so presumably, he was under arrest. That m than anything had taken the wind out of his sails. He was too much a part of the soc establishment for it not to have done so. There could be no doubting the seriousness the matter. And yet . . . of what matter? He would have sworn that all the deals which police might have been interested in were absolutely watertight - no leaks. It would be the interests of everyone involved that this should be so. The fact remained, howev that someone had betrayed him. There was no other explanation.

As he stood, inwardly seething, waiting to be told his fate by the senior police officer present, it occurred to him, having watched it for a little while, that the search was a somewhat curious one for an investigation into his financial affairs. The three policemen who were searching his study were taking a great interest in things which could have no conceivable relevance to a financial investigation. Perhaps it was just a display of arrogance on their part - that they now had the power to do whatever they liked in this house. Harrison was mystified; but he was also given cause to wonder if, just perhaps, there had been a mistake.

.Beside him stood Stella, quiet and impassive, with only the drawn whiteness of her face betraying her intense shock. For the mistress of the house even more than the master, this legalised assault was painful to bear. Harrison, at least, had other sides to his life, in Carlisle, and elsewhere, which took him out of the house; but this place was her domain, and its violation was felt by Stella in a much more personal way than by Harrison. As she stood there beside Harrison, her initial shock began to give way to anger, not just against the police, but also against her husband. For Stella, as for most women, the essence of her relationship with her husband was the security and status the marriage brought her. She was the wife of her husband; he was a man of substance and position, and this was now her security, her life. In the space of a few minutes, that security had been shattered. What for most women was no more than an imagined nightmare, had come to her in reality. So strained had their relationship become in the past few weeks that, within a few minutes her conviction grew that Harrison's own actions were responsible for what was happening. For some time she had been increasingly apprehensive that her husband's rather arrogant boldness in his conduct of business would become reckless, and lead to precisely what had now happened.

Her anger boiled up inside her. Robert had been totally selfish. When he had taken the risk that had led to this, he had taken it for himself only, thinking only of himself. She had not counted - the consequences for her if something like this did happen had evidently been set at naught. She wondered if he had even thought about the matter. If Robert were to be bankrupted or jailed, not only would she be left destitute, but she would never again be able to hold her head up in society. To lose one's husband was terrible in any circumstances - to lose him because he was a criminal . . . She did not know if she would be able to endure the shame of it. A woman without a husband must explain herself. That was the way of the world. She would either have to lie, or tell the truth, and either would be a humiliation which she should not have to bear. It was so unjust, when she was innocent of any wrong. She had done nothing, but she would have to suffer nevertheless. But she was the wife of her husband, and she knew that this also was the way of the world.

All this passed through her mind in a few moments - she seemed to see the future in appalling clarity, and she could contain herself no longer.

"Robert, what is this about? Why is this happening to us?"

Her voice was low and tightly controlled, but she could not entirely keep the fear out of it. But Harrison, when he turned to her, seemed shaken and helpless. He scarcely seemed to recognise her as he looked at her. She might almost have spoken to a stranger.

"I don't know," he said at last, almost to himself. "God's truth, I don't know."

She was exasperated.

"You must know. You must have some notion of why this is happening. What have you done? What have you done that has brought the police here?"

"I don't know, I tell you, I don't know. You must not tax me with it, not here, not . . ." His eyes turned involuntarily across the room. He had spoken in a quietly savage undertone, but in the sudden silence of the room it sounded almost like a shout. The three policemen were listening intently.

But Stella's exasperation was complete.

"You must have some idea. This cannot be happening for no reason. And what is to become of us? What is to become of us?"

But Harrison was silent, and her appeal was met only by the quiet of the study, in which papers rustled and books thumped as the policemen continued with their search. It was macabre, unreal, and for a moment, Stella doubted her eyes or her sanity. But long minutes passed and the policemen continued their methodical search, while the two of them stood mute and still by the study wall, afraid to move, because to do so would only bring further humiliation. Perhaps they would be forcibly restrained. Outside the room the other policemen moved about with more noise, directed from time to time by the authoritative voice of the officer who was in charge of them. When he came back into the study, where he had sent them, he would complete their humiliation - in a few minutes, in half an hour, whenever he chose. In the meantime, they had been told to stand there and they could do no other.

Stella's eyes began to take in the details of the room as she looked about her - the leather upholstered furniture, the walnut cabinets and maple wood panelling, the oak bureau now standing open with its contents scattered, the three-light stone mullioned window overlooking the square - everything spoke of success. The policemen, and the disorder they had created during their search, seemed like a vision from a dream. Surely all this could not be taken away from them so quickly, so easily, as though it had never

152

been. The permanence and stability of English middle class life is an illusion; and yet those who take part in it are always trying to forget this, behaving as though it were as permanent as the artefacts that make it up. The artefacts - the fine houses, furniture, clothes, and all the rest, remain, to be re-arranged perhaps, as an illusion for someone else; but for individuals the illusion must remain an illusion, and if Fortune decrees that it should end, then they must perforce return to the noise and squalor of the streets beyond the net curtains and fine doorways, and make way for someone else on whom Fortune has smiled.

To be able to forget this was as sweet as it was dangerous, and although Stella had not forgotten it, it had been possible for her to push it to the back of her mind for much of the time. Her marriage was still only young, but it had been eventful, and the memories she had of it were equally varied: some of them joyous, pleasurable, others dark. Sometimes she had been so happy that it had been easy to believe in herself, and in Robert, with unsullied completeness. But there had been other times when she had not been able to forget the fear, and the memories were dark. She held one such memory now, a memory of herself, in this very room, confronting her husband's anger.

She glanced at him suddenly. A suspicion was hardening in her mind, and as she looked at him, she could see that his anger was dissipating - he seemed beaten, waiting to accept his fate.

"Robert."

She had to clutch his arm to drag him back to the present, so frantically had his mind been operating on another level.

"Robert - does this have anything to do with that business with Edward Chisam? Is it because of Chisam that this has happened?"

Had it mattered, it would have been a gross indiscretion for her to have spoken aloud; but as it happened, it did not matter - it was an irrelevance. That at least was what Harrison concluded after a moment's confusion while he re-orientated himself.

"Chisam? Edward Chisam? Of course not. It can't possibly have anything to do with him. What do you mean?"

"I mean the way you were hounding the man. I told you no good would come of it, and if this is the result, then you are the greatest fool alive. You had no cause, Robert. I tell you, you had no cause. I wish only that you would believe me. Chisam is nothing to me, or to you. He simply isn't worth it. And if your motives were financial, if you were simply using it as a way to gain an interest in an overseas trading company . . ."

"Stella, will you hold your tongue! I do not want to hear another word."

Harrison had regained some of his composure. His mind had started working on ordinary lines again, and he was able to start planning his defence rationally. Th business with Chisam was not important, but once Stella started prattling about hi personal and financial business, there was no knowing where it might stop. He was unde arrest, and the least said the better, therefore. The mention of Chisam had put on thought in his head, however. His contempt for the man had been added to by the fac that the precariousness of his financial position had meant that Chisam had not been ab to afford a lawyer to defend his interests. In Harrison's eyes that meant that Chisar deserved what he got. The man was feckless, and fecklessness was an offence which wa justifiably punished.

But now he was mentally kicking himself for the same reason. He who had sneered Chisam to his face, had stood for more than a quarter of an hour in sheepish silence, lik some lower class nonentity who had fallen foul of the law. So devastating had been th impact of the police bursting in, in the way they had done, with signed warrants an apparently irresistible force, that he had been temporarily stunned, which was of cours the intended effect. Now the mental paralysis was beginning to wear off. He conscious took a grip on himself. Turning to Stella, he took hold of her by the shoulders.

"Stella, it's important for both of us that you don't say anything about our personal business affairs - not here, where they are listening." He gestured at the police. " Yc must believe me when I tell you that I am as completely taken by surprise by this as yc are. Until the police tell me what this is about, I am completely at a loss to know. It ma even be a mistake. However, I intend to do something about it at least."

Something of the renewal of his personality, the return of his command over himsel communicated itself to her, and he felt some of the tension and the tautness go out of he He held her still, and for a space, something of what they had lost they held again, an for a moment, they were alone.

Only for a moment. The study door was pushed open, and Stella stiffened when sl saw that, framed in the doorway stood the officer with the imperious voice, who was i charge of the police. It was as imperious as ever as he used it now.

"Right, you two - outside." He gestured with an equally imperious tilt of the head.

Harrison turned to face him, assessing the man, trying to gauge his quality. He did n like what he saw, and felt his anger rising inside him.

"I do not move from this house until I have arranged to see my lawyer. I don't kno the exact legal basis of your intrusion, but I intend to find out."

"You will be permitted a lawyer when we decide you may have one, and for the tin being you may not have one. Now, outside, the pair of you."

Inspector Vernier rather enjoyed these little confrontations. They were a compensatic for the routine of police work, and for the disappointments when the quarry, for whatever reason, managed to slip away, wasting so much careful preparation. When, in a case like this, you'd got them cold, there was no doubt about the outcome. You'd got the warrant, the bird was in his nest, and it was all cut and dried. No amount of squirming or manoeuvring was any use - you'd got them exactly where you wanted them. It was especially pleasurable when you took a dislike to them, and Vernier had taken an instant dislike to Harrison. He was going to enjoy taking this arrogant bastard down a peg or two. "Very touching," he had sneered to himself when he had come into the room and seen them together. "Well, we'll see how touching it gets."

"Outside, I said."

Harrison took a step forward. The desire to punch the man's face was overwhelming, and the satisfaction it would afford equally so. But now he had control of himself again, and he knew from experience that more would be gained from letting the other side make the mistakes. He ignored the policeman and strode to the doorway. The toggle for the servant bell was by the door, and Harrison pulled at it sharply. He pulled again, impatient for a response. After a few moments, footsteps were heard coming up the stairs from the servants' quarters.

Mary, the maidservant, hesitated as she neared the top of the stairs, intimidated by the police, and the disorder, and the atmosphere of disaster which lay upon the house. She almost lost her nerve, and prepared to scuttle back down to the illusory safety of the servants' quarters. So swift had been the police raid that the servants had only a confused idea of what was going on, and they had cowered in the servants' kitchen, afraid to move, hoping that the tide of the law would wash over without noticing them. The summons of the bell, when it came, was startling and horrible. It was peremptory, however, and a life of service meant that it could not be ignored. It was the maid's bell, and so Mary was thus selected as the victim. Just before Mary faltered at the top of the stairs, however, Harrison caught sight of her.

"Mary!"

His voice made her jump, but she went to him at once.

"Mary, you are to go at once to Mr Ritchie, of Ritchie and Grainger, the solicitors, and tell him that I require his services immediately. The police have entered this house with a warrant without giving any reason, and they intend to take me away under arrest. If I am not here when you come back, he is to go to the police station. Can you remember that?"

"Yes, sir."

Her answer was little more than a whisper.

Vernier interrupted brusquely. He had been uncertain for a moment what Harrison was going to do, thinking that he might be calling for assistance to try and resist arrest b force. He was sure of where he stood now, and moved to end this prevarication.

"No lawyer, I said, until we decide otherwise. You will not do as he says Miss otherwise you may get into trouble with the law too. We'll tell him when he can have lawyer. Now, outside you two. I won't tell you again."

He motioned to two of the constables in the room, who closed in behind Harrison.

"You will go, on pain of dismissal, Mary. Wait until after they've gone if you have to, Harrison shouted to her as he was marched down the stairs. Then they were gone, an Mary was left alone with her dilemma. A little moan escaped her.

"Oh, dear God, what shall I do? What shall I do?"

It seemed as if the world had finally taken leave of its senses; as if the last of th certainties that she had taken for granted, that had given life a predictable, if dour an grim solidity, had suddenly evaporated, as if they had been no more substantial than th flickering image of a cinematograph picture. Abruptly, she turned and ran back down th stairs to the servants' quarters, to seek the comfort and solace of her kind.

20

The port of Wilhelmshaven was founded by the Prussians in 1869, on the eve of the creation of the new Germany. As well as being Prussian in inspiration, there was something unmistakably Prussian in the character of the place, as though it was intended as a kind of proclamation in physical form of what Wilhelm I's German Empire was to be all about, in case there were those who were in any doubt about the matter. Certainly all those who served there would never forget it. It was an embodiment of military bureaucracy - seemingly endless rows of single storey blockhouses regimented alongside the miles of quays which flanked the muddy waters of the Jade Busen, the dreary inlet of the North Sea in the flat and sodden coast of the North German Plain, on which the port stood.

Only the ships themselves - the tripod-masted battleships, the angular destroyers, the supply ships, the tugs and the tenders - brought variety and interest to the place. The ships were living things, engines of power and destruction, charged with the romance of the sea, and of the faraway places to which they had been and to which they might go, even if not many of them ever actually did. The land, in contrast, was dead; smothered with regimented buildings and regimented people, with bureaucracy, with order and correctness, and with something even more sinister - the power of dead, dull minds over the smallest particle of humanity in the place - a sort of cunning stupidity that seemed to characterise authority in its worst manifestations. The place was deader even than the quiet marsh which had been there before the port was built, and which still stretched out vastly in every direction on the landward side - a solitude of stagnant water under bright green bog, tussocks of coarse grass, sad booming bitterns, cloudscapes and cold winds.

Wilhelmshaven was only tolerable as a place to live when one did not have to think about it; when one was absorbed in work, in routine, in the war, in love, in any of the passions that can fill the human mind to the exclusion of its surroundings. Such passions anaesthetise the sense of the aesthetic, so that the ugliest places can seem beautiful; or one is oblivious of their ugliness.

For Korvettenkapitän Fritz Seebohm, it had been the war that had enabled him to tolerate Wilhelmshaven; that had masked the contrast between the hills and forests, the pretty villages and Romanesque sumptuousness of his native South, and this Prussian mudflat. Germany had not seen war for more than a generation, and for a peacetime reserve officer, war, even this war, was the most tremendous experience imaginable. Up to now, he had been lucky. His boats had had remarkable success against Allied shipping, and this had been recognised in official quarters. The possibility of promotion had been hinted at, although so absorbed had he become in what he was doing that he could no longer respond to such rewards as he might have done in peacetime. The prospect of promotion was actually alarming. So successful had his private war been, that to be removed from the operational command that enabled him to conduct that war, he now regarded as a calamity. His life was now like the progress of a tightrope walker, dependent on the most delicate balance in certain financial markets: anything that threatened to take away the tightrope would be disastrous. It was nerve-racking, it was exhilarating, to the oblivion of all else, including Wilhelmshaven and all its dreariness.

His main fears centred on Edward Chisam, who, following the sinking of the 'Lusitania' in May, had suddenly proved unreliable. Since the sinking of the British cruiser 'Wrathful', there had been nothing from Chisam. The silence was ominous, and he had urgently been trying to re-secure his position. If Chisam was now unreliable, his operational command no longer held such significance; but the arrangement with Chisam was central to everything, and so far, he had nothing to replace it with.

It had been since the sinking of the 'Wrathful' that everything had started going wrong. The 'Heidelberg', the ship the 'Wrathful' had evidently been intending to intercept, had got away, and had managed to bring its cargo, which included a large consignment of Brazilian sugar, into Hamburg, and into the warehouses of one of Seebohm's principal business rivals. Since then, no ships carrying South American sugar had been intercepted by the Royal Navy. The markets had already started to adjust, and although futures in Seebohm u. Sohn's sugar were still buoyant, he knew that wouldn' last. It looked as if the whole business was coming to an end. It was not how he had envisaged it ending, and if he wasn't fairly adroit in the next few days and weeks, he could be in deep financial trouble. As long as the flow of money coming in was uninterrupted, he was alright. If the flow of money dried up, and he was not able to sell his holdings at the right price, he would be left over-committed, the possessor of a lot of worthless pieces of paper.

The ensuing embarrassment would be more than simply financial. Other eyes than those of his creditors would turn to scrutinise him. However, it had been the financial side of the business, the movement of prices in futures markets and in commodity markets that had been the dominant interest. From that point of view, the operational side of it had always been subsidiary, a means to an end. Day to day, it was a sober reality rather than a source of excitement. In the day or two following a hoped for interception, he would discreetly scan his intelligence sources with as much anxiety as he daily combed his more private sources of information. There was, nevertheless, a certain elegance in the way the thing worked, an elegance that derived from its appearance of

158

being almost detached from reality. You supplied just the right amount of information in the right place, and almost miraculously, there was the result, in cold print. It had been a game, however; a clever, sophisticated game, which had appeared to be essentially ancillary to the real world of money.

And then, in the course of a morning, it was suddenly no longer a game, and he had been made aware of forces more sinister than anything in the world of credit, debt and money. That morning, an officer from the naval ministry in Berlin, accompanied by two aides, had arrived in Wilhelmshaven. They had apparently spent some time closeted with the Vize-Admiral, whose command included the submarine flotillas, before Seebohm was summoned to see them. The Admiral told him simply that the officers from Berlin wished to speak with him in connection with an inquiry they were conducting, and that he was to answer their questions to the best of his ability. They would interview him alone. None of this in itself was particularly alarming - it was typical of the way the navy conducted official business, and especially typical of what one would expect from Berlin. It was only after the interview began that Seebohm started to realise what it was about.

The principal of the three officers from Berlin, Kommodore Bräuer, was a divisional commander in Naval Intelligence. His divisional brief covered merchant shipping, which made it, as a brief, an unusually varied one. Bereft of many natural resources, Germany relied on imports from overseas for vital commodities without which the war could not be carried on. Anything that threatened those essential sea lifelines was a matter of interest to Naval Intelligence, and to Bräuer in particular. To beat the British blockade you always had to be a step ahead in the intelligence war, because all too often, it was either your ship or theirs. Sometimes you had a run of good luck; sometimes you had bad luck; and sometimes it was so bad that you knew it was no longer a matter of luck - someone had to be found and stopped.

The interview took place in an ante-room to the Vize-Admiral's office. It was conducted formally, Seebohm entering the room as an interviewee, to find Bräuer seated at a desk, and an empty chair for himself on the other side of the desk. Bräuer was, to begin with at least, formal in his manner, and used his superiority in rank to enable him to dictate the tone of the interview. Seebohm was not told what the interview was about, but simply that he was being asked some questions in connection with an enquiry which Bräuer was engaged in. Bräuer's first questions were disarmingly routine, establishing facts about his career and his present position, facts which he could just as well have obtained from official files. No such files were in evidence in the room, and Bräuer made reference only to a small notebook. He seemed in no hurry to come to the point, even asking about details of Seebohm's schooldays in Freiburg, and childhood holidays in

159

Switzerland and Bavaria. Seebohm answered as well as he could, feeling increasingly puzzled as the interview progressed. Bräuer himself seemed to relax a little - it was a warm day, and one of the windows was open, admitting a gentle breeze which brought with it the shrieking of nesting swallows as they swooped over the idle waters of the river.

"Tell me why we are fighting this war, Korvettenkapitän."

The question brought Seebohm the first twinge of alarm. It was the first indication that the matter which Bräuer wished to discuss with him was not routine. Such questions were not asked by officers conducting a routine inquiry - certainly not by high ranking officers from Berlin. One was not supposed to entertain such questions. To do so was dangerous, unless one was very sure of one's friends. For a moment, Seebohm even wondered if Bräuer was a dissident, carefully sounding out possible support; but he only needed a few moments thought, and to glance at Bräuer himself, to dismiss the idea a fantastic.

Why were they fighting this war? The question was idly put, but it was not idly meant. The twinge of alarm prompted caution.

"We . . . went to the assistance of our allies, the Austrians, by engaging the enemies of the Alliance - the Russians, the French, and the English, sir."

"So! German soldiers have died in thousands in France, and in Poland, and German sailors are engaging the English navy on the seven seas, all for the sake of those bumpkins in Vienna!" Bräuer smiled as though it were a joke; but the smile was brittle and disappeared abruptly as Bräuer continued brusquely.

"You command a flotilla of submarines, Korvettenkapitän. Where are they operational?"

"At the moment sir, mostly in the western approaches to the English Channel."

"And your orders?"

"My orders are to intercept and sink any English or Allied shipping, and also any other ships which trade with the enemy, according to the laws of war, sir."

"And what success have you had?"

"We have had much success, sir. Thirty four ships definitely sunk during the last tour of operations, and seven more which were unconfirmed. We lost one boat during the same period, sir. That was in May."

Seebohm had known many of those on board - there had been no survivors - and he was still affected by the shock of it. He felt he would have liked to talk about it now, having had little opportunity to do so with anyone else, other than with Sophia, his wife who, while sympathetic, could not understand in the way that a fellow serving officer

160

would.

But Bräuer accepted the loss without comment. He had no intention of being diverted from his purpose.

"Why was it important that those ships were sunk, Korvettenkapitän?"

"Why, sir? Because the English are dependent on overseas trade for vital supplies, especially food. If those supplies are cut off, if the sea lanes are cut, then the English will surely starve."

"I see. And would you say therefore, that it is important to sink ships carrying food in particular?"

"Yes, indeed I would, sir."

"For the reasons you have just given?"

"Yes, sir"

"Not for any other reason?"

"Other reason, sir?"

"Yes, any other reason."

The sense of alarm was no longer a twinge. The atmosphere in the spartan ante-room was suddenly charged, as a suspicion of the truth of the matter began to dawn on Seebohm. But it was as if Bräuer was able to read Seebohm's mind and predict his reactions precisely.

"Come, come, Seebohm, you're surely not suggesting that when a ship carrying a cargo of food is sunk, the only consequence is that the mass of the English population have to tighten their belts another notch. Other people are affected more directly and more immediately - the owners of the ship, for example, and the insurance companies; also those whose cargo it was. Do you follow me?"

"I'm not sure that I do, sir," Seebohm replied stiffly. He suddenly needed time to think; but Bräuer was not to be deflected now.

"Perhaps if I proceed by way of an analogy. I understand that in your private life, you are a trader in sugar in connection with your family's confectionery business."

"Yes, sir."

"These must be interesting times for traders in sugar, and other overseas commodities, especially those vital for Germany's war effort. Prices will be high because of the war, and the uncertainty of supply, and the trade will be valuable. Of course, if you lose a cargo it will be a great blow because of the money tied up in it, the more so, perhaps, because for every cargo lost, prices will tend to rise even more. You will note," he said by way of an aside, "that I have taken the trouble to inform myself about the general outline of these matters; and most interesting it has proved.

161

"So! To lose a cargo is bad, a most serious matter, especially if you don't know if the next ship will get through safely, either. But if one of your rivals in the same trade loses a cargo, why, that is good. From a purely selfish point of view - and you will admit that trade is a very selfish business, is it not, Korvettenkapitän? - from a purely selfish point of view, for one of your rivals to lose a cargo can only be good. You benefit from the rise in price without having lost anything. And the expectation of further shortage only fuels the rise in prices even more - the expectation of an even greater prize. It must be exhilarating to live on expectation, must it not, Korvettenkapitän? - to place all one's hopes in the future on the uncertainty of chance events, on the expectation that this ship and not that ship, will fall a prey to the enemy."

Bräuer had risen to his feet, and had walked over to the window, seemingly carried away by his own eloquence, his attention diverted for the moment from the person of Seebohm. Every few moments, however, at the end of each telling point, he would turn quickly to observe Seebohm's reaction, watching him minutely and missing nothing.

"It would be," he went on, "nothing less than the exhilaration of the gambler, of one who stakes his future on the turn of the roulette wheel, or the roll of dice; of one who lived in the present by gambling on the future. What strikes me as strange, even from my limited acquaintance with trade and commerce, is that that kind of risk taking, that kind of exhilaration in future uncertainty, is entirely alien to the solid, comfortable citizens of our trading and financial community. They aren't really interested in risks. What they seek above all else is a safe, dependable source of income that they can squeeze regularly like a milch cow. Even in normal times, taking risks was something to be avoided if at all possible. One of the most improbable things imaginable, after all, is the idea of a banker taking a risk - as improbable as finding a nun running a brothel. Now, it seems to me that, under the present circumstances, to trade in overseas commodities is such a risky business that the natural inclination of the average businessman would be to minimise his involvement in it as far as possible. The last thing that would occur to him would be to maintain his dependence on such trade, or even to increase it - unless unless, of course," and Bräuer turned to face Seebohm suddenly, walking towards him spreading his hands on the table edge so as to lean over towards the other, "unless some way was found of minimising the risks by, how shall we say, by fixing the odds Supposing some means had been found - if you will allow your imagination to encompass such a thing - some means of ensuring that only ships and cargoes belonging to rival traders were lost to the enemy, while leaving one's own relatively secure Supposing that somehow, such a thing could be accomplished, would that not make overseas commodities a more than attractive proposition for a trader? Now, what would

162

you say to that, Korvettenkapitän? How would that strike you as a proposition?"

Seebohm smiled ruefully as he returned Bräuer's unblinking gaze. He had met his match in this man, and was now most certainly in a very tight corner. He nevertheless had the detachment to admire the performance he had just witnessed. The art of interrogation is precise, and subtle, and of great range; and however black the art, as practised, however much the practitioner may descend towards the darker end of the range, if he does it well, then he is an artist of rare talent. Bräuer was such an artist, and although it gave him no comfort, Seebohm acknowledged the fact. The spider had spun his web and caught the fly.

"That would be . . . a proposition difficult to refuse, sir."

"Indeed? Difficult to refuse, regardless of the circumstances?"

"Well, sir, they would have to be clarified, of course."

"Why 'of course'? It must be obvious, surely, that the general circumstance will be the present war, precisely because of the nature of the business."

"Of course, that is correct, sir. But in that case, it would need to be established what other factors might be involved. If we are speaking of the war with England, the war at sea, then the objectives of the war itself might be expected to take the first priority."

"Explain yourself."

"What I meant, sir, was that merchant shipping, and the business of beating the blockades are not carried on in isolation from the naval war with England. They are, as often as not, an integral part of that war, and therefore may be subordinated to it. In other words, it can sometimes be necessary, as it were, to set a sprat to catch a mackerel."

Bräuer continued to stare at him with an expressionless face for several long seconds before he straightened up and turned away for a moment, looking thoughtful. It was a long shot, but it was the best Seebohm could do. Perhaps Bräuer already knew that the sinking of the 'Wrathful' was a chance event. But such was the nature of intelligence, that it was possible that Bräuer would have to go back to his own sources to confirm that there was not, contrary to what he may have been told, some covert operation, jealously guarded in one of the more obscure sections of Naval Intelligence, which even he had been kept in ignorance of. At most, it would gain for him only a little more time.

Somewhat to Seebohm's surprise, it appeared to work. Bräuer did not immediately press home the advantage after thus tacitly establishing his victory. Thus the interview ended, in an atmosphere of uncertainty, but with Seebohm knowing that Bräuer knew virtually everything, and certainly enough to have him arrested; and knowing also that Bräuer knew that he knew. But the obvious consequence did not follow, even though Bräuer, to have gone so far, must have had the requisite evidence. When he was escorted back to the Vize-Admiral's office, it was to be told simply that Kommodore Bräue would interview him again on the day after the morrow. In the meantime, the Vize Admiral ordered that he was not under any circumstances or for any reason , to leave th Wilhelmshaven naval base. He was dismissed without further explanation.

What in God's name did it mean? It surely must at least mean that the Vize-Admira knew as well as Bräuer, for he had been placed under virtual open arrest, even if norma arrest procedures had not been followed. Why had they approached the matter in such strange way? Why had he not been arrested outright? Did they still lack enoug evidence? If so, how long did he have before they got their evidence?

The dark waters of the dock stared back at him blankly as he leaned on a bollar gazing down into it. He had not returned to his office, and his wandering feet had, as of their own volition, brought him down to the docks, to the place where all his wor here had fruition, the place from which the boats - his boats - set out on their patrols, an to which they returned, sometimes shaken and subdued, more often triumphant, an always victorious, with a list of kills to report. At least he had not let them down, as the had not let him down; and he felt sure that, if he needed to ask anything further of then then they would respond to his call.

What immediately concerned him was to understand what had happened, an especially why it had happened. However many possibilities he examined, one alway returned to the centre of his thoughts; and to confirm his principal suspicion, he had know if Chisam had been in Amsterdam recently without his knowledge.

If Chisam was responsible for this, then he had cause to be rueful as well as angr Ever since the business over the 'Lusitania', Chisam's position had been in doubt, and was partly his own fault that it had remained so. He should have arranged to see Chisa personally rather than attempting to deal with the matter by letter, using lack of time ar opportunity as an excuse. He had been so taken up with the success of the thing that had no longer seemed that important; yet he had always been aware of Chisam discontent as a loose end that needed to be tied up. Now it was a loose end that ha unravelled the whole business, or so he suspected. To be sure, certain checks had to l made in Amsterdam.

He pulled out his watch. He was, nominally at least, a wealthy man; so wealthy, that was not sure how much he was worth to within ten thousand marks, which is not at a unusual among those whose wealth is rising rapidly. But now the most valuab commodity he had was time, because it was suddenly so scarce. Until the ne interrogation he had a sort of liberty at least. He could not imagine this curious state affairs being allowed to persist thereafter. If he wasted this time it would be a great

164

waste than if he threw away all the money he ever had. As it was, he was going to lose a great deal of money as a result of this. But the threat to his liberty was now sinking in, and as it did with almost all others in a similar situation, he discovered that his liberty meant more to him than his money. It had not yet sunk in that it was not just his liberty but his life that was in danger; that he might face a firing squad following the court martial that now hung over him. Perhaps when that realisation did sink in, his judgement would be shaken by the resultant panic, and he would become his own worst enemy.

At that moment, he was cool and rational. Once he had accepted that the game was up, that he wasn't going to bluff his way out of this, he was able to decide very quickly what needed to be done. First, someone had to be sent to Amsterdam to check for evidence of a visit by Chisam. Could that not wait until later? It was essentially irrelevant to the problem of his getting away. No, it could not wait. He did not intend merely to scuttle away, tail between his legs, like some cur of a thief. He had decided on the manner of his going, and it was necessary for him to have confirmation of Chisam's treachery before he left Wilhelmshaven. Therefore, someone must go to Amsterdam at once, and be back in Wilhelmshaven before tomorrow night. Amsterdam was only some two hundred kilometres away, but if there were any problems or delays there, it might not be easy to keep to such a timetable.

But that was nothing, nothing at all, compared with the second journey he had determined upon. He saw no reason why he should be left penniless at the end of this affair, which had so far been so enormously profitable to him. He had lost one life, and had created another, created it with nothing less than his own skill and judgement, with the very best of himself, putting forth his greatest strength. Now this too was gone; and yet it could not be dismissed as easily as he had dismissed the first. If it was just a matter of money, blind godless money, money that has no other attribute than quantity, than purchasing power, than the satiation of appetite, a belch of self satisfied greed, then he could lose every last penny of it, and have lost nothing of importance. It was, indeed, in that spirit that he contemplated the loss of most of his fortune with no more than a passing regret. It was pride - a feeling of having invested something of himself in the affair - that made him reluctant to throw it all away. A man may have many chances or few, but each chance that comes, each opportunity seized, takes up a little more of that resource which for every man is the most finite - time. It was, as Seebohm had just discovered, the most valuable resource a man has. He had invested a part of himself in his affair, and to throw it all away now would be to deny that part of himself, to admit that it had been a waste, a negation of his time, his strength, his life. It was a touch of old

165

mortality.

It would be better, nevertheless, to resign himself to the loss of it all. The papers whic would give him title to the only part of the business that looked as if it might be salvage being outside Germany, or German jurisdiction, were at his family home in Freiburg. 1 convert bonds or securities into cash or gold was now out of the question - the pape themselves were all he could hope to get out. Freiburg, however, was seven hundre kilometres from Wilhelmshaven. The chances of anyone without an official warrant speed their passage being able to accomplish such a long journey there and back by tl following night were not good, to put it at its most optimistic. And yet the journey had be at least attempted, not just for the sake of the papers, and what they represented, b for the sake of Sophia, his wife. When the news broke, Sophia would take it badly. F all that she had married him against the wishes of her family, because he lived by trac and for all that she had visibly enjoyed the prosperity that trade had brought ther particularly since the scheme with Chisam had boosted his income so spectacularly, si had never entirely ceased to be a Hochberg, and when the nature of his disgrace becar known, all the Hochberg in her would come to the fore. He could almost hear the bare concealed satisfaction in the remarks her family would make to her.

"Really, Sophia, you might have spared yourself all this trouble if only you had listen to us in the beginning. We told you no good comes of that sort, so perhaps now you w be more prepared to listen to us."

There would be strong pressure on her to break with him and return to the fami Quite possibly a divorce or annulment would be offered her - the Hochbergs we certainly influential enough to be able to procure such a dispensation. And it was ve likely that she would be persuaded, particularly if she got the news first through them. she did not hear the news from himself first, even if indirectly through a courier, he f fairly sure he would lose her. And not only her, but their two small children, Hans a Theresa. It was when he thought of them, picturing their faces, hearing in his mind's e their childish voices that he felt the worst. Sophia would not go into exile with t children. Her family, knowing this, would use the children to maximum effect in th favour. And what would they think of him, those little ones, when they were old enou to understand? Would they understand? Would they forgive? He had a sudden vision Hans aged about eighteen, rebellious, idealistic, confronting him in his old age with the self-righteous indignation of youth, confronting a father tainted with the sins of t world, compromised, having sold his honour, his family, his country . . .

He pulled himself out of his reverie. What foolishness was this! In a week he mig well be dead. All he could do was to write to Sophia. If he did not write, there would

166

no possibility of a reconciliation. And above all, he must do it now, quickly. There was no more time for regrets or recriminations. The message must be written and a messenger found. The fact that his death might be imminent was now starting to impress itself upon him.

The hands of his watch stood at ten minutes to twelve. He looked across the oil scummed water to the submarine dock. Three submarines were there, moored together, long and slender-hulled, so low in the water as to be reminiscent of some great cetaceans, their clean lines broken only by the superstructure of their conning towers amidships. One of them was preparing to put to sea, and was the centre of a hive of activity. Stores were stacked up on the dockside waiting to be loaded, and a torpedo, upended and dangling from a dockyard crane, was being swayed into the forward hatch. There was much coming and going along catwalks, and every now and then the sound of a voice raised to a shout would reach him across the water. The submarine looked indistinguishable from the other two, but he knew that it was the U24, and that it was due to sail with the high tide on the evening of the morrow. His luck had not entirely deserted him. What he needed now above all else was three or four people whom he could trust - trust with his life if necessary. If anyone here in Wilhelmshaven came into that category, U24's commander, Rudolf Schneider did. They had known each other since before the war, and had become personal friends, and it was largely as a result of Seebohm's influence that Schneider had received his command. It was a debt, and it was a debt which Seebohm now needed to call in.

But that would be for tomorrow. Today, there were other debts he needed to call in. He straightened up, and began to saunter casually in the direction of the officers' mess. A hundred metres away, another man stood up from where he had been leaning against a bollard, half hidden by a stack of oil drums, and equally casually began to follow. It was one of the two officers who had accompanied Kommodore Bräuer to Wilhelmshaven.

The lounge of the officers' mess was beginning to fill up as members and guests assembled to await the gong announcing lunch. Seebohm stood against a wall where he could see the whole room. There were always strange faces to be seen, and not infrequently, strange uniforms as well - officers from visiting ships, army officers, even the occasional Austrian; and so Seebohm did not pay any special attention when the man who had followed him up from the quayside entered the room. The man quickly identified Seebohm and took up a position where he could watch him.

Seebohm knew he was being watched. He had not yet identified the man, but he knew that it was important that he did so within the next few hours, otherwise his chances of getting away would be greatly diminished. In the meantime he would have to be constrained by extreme caution. At least Dietrich was here. It was Viktor Dietrich whom he had thought of first when he knew he was going to need help, and finding him here now meant that his luck was still holding. However, Dietrich was engaged in conversation, and Seebohm had to wait agonising minutes until Dietrich's companion moved away. Once the lunch gong had sounded the opportunity would be lost. He nudged Dietrich gently with his elbow while continuing to stare fixedly in front of him.

"Don't look at me," he muttered in a low voice. "I'm in a fix and I need help. Don't look at me!" He pushed a piece of paper screwed into a ball into Dietrich's hand. "Don't read it here. Read it where no-one can see you."

The astonished Dietrich was phlegmatic enough not to allow his astonishment to show for more than a moment. He was no actor though, and could not restrain himself from staring at Seebohm's retreating back as he made his way towards the door. Seebohm had engaged the attention of another officer and they left the room as the gong sounded apparently deep in conversation.

The waiting had been the worst, at times almost unbearable as the long afternoon dragged into an even longer night. He had accomplished two things during the afternoon, however, by the simple expedient of going for a walk. His apparently idle steps had taken him wandering downstream in the direction of the sea, until at length he stood within sight of the northern perimeter of the naval base. From where he stood he also had a clear view of the most northerly of the jetties which stood out into the river. It looked promising. Yes, it would suit his purpose. The end of the jetty stood in the deep channel, and yet it did not stand too high out of the water. It looked fairly dilapidated which meant that it would not be used much. It was an excellent discovery, and he continued his walk with a feeling of satisfaction.

He had paused only a few moments to look down on the jetty, one of many such pauses during his perambulation. As he started off again, he had time to glance at the man behind him. He had marked the man clearly once he had left the main area of the base and wandered into the area of riverfront clear of buildings and other obstructions which would give the man cover. The man did not approach to within a hundred metres and Seebohm was unable to get a good look at his face; however, once they were clear of cover it was impossible for the man to maintain any pretence as to his purpose, and so simply followed Seebohm at a fixed distance, keeping him in view. By the time Seebohm stood looking down at the jetty, he knew the other man must be armed. He was only a few hundred metres from the perimeter, no-one else was in the vicinity, and a pistol would be the only way of stopping him if he decided to make a dash for it. Perhaps the

168

both knew he would not, but doubtless the man had his orders, and the thought of the pistol gave Seebohm a momentary feeling of chill, the more so because he had still not decided how he was going to deal with the man when the time came. He wondered if he would have to kill him; but things would have to be desperate indeed before he resorted to that.

He lay awake most of that night, staring up at the ceiling, listening to the noises of the river coming through the open window. It was a stifling, sweaty August night, and he probably would not have slept anyway; but tonight was his last night in Germany and he had much to remember. If he had had the choice, he would have liked to have spent his last hours on German soil in Freiburg, the scene of his childhood, where the dark menace of the Black Forest lowered over the green valleys and the dusty little mediaeval villages and hamlets where he had roamed as a boy, had shot at game with a home made crossbow and run away from farmers and gamekeepers; had ogled girls at dances in the company of the other gawky, callow youths who represented the hopes and aspirations of Freiburg's gentry; had become a man. And from Freiburg, it would be easy to escape to Switzerland, as he had done as a youth, to the Bernese Alps, where to climb above the pine forests to the vastness of the eternal snow, to the arid, terrifying splendour of ridge upon sharp ridge, to the wind restless with the violence of death, and bitter with the freshness of new life, to the silence, was to be purged and cleansed of all sin, to stand as Adam had stood at the beginning of time. Perhaps, when all this was over, he would go to Switzerland again; but such thoughts were futile, and only served to make him even more irritable. He slept for an hour or two, but felt little better when he rose to meet the day. It was to be a long day - the longest day of his life. The worst part of the waiting was not knowing how it would end. He was afraid that Bräuer was playing with him, that they would come for him today and not tomorrow, and that all this desperate scheming was quite futile, and that Bräuer knew, knew it all for what it was, and would break him with it.

He was ready by nine o'clock, with a small attaché case packed with what he intended to take with him. It was surprising how little was absolutely necessary: the year he had spent living under the spartan conditions of Wilhelmshaven had detached him from the need to live amongst a wealth of personal possessions. All that had been left behind in Freiburg and Berlin - wealth he would never see now, and in the case of some of it, had never yet seen.

The man who watched still shadowed him at a discreet distance - never too close, but never out of pistol range. The problem of how to deal with the man Seebohm had in the end resolved by the manner in which he intended to depart. Seebohm also had a gun, a small Mauser automatic pistol. It was not a Service weapon, but his own gun, and it wa[s] packed into the travelling case. If he carried it on his person he would be tempted to us[e] it, and he was still calm enough to realise that that would be the worst mistake he coul[d] make. He was going to have to rely on the quickness of his wits.

The waiting was interminable. He had nothing with which to occupy the empty hour[s] the slowly dragging minutes. He had been suspended from duty - officially he was Abser[t] On Duty, to deflect, for the time being, embarrassing questions from the idly curious but he could not enter his own office, and it was out of the question to wait in th[e] officers' mess, where he would inevitably face questions from those who knew him, an[d] so he was in effect confined to his room. It was a spartan prison, three metres squar[e] containing a regulation issue bed, chair, dresser and washstand, and a square [of] threadbare carpet. It provided the minimum of comfort necessary for an officer to slee[p] there and no more, and it had served that purpose for him as it had done for an unknow[n] number of other naval officers who had been billeted there before him. Had any of thos[e] others been forced to spend long hours pacing up and down, apprehensive to know the[ir] fate, with taut stomach and dry mouth, in a morass of uncertainty? In Wilhelmshave[n] But this was the navy, and the navy was unforgiving and unrelenting. When you we[re] subject to its discipline, that discipline held you in its thrall no matter where you wer[e] whether in the heart of Germany or on the most distant shore of the seven seas. You we[re] a pawn, a part of something infinitely bigger than yourself. But he was finished with th[is] now, even as he paced up and down in this small cell, finished with it as surely as if [he] were to make an end of it with the sleek little Mauser tucked into the attaché cas[e] Perhaps that was what Bräuer wanted him to do - expected him to do. Perhaps that w[as] why they held off, waiting, watching. Perhaps . . .

The spell was broken shortly before three o'clock. Through the window, he caug[ht] sight of a figure striding up towards the officers' mess from the direction of the ma[in] road. It was Petersen, Max Petersen, whom he had sent to Amsterdam. Max had do[ne] splendidly to be back so quickly. He could only guess at the difficulties and delays whi[ch] he had overcome to have completed the journey in time. There would be no opportun[ity] to talk to Max, or even to thank him for what he had done. That was part of t[he] arrangement. Petersen's journey may or may not have attracted official attentic[n] depending in part on how discreet he had been; but further contact with Seebohm was [an] avoidable risk, and he owed it to Max not to put him in any further jeopardy.

He forced himself to wait for another quarter of an hour before making his way over the mess. As before, he was followed, but he paced his progress to give himself t[he] maximum amount of time unobserved. He was still in luck. Just for those few momen[ts] there was no-one else in the alcove which contained the mail boxes, and he had about twelve seconds before his shadow came round the corner. It was there - a bulky envelope in Petersen's box. Time enough to check that it was the right one and shove it under his lapel. Back in his room he locked the door and made preparations to burn the contents of the envelope as soon as he had read and noted them.

The contents were infamous - monstrous. Chisam, or at least, his messenger, had been in Amsterdam alright, and there had been no need for Petersen to look for evidence of it, for there was a letter. Seebohm could scarcely believe his eyes when the thing tumbled out from the pages of notes Petersen had written about his findings, and had folded the letter into. Chisam's light, scrappy hand on the envelope immediately stood out in contrast to Petersen's notes in standard German script. He quickly read Petersen's notes first to get an impression of what he had found. Petersen had had no difficulty in contacting the names he had been given, but when he had asked for anything in the name of 'Pieter van Dijl', had been given a negative response. A letter had been left, not for Pieter van Dijl, but for Fritz Seebohm. When Petersen had asked whether the letter had been delivered by hand, he was told that it had been. The man had apparently not left a name, and the description given by the contact at the hotel was too vague definitely to identify the man as Chisam. But for the moment, Seebohm was convinced it must have been Chisam: he was so angry that he could not bring himself to read the letter immediately; but when he did so his anger only increased, as he saw at once that Chisam had made no attempt to disguise the identity of the addressee.

"I have taken this step," Chisam had written, "because this business is finished, and because there is only one conclusion to it. You seem almost to forget that, unlike you, I did not know how it would end, and had made no preparation for such an end. I have been used, deliberately and cynically; but I do not intend simply to be discarded. The authorities here will be in a frenzy to lay their hands on those responsible for the ambush of HMS 'Wrathful', and they are not far behind me now. I may have only days left. And so, my dear Fritz, I want out, and you are the man to help me do it. After all, I could hardly have turned up at the German frontier unannounced, claiming as my credentials the role I played in helping the German navy to bag one British cruiser - think how embarrassing that would have been for you. We shall have to agree on something more appropriate. But it will have to be soon, very soon, because things are getting very difficult for me here now. Think of it, if you like, as an insurance policy, rather than the helping out of trouble of a former colleague. If they arrest me before I am able to leave England, then it may be that your people will start to ask you awkward questions about the 'Wrathful' soon after; or rather, about the 'Heidelberg', if they have not already begun to do so, that is. For I am sure that there are more channels of communication than this one, between England and Germany. And so, as your insurance policy, you will supply me with a means of escape. You will send a submarine to Whitehaven to take me off. I will wait at dawn each day from the fifteenth to the twentieth of this month inclusive, on the outer mole of the harbour. When the submarine arrives, the commander is to send in a boat. I know I can rely on you Fritz because once again, our mutual interests are involved. And perhaps it may be that, in the end, we will not have lost everything of this business . . ."

Seebohm almost choked with rage. The scoundrel! The absolute scoundrel! The man was utterly contemptible. More, he was beyond contempt. What depth of hatred, or twisted bitterness had brought him to this? The letter reeked of vitriol, and yet it was meaningless. Where was the sense in it? What was the purpose of it? As far as he could see it seemed only to be hatred, pure hatred and vitriol for its own sake. Only a deranged mind could have produced such a letter, and Seebohm tried and failed to imagine what Chisam must be like now. In this foul treachery he could see nothing of the man he had come to know at Lowther, and whose acquaintance, indeed, whose friendship, he had renewed in Amsterdam. Could fortune alone have wrought such a change, or were the seeds of the man's derangement there, even at Amsterdam, even at Lowther? Well, there was no doubt about the man now. He was a serpent, a poisonous serpent, and must be dealt with swiftly. Seebohm pounded the chair arm with his fist in his anger. The scoundrel had actually taunted him with his betrayal, flaunted it before him like a trophy of battle. How could any man be so devoid of self respect and shame? It was repulsive, horrible. To be brought down by such a man was utterly humiliating. The wound of yesterday which he had anaesthetised with the discipline of his mind was re-opened, and the pain of it struck him with renewed force. What a stupid meaningless waste! All those hopes and fears, all the effort and the risk, all the triumph and the success - suddenly was all finished; suddenly it was no more than a noise echoing in the past.

"So, Edward Chisam," he said aloud, "this is how it will end."

The letter changed nothing, then. It only strengthened his resolve to do what he had already had in mind once he suspected Chisam's treachery. And he would do it, not simply out of revenge, which at most was what motivated Chisam, but out of necessity, as one scotches a snake, because it must be done.

And Chisam's revenge? This pathetic, ridiculous attempt to atone for the burden he had taken upon himself in his madness, in his derangement - a German submarine for British cruiser. Would he be afraid when the time came? He, Seebohm, afraid? He picked up Chisam's letter suddenly and tore it in two, screwed the pieces into a ball and flung

172

from him. Well, he would have answer to that. And perhaps, too, he would even have a use for the little Mauser pistol he had packed into the attaché case.

Evening had come, and the sun hung low in the sky, its force spent. The air above the rooftops was now golden with the clear, thin light, and grey shadows had filled the spaces between the buildings like a soft mist. The tide was full, and across the quays, the distant Jade sparkled wanly in the failing light; and it was time to go. Dietrich had not made it back. Seebohm had no regrets. He had done as much as he could, and he trusted Dietrich as much as he trusted any man. If Dietrich had managed to get to Freiburg before any hue and cry started, then he could still entertain hopes in that direction.

He buttoned up his coat and picked up the attaché case. He stepped out of the room and closed the door quietly behind him, locking it from the outside. A minute later he was outside, walking slowly but purposefully down to the quays and the submarine dock. As ever, his shadow followed discreetly behind. A small crowd had gathered to see the U24 off - mostly the usual loafers, stevedores and dockside labourers, but also some crew members of the other submarines in the dock. But there were others there too who were not normally part of such an occasion. Seebohm noticed that the quayside end of the gangplank to U24 was guarded by two armed marines, one on each side of it, each steel-helmeted and with a rifle slung behind him. His gaze shifted as he noticed another figure standing on the edge of the group - Bräuer. He felt his insides twist with the shock of seeing the man again, and he knew he was afraid. What was Bräuer doing here? But he knew very well. Bräuer knew that Seebohm would be expected to make an appearance to see the U24 off, and precautions had been taken to ensure that Seebohm did not attempt to escape with the vessel. And from Bräuer's point of view it was no doubt an interesting exercise in psychological pressure. How would the victim react to having to stand and watch while his last possible means of escape sailed away without him? Whether Bräuer derived active pleasure from such an observation would be hard to say.

Bräuer stood watching with interest now as Seebohm stood by himself a little way away from the group of watchers around the end of the gangplank. He was the commander again, watching one of his submarines begin another tour of operations. Bräuer, watching, saw him standing, aloof and detached, his coat buttoned up and his uniform cap squarely on his head, the braid on his epaulettes gleaming in the evening sunlight, as if he were no more than what he seemed, and there was nothing untoward about the little ceremony which was unfolding before him. How deceptive appearances were, and how easy it was for some men to cross the divide between decency and dishonour. Who would have guessed that this man was a traitor? Bräuer's instinct was to end this charade at

173

once, to stop this travesty, this insult to the uniform and the flag. But he was not all-powerful here. He was regarded, as were all of his profession, with a certain mistrust, even a certain unease, by the naval command here, lest the probing scalpel of his curiosity should come too close to them, should disturb traditions comfortably assumed and the easy familiarity of years; and so he had had to agree that certain procedures should be followed before he took any further action - unless Seebohm himself gave him cause to act before then.

But it seemed as if Seebohm had given up. He continued to stand quite still, watching impassively as the final preparations were completed. The marines stood aside and the crowd fell back a little as the gangplank was pulled away. There were shouts of command from the officer of the watch, and the mooring lines were cast off forward and aft and hauled in. The water around the submarine's stern began to churn gently as the propellers gave her steerage way, and a haze of dark smoke eddied up from the exhausts as the throbbing of the diesels quickened. Slowly, but with purpose, the long whaleback hull swung out into the dock, and began to slide with deceptive idleness towards the entrance to the canal. A brief cheer went up from the crowd. Kapitänleutnant Schneider now stood on the conning tower beside the officer of the watch, and the commander of U24 took off his cap and waved with it. Only Seebohm knew that Schneider was waving at him in particular, and he raised his hand and waved back. Now the submarine was through the dock entrance and into the canal, and only the top of the conning tower and the masts were visible as she moved along the canal and out of sight, down towards the sea locks. Seebohm watched until the last of her was gone before turning and walking slowly in the direction of the Bismarckstrasse. With the tide now full, U24 would only be delayed by a few minutes at the locks, and Seebohm found it extremely hard to curb his impatience; but it was essential to preserve an outward appearance of calm until the last moment. Seebohm's shadow had also detached himself from the now dispersing group on the dockside and was following Seebohm again; but the crisis seemed to have passed and Seebohm's slow, thoughtful pace up towards the Bismarckstrasse did not necessitat any urgency. Seebohm, however, was glancing surreptitiously at his watch as he walked and as he turned into the Bismarckstrasse he began to quicken his pace as imperceptibl as he could. Just ahead was the central registry, and beside it was the messengers' hut. Here the messenger on duty would wait until summoned by a bell to the registry to collect an urgent message, or until the next bag of routine mail was ready. He would then collect a bicycle from the lean-to on the far side of the hut and proceed on his errand. As he drew level with the hut, Seebohm, glancing behind, saw with satisfaction, that his shadow had allowed more than a hundred and fifty metres to open up between them. He stepped suddenly into the hut. Only the off-duty messenger was there, slumped over a newspaper spread out on the table: his colleague was presumably out on his rounds. He stood up, startled at Seebohm's sudden appearance. It was unusual for officers even to acknowledge the existence of mere messengers; for one to come into the messengers' hut was almost unheard of.

Seebohm wasted no time on preliminaries.

"I must go into the town at once. It is a matter of the greatest urgency. Do you have a bicycle here?"

"Er, yes . . . yes, sir," the man stammered in response.

"Lead me to it at once."

"Yes, sir. I must ask you to sign for it, sir. It is the regulations."

Seebohm ground his teeth at the delay; but this was Germany, and the regulations were the regulations, no matter what the crisis. The registry was only next door if the man needed any authority to back up his regulations. Seebohm scrawled his name illegibly on the clipboard offered to him, then thrust it from him.

"At once, man, at once!" he exclaimed in his impatience. His shadow more than likely had already started running. The messenger led him out of the back of the hut to the lean-to where a couple of spare bicycles were standing. As Seebohm seized one and mounted it, the thought crossed his mind that he might disable the other bicycle to delay pursuit. But there was no time - even a few seconds' delay might be fatal. It would also make the messenger suspicious - it would certainly be against the regulations.

He wobbled uncertainly over the first few metres - it had been a good while since he last rode a bicycle - but then he was back on the Bismarckstrasse and pedalling hard in the direction of town. He glanced over his shoulder and saw that his shadow had closed to within thirty metres of him and was running hard. He was also panting hard, being unused to this kind of exercise, and when he saw Seebohm he began groping under his lapel as he ran. Bang! The report of the pistol sounded horribly loud, and Seebohm heard the bullet whistle past his head. A second shot was followed by a third, and Seebohm felt his spine crawl in anticipation of the jarring impact of a bullet, even though he knew it was highly unlikely that the man would hit a moving target while panting for breath after running. And now the distance had opened up again as Seebohm got the hang of the bicycle - fifty metres, a hundred metres, a hundred and fifty. His shadow had reached the central registry and had stopped. A dilemma presented itself. Should he seize another bicycle and continue pursuit, or go into the registry to raise a general alarm. After a moment's indecision, the man plunged into the registry, remembering at the last moment to pocket the pistol. It was well over a minute before he emerged again and dashed to the

175

messengers' hut. By this time, Seebohm was almost out of sight. The Bismarckstrasse was not a straight road, but turned a slight bend about half way down. Once Seebohm had passed the bend he was hidden from view from the central registry and that stretch of the road. Glancing behind to make sure there was no pursuit, he took the first turning on the right, and within a minute was pedalling hard along the Mühlenweg in almost the opposite direction, and making for the coast road. He reached the coast road four minutes later, and there was still no sign of pursuit. Now he could see the sea, and he began looking desperately for a sight of U24. He passed the end of the canal and there was no sign of her there, so she must already have left the canal. Please God she was not delayed. He pressed on, with the still waters of the Jade on his right, now turquoise under an eggshell-blue sky, and a drab expanse of open wasteland on his left, already becoming dark with the shadows of the night. He was tiring now and beginning to pant with the exertion of pedalling the cycle. He glanced behind, and then looked again. There was something on the road behind him - another cyclist. He looked a third time to make sure but there was no doubt, and although he was nearly a kilometre behind and the light was failing fast, there was no doubt as to who it was. The man was a devil! He had guessed. He had remembered the previous day's events, had guessed where Seebohm would be making for once he had seen through the ruse, and he had taken a short cut. Now the margin of error was almost nothing - a minute perhaps, if he was lucky. It wouldn't be enough.

Seebohm redoubled his efforts, his tiredness forgotten as he tore down the road toward the distant jetty. Then he saw it, the long, low shape off to the right, jet black against the ghostly phosphorescence of the water. It was still a little ahead of him, but he was travelling faster; and there at last was the jetty. When he reached it, his pursuer was still about a kilometre down the road. He had less than two minutes before the man caught up with him. But here was the U24. She seemed to drift in towards the jetty with agonising slowness. Schneider was alone on the conning tower as he brought the submarine smoothly in to bump gently against the end of the jetty. At the last moment Seebohm threw the bicycle into the water - it would be one more piece of evidence against him then jumped down, clutching his hat and attaché case. The hard steel casing jarred his shins as he landed and he stumbled a little. Immediately he felt the submarine tremble beneath him as the diesels picked up and she began to move out into the stream again.

He was possessed by a triumphant elation, as if he had cheated fate, had denied the wilfulness of a scornful Fortune. He was not at that moment conscious of the burden of what lay ahead, only of what he had just achieved, even as he still panted from the exertion of his escape. He had done it! He was even a little surprised at how easy it had been. He had been increasingly oppressed over the last thirty six hours by the conviction that it would not be so easy to escape someone of Bräuer's calibre by means of such a simple ruse. But he had done it! Fritz Seebohm was master of his own fate again, and he would yet have something to show Herr Kommodore Bräuer and his masters in Berlin; and Edward Chisam and the British. And Sophia? Oh, Sophia, Sophia, Sophia!

The sound of Schneider's voice from the submarine's conning tower recalled him to his immediate danger. He moved along the casing to the conning tower to put himself out of sight and out of the line of fire from the jetty, behind the bulk of the structure. He had managed to board the submarine with less than thirty seconds to spare, for when his shadow reached the end of the jetty, Seebohm was still stumbling on the submarine's casing within pistol shot, and the man might still have finished him. But it would have been a chance shot, and an unlikely chance, for like Seebohm, he was by then near the end of his strength and could no longer rely on his marksmanship. It did not occur to the man at that moment that to have shot and missed would have been as effective as to have shot and hit his quarry; for at that moment he saw only conspiracy, and was dumbfounded by it.

When at length Seebohm found the conning tower ladder and swung himself up onto the little platform, the U24 was several hundred metres out from the shore and well out of pistol range. Kapitänleutnant Schneider greeted his commander warmly, if a little quizzically, as they shook hands, for he still awaited a reason for Seebohm's unorthodox method of embarkation. Seebohm, however, was still breathless, and not inclined to talk. Explanations could wait now. He turned to look back at the jetty, and at the small figure now standing on the end of it, a mere black silhouette against the western sky, a sky now silver with the palest ghost of day, still touched with the most fragile pastel pinks and greys where a wisp of cirrus caught the sun and held its light to the last before the mist of night enveloped it. The small figure stood motionless on the jetty at the sea's edge, at the very edge of Germany, watching the receding vessel. He had lost his quarry, the quarry he had been detailed to guard and to follow and even to kill, and for that he would have to face the wrath of his superiors; but now he could only watch in the stillness of the evening as the submarine was gradually lost in the quicksilver of the sea.

Seebohm, on an impulse, raised his arm and waved at the still visible figure, but the man made no move to reply.

"Who is that?" Schneider asked him.

"Do you know," said Seebohm, with a touch of breathless surprise, "I haven't the faintest idea."

21

Inspector Vernier stood up wearily and looked across the desk to where Robert Harrison sat, equally weary, in an uncomfortable high backed chair.

"Just to make myself abundantly clear, Harrison, I'll repeat what I said before. This country is at war, and this is an extremely grave matter of national security. Anyone suspected of complicity in it is in very serious trouble indeed. I'm talking about treason and treason is a hanging matter. Nothing you have said so far refutes the evidence we have against you, and your lack of cooperation will be taken note of as part of that evidence."

Vernier had come round the desk and was leaning over the man as he went on:

"I've got you in my sights Harrison, and I'm going to make bloody sure you won't squirm out of this one. I'm going to nail you. We're holding you under special wartime regulations, and we'll hold you for as long as it takes."

"I keep telling you," Harrison said, his speech becoming slurred with fatigue, "I keep telling you you're making a mistake. I do not know what this is about. I cannot tell you because I do not know."

Vernier turned away and pressed his knuckles into his eyes as if to try and press out the tiredness that was slowing his thoughts. Something was wrong with all this, something was very wrong. The browbeating technique had produced nothing, absolutely nothing and the whisper of his intuition was telling him that this was a blind alley. If Harrison was the man he was looking for, there would have been something, some hint, no matter how small, to satisfy his intuition that Harrison was lying.

He returned to the desk and riffled through his notes. He was not going to admit defeat although there was not a lot left. Either the evidence was there, and he was simply going to have to work harder to extract it, or . . . His hand paused at one page.

"Who is Edward Chisam?" he asked suddenly.

Harrison looked up, startled.

"Edward Chisam? What's he got to do with this?"

"I'm asking the questions. Who is he?"

"Well, he's a deputy manager of the Whitehaven Cocoa and Coffee House Company. They're mostly traders in commodities - importers and wholesalers of cocoa, coffee, tea, sugar, that kind of thing. As far as I know, Chisam deals mostly with the shipping side of it - the import business."

"And what's your connection with him?"

"It's . . . a professional connection. Chisam is a client of the firm of which I am partner."

"Is he a friend of yours? You seemed to recognise the name more readily than if he was just another client."

"Indeed, he is not," said Harrison with feeling. "If one wishes to preserve one's standing in society, one does not associate with individuals of Chisam's ilk."

"But you know enough about him to have formed such an opinion of him."

Harrison reflected for a moment before replying.

"Chisam is heavily in debt, largely as a result of his own irresponsibility and fecklessness. We manage his debt, and therefore supervise his personal financial affairs, and will continue to do so as long as he is unable to redeem them himself."

"Seriously in debt, you say?"

"I cannot see it going on for much longer, to be frank. We will have to foreclose on him if he cannot pay off the debt soon."

"And he is aware of that?"

"I presume he must be, although as I say, the man is feckless."

"Is it possible that this man has a grudge against you? You say you manage his personal financial affairs because of his debt, and you clearly have a low opinion of him which you don't trouble to conceal. Perhaps he might feel hard done by. Regard you as an enemy."

"An enemy? Don't be ridiculous. A social inferior cannot be an enemy. If such people don't know their place then they are very quickly put there. And Edward Chisam will most certainly be put in his place. Besides, it's the firm that manages his debt, and it's entirely his own fault that he's got himself into such debt, not ours."

"Could he ever have had access to your personal stationery?"

Harrison thought. "I keep a stock of it in my Whitehaven office, and I have interviewed Chisam in that office."

"Was he ever alone in the office, even for a minute? Perhaps you went out to speak to someone, or to fetch something."

"I cannot distinctly recall such an occasion, but it is possible."

"So on at least some occasions, you dealt with the man on behalf of your firm. Was it mostly you who dealt with him?"

"I don't know if it was mostly me, but I suppose I dealt with him as much as any of the other partners."

"And it's possible he might have a grudge against you?"

Harrison shrugged noncommittally. "I suppose it's possible he might; I really couldn't say."

"Is it possible that you have a grudge against him?"

"I'm sure I don't know what you mean," replied Harrison coldly.

But Vernier was no longer looking at him. His eyes were unseeing as he turned over i his mind this curious assemblage of facts. Ships and shipping. Traders in cocoa, coffee sugar. Sugar . . . Heavily in debt. Possible access to the stationery. He still couldn't se any pattern, see how it fitted in with Maxwell's case, but he was receiving stron vibrations from his intuition. He turned to Harrison again.

"Do you know if this Edward Chisam had any connections with Germany, or wit Germans? Before the war, I mean."

"I'm afraid I don't. Am I to understand," Harrison continued as he began to take in th implications of the turn the line of questioning had taken, "am I to understand that it on Edward Chisam's account that I have been subjected to this monstrous imposition?"

"You're to understand nothing of the sort. Not, at least, until we've had a chance have a word with this Edward Chisam. The trail has led to you, Harrison, and we'l holding you until we're sure of the facts."

The interview, however, was over. Indeed, Vernier could not wait to get Harrison of of his sight. He was now ninety percent sure that Harrison was a dead end. But Chisai was still only a hunch, and he could not yet afford to relax his grip on the situation. F pressed his knuckles into his eyes again. Curse these damned provincial enquiries. It wa always the same. Just when you had critical decisions to take, and some supportin information from central files and a little consultation with Head Office would be mo useful, you were in the middle of the desert hundreds of miles from civilisation, an absolutely on your own. In addition to which, it was Sunday evening: not the best times, even in London, but out here . . .

"Where does this man Chisam live?" he asked Harrison.

"Whitehaven," Harrison answered dully.

"Whitehaven? Where the hell's Whitehaven? How far away is it?"

Harrison explained, and Vernier swore an oath. It would take at least two hours to g there, even if there were any trains, and if it proved to be a wild goose chase they'd the be stuck there at least until the following morning. Well, it looked as if this Edwar Chisam would have to wait until the morning. He'd had enough for today, anyway. The he remembered that the warrant under which he was holding Harrison expired in tl morning. Harrison didn't know that, at least, not yet; but if that maidservant had gone the lawyer's office, a lawyer might turn up at any time - might already have been turne away by the local police, although they hadn't said anything. The lawyer would stymied if they had left Carlisle for another town. And of course, he would need to ta

180

Harrison with him to help identify this Chisam.

He swore aloud again. Well, at least the local constabulary could sort out the transport and accommodation for them. In the meantime, perhaps they could also rustle up a bit of grub.

"Alright, Harrison," he said wearily, "we'll take a break."

Three hours later, the last train from Carlisle pulled into Whitehaven station. A rather grim little group of five men stepped down one by one onto the platform into the wan yellow gaslight of one of the station lamps. They stood for a few moments drinking in the cool night air after the stuffy atmosphere of the carriage. Steam hissed gently from leaky pipes and a large moth battered itself determinedly against the glass of the gas lamp. The pungent, evocative smell of the sea was in the air. Inspector Vernier looked around with disfavour. So this was Whitehaven. He couldn't see much of it, but from what he could see, it was even more of a Godforsaken hole than Carlisle, and Carlisle had been bad enough. Why did all towns in the north of England look so dreary, and so drearily alike? And what kind of people could bear to live in such places? They must be a different species. Oh, to be back in London, tucked up with his mistress in her nice warm bed - or even with his wife. God! This case was really getting to him.

Here was the local constabulary, anyway - he noted two uniformed policemen making their way down the platform towards them. The Carlisle police had wired ahead to warn them of his arrival, and of his requirements when he did arrive, so he was expecting their story to be a good one. Inspector Vernier had a fairly short fuse, and he had just about reached the end of it. He had almost reached the end of it even before they had left Carlisle. Harrison, when he learned that he was to be taken to Whitehaven that night had at first refused point blank to go. Vernier, already worried about the warrant, had blustered, then threatened Harrison in increasingly abusive terms, and in the end, Harrison had only agreed to go if he could see his wife first. It had been an uncomfortably emotional meeting, made worse by the fact that it had only been with great difficulty that Mrs Harrison had been dissuaded from accompanying her husband to Whitehaven. She had gone with them as far as the station, and Harrison had become physically angry when Vernier's men had none too gently prevented her from going any further.

At the end, Stella had stood on the platform watching the train recede into the darkness of the night. Harrison had managed to say enough to indicate what had happened, before he was silenced by Vernier. As she stood watching, it was as if the world she knew had ended as the tail lamp of the train was finally extinguished in the darkness.

On the train, the journey had been completed in tense silence. Now, Harrison stoo
sullen and indifferent among the four policemen on the platform. The two Whitehave
officers, a sergeant and a constable, exchanged greetings with Vernier, the sergea
touching his cap on seeing Vernier's identification papers. Vernier drew them aside,
be out of earshot of Harrison, before questioning the sergeant. Yes, he was tol
transport had been provided - a Black Maria was waiting outside the station. Ye
accommodation had been arranged at a local rooming house - perhaps the Inspect
would arrange to pay off the landlady. She had been helpful in the past and th
Whitehaven police wished the arrangement to continue. Unfortunately, no, the loc
magistrate whom they had dragged from his bed at this uncivilised hour had refused
sign the search warrant - not, at least, before speaking to Vernier himself fir
Apparently he knew Chisam personally, and was quite shocked at what was bei
proposed. He was waiting at the police station for their arrival. It was only with difficul
that Vernier restrained himself from venting his irritation on the hapless sergea
confining himself to a curt nod of assent.

They made their way outside to where the horse-drawn Black Maria was waiting in t
station yard. Vernier's four men and the Whitehaven constable sat inside with Harriso
while Vernier and the sergeant climbed up onto the dickey with the driver. The clatter
hooves and wheels on the cobbles echoed in the empty streets as they made their w
through the town. The only signs of life were the late night drunks, and the vagrants w
were always there, the lice of a city, deranged by misfortune beyond humanity, a
beyond its understanding or its pity. Tonight, at least, the local constabulary had mc
important matters on hand than knocking the heads of drunkards with police staves. T
Black Maria stopped only once, outside the rooming house in Tangier Street, to all
one of Vernier's men to claim the rooms and confirm their availability. On reaching t
police station, they passed under the entrance arch and clattered into the yard. Inside t
station, the yellow light from gas lamps fell depressingly on stained woodwork, flyblo
brown paint and worn linoleum floors, and in the air was a smell of stale sweat.

The duty sergeant stood up as they all trooped in, as much in surprise as anything el
The Special Branch was rarely seen in Whitehaven - their very appearance had alrea
made the duty sergeant's night, and by its end he would have enough saloon l
conversation to last him for weeks. Introductions were once again effected, and the d
sergeant also touched his cap when Vernier identified himself; he then retreated a f
steps down a passage leading to the rear of the place, and knocked discreetly on a do
After a moment, two men emerged and accompanied the sergeant to the front offi
They were the luckless magistrate, who was still holding out on the warrant, a

Superintendent Hogg, senior officer in charge of the Whitehaven police. The duty sergeant would ever afterwards point to that night, and to his foresight in calling in Superintendent Hogg as soon as the telegram from Carlisle arrived, as a turning point in his career.

"If I hadn't called in the Super when I did," he would assure his audience as they surveyed each other across two thirds empty tankards in a smoke filled bar, "I would still be a sergeant now, as sure as I'm sitting here."

It was as a sergeant, however, that he watched the proceedings unfold.

Vernier was disconcerted by the appearance of so senior an officer at this juncture. It threw him out of his stride. He had been intending to give the obstinate magistrate, whoever he was, the full benefit of his pent up frustration - now he would have to clamp the lid on his frustration yet again. Superintendent Hogg examined his credentials thoughtfully.

"What seems to be the problem, Inspector?" he asked, in a voice that suggested that perhaps there needn't be a problem at all if Vernier would only hold his peace. "Mr Kennard here tells me that you've asked for a search warrant, and he has serious reservations about a warrant in this case, which I can well understand."

Kennard was short, with frizzy ginger hair, and a somewhat irascible temper. He was a local mill owner, and as a magistrate he was feared by the local ne'er-do-wells who came before him on the bench; but now he was out of his depth, even if he did not yet appreciate it.

"I'm sorry if this man Chisam is a friend of yours," began Vernier, "but I'm afraid this is absolutely necessary. A very grave matter of national security is involved, and personal feelings must take second place."

Kennard expostulated noisily, as much to preserve his sense of importance as to make his point. He was not used to seeing this side of the law, and a close acquaintance with dingy police stations at such an hour of the night he found, to his discomfort, was a strongly deflating experience.

"Not a personal friend, exactly, but I know the man; he's in business - damn it man, he's a member of the Conservative Party - it's a preposterous idea that he's involved in . . what you're suggesting, absolutely preposterous. Where's your evidence? I demand to see some evidence. Coming here with your fancy London ways . . ." he was warming to his theme as his confidence grew . . . "we're not all bumpkins, you know, and in a small community like Whitehaven . . ."

Vernier was no longer listening. He was eying Superintendent Hogg, trying to gauge his reaction to all this parochial claptrap. For that was the point - these people actually

183

believed that they were as sophisticated and worldly-wise as any Londoner; that becaus
they ruled the roost here in this little backwater, they knew all there was to know abo
the ways of the world. And perhaps they did in their own way. They were foxes in
jungle where there were only foxes; whereas he, Vernier, was used to dealing with tiger
Out here, their dealings with tigers were so infrequent that they could easily imagir
themselves to be the equals of tigers, and expect to be treated accordingly. They had r
real understanding of the level of society above them, because it hardly existed i
Whitehaven and places like it. It was too easy for them to believe that because they he
set themselves up with a bit of a mill, or a local grocery business, or a miserable secor
rate trading schooner running coal to Dublin, or whatever, that not only did this confir
their *savoir-vivre*, but also that they stood in some sense as equals in the democracy
property. They stood on their own feet and answered to no-one, any more than did tl
greatest in the land. In Whitehaven, the roar of the tiger rarely sounded more than
mutter, and when it did sound as a roar, they scarcely knew whence it came. Vernier p
it down to the spread of democracy. Democracy would be the downfall of the country o
day, as people like this prevailed by mere weight of numbers. One day, some jumped
grocer would get his hands on the levers of power, and it would be the end of England.

He could see that Superintendent Hogg was going to need talking to. He was clear
impressed by Kennard and his bluster; and was he not after all, one of them - indee
barely even that, for he was only a public official, dependent on a salary. To Hogg
much as to Kennard, Vernier was an unwelcome intruder. Ignoring the irate Kennar
Vernier stepped over to Hogg and murmured: "If I could have a quiet word, sir." Verni
regretted having to divulge information unless it was absolutely necessary; but
evidently was necessary, and in the end, the Superintendent went like a lamb. His on
stipulation was that he would have to divulge at least the outline of the business to t
obstinate Kennard to ensure his cooperation; but he assured Vernier that he would ma
himself responsible for Kennard. It was not for nothing that Vernier was seen as havi
a bright future in front of him.

Superintendent Hogg had been unmistakeably impressed by what Vernier had told hi
even though it had been a heavily edited version of the available facts. Within half
hour, several extra constables had been called in, and with Vernier and his men, t
party was sufficient to require two Black Marias for transport.

Edward Chisam's residence, No 6 Victoria Road, a modest, mid-terrace town hou
was in darkness when the two Black Marias drew up in the street outside. It was t
minutes past eleven, and all the windows in the street were in darkness: only the yell
light from the street lamps lit this still and empty suburb late on a Sunday evening. W

184

the silence broken by the noise of hooves and wheels, and the sound of boots clashing on cobbles as heavily shod policemen jumped down from the vehicles, it was possible to see curtains twitching here and there as light sleepers roused from their beds peeped out to see what was going on. No curtains twitched in the windows of No 6, however, which remained dark and mute and unresponsive. Four men were sent to find the back entrance, and a brief whistle was the signal that they had taken up position. Vernier stepped up and rapped peremptorily on the front door knocker, a heavy cast iron ring suspended from the mouth of a cast iron lion's head. The stout wooden door reverberated like a drum, and they could hear the sound of the knocking echoing within the house. Many more curtains twitched along the street, and one window was even thrown open as someone less discreet stuck his head out for a better view. Somewhere, a dog started barking, with an irritating urgency. Four times Vernier knocked, each time listening to the echoes dying away into the silence within. After the fourth time he stepped down and turned to the Superintendent.

"I think it would be best if we went in by the back way, sir - less public, and the door may well be easier."

Hogg concurred, and they made their way to the back entrance. The yard was already occupied by the four policemen guarding the back. At a word from Hogg, one of them began battering at the door with a fireman's axe. The door proved stouter than was anticipated, and it was evidently bolted as well as locked. By the time two constables, taking it in turns, had reduced the door to its constituent planks, heads were protruding from the windows of most of the neighbouring houses. Vernier stepped cautiously inside. The light from the police lantern revealed the scullery to be empty. The air smelt stale, and still carried faint traces of cooking odours, from a meal eaten many hours or even days earlier. No dirty crockery had been left on the table or in the sink, however, and everything had been cleared away for the next meal. They pushed open the door into the living room, where Vernier lit the lamp. Again, no signs of life - it was a simply furnished room, and the high backed dining chairs had been neatly pushed in against the polished dining table, as if awaiting Chisam to descend for breakfast the following morning. The fireplace was completely empty. The farther door opened into the hall and stairwell, and the front door was opened to allow the others in.

Slowly, Vernier ascended the stairs, the light from the lantern casting weird shadows from the bannister rails and newel posts. At the top they paused. The house was absolutely still and silent, and Vernier was already sure that there was no-one alive in the house other than themselves. The back bedroom was empty, with not even a carpet on the floor - clearly it was never used. The spare room also seemed to be unused, other than as

185

a storeroom: there was furniture stacked up at one end, and also a couple of trunks which Vernier eyed with interest.

The door to the main bedroom was locked. Vernier tightened his lips in a little grimace. He hoped very much that it wasn't going to be messy. This was a side of police work that he liked the least; was even a little squeamish about, although he would never have admitted it even to his closest colleagues. It was a weakness that was not acceptable, least of all in a policeman, and on occasions when he was prey to it, it was only shame and a fear of discovery that helped him maintain his self control. Who would have thought that this case might produce such an occasion?

He exchanged glances with Hogg, who in turn made a little grimace, before nodding to the constable with the axe. It took several heavy blows with the back of the blade before the lock was smashed and the constable could push the door open with his boot. Vernier swallowed, his throat dry, hoping no-one would notice the bobbing of his Adam's apple as he lifted the lantern to illuminate the room. There was a momentary glare as the light from the lantern was reflected back by a dressing table mirror, before Vernier swung the lantern, and its light swept across the room, fleetingly illuminating a wardrobe, chairs, a side dresser, a bed, a bookcase, and . . . He stepped into the room and swung the lantern round to check again. But the room was empty. Edward Chisam was gone.

Even when they had lit the lamp and examined the room again in its bright light, it was still impossible to divine any definite impression of its former occupant's presence. Chisam was gone, and yet, as to whether his absence was to be lengthy or brief, the empty room told them nothing. A raincoat hung in the wardrobe; there were clothes in the dressing table drawers, and yet there was room in both for clothes which might have been taken away. A slight depression in the bedspread where the occupant had sat down perhaps to tie his shoelaces before leaving, seemed to be the only mark of his physical presence which he had left in the room. It was almost as if it were a hotel room, and the occupant had no intention of staying or leaving any permanent impression on the place. Only the bookcase gave some indication of the character of the man, or that this had been more than a mere hotel room. It was stuffed almost to overflowing with books, pamphlets, leaflets, papers, paperweights. A small model of a sailing vessel, done in wood, stood on the top of it. There were books on commerce and business practice, a nautical almanac of some sort, books on the west African colonies, a home study course in German - Vernier noted it with interest - mathematical tables, an atlas, various novels from Conan Doyle to Conrad, and a scatter of more obscure works with names like Aristotle, Machiavelli and Plato on the spines. The man clearly had pretensions of being an intellectual. And intellectuals, as far as Vernier was concerned, were troublemakers

More than half the trouble in the world these days was caused by intellectuals and their stirrings and rabble-rousing, and the world would generally be a better place without them, of that Vernier had no doubt. To nobble an intellectual would give him even more pleasure than nobbling that prig of a banker had done.

He stood up to ease a momentary cramp in his legs. All those papers in amongst the books would have to be gone through in detail, and that looked like being a job in itself. His eye was caught by the fireplace. Unlike the one downstairs, this one had not been cleared of ash. A heap of pale coal ash spilled out from under the grate onto the hearth. On top of the grate was another pile of what looked like darker ash. Vernier stepped over and knelt down to have a look. The darker ash was the ash of burnt paper. Gingerly he picked up one or two fragments from the pile and held them up to the light. There didn't seem to be any writing on them. Something else caught his eye. Gently, he lifted the grate up out of the fireplace and set it down on the hearth. Had he missed it? His fingers sifted slowly through the coal ash, and then he had it. It was a small fragment of the paper which had escaped being burned and had fallen down through the grate. He held it up. Could it be . . ? With his other hand he reached into his breast pocket and after a moment pulled out a piece of paper. It was a piece of light pearly grey bond notepaper. The fragment from the fireplace matched it exactly.

Vernier stood up, a grim smile slowly spreading over his face. He'd cracked it! It had only been a hunch, from a chance question, but he'd cracked it. He felt very good at that moment. It had been a good night's work, and he was feeling extremely pleased with himself, his nerves of a few minutes earlier now entirely forgotten. No doubt the house would furnish other evidence in corroboration, but this - this small fragment of paper, still edged with ash, was the key to the case, and what he had come all the way from London to find.

He looked up to find Superintendent Hogg gazing at him curiously.

"Found something interesting, Inspector?" Hogg asked him.

"Indeed I have, sir." He stepped over to show the Superintendent. "These two samples of paper are identical, wouldn't you say, sir?"

After squinting at them for a moment, Hogg agreed that they were.

"This notepaper is from the stock on which the message I referred to earlier was sent. Because this paper was specially prepared for a single customer, there can't be any doubt about the source. I'm pretty sure now that Harrison wasn't responsible; and I think this settles it. This Edward Chisam is our man."

Hogg gave him a wintry smile. "I'm impressed, Inspector. It's a neat bit of work."

"Thank you sir," Vernier replied, as modestly as his pride would allow.

"However," Hogg continued, "there's still the matter of laying our hands on the man Where is he?"

It was agreed that nothing more could be done that night. The burnt paper in the grate suggested that Chisam wasn't coming back. Nevertheless, a guard would be stationed in the house in case he did return. Meanwhile, there was the problem of what to do about Harrison, who at that moment was locked in one of the Black Marias outside. He had been brought along in case Edward Chisam had been found at home, and identification was needed. Now that that didn't seem to be immediately in prospect, there couldn't really be any justification for continuing to drag Harrison around with them, even if the warrant was not due to expire in the morning. But although he was no longer the main suspect, Vernier remained suspicious about Harrison, and felt reluctant to release hi grip. Perhaps it was just prejudice. The dislike he had conceived of the man was hard to shake off, and perhaps that, in the end, was all it was. But he didn't have to make an decision about Harrison until the morrow anyway. Harrison still didn't know about th expiry of the warrant; but in any case, he was more or less obliged to spend the night with them in the lodging house, as there was practically no alternative at that hour of th night. Even if he was released now, Vernier couldn't see the man turning up on th doorstep of a local acquaintance in the small hours of Monday morning with a story tha he had just been released from police custody. After tomorrow, Vernier would have t rely on the local police to watch Harrison until the case was sewn up.

In fact, for Robert Harrison, the worst was largely over, although it would still be man hours before that thought occurred to him. At that moment, he was nevertheless experiencing a certain lightness of mood. Although he could see very little from inside the Black Maria, he could hear well enough, and he had been able to gain a fai impression of what had been going on. It was balm to his soul. What he had been pu through on Chisam's account had now been visited on Chisam himself, and he was now taking pleasure in the sweetness of revenge, even if it had hardly been intentiona Indeed, his own plan for finishing Chisam had not included anything so dramatic as th midnight raid. The assault on Chisam's front door, the thudding and crashing of othe doors being broken down was music to his ears, and the mental images of it worked o him like a benediction. It helped restore his faith in the rightful order of things. His on worry was about meeting Chisam when the man was finally brought out. Would it b clear to Chisam who had won; who had been revenged on whom, if he himself was sti in custody, locked in the Black Maria? It was important to Harrison that Chisam shou know who was the victor. And he could expect no consideration from Vernier, wh would fully understand what he was doing if he humiliated him in front of Chisam

188

Harrison's mood swung from exhilaration to anxiety and back again, as many times in as many minutes, as the minutes dragged by and there was no further sound from the house.

But when Vernier did return, there was no sign of Chisam, and no mention of him either. Despite his apprehensions, Harrison was disappointed; but Vernier was incommunicative and refused to answer his questions. The Black Maria moved off, and when it stopped again and the door was opened, Harrison saw that they were not at the police station, but in Tangier Street. Vernier led the way to a rather dingy looking lodging house which Harrison did not remember having noticed before.

The landlady, an elderly woman with a hard face, and dressed in clothes that looked none too clean, had evidently been waiting up for them, for she greeted them angrily with a stream of abuse, complaining, insofar as Vernier could make out the Cumberland dialect, about the lateness of their arrival. She stood in the doorway, apparently refusing to move to let them in. Vernier, now extremely tired, had also reached the end of his patience, and would have been perfectly willing to have her arrested and thrown into the Black Maria if she continued to be obstreperous. However, when he took out his wallet and peeled off a ten shilling note from a wad of such notes, she gave a scornful snort and gave way. She continued to mutter under her breath as she led them up the stairs to their room. It was an extremely dingy room, containing a most unprepossessing looking bed, a couple of armchairs whose torn upholstery was slowly shedding the stuffing, and nothing else. Some more chairs were fetched, and a couple of candles - the gas seemed to be off - and then the old woman left them to it.

Harrison, who had been both appalled and amazed by these proceedings, at length found voice to ask a question. Vernier, under the circumstances, remained brusque.

"You'll be going back to Carlisle in the morning, where you may be released on bail. In the meantime, I'm afraid you'll have to spend the night here - there's no practical alternative at this time of night."

Harrison didn't argue. He had a sufficient inkling of the way the wind was blowing to satisfy him for the moment, and he was much too tired to care. He had been allowed very little sleep over the last forty-eight hours, and he suddenly found that his head was swimming with fatigue. Even when Vernier indicated that he could have first refusal of the decrepit-looking bed, which they had all been eying with dismay, he hesitated only a second before allowing himself to collapse onto it. The policemen settled themselves as best they could in the chairs, and Vernier blew out the candle.

Dreams are strange things in which the strangest things can happen: so strange sometimes, that one is even aware, in some sense, of their unreality while one is yet asleep and the dream is still in full possession of the mind. But no dream, surely was stranger than this. It had been one of those deeply joyous dreams of reminiscence, o' happy times long ago, of boyhood homes, and school, and green summers filled with adventure; but Stella was also there, mixed up with childhood friends, and it only made the dream the sweeter. But suddenly, appallingly suddenly, everything was black with the wrath of God: the world shook to the thunder of His rage, mountainsides collapsed, grea' buildings crumbled, a great wind blew, screaming, shrieking . . .

He was conscious again, and aware that he had been dreaming; but for a moment, the dream still seemed to hold him. Something tremendous had woken him up, shaken him out of a deep sleep; but he did not know what it was. But the shriek of the wind which he had heard in his dream was still there - he could still hear it even now he was awake, and the shriek was getting louder and nearer. But the shriek was not the wind, it was . . . I was a sound he had never heard before - it was the whistle of a shell. Seconds later, there was an enormous explosion close by, which shook the dingy boarding house to its foundations.

He sprang off the bed, almost impelled by the sheer force, the sheer volume of noise from the explosion. The others had risen from their chairs, and had all assumed a similar, slightly crouching posture of startled alarm, as if they were about to take flight. The room was no longer dark - their forms, and the features of the room were already distinct in the thin light of early dawn.

"What was it?" someone asked. But a bewildered shake of the head was the only reply. Vernier went to the window, pulled aside the filthy bit of curtain that covered it, and pushed up the sash. People were visible in the street below. Some were early morning workers, miners and railway workers in rough working clothes, clogs and canvas knapsacks; a newspaper boy, caught, as it were in the act of pulling a newspaper from large bag slung over his shoulder; some were in night attire, having ventured out into the street to see if they could see the cause of the explosion; others, like Vernier, were leaning out of upstairs windows. All were clearly startled and confused - no-one seemed to know what to do.

"What is it? What can you see?" Harrison asked Vernier; but Vernier ignored him. At that moment, a man appeared in the street, having emerged from one of the alleys that led to the harbour. He was shouting and gesticulating, pointing in the general direction of the harbour. Vernier could not hear what the man was shouting - he was too far down the street. As he strained to listen and catch the man's words, his ears became aware of another sound. Harrison and the others heard it too - a whistling sound, rapidly falling in pitch, and increasing in volume. Vernier instinctively ducked back into the room just a

190

the whistle, a noise of horrible menace, reached a crescendo as it seemed to flash right overhead, to be followed immediately by another appalling explosion. They all dropped to the floor in panic. Harrison found himself crouching by the bed, clutching it for support. He was still sufficiently detached to notice a flea jumping on the bed, and to feel a sense of dismay that he was probably infested from having spent the night on it.

Vernier, who had been crouching below the window sill, cautiously raised his head after a few moments. In the street below, some people had started running, although no-one seemed to know where to run to - some ran up the street, others down. Other people remained in the same frozen attitude as before, as if aware that there was no escape from this unknown terror. Vernier had the feeling that this was a complete unreality - it was so inexplicably bizarre that it couldn't be happening, even if one understood what it was. Then he caught sight of a great pall of dense, dark smoke rising into the air against the dawn sky to the east. As he gazed at it stupidly, still not realising what it was, he became aware that the man who had been shouting down the street just before, was still shouting, but now within earshot.

"... ship ... ship ... it's a ship. It's a ship. There's a ship out there. There's a ship in the bay firing its guns at us. It's a ship ..."

Then he heard the whistling noise again, a noise which even in the space of two or three minutes had acquired the power to turn his blood to water. He dropped to his hands and knees; but before he was properly down, the shell landed. The explosion was much closer, and the force of the blast shattered the bedroom window. Harrison felt the floor move and the bed beside him jolt as he clung to it. After a few moments, Vernier felt something wet on his neck, and his sleeve also felt wet. Looking down, he saw that he had been badly cut by flying glass from the imploding window. His right cheek was bleeding profusely, and another piece of glass had embedded itself in his right forearm, and his lower sleeve was already wet with a spreading stain of bright red blood. One of his men noticed that he was hurt, and came forward to help him.

"Jesus," Vernier heard himself say in a dazed voice. "Jesus . . ." He couldn't speak properly - the glass in his cheek had gone right through and he could feel it grating against his teeth. As gently as he could, his sergeant pulled out the glass. He dabbed at Vernier's wounds with a handkerchief that soon became saturated.

"I'd better have a look at that arm, sir. I don't like the looks of it."

"Yes . . . thank you, Wilson." Vernier was shaken, and the sight of his own blood had temporarily unmanned him. As Wilson began to help Vernier with his jacket, they all became aware of the sound of someone screaming. It was coming from outside. Vernier, looking at the window, saw, with a sense of shock, that the shell had landed in Tangier

Street, about fifty yards down the street. The front of a building had collapsed and a grea heap of rubble and lumps of broken masonry spilled right across the street. There were bodies lying on the cobbles of the street - some were still, others were moving feebly; and it was one of these who was screaming, a heartrending sound which tore at the nerves, so directly did it communicate the agony and terror of the unfortunate wretch.

"For God's sake . . ." Vernier began, wincing in distaste at the screams. "We'd bette go down and help. No sign of the local constabulary yet, and we can't stay here." He fel trapped in this verminous little rooming house, and it was a desire to get out of it a much as an awareness of his duty that motivated his words. He stood up unsteadily.

Sergeant Wilson, a veteran of the Boer War, was equally certain that they should sta' put. He had been under fire before, whereas Vernier had not.

"Indeed, sir," he began, "but I'm not sure . . ."

For some reason they did not hear the approach of the next shell. Perhaps th screaming from the wounded man obscured its whistling, or perhaps the sound of thei voices; but when it landed, they were completely off guard. The shell struck the buildin; next door. When it exploded, they hardly heard it as an explosion. It was as though giant sledge hammer had smashed into the house, jolting and shaking it as if it was doll's house kicked by an angry giant. The visceral shock of it stopped hearts, pulverise bowels, blinded eyes and deafened ears. They were thrown to the floor or against walls bricks and plaster fell, filling the room with choking dust. Harrison, still crouching b the bed which had given him a little more protection than the others, had an insan moment of clarity. He saw Vernier, still against the wall where the shock had throw him. He was slowly sliding down to the floor. As he slid down, Harrison noticed, wit the sharpness of a dream, a dark stain spreading down the front of Vernier's trouser: The Inspector had lost control of his bladder and was wetting himself. Harrison felt a hysterical desire to giggle, to laugh, to shout. In the midst of calamity, of chaos an death, here, like the eye of calm in the centre of a storm, was a moment of pure joy. H only beheld the sight for a few seconds, but he beheld it, and it was enough: Inspecto bloody Vernier, the arrogant bastard, was wetting his pants. It made up for all the hour of humiliation he had had to endure over the past two days. A makeweight had bee thrown onto the scales, and he knew that there was a divine justice: first Chisam, an now this. He was avenged, and whatever else might happen, he was content. What di happen, a few seconds later, was that the ceiling collapsed. Something solid struc Harrison on the back of the head, and he went out like a light.

22

As the dawn gradually grew stronger, the shades of night took on substance, detail and colour. Dawn filled the world, asserting the dominion of day. On the old sandstone of the garden wall, the silvery trails left by snails during their nocturnal wanderings became visible - crazy, aimless patterns on the rough red stones. The amorphous presence of the tall privet hedge became a mass of small glossy dark green leaves stirring restlessly in the light morning airs, and there were hints of a gentler, paler green under the grey carpet of dew covering the lawn. The red roof tiles of the house emerged from the darkness first as a gentle pink in this first light, still long before sunrise. A blackbird sang somewhere nearby, his chirring whistle sharply and insistently announcing that the day had begun, even at this early hour.

Edward Chisam stepped back a little to survey the result of his labours. Three quarters of an hour of steady digging had produced a hole some three feet deep and nearly three feet across at the top. A sizeable mound of earth had been thrown against the garden wall. He looked up at the sky, and then towards the house. But it was still far too early for anyone to be stirring yet. Indeed, this was a Sunday, and it would still be two or three hours before the first curtains would be pulled back from bedroom windows, the sound of crockery heralded breakfast, and the smell of fried bacon scented the morning air; and another hour after that before the twin bells of St Cuthbert's parish church would begin half an hour of pealing a mellow, monotonously soporific two note chime, calling the people to come and be seen in church. For this was the country, where life was lived at a more genteel pace; and the village of Seascale, about ten miles south of Whitehaven, was an especially genteel place.

Three or four years ago, Chisam had been a regular visitor to the place where his uncle, Joseph Chisam, had built himself a retirement home by the sea. Uncle Joseph had been the manager of the Whitehaven Cocoa and Coffee House Company, and had retired as a wealthy man. Among other properties, he owned the modest terraced house in Whitehaven which was Chisam's present home, as well as a substantial share of the business, and at that time, Chisam had based much of his hope for the future on his uncle's good favour. "And why not?" he would have said, had he been questioned about his motives - it was the way of the world. If families could not look after their own, what else was there? But the world had followed a different way. Uncle Joseph had been slow to advance the hoped-for favours. Perhaps the old man had had doubts about his nephew even then, or perhaps he was just taking his own time in the matter; but in the end, Chisam's impatience had led him into other, ill fated ventures.

Now of course, things were different. He was not exactly *persona non grata* - not yet but no longer was he a regular and welcome visitor for Sunday lunch, or even for whol weekends spent enjoying the quiet of life in the country as lived by civilised people Sunday newspapers and coffee in the lounge, pottering in the garden, promenading alon the beach, port and conversation after dinner. Failure is an unwelcome guest, and a Chisam saw his prospects in the firm fading, with an outsider appointed as manager c the company, and others taking his place in the line of advancement, so here too, at hi uncle's house, the welcome was no longer warm, and his visits had become infrequen Now they were the minimum required by convention for formal relations to be kept uр But no formal breach had been made and nothing had been said; and that kind c rejection is the hardest to accept. For Chisam, his family had been one of his last refuge and one of the wellsprings of his disillusionment was what he came to see as the paucit of middle class life once the esteem of money and property is set aside, and th unforgiving small-mindedness of their relationships. It was not a lesson he took well i any sense, for in the end his chief reaction had merely been a kind of counter grudge: fc Edward Chisam was still middle class, and could be as small-minded as the rest of then But he had been driven farther than most, far beyond the bounds of any ordinary grudg of social misfortune, and had acquired the outcast's sharp cynicism, which held a humanity at arm's length in contempt. But it was a feeling of grudge which als persisted, and it had amused him when expediency had coincided with an opportunity work off a little of the grudge. As no formal breach had occurred between himself and h uncle, no formal objection existed to his requesting that he might visit them; and n only visit, but stay overnight. It would be an imposition, a gross breach of manners to g against the unwritten and unspoken codes of propriety and form. But as he would almo certainly never see them again, never be beholden to them for his very existence, he nee no longer fear the consequences. It might actually be enjoyable. Indeed, if the mood too him, he might make a proper job of it and be outrageously boorish: at least it would gi him something pleasant to think about. But the reality of the matter might well furnis him with a touch, just a touch of satisfaction. Would the police come here too? He rath thought they would, if only to interview his Uncle Joseph about his former tenant. Whic meant, of course, that he would have to exercise self restraint until the very last - f what in part had driven him here was the feeling, almost akin to an animal instin which had at last become imperative, that his own house was no longer safe; that it w no longer safe even to be in Whitehaven, and that he must flee. And now he w running.

And when the police had departed from this place, leaving behind them outrage ar moral indignation that the names of respectable people had been associated, however peripherally, with such matters; that they had been used and let down by such a scoundrel; would they not also leave behind a certain satisfaction, a certain feeling of righteousness vindicated, a certain - *Schadenfreude* was the German word for it, and perhaps that summed it up the best? Yes, *Schadenfreude* would be a good word to use. The family, and especially Uncle Joseph, would see that he had received his just deserts, and he felt sure that they would take a certain grim pleasure in it. Well, he would have his *Schadenfreude* too. Scandal was scandal, and in a place like Seascale, memories would be long. He thought it would be quite some time before his uncle and aunt would feel comfortable in church again. And if they were not able to demonstrate their appearance in church every Sunday, it would be noted; tongues would wag. "Perhaps," people would say, "perhaps . . ." Yes, he would have his *Schadenfreude*, if only at second hand.

At least the police would not devote such detailed attention to his uncle's house as they would at Victoria Road, although whether his uncle would appreciate that was another matter. But even if the police knew he had been here, as long as they had no reason to suspect that he had been up to anything unusual, there would be no cause, for example, for them to search the garden - provided he covered up all traces of his excavations.

He stuck the spade into the earth and knelt down by the hole to scoop out the loose soil that had fallen back in. When he was satisfied, he picked up a small, stout metal cash box from where he had left it on the edge of the lawn, and carefully lowered it into the hole. The disposal of this cashbox was the principal reason for his visit to Seascale. Its contents, wrapped in oilcloth, included the remaining cocoa futures which he had been unable to sell before he left, and certain other documents which it would now be most embarrassing to be found with. To be truly secure, he should have burned them, as he had already burned other things before he left Victoria Road: but apart from the fact that they represented a not inconsiderable sum of money, he, in common with others who found themselves in a similar position, had been unable fully to bring himself to terms with the fact that he would not be coming back. It was an irrational hope, a kind of sentimental romanticism, a last vestige of naivety, and it was this side of him that was burying the cash box. Effectively, he buried that part of himself with it

It took him only about ten minutes to shovel back the earth and fill in the hole, but a good half hour longer than that before he had removed the traces of his digging sufficiently for them to be invisible to all but the most searching look. He returned the spade to the shed, and then crept back up to his room. He did not immediately go back to bed, but opened the window and leaned out to watch the sun coming up over the

195

mountains. The window looked out over the back garden, and he watched until all sign of his guilty footprints through the dew on the lawn had evaporated away. The sun ha risen blindingly into a cloudless, already oppressive sky. It was going to be another h day.

He made his farewells shortly before noon. He had slept in late, partly to avoid th possibility of being expected to go to church, which he would have loathed, and had the been oblivious of the pealing of St Cuthbert's two bells, the last time he might hav heard them. He breakfasted while the others were having their elevenses on their retur from church. This breach of what his hosts at least, considered good manners, wa sufficient to ensure that when he did leave, his farewells were scarcely acknowledged. H might have considered it regrettable that things had ended thus; but he did not. He ha no regrets at all, for there was nothing left to regret. Such things belonged to the past.

He had given out before he left that he would be catching a lunchtime train back Whitehaven; but in fact he intended to stay in Seascale until evening. He had alread started running, and like a hare running from a stoat, he would try to make his course difficult to follow as possible, even if, like the hare's, his ultimate objective would not too difficult to predict.

On the recreation ground near the station he found some sort of village fete in progres There were marquees, stalls, a band, children's races, and a Master of Ceremonies whos voice could be heard every now and then booming out over the proceedings through megaphone. Chisam stood looking down on the scene, hesitating; and then, feelir slightly foolish, he descended the steps down to the field, drawn, almost against his wil by the meretricious hubbub of sound. He lost himself in the crowd, and slowly wandere past the various attractions. As he did so, he gradually forgot himself, forgot why he wa there, forgot the past and the future, even that he was a grown man bordering on midd age. He discovered the magic of a fair, that one can publicly experience the delights childhood in complete anonymity, because that is what a fair is all about. No-one kne or cared who you were, and you could take your pleasure as privately as in a dream.

The bright, noisy music of a barrel organ washed over him, washed away his identi so that, while it held him in its breathy, fluting, shallow embrace, he floated in it only the most peripheral, superficial level of consciousness. To be a child again, he who ha almost forgotten that such delights existed, was to experience the strangest form of se indulgence: strange, because it could only be a fantasy as unreal as the painted wood figurines that adorned the barrel organ; indulgent because a fair is an interlude indulgence for any and all who care to allow it to embrace them, an interlude which multitude of people share for a brief time in each of their disparate journeys. It took hi as it took a child, perhaps because it was so unexpected; because he hardly had time to think before he was enveloped and whirled away in its merry-go-round of gilt and sawdust, coconut shy and candy floss, its din and jingle, its aromas of farmyard and fried onions, its promise of desires immediately fulfilled: a very English caravanserai. Ah, to be a ten-year-old, with a ten-year-old's capacity to be oblivious of all but the passing moment. He bought an ice cream, and watched the coconut shy as excited children, and fathers in shirt sleeves and braces, tried their luck; he had a go at the quoits and managed to win some little trinket which he stuffed into his pocket; he watched the donkey rides, seeing one very small girl, crying miserably because she was afraid of the donkeys, who had to be taken off and comforted in her mother's arms, and he was touched with pity as only a childless man can be. A minute later, the child's face was wreathed in smiles. A little further on, he came upon a fortune teller's tent, and out of curiosity he went inside. It was dark and close within, and in the centre of the tent was a small round table draped with a cloth, with a folding chair on either side. One was suddenly aware of the grass of the field, a kind of raw presence, which formed the floor. He found the tent empty, however, and after a moment, he re-emerged into the sunlight. He immediately saw a woman, strikingly dressed in gypsy costume complete with a brightly coloured scarf wrapped around her head and large gold ear rings, striding purposefully towards him. She had been talking to another stallholder and had seen him go into her tent. Perhaps she was pleased to have a customer; or perhaps she was apprehensive about her takings, which she had left in the tent.

"You are desirous of having a reading, sir?" she asked him in a husky contralto voice. She was perfect, down to the darkness of her skin, even if that was due to walnut juice rather than the sun of southern climes: the finest fair in the land could not wish for a more authentic gypsy queen. With a flourish she preceded him into the tent and bade him be seated. She picked up a lamp from the floor, placed it on the table and lit it. She then took his left hand in hers and held it palm upwards, kneading his fingers for a few moments in a way which was quite erotic, before pressing his hand down onto the table, palm still upwards, where she could study it in the lamplight. Once or twice she looked up quickly and gave him a searching look through narrowed eyes before concentrating on his hand. If she was not actually a gipsy then she was doing it very well, and he was impressed despite himself. Her husky voice interrupted his thoughts.

"You have known much prosperity," she said suddenly. Well, not too difficult to guess, perhaps. Even during the worst times, he had not allowed his appearance to deteriorate, and he still looked what he had once been, a comfortably-off member of the middle class. And in a curious sense he was at that moment, very prosperous in money

197

terms.

"You have been prosperous, but you walk alone," she continued, still looking down
his hand. Now that was a much shrewder observation. Not all married men wo
wedding rings - and she had squeezed his fourth finger thoroughly to see if there was ar
mark of a ring there - and it was generally most unusual for a man of prosperity to I
without a wife. A fair, or village fete was after all mainly seen as a family occasion, eve
if, as he had himself discovered, anyone, whatever their age or condition, might I
charmed back to childhood for a day, or an hour, by its transient brightness. Was the
something, some subtle chemistry which only a woman could perceive? An unsettlir
thought; and he was suddenly disturbed also by memories of Stella. He cleared his thro
to answer her.

"Yes, yes, I suppose that's true also. You are most perceptive Madame."

She looked up, and then acknowledged his complement with a bow of the head. S
scrutinised his hand again.

"You have travelled over water," she went on, her voice lower now. He thought of t
trip he had made to Amsterdam; but most people had travelled overseas these days,
there was nothing very remarkable in such a pronouncement.

"And you will travel over water again, and soon," she continued, her voice quickenir
now. Chisam sat up, a little surprised. This was interesting.

"Yes, soon," she repeated, "you will travel over water; but after that - after that . .
her voice faltered, and she looked up at him. It was extraordinary. Her face was drav
with - was it fear? Disgust? He could not tell, but he was slightly alarmed.

"After that, there is nothing," she breathed, still staring at him.

"Nothing? What do you mean, nothing?"

"I mean that you will travel over water soon, but after that, it is a blank, I can s
nothing. There is nothing after that."

He was nonplussed.

"But . . . are you saying . . . are you suggesting that . . . that my life will soon come
an end? That's not a very nice thing to say."

"You came here willingly, sir, of your own free will to ask me for a reading, and I ha
given you of my art. It is not up to me whether what I read is good or bad. I merely t
you what I can see," she answered, her voice low and reverential. "I did not say your l
will come to an end soon. I said only that after you have crossed the water, I can re
nothing. I can see nothing beyond that." She withdrew her hands from his. "I am sor
sir, but I can tell you nothing more."

It was extraordinary, most extraordinary, and disturbing. There in the dark tent, w the flaring lamplight glistening on her gold earrings and illuminating her flashing eyes when she looked up at him, it was hard not to believe in her, hard not to believe that she was a true Romany, a witch, a seer, who had given him some foreknowledge of his fate. He was uncomfortable and embarrassed, and stumbled a little clumsily as he got up from his chair and picked up his travelling case. He reached into his pocket for her fee. She glanced up at him quickly as he laid the coins on the table, before casting her eyes down again. He turned and pushed his way out into the light.

The sudden change from the darkness of the tent to the bright afternoon sunlight and the noise and bustle of the fete was startling. Why, he was still a child, a child of the fairground, to allow himself to be frightened by such hocus pocus. What else, indeed, was it for? The woman was simply a part of the whole: she was absolutely superb, and she knew it. Clearly bored by playing the routine to a series of dull children, she had given full vent to her talents on this middle-aged stranger who ought to have known better. Was she laughing at him? She would be less than human if she was not. But suppose she was not laughing at him. Suppose . . . He had a sudden desire to whip the tent flap aside to catch her unawares; to see if she was laughing and human, or . . . He picked up his case and walked briskly away from the tent. What a child! She had, of course, seen his travelling case. "Elementary, my dear Watson!" a voice inside him seemed to say.

The spell, however, was broken. The atmosphere of carnival and fete which had lulled him and spirited him away had suddenly been chilled by the fortune teller's words, however quickly he had regained his equilibrium. Through luck or shrewdness, her words had cut through his gentle daydream and touched his fears, reminding him of what, for an hour, for an indefinable interval, he had put to the back of his mind. Of course, her words meant nothing - she had merely been using the tricks of her trade, even if she had used them rather more zealously than might be considered appropriate for a village fete: but the daydream was gone, and he could not call it back. With its spell broken, he found that the atmosphere of the fairground was starting to jar on him. He now noticed the children more by their piercing shrieks, or their faces slobbered with ice cream or candy; the music from the barrel organ was really very cheap and shallow; and people would push and shove so. But he had yet to exhaust the fair's variety.

One of the principal attractions of the afternoon was to be a display of some of the arts of war by the army. A platoon of soldiers would stage a mock battle for the general entertainment of all present, as well as for the more specific purpose of encouraging volunteers. Young men of military age who had so far failed to succumb to the call of patriotism might be seduced by a touch of excitement; and if the war proved to be a long one, it would also be useful to catch the imagination of the next generation of boys. Not

199

that the boys needed any encouraging. Groups of them hung around entranced, as th
soldiers, in khaki and with large boots and large rifles, prepared to do battle. Under th
direction of their sergeant, equipment was unloaded from the canvas covered motor lor
in which they had arrived, and they took up their positions. The attacking group forme
up next to the lorry, using it as cover: the defending group concealed themselves as be
they could in the long grass of the embankment which flanked the field. When the wo
was given, both sides opened fire with a will. The cartridges were blanks but the noi
was real, with both sides keeping up a deafening fusillade with a dozen rifles a side f
several minutes. The attacking side then fixed bayonets, and in the face of spirited firir
from the defenders, charged the embankment, yelling at the tops of their voices. Within
minute it was all over, and the small boys were scrambling to pick up the shiny bra
spent cartridges that littered the field of battle.

The highlight of the display, however, was to be the firing of a field gun. The gun h
already been unhitched from the lorry, and half a dozen soldiers now swung it in
position facing out across the fields to the south. Turns of a wheel elevated its muzz
until it pointed defiantly and menacingly upwards. A blank charge was loaded into t
breech which was then closed. The sergeant shouted a command, and a hush fell over t
field. The soldiers nearest the gun stuck their fingers into their ears. The gunner stepp
forward and waited for the sergeant's command, stilled for a moment, for an eternity.
was a tableau that was being repeated a hundred fold, a thousand fold, in France,
Belgium, Poland, Serbia, Gallipoli, Mesopotamia, Africa; where ten million men, to
from wives, children, parents, the familiarities of home, from life itself, marched acrc
the battlefields and the graves of their forefathers to a tune as old as humanity;
discordant tune, a banshee wail that sounded more harshly than the music of the cheap
barrel organ.

"Fire!"

The sergeant's command was almost lost as the gun went off with a great noise,
crash of human thunder which echoed against the sky and knocked mockingly at t
gates of heaven. Smoke rolled away from the gun and the soldiers unstopped their ea
The dying echo was the only reply from heaven.

The last train of the day to wind its slow and laborious way around the Cumberla
coastline slid gently to a halt with squeaking brakes and clouds of steam alongsi
platform two of Carlisle station. The journey up from west Cumberland was one whi
Chisam always found rather wearisome, and as he walked along the platform he thoug
about the pleasant prospect of a bath, dinner, and bed, for it had been a long day. T

200

might be the last day when he could predict what his movements might be, so for this night he would spend a little money on a comfortable hotel. Tomorrow might find him a long way from such comforts, and tomorrow . . .

He stopped dead. He had almost walked past her before his subconscious had registered recognition: a woman who sat small and still and alone on one of the station benches. Her aloneness, her presence, almost like an electric field, an alarm of some personal travail, would have commanded attention even if one did not recognise her.

"Stella!"

His voice was faint with surprise, almost inaudible, but she looked up slowly on hearing her name spoken. They stared at each other for several seconds, each held by the surprise of the moment. Stella seemed only gradually to recognise him, and when she did, she seemed only to be perplexed.

"You - what are you doing here?"

Chisam's temporary and precarious sense of equilibrium was suddenly shattered. Any meeting with Stella would have been traumatic, given everything that had happened; but this was fate. Stella seemed shrunken and frail, her face, when she looked up at him, was the face almost of an old woman. She had been crying, and she seemed hardly to be aware of what was going on around her. It was horrible to see her thus, not simply because of her physical state, but because he hardly recognised her as the person he once knew. Something terrible had happened to her and she had been defeated - her spirit had been broken, and it was a shock to see her in this place, on a station bench like a vagabond, passive and listless, not knowing what to do or where to go.

"Stella," he said again, gently, "why are you here like this? What has happened?"

"They have taken him away," she said, her voice little more than a whisper. "They have taken him away, and everything is ruined."

"Who? Your husband? Who has taken him away?"

But now that he had had a chance to collect his thoughts, he knew, before she answered, what had happened. Her words only confirmed what he had already known.

"The police have taken him away. They have taken Robert away and they would not let me come with him. And . . . I have lost everything, for they have destroyed everything."

"Taken him away. Taken him where?"

"To Whitehaven. They refused to let me come with him. They would not let me board the train."

"How long ago was this?"

"How long? How long have I been sitting here? An hour - two hours? I'm not sure. I cannot think what to."

She was distracted still, but for Chisam, looking down at her, the pattern of events wa
all too clear. For it was a tragedy of his making, even this, which he had never intende
because he had not thought sufficiently about the consequences of what he had done. An
he himself was now also a victim of it.

"Do you know . . . why they took him?" he asked hesitantly.

"They would not tell me why, but . . ." her eyes remained downcast as she went on, "
believe from what was said that it was something to do with you. With . . . the wa
Robert had dealt with you because of your debt. I can understand if you feel that this i
only our just deserts in consequence, but," she looked up at him then, "if it is that, then
at least would like to say how sorry I am that it happened."

"Oh, Stella, Stella, there's no need for you to apologise."

She still did not know the truth. He felt his insides twist with shame. How could h
have done this to her - to himself? For when she knew the truth, her memory of th
meeting would be doubly bitter. He must not let her go on. And yet, was it so wholl
unjust? Had not Harrison in all truth had a hand, at least morally, in his ow
predicament? Had he not lent a willing hand to help pay out the rope with which h
Chisam, had attempted to hang him? Perhaps he might draw some solace from tha
indeed, he must - he could not leave her like this, and he could not leave himself withou
something with which to assuage the pain and the bitterness of this moment, whic
would remain with him for ever. For it was he, Chisam, who had destroyed her spiri
had brought her to the nadir of humiliation. She was apologising to him, and he cou
do nothing. Now was the moment when, in justice, he should account for himself; b
there was no time left to do so. And he wanted, oh! how much he wanted to comfort he
because he knew that it was within his power to do so, now at this moment: but he cou
not, because he was afraid - afraid for his life. She would betray him in her fury whe
she understood the truth, just as he had betrayed her. She would have no pity for hir
and he could not face the thought of that.

And there was nothing he could do. She had unwittingly saved him by warning him
how close the pursuit now was, and for the same reason, he could not help her now. F
wanted to run, to put as much distance as possible between himself and these despera
tidings of pursuit, and between himself and the shame of this moment. But it was al
shame, and what Stella still meant to him, that stayed his flight. He set his case dov
and gently held her by the shoulders.

"Stella, you mustn't apologise, because you have nothing to apologise for. It is as y
say, partly because of . . ." it was difficult for him to speak Harrison's name, especially
Stella " . . . of your husband's dealings with me that the police have taken him. But on

202

partly for that reason. The police have made a mistake, and when they realise it, if they have not already realised it, they will release him." He could imagine only too clearly what was likely to be happening in Whitehaven.

"But . . . why Robert? Why did it have to be Robert; and why did they have to be so harsh?"

"Because he was involved. Not in the way that they thought, and when they realise that, they will release him; but he was involved. He didn't perhaps foresee these consequences when he took the actions he did. But then we don't always foresee the consequences of our actions, even when some of us . . . regret those consequences. And even if we foresee the consequences, we cannot always help ourselves if we are subject to forces beyond our control."

"And Robert - you say he will be released?"

"When the police realise they have made a mistake in his case, I am sure they will release him, yes."

She seemed to seize on this eagerly, her face lighting up as she gazed at him.

"Then," she said, "if you are sure of this, will you come to Whitehaven with me to help me get him released?"

"Oh, Stella, you don't know what you are asking. There is another train I must catch tonight, within the hour. If I don't, then I as good as forfeit my life. We could not get to Whitehaven now before morning, and by then I am certain your husband will have been freed. You must believe me, Stella. I am sure of what I am saying."

"Then, you cannot help me."

"I cannot go with you. I must catch another train tonight. Go home now, and travel to Whitehaven in the morning. You will see your husband then."

He let his hands fall from her shoulders, and stood back a pace. She stood immobile, however, her eyes staring into his.

"I . . . cannot go home. The house has been violated. The police are still there, and I could not return there alone tonight."

He had picked up his case and was turning to go, but now stopped again.

"Can you not stay with a friend, just for tonight?"

"There is no-one who would acknowledge me as a friend, not now. When I appealed to some of those whom I had counted as friends for help, it was suddenly very inconvenient, and they regretted their inability to help me. And now you also, it seems, can only regret your inability to help me."

"If I am not gone within the hour, I am lost," he said; and then more gently: "If you get your maidservant to attend you, you could seek shelter with her, or she would enable you to seek help in ways which, for a respectable lady on her own would not be possible. But I cannot delay any longer. I have to go. I am in danger for my life. I have become as much a victim of chance and circumstance as you, and I cannot choose my path any more than you."

Her eyes would not leave him, but he could not say any more. He was now desperate to be away, to flee, now that he had been reminded that the police hunting him were also in Carlisle and he was in appalling danger. It was horrible that it should end like this, for he would never see her again; but to stay any longer would only make things worse for both of them. She would not understand this, not now, or ever. When she knew the whole truth, she would have only hate for him.

"Edward!"

The desperate appeal in her voice cut into him like a stiletto. Her eyes were enormous, as if she hoped that by thus encompassing him she might yet somehow stay his departure. Her hands were held out in an unconscious appeal like those of a child. Yet she stood alone and already separated from him by a gulf wider than either of them could know; wider almost than life itself. They were too far apart for Fate to be defied now. It was a barbaric Fate that demanded this of him, that he should turn away from her at her moment of greatest need. It seemed to extinguish the last spark of humanity in him that such a Fate would deny even the most basic instinct of charity. All the pain of the past and all the folly of the present were charged into that moment, and he was suddenly weary of it, as a sick man is weary of a long illness. To walk away from her was the hardest thing he ever did.

"Goodbye, Stella."

She said nothing, only her eyes registering gradual realisation of his rejection of her appeal. She remained quite still, even when a through express train suddenly filled the station with a clattering roar, that drowned his echoing footsteps on the empty platform. He could not look back.

23

Chisam did not get his bath that night, nor the meal he had been looking forward to, and such sleep as he did get was fitful and intermittent, under uncomfortable circumstances. By the time he had been expecting to be enjoying these comforts in a Carlisle hotel, he was already many miles south of Carlisle on a night express from Glasgow, enduring that most depressing experience, a long railway journey through the night.

The shock he had received at Carlisle station had been a double one. He had been confronted, in his meeting with Stella, with the consequences of his own actions, with the pettiness and futility of revenge; and beyond that, with a kind of brutal sanity that had wrested from him the illusion of revenge, from the idea that, in the world of power and money, the taking of revenge would be permitted to one such as he. Its brutality had been to reveal him to himself as what he really was, and to compel him to face that reality, and the understanding of what his world had contracted to as he witnessed Stella's distress. He could not have waited to see her distress turn to hatred, and to walk away from her had been an act of self preservation, the first manifestation of a renewed sense of sanity, even if it was the sanity of the world of power, which in the end reduces everything to its own level. It left him with almost nothing, peeling away the last layers of self delusion; and only a tenacious inner dignity and the most basic instinct of self preservation enabled him to carry on.

It was the instinct of self preservation that had given him his other shock. Stella, in her misery, had been unaware of the import of her words; but the information that the authorities were now only hours behind him jolted him out of his temporary state of complacency and left him feeling horribly sick. Chisam was no desperado, and he had no illusions about his chances if the authorities were to catch up with him. There was no heroism in him that relished such danger, and he was still middle class enough to fear, almost above all else, the humiliation that would follow if he was apprehended, however irrational such fears were by then. The general and undefined apprehension of the previous few days had suddenly become reality, and the suddenness of it had found him badly prepared, badly flustered and badly afraid.

He had managed to find an empty compartment, and for a long time he remained slumped in the same position in which he had first thrown himself onto the seat. The window was a great inky pool as the train crossed the wide barren moors of the Shap summit, only the twinkling light of an occasional farm relieving the absolute blackness of the night, ghostly fireflies disturbing the reflection in the glass. His thoughts wandered, seeing now a face, now a memory of an incident, or a scene, or a place, but without any coherence. He had a sudden vision of Kerry Dancer being led into the winners' enclosure at Newmarket, the blanket for his steaming back, the silken sash for second place, the disappointment tempering the pride, and the memory of how pride had triumphed; and then another memory, of the Kaiser, and of the instant when he had looked into those cold blue eyes and had seen only pride reflected back at him, like a palace of glass; as if he was a warrior who had stormed the inner citadel of a fortress only to find it empty. He could not have imagined then, that this was how it would end in the blackness of the night, with the world gone mad, and himself with it, and the only sanity to grab and run, or be killed, and the palace of glass shivered into a million fragments. Who could believe, except with hindsight, that perhaps all the elements of such an end had always been there, and it only lacked the one ingredient, time, to bring them all together? While tigers fought and gods laughed, and the noise of their commotion confounded the earth, the fox that tweaked a tiger's tail must needs discover the ways of a fox when the pack is running in his wake. Even a week ago, he had no thought it would end like this, and his carefully laid plans, already dangerously thinned by the adversity of chance, were now precarious indeed.

The dim lights of a town disturbed the unreal images in the glass of the window, and the train wheels boomed gently over a bridge as they crossed a river before pulling to a stop in a station. It was Lancaster. Cautiously, Chisam stood up and opened the window to peer up and down the platform; but nothing appeared to be out of the ordinary, and there were no signs of the police. The only uniforms in sight were those of the railway company, and that of a solitary sailor, his dunnage piled on the station bench beside him waiting for heaven knew what connection at that hour on a Sunday night. The hue and cry had evidently not reached this far yet; but he could not assume that he was safe. Telegraph wires ran alongside the line, and at the next station, or the next, it might be different.

After Lancaster the train plunged into rural blackness again, but the towns and the stations became more frequent. The train seemed to travel more slowly the further south it went, as though the increasing density of settlement through which it travelled somehow impeded its progress.

Chisam left the train at Preston. At Carlisle he had bought a ticket to Southampton in an attempt to deceive his pursuers: whether the money thus lost was worth the loss, only time would tell. His immediate objective was Liverpool, and he had an hour to wait until the next Liverpool train. He waited on a bench, not daring to go into the waiting room or the buffet in case they were being watched. At any moment he expected to see a posse of police striding up the platform towards him. His overwrought imagination was in

206

contrast to the dreary, almost deserted stillness of the station, disturbed once by a coal train going north, and occasionally by the rumble of a platform trolley laden with mail bags being pushed along by a couple of porters. A shunting engine, apparently abandoned, steamed quietly away by itself on one of the middle tracks. There is a special kind of eeriness about a railway station late at night which is unlike anything else - a kind of soporific tenseness, because it is not a place to be in, but a place to wait in, and in the experience of waiting, one is often most alone with oneself. It was an experience that did little to calm Chisam's nerves, and it was as much as he could do to prevent himself from pacing up and down, which he felt would draw attention to himself.

The Liverpool train was ten minutes late arriving, and when it did arrive it delayed in the station for a further ten minutes. Chisam waited on the platform near the train, and boarded the train at the last moment, with the idea of avoiding being followed. It was a piece of foolishness which indicated how much he was being affected by nerves, by lack of sleep and lack of food. The journey to Liverpool was even worse than the journey from Carlisle had been, and took almost as long. For nearly an hour the train crawled along in stops and starts through the dreary approaches and suburbs of Liverpool. For long periods it would stand apparently immobile, the only view being one of the endless ugly brick terraces, weirdly illuminated by the ghastly light from the street lamps, to resemble a scene from a nightmare. When at last the train pulled into Liverpool's Exchange station it seemed for the moment like a blessed relief from the nightmare. It was however, only the end of an episode in the nightmare. His precipitate flight had meant that all his plans had been thrown into confusion, in addition to which, the closeness of the pursuit meant that there were severe constraints on what he could do and remain safe. Not that there would be much safety for him in Liverpool now. Once the police knew he was on the run, it would be one of the first places where they would set a watch. Indeed, not only would they watch for him, they would actively search for him, or for evidence of his having been there. If he allowed them to find such evidence, he would be reducing his chances still further. It meant that he was faced with an uncomfortable day, beginning with the long remainder of the night. He would have to be on his guard all the time, and he could not count on getting any rest.

Exchange station was still restless with activity even in the small hours of the morning. On the opposite platform was a large group of soldiers who were mostly sprawled on platform trolleys or on improvised beds made from backpacks, evidently bivouacked for the night, or awaiting an overdue train. All the trains seemed to be late these days, part of the disruption caused by the war. Elsewhere, there seemed to be a lot of coming and going by railway officials, porters pushing platform trolleys, groups of people standing about: the presence of so many people, and in particular of so many uniforms was alarming, and Chisam found it difficult not to look furtive. It was impossible to tell whether the train was being watched, even though he could not immediately see any police. He walked quickly away from the train and made his way towards the exit. He slowed as he approached the exit so that he could have a good look at it before getting too close; but still there were no police in sight. The solitary railway clerk took his ticket with scarcely a glance at him, and moments later, he was on the streets of Liverpool.

It was a quarter past three in the morning. He had nowhere to go, and Liverpool was a city he did not know well. It would not be easy to find lodgings at this hour of the night and it would be dangerous to attempt to do so. The small hotels and boarding house would not be open at this hour, and if he attempted to book into one of the larger hotels he would be remembered. He would have to spend the night on the streets of the city either keeping on the move, or finding some corner where he could rest without being seen. For someone of Chisam's class, this would be a daunting prospect under any circumstances; for Chisam now, tired from lack of sleep and hungry, it was to be an ordeal. Only luck, and his native wit, sharpened by the sense of danger, enabled him to face it.

In the street outside the station he found a whelk stall, one of the sort that would trade all night in the centre of some of the bigger cities. This one was run by a rather short and very fat woman who wore a man's cloth cap over close cropped hair, and smoked a clay pipe. She also sold cockles and oysters, hot roast chestnuts, hot pies, and tea dispensed from an urn. The tea was a penny per cup, and the chestnuts twopence a packet, and Chisam consumed a considerable quantity of both by the light of the two flaring gas jets that illuminated the stall. The chestnuts were mouthwateringly sweet, and his hunger was such that he could not have enjoyed the finest meal at the most expensive hotel in Liverpool more than he did those chestnuts.

"Looks like you 'aven't 'ad a square meal in a long time," the woman observed as she watched him stuffing himself. He mumbled agreement through a mouthful of chestnuts. He bought several more packets of chestnuts and a hot pie, stuffed these into his pockets and set off down the street.

In Liverpool, all streets ultimately led to the waterfront, to the river, and thus to the ends of the earth. The pulse of the city's life beat to the rhythm of the tides that bore the ships out to the open sea, or in to the docks, through which passed a wealth of goods more varied, more lustrous, cheaper and more abundant than in all the previous history of trade by sea. Liverpool was the grandeur and the squalor of industrial wealth; it was a harsh place, a place where men fought each other to make fortunes, or to earn enough for

208

a crust to stave off hunger. It was a place where thousands lived from day to day in the squalor of the struggle for existence, and where thousands more who had lost or abandoned the struggle came to seek a haven or refuge beyond the sea.

Chisam walked down a grim chasm of stone, lit by the light of street lamps that gleamed on the tram lines set among the cobbles, and half revealed the grey, closed faces of the warehouse-like blocks of buildings that formed the sides of the chasm. The lamps cast a dreary light that made one conscious, more even than in the light of day, of the grime of the city on every stone. The streets were quiet, but not empty of people. Shift workers in ones and twos were walking in both directions along the street; twice Chisam was accosted by Irish beggars, unbelievably filthy individuals, one with an enormous shaggy beard as though it was a mark of his rank, who managed to persuade him to part with half a crown. Further down the street he was suddenly face to face with two policemen who emerged out of the gloom between the street lamps. There was no possibility of avoiding them, for they were right in front of him and coming towards him, capes around their shoulders and night sticks in their hands, one of them also carrying a lantern. He checked momentarily at the sight of them - he would have been less than human if he had not. They were walking slowly and in step, and were apparently absorbed in conversation. If he lost his nerve and ran, they would certainly run after him, if only to find out the reason for his suspicious behaviour, whereas if he didn't draw attention to himself . . . They continued to stroll forward. As they passed him, the nearer one looked up and gave him a searching stare for a moment or two. Chisam nodded to him, marvelling at his own audacity. The policeman gave no acknowledgement, but only continued to stare, before looking away and continuing his conversation. When they were past, Chisam found it hard not to stop and look back, as if he could not believe his luck. But it was unlikely to be mere luck: much more likely that they were not looking for him in Liverpool yet. This discovery raised his spirits considerably, and his hopes that he might get out of this after all. He was a long way from relishing the prospect before him, but it made it easier to face.

There was a church to his left, the silhouette of its spire looming half seen into the night, and before him, blocking the road, was a forbidding, low rectangular gateway, which turned out to be part of the framework of the overhead railway. When he had passed under its noisome darkness, he was immediately aware of a change of air. To his left was the vast bulk of the Royal Liver Building, all its many windows in darkness. Ahead of him, beyond the empty, windswept Pierhead, light glistened on black water, and in the distance, seeming very far away and faint, were the lights of Birkenhead. A fresh breeze blustered against his face, and there was a hint of the sea in it. He had reached his point of departure.

The breeze revived him momentarily, but it could not stave off the exhaustion that now threatened to overwhelm him. He was stupid with fatigue, and if he did not fin somewhere to rest soon, he would drop where he stood. He walked forward until he came to the head of one of the ramps leading down to the landing stages, and he could se funnels and masts of vessels tied alongside. They would be the Mersey ferries, an perhaps one of the ferries to Dublin or Belfast. He would have to wait till morning to fin out. All was quiet there at the moment, but there was no place for him to hide there. H was drawn instinctively downstream, towards the Prince's landing stage, where th transatlantic liners berthed. It was there that his fate would be decided, and exhausted or not, he had to see it at least, even now, in the darkness. The barriers prevented him from getting onto the landing stage itself, and the nearest he could get was the access from Riverside station, from where he could see nothing; but from the southern end of th Prince's landing stage he could clearly see two big ships, one behind the other, tied up against the quay. He could learn nothing more during the hours of darkness, but he stood for some minutes watching the activity on the quay - men walking up and down th gangplanks and on the decks of the ships. The sight of the ships mesmerised him, fille him with excitement, anticipation, horror and fear. He dreaded the sea voyage that face him; he had a physical dread of the rage of the sea, of drowning, of the discomfort an the seasickness. But this was his escape, and the image of the ships, great presences ha seen in the lights of the quayside, lights glittering in portholes and on masthead creatures of the wide ocean pregnant with the spirit of far continents, caught his spirit a it had caught the spirit of thousands upon unknown thousands who had gone there befor him, and he felt as if he was being pulled by the tide of their passing.

Riverside station was a hive of activity. Cargo was evidently being unloaded from on of the big ships. Dockers were bringing scores of long wooden crates into the static from the goods entrance to the landing stage and loading them directly onto a goods trai that stood in the station. Despite all the bustle and activity, there was something furtiv about the business, an impression very much enhanced by the presence of at least a doze uniformed policemen. Their presence meant that Chisam's view of it was limited to surreptitious glimpse before he retreated to the safety of the darkness again. It was glimpse that gave disturbing food for thought, however. He suspected that arms an ammunition were being unloaded, and this from a transatlantic liner. He remember what they had said about the 'Lusitania'.

On the other side of the station there was more activity as cargo vessels in the doc were being unloaded. There were no police in evidence here, and the cargo seemed to b mostly agricultural: bales of wool, sacks of potatoes, crates of Australian apples - he could read the legend stencilled on the crates by the light of powerful electric lamps illuminating the quayside - and a large number of barrels. A dockside crane was helping to unload the cargo, and most of it was being wheeled into the long warehouses that ran along the quayside. It was strange to see such work going on at night, but Chisam assumed it was part of the exigency of war.

As he watched, Chisam noticed that a door in the end of the nearest warehouse was ajar, and nobody had gone near it during the time he had been watching. It gave him an idea. He moved to a point where he was out of sight of the activity on the quaysides, and then hoisted himself over the barrier. Judging his moment, he walked quickly across to the warehouse and stood by the door. He stood quite still for a minute, but there was only darkness and silence within, so he gently pushed the door open and stepped inside. The space he had stepped into was not large. As far as he could judge it was an office of some kind - he could feel a chair and desk on one side of him and some sort of cabinet on the other. At the farther end, his groping hand touched a door handle. He turned it, and found the door unlocked. As soon as the door was opened a little, both the sound and the light thus revealed indicated that it opened into the main body of the warehouse. Cautiously, he peered out. His immediate view was blocked by a large stack of crates, and to the left and right were further stacks, piles of sacks, stacks of bales and barrels. The current activity seemed to be some way off down the length of the long building, which was what Chisam had expected from the outside view. He emerged from the office, closed the door, and got into the shadow of the nearest stack of crates. From there, he found nearby a large stack of bales of wool, perhaps fifty feet square. He managed with difficulty to scramble up to the top of the stack, where he was some fifteen feet above the floor. He reckoned that if they were still loading goods into the warehouse, they would not be taking them out of the warehouse again during the next few hours at least. He would be as safe there as anywhere in Liverpool.

He awoke after profound sleep, and at first he could not think where he was. The great pile of wool bales he was lying on formed an uneven, but not uncomfortable resting place, which, suspended so far above the ground, gave no immediate clue as to the nature of the place. Above him, bright sunlight streamed through wide skylights among the cast ironwork of a vast roof. No-one was in sight, and he lay in a suspended solitude out of the sight and knowledge of the rest of humanity. That he was not alone, however, was evidenced by the occasional echo of a voice, or of the clash of iron on stone which was reflected down to him by the roof. Before the memories of the previous night came

211

flooding back, it might have been the continuation of a dream, so strange did th
situation seem. He sat up cautiously, and the rest of the warehouse was revealed to hin
stretching away into the distance. Most of the floor space was filled with stacks of crate
or bales, so it was difficult to see where the occasional noises he could hear were comin
from. His watch had stopped, and he had no idea what time it was, but from the angle o
the sunbeams coming through the skylights, the day was well advanced. He stirre
himself and scrambled down to the ground. The door he had come through into th
warehouse the previous night was still closed, but it would be too risky to attempt tha
way now - more than likely, the office would be occupied. He would have to find anothe
way out. The great piles of goods made it easy to move about without being conspicuou
and at length he found an unlocked door that gave access to the quayside. He opened it
crack and peered out. The sunlight was blinding and sparkled gaily on the water of th
dock. The freighter that had been alongside the previous night was gone, but men sti
walked along the quayside. He had to wait for what seemed an agonisingly long tin
before that end of the quay was clear and he could risk stepping out. He walked past th
end of the warehouse and on to the barrier which he proceeded to climb over. As he d
so, he glanced back at the end of the warehouse, and noticed that beside the door he ha
entered during the night was a window. Someone was now looking out of this windov
clearly watching him climb over the barrier. The face disappeared from the window ar
the door opened. There was a shout, and the sound of running feet. Hastily, Chisa
scrambled down from the barrier and started to walk briskly away. But this did not dete
his pursuer. Looking back, Chisam saw the man climbing over the barrier after him. F
walked even more briskly, trying to lose himself among the many people now throngir
the Pierhead. But the man had broken into a run and was fast catching him up. Chisa
dodged round a cart laden with barrels and broke into a trot. The cart hid him from h
pursuer for a few moments; when the man rounded the cart, he had to stop until he ha
identified his quarry. He then gave a loud shout: "Stop, thief!" and set off at a run. On
or two people turned their heads and Chisam was fearful that someone might try ar
intervene. If the man caught up with him he would probably attempt to detain him un
the police could be called. He reached the road that ran round the Pierhead, but he w
still a long way from the nearest building. As he crossed the road he passed in front of
tram that was standing at a tramstop. At that moment, he heard the 'ting-ting' of th
conductor's bell, and without waiting to think about it, he doubled back and jumped on
the rear platform just as the tram started to move off. The conductor made an abusi
protest, but he ignored it and dived inside. His pursuer, having seen him board the tram
made to do likewise; but he made the mistake of trying to board the front platform. F

212

was unceremoniously shoved off again by the driver, and sent sprawling into the dust of the gutter as the tram gathered speed. Chisam gazed at this scene with satisfaction, but realised too late that the man had not lost sight of him despite his misfortune, and for two or three seconds they stared at each other through the tram window, separated by only a few yards. Too late, Chisam turned his face away. The man had got a good look at him, and would remember his face. He mentally kicked himself for being so slow-witted. As a result of this one stupid incident his position had become even more dangerous. The time advantage he seemed to have gained by his precipitate flight had been wiped out at a stroke, or so he judged. As soon as the police knew he was in Liverpool, this incident would take on additional significance. As it was, it might now be too dangerous to return to the Pierhead - but return he must if he was to get away.

The tram rounded the corner of the Royal Liver Building and passed beneath the overhead railway on its way into the city. Chisam waited for two stops before getting off. He started to make his way back towards the river. He had previously been unsure of exactly how to proceed when he got to Liverpool. The ridiculous and unfortunate incident on the Pierhead had now made up his mind for him - his flight must not be delayed by an instant, and he should leave at the first opportunity.

In order to apprise himself of what those opportunities were, he had to return to the vicinity of the Pierhead, where most of the major shipping lines had their offices. The streets were now thronging with people, and a clock above a bank read twenty past eleven. He now felt safe enough for the time being, and able to move about freely, as long as he moved in a crowded place. By one o'clock, he had managed to establish the pattern of shipping departures from Liverpool, from discreet enquiries, and the perusal of notices and advertisements at the various shipping company offices. He learned that the only ferry departures on that day were to Belfast and Dublin, neither of which were of any use to him. The next ferry to Cork was not until Wednesday, and he could not risk waiting that long. The real news had come from the White Star office on James Street, and the new Cunard building on the Pierhead. The two big ships he had seen the previous night alongside the Prince's landing stage were the 'Orduña', which was under charter to Cunard, and the White Star liner 'Arabic'. The 'Arabic' had berthed on the previous day, and the stores he had glimpsed being hastily unloaded during the night were presumably from the 'Arabic's holds. He already knew about the 'Arabic', for it was the ship he had originally earmarked when he had drawn up his carefully laid plans for departure, and he confirmed at the White Star office that the ship was still scheduled to depart on Wednesday at seven-thirty pm. The 'Orduña' was making ready to sail that night, at nine pm. Both were bound for New York.

He considered the matter thoughtfully while consuming a plateful of fried sausage a‎ chips at a cheap eating house which was full of office workers taking their lunch brea‎ The problem was the closeness of the pursuit by the police. The fact that they had gone ‎ Whitehaven meant that they were now looking specifically for him, and whether the‎ traced him to Liverpool or mounted a search for him there as a logical precaution, it w‎ now unsafe for him to stay in Liverpool. He must assume that every passing hour wou‎ increase the thoroughness of the police search, and the likelihood of his being picked u‎ But the closeness of the pursuit made getting away more difficult. He had expected th‎ the police would eventually trace his movements to Liverpool, and would probab‎ identify him as having boarded a ship to New York. But his original expectation h‎ been that by the time they had traced him thus far, the ship would have docked at N‎ York, and he would have escaped into the vastness of the United States.

He would not be safe until he had reached New York. Most modern ships carri‎ wireless telegraphs, and the British authorities would thus still be able to secure his arr‎ while the ship was at sea. If the pursuit was as close as he feared, then it was more th‎ likely that that was what would happen - if the authorities knew which ship he w‎ travelling on. He could not now wait until the 'Arabic' departed Liverpool ‎ Wednesday. But even if he travelled on the 'Orduña', the only other ship available, t‎ authorities would probably still succeed in detaining him, because of the ship's wireless‎

The noise and bustle of the eating house, the jostle of newcomers trying to squee‎ their way to a seat, the pungent odours of fried fat, vinegar and tobacco smoke served ‎ irritate him to the point where he could not prevent his attention being distracted. ‎ needed to be in the open air again to think clearly. He left the eating house and walk‎ down Dale Street back towards the river. He found himself drawn towards the waterfro‎ as if proximity to the two ships that were the focus of his attention would somehow he‎ him solve the problem.

From the front of the Royal Liver Building, the river was a splendid vista, a gre‎ expanse of water three quarters of a mile wide. The opening out of the horizon seemed‎ sharpen his vision, so that when he looked across to the Birkenhead side, he could s‎ the cranes of the dockyard clearly etched against the sky, and to the left of them, ‎ buildings of the town. The ferries were passing each other in mid stream, and as ‎ Birkenhead ferry grew visibly smaller by the minute, the Liverpool ferry loomed larg‎ so that he could see the people crowding its decks, and hanging over the rail and looki‎ down at the bow wave that foamed around the vessel's broad squat stem. As it swu‎ round to come alongside, Chisam could see people on board already moving towards ‎ gangway entrances, while on land there was a stir among the people and vehicles wait‎

214

on the main ramp down to the landing stage. Looking down on the scene from where he stood, Chisam's gaze suddenly fell on two figures standing at the entrance to the ramp - they were policemen. He was sure they had not been there before. As he watched them, he could see that they were checking the traffic on the ramp. Instinctively, his gaze shifted to the entrance to the Prince's landing stage. Although it was farther away, there too he could just make out the figures of two policemen standing guard at the entrance.

He was trapped! He turned away in dismay. So it would be as simple as that. All the travail he had put himself through had been for nothing, and the end would be as undramatic and as humiliating as if he had waited for the police to come for him in Whitehaven. Shock turned to anger, to an inner rage which, for a moment, made him tremble physically with its intensity. Damn them! Damn their efficiency and their organisation. Damn their arrogant assumption that he would tamely surrender. He had not come this far simply to give up now.

All he had were his wits. Well, he would see what use he could make of them. He knew what the risks were, what he would be letting himself in for. He turned back to look at the policemen again. Watching them for several minutes, he could see that they were not checking people's travel documents or other forms of identification, but simply observing the people who went through the gate, presumably watching for someone with a particular description.

The idea came to him as he stood staring intently with narrowed eyes at the distant entrance to the Prince's landing stage, watching the police as they checked the traffic in and out. His first incoherent thoughts about how he might use the two ships became clarified as he stood in the bright August sunlight, and he knew exactly what he was going to do. He stood for a few minutes longer, running through the idea in his mind to see if it had any obvious flaws. There were certain risks, but these he was fully aware of and was prepared to take. It was probably the best scheme he could hope for under the circumstances. He turned away from the waterfront for the last time and slowly began to retrace his steps towards the city. His confidence had returned as suddenly as it had deserted him. He knew his plan was a good one, because his natural pessimism which had given it birth had been tempered by the years of adversity, years that had made him introverted and calculating, and alien to the ways of those around him, but which had sharpened his wits and his instinct for survival. He now had enough confidence in that instinct to pit it against even a foe as daunting as this.

As the sun declined, it set the sky in the west on fire; an incandescent furnace of light that seared all but the heaviest and most leaden clouds into a blaze of silver - a light

215

which suggested the very hope of heaven beyond the grim skyline of the city. The blaz
of light in the west may have been a symbol of hope for some of those who now stood i
the long queue of people waiting to gain access to the Prince's landing stage; but if
was, few of them showed any outward sign of it. The SS 'Orduña' was due to sail th
evening, and these were the steerage class passengers waiting to board the ship. The
stood quietly, some alone, some in family groups, picking up and putting down their bag
and bundles as the queue shuffled along. Most had the slightly shabby appearance
those who are poor but not destitute: coats, hats, dresses were thin or worn or sometim
soiled; many were in the styles of twenty or thirty years earlier. Some of the costum
were outlandish, for there were many nationalities here - Swedes, Finns, Dane
Norwegians, Dutch, Belgians, Spanish, Irish - to move along the line would be to he
half the languages of Europe, spoken in subdued murmurs, as each group sought
maintain a certain privacy and identity, even as they were about to be absorbed into tl
melting pot of steerage. There was no room in the holds for steerage class baggage,
the bundles they carried were all they would take with them into the New World. Th
moved like nomads, with all their worldly possessions about them. Some had lar
bundles, others had nothing but the clothes they wore - the merest human baggage add
to the tide of European refugees that was the new America. They waited with tl
patience of those who were used to being made to wait, and for the most part, the
demeanour was subdued. Theirs would be the worst sea voyage, with none of tl
comforts with which First and Second Class passengers would be pampered. If tl
weather was bad, then conditions in steerage would be abominable, and they would
confined to the dimly lit, overcrowded cabins, foetid with the stench of vomit, urine a
sweat. Some of the weaker among them, the frail and elderly, the weaker children, wou
not survive the voyage. For the most part, they knew this; but it was still preferable to t
forces and pressures that had driven them to cross the sea as refugees. It was in Ameri
that their dreams began, whether these would be fulfilled or not. The sea voyage, and t
ship, were a necessary purgatory that they all had to face.

The two policemen watching the queue as it passed them saw only a long line of rath
shabby people. Apart from the fact that they were obviously poor, and many of them al
foreign, their aspiration to travel to a distant continent and start another life the
somehow set them apart and made them objects of a certain contempt to those who h
never been subject to any such necessity. It was a contempt that had the effect of a veil
screen of prejudice through which the individuality of those surveyed was lost, maki
them appear uniform, characterless, without identity. If a man was well dressed a
visibly affluent, respect made one conscious of his identity, his personality: if the sat

216

man was seen shabbily dressed, it was his poverty that was seen, not the man behind the poverty.

Thus, the man who appeared to be walking in the company of a large, plump Dutchwoman, who was trailing two small, rather dirty children, both of whom were grizzling quietly with a desolate hopelessness, a man dressed in a visibly dirty overcoat that was patched at the elbows, and a nearly shapeless tall black hat, and who carried his worldly goods in an old blanket slung over his shoulder, a man whose face was unshaven and dirty, and wore the expressionless vacancy of the poor, was allowed to pass without comment. Neither of the two policemen connected him in any way with the well-dressed middle class gentleman whom they were looking out for, and of whom they had a fairly precise description. They were, after all, looking for a gentleman, not a dirty, impoverished emigrant among the long queue for steerage class.

As the queue passed within the gates, Chisam found it difficult to remain expressionless. The worst part had been the waiting as the queue moved slowly up to the gates: a moment of intense anxiety as he had come under the scrutiny of the nearer of the two policemen, and then he was through. The queue had progressed twenty or thirty yards within the gates before he dared to admit even to himself that he had done it. He had crossed what must have been the main barrier to freedom. He was through! It was with the greatest difficulty that he prevented himself from looking back to see if the police had had second thoughts. He did not want to do anything to draw attention to himself now. He did, however, permit himself a slow smile.

It was another half hour before the boarding formalities were completed; and then suddenly he was clumping up the long wooden gangplank, still in front of the plump Dutchwoman, and behind an elderly man with no hat and long grey locks. Water glinted briefly below, and then he stepped off the gangplank down onto a steel deck through the rectangular hatch in the side of the ship that was the entrance for steerage passengers. There followed a confused impression of long, dimly lit grey painted steel corridors, steel walls, decks and deckheads, an endless tangle of pipes, and an all-enveloping hum of machinery that gave the ship the aura of a living thing. In a 'tweendecks space between D and E decks, the men and boys were separated from the women and children by Third Class stewards, who then led them to their separate accommodation. Chisam was confronted with a large, low-ceilinged space that ran half way across the ship, filled with tiers of bunks stacked like racks of shelving in a warehouse. The tops of the racks were bolted to the deckhead, and the bunks were fitted with boards to stop the occupants from sliding out. Most of the bunks were taken when Chisam arrived and he had to make do with a bottom bunk - the least desirable - at one side of the ship. Each bunk was provided with a palliasse and a pillow, and covered in a blanket on which was stencilled in large letters: 'Pacific Steam Navigation Co'. On top of each unoccupied bunk were a tin mug and a tin plate, also stamped with the name of the Pacific Steam Navigation Co.

The hubbub grew louder as men settled themselves into their bunks, establishing little colonies of their own particular nationality, sometimes unceremoniously ejecting foreign intruder who had claimed a bunk in their midst. At one point a fight broke out but on the whole the intruders went quietly and found other berths where they could Clouds of tobacco smoke thickened the air, and in the next tier of bunks to Chisam, group of Irish labourers, already the worse for drink, began singing a bawdy song singing it slowly, draggingly, badly out of tune, in the manner of drunks who are going to make a night of it.

Before long, there was a general movement out of the dormitory for the evening meal Chisam picked up his bundle and his mug and plate and joined it, feeling glad of the excuse to get out of the dormitory. The Third Class refectory was a long room filled with long tables flanked by rows of long benches. Diners queued up at one end to have their plates filled with a ladle full of vegetable stew, and their mugs with tea or cocoa. From where he sat, Chisam had a view of the quayside, towering like a great wall high above the porthole through which he peered. The daylight was nearly gone, and the quayside showed merely as an expanse of blackness, with a strip of pale sky above. Standing on the edge of the quayside directly opposite, their tall helmets unmistakeable in silhouette against the pale sky, were three policemen. They stood in a group, talking, and were not looking at the ship, but Chisam instinctively looked down to hide his face. His elation having managed to board the 'Orduña' was quickly dispelled by this reminder that he was as much in danger as ever, and would remain so at least until the ship sailed. As if emphasise this fear, when he surreptitiously glanced up again, it was to see the group of the quayside breaking up, two policemen walking purposefully one way, the third in the opposite direction, as if they had agreed on some plan. He knew, as though he could read their minds, that they were looking for him.

He could not allow himself to be trapped in the rabbit warren of the ship, if the danger was as close as that. He followed a number of others who evidently had no stomach for another sight of the dormitory just yet, forward along D deck and then up to the forward well deck, which served as the Third Class promenade. A number of steerage passengers had gathered there to watch the proceedings as the ship prepared to sail, and Chisam did not feel conspicuous when he joined them there, his blanket bundle over his shoulder and clutching his tin mug and plate.

All the indications were that the 'Orduña' would sail on time. Two tugs had come alongside and were marking time, holding their own against the current. On the quayside, two of the gangways had been withdrawn, and loafers were beginning to gather to watch the departure. A movement above and to his right caught his eye. B deck promenade, which overlooked the forward well deck, was Second Class accommodation. Two of the policemen whom he had seen on the quayside had just emerged from the Second Class saloon on B deck. Chisam froze and looked away, trying at the same time to keep them in sight out of the corner of his eye. Did they know he was on the ship, or was this a last minute check before the ship sailed? The policemen stood and surveyed the steerage passengers in the forward well deck for a minute or so, then turned and disappeared aft. Mentally, Chisam held his breath. They were still looking for a gentleman.

Ten minutes later, there was no doubt. There was a rattle and scrape as the last gangway was withdrawn, mooring lines splashed into the water to be hauled in by the 'Orduña's crewmen, and the tugs moved in to help nudge the big ship out into the stream. The deck trembled as the engines increased, and the thump of the pistons could be felt. They were moving. An expanse of dark water opened up between the ship and the quayside: it represented the distance, still only small, but growing by the second, between himself and his past. His old life ended there on the quayside, where the people who had gathered to watch the ship depart now stood in the bright light of the electric lamps. Everything it represented, good or evil, hateful or blissful, from childhood memories to the memory of Stella as he had left her in Carlisle, his whole existence was now separating from him as the ship drifted farther and farther out into the stream. The sky was barred with black wracks of cloud, and the water was black, its blackness emphasised by the stipple of light reflected from the quayside. Chisam gripped the rail as he stared at the shore, and stared and stared. The blackness of the water was like the darkness that obscures the future from the past, the darkness of fate, into which every individual, alone finally in the darkness of his own isolation, with every degree of hope or of resignation, plunges towards oblivion.

The 'Orduña's siren boomed out into the gathering night, the echoes rolling back across the wide river. It was answered by the tugs and other ships berthed on both sides of the river, the brief wailing cacophony of their sirens at once a gesture of farewell, and of solidarity with another vessel which, in a few hours, might be facing the shells and torpedoes of the enemy. The sirens died away, and for those watching on the quayside, the great ship was suddenly gone, lost among the confused glimmer of lights that marked the farther, darkened shore.

24

For a long time the submarine had remained almost motionless, its motors turning ove just sufficiently to give it steerage way against the current. The sea here was dangerousl shallow, in places as little as twelve metres, which would mean that the submarine although submerged, would be visible from the surface. Several times the keel ha scraped menacingly through shingle on the sea bed, and the crew had held its breath les the boat should run aground. They had only been submerged for two hours, but alread the air was noticeably stale, and during that time, very little progress eastward had bee made. The U24 had come through the North Channel during the night, taking advantag of the darkness to run on the surface for most of the way so that the batteries could b recharged and the boat flushed out with the cool night air.

Most of the previous day had been spent submerged in the approaches to the Nort Channel, playing hide and seek with a Royal Navy destroyer which, while never comin close enough to be dangerous, they had not been able to shake off, and they had had t suffer several attacks by depth charges. Only with the coming of darkness had they give their pursuer the slip. The tension had built up during the day in the increasingly fou sweat-laden air which they could not renew through having to remain submerged; an the tension was increased by hearing the sound of the destroyer's propellers fade, only t return again and again, until it seemed they would never shake the bastard off - tensio that threatened to break into uncontrolled fear each time the boat was shaken b successive shocks from depth charges, each one closer than the last, as the destroyer ha laid down a pattern, with the submarine's crew waiting to see how close the patter came, each man alone with his fear, staring up at the deckhead, where at any moment th sea might burst in with appalling violence as the pressure hull collapsed. Only with th coming of darkness had they been able to escape by the simple expedient of surfacing an running at speed on the diesels to put as many kilometres as possible between themselv and their pursuer; and the tension had been flushed out with the foul air into the co August night.

Nevertheless, it had been a bad day, a bad beginning to a tour of operations that h been unusual, if not inauspicious from the start. Once at sea, a submarine was an isolate unit acting on its own with little or no contact or support from the rest of the nav Submarine skippers enjoyed a very independent command, an independence that test their abilities as leaders and commanders to the limit, and made of them a special bre of men. For Kapitänleutnant Schneider, the presence on board of his commandi officer had inevitably had an inhibiting effect on his command, however well in gener he got on with Seebohm; and the skipper's unsettled mood had communicated itself to the crew. However much Seebohm tried to remain aloof from the day to day running of the boat, in the confined space of such a small vessel, his presence was unavoidable; and the occasions when it was necessary, for courtesy's sake at least, for Schneider to seek Seebohm's approval of an order were sufficiently frequent to transform the usually easygoing discipline of a normal voyage into something appreciably more strained. A certain mysteriousness about the reasons for Seebohm's presence on this voyage only added to the strain. Seebohm had not explained his unorthodox embarkation on the evening of their departure, and had so far committed himself only to an explanation that he was acting under special orders, with a hint that these had to do with intelligence or espionage. More extraordinary was Seebohm's order that U24 maintain strict wireless silence throughout the voyage. Wireless communication with Wilhelmshaven was normally at best intermittent; but Seebohm's stipulation only added to the strangeness of the situation.

Of more immediate concern to Schneider were the sailing orders that Seebohm had given. Normally they would have run down the west coast of Ireland to reach their area of operations across the main shipping routes through the western approaches to the English Channel and the southern Irish Sea. The North Channel route was risky - there was a standing order from Naval High Command to that effect - and the northern Irish Sea was dangerous for submarines because the water was very shallow; in addition to which, there were no ports or sea lanes of any importance there. Whitehaven, which was the port Seebohm had ordered him to proceed to, was known to Schneider only as a name on a chart. It was too small to be a military target of any significance, and according to the pilots' manual for that part of the English coast, was not capable of berthing large, modern vessels, which only confirmed its unworthiness as a target.

The suspicion that the main object of the voyage had to do with the espionage that Seebohm had hinted at did nothing to allay Schneider's misgivings. The business of espionage was something he viewed with profound distaste.

Seebohm himself had been subdued throughout the voyage; far more subdued than Schneider had ever known him to be. He had lost his usual ebullience, which, despite his background, had made him a surprisingly good commander of submarines, one with whom Schneider had worked well. He had withdrawn into himself, and would not share his preoccupations with Schneider. Schneider was sufficiently irritated by this state of affairs to contemplate breaking Seebohm's order about wireless silence - waiting until Seebohm was asleep and then asking the wireless operator to see what information might be had from Wilhelmshaven or Berlin. But by doing so, he would be involving himself in

221

the business - that shadowy world of suspicion and counter-suspicion, where no man can trust another, and the very basis of civilised human behaviour is destroyed; a world he despised, and he recoiled from it. In the end, he did nothing, even though the price of his inactivity was high. He felt almost that he had been humiliated in front of his crew, who, he felt, were expecting him to stand between them and this dour shadow of their commander, who so disturbed and offended the spirit of the boat. There was, nevertheless, a sense of expectancy, a sense that they were involved in something unusual, out of the ordinary: the lowliest seaman was as full of interest about what was going to happen as Schneider himself, even if he did not share Schneider's apprehensions as skipper.

For the last two hours, nothing had happened. They had had the Point of Ayre light abeam to starboard when the bridge watch had spotted a ship dead astern. It had been overhauling them fast, the two phosphorescent plumes of an impressive bow wave being the first thing the watch had seen of it, and there had been no time to wait to identify it. The alarm had been sounded, and they had dived immediately. They could not dive deep because the water was so shallow, and all they could do was take evasive action, turning sharply to starboard and closing everything down for silent running. Once they were submerged, the sound of the ship's propellers became audible, and they sounded ominously like those of the destroyer that had hunted them the previous day. They had waited while the sound of the propellers grew nearer: only Schneider had known how dangerous their situation was if the ship had seen them. Immediately ahead to the south were the submarine banks that lay between the Point of Ayre and St Bees Head, which they could not cross while submerged. They had no sea room to take appropriate evasive action if the ship attacked: they would have to submit to its depth charges, or surface to face its guns. No more pointed justification of the Naval High Command's warning about the north Irish Sea could be had than this. Schneider had glanced across at Seebohm, but the latter remained aloof and impassive, gazing straight ahead of him, looking at nothing or no-one in particular. Schneider had the sudden impression that Seebohm was waiting for something, some time or event that only he knew about; waiting with an impassive confidence that enabled him to face the present danger with an almost unreasonable equanimity.

The sound of the propellers reached a climax as the ship crossed their stern, then slowly died away to port. It sounded as if the ship had just been passing and had not seen them. After the experience of the previous day, however, Schneider wasn't taking any risks. For a long time after the last sound of the ship's propellers had died away, they waited, each man listening in a studied concentration in the dim, sweat-laden silence

When Schneider risked a look through the periscope, there was no sign of the ship. To starboard, the Point of Ayre light still gleamed intermittently in the blackness of the night, but to port, the mountains of Cumberland were showing in sharp-etched silhouette against the redness of dawn. He was able to take bearings, and slowly the boat was swung round so that they resumed their former course, making cautiously eastwards into the dawn.

At last Schneider stood up from the periscope and turned to face Seebohm.

"We have arrived, sir," he announced quietly. There was a stir of interest in the Control Room as Seebohm took the periscope and had a look for himself. But Seebohm remained non-committal and aloof, and those who had hoped to hear his intentions, and therefore what the immediate future might hold, were disappointed. When Seebohm stepped back from the periscope, he joined Schneider to consult the chart for a moment, and then said merely:

"Keep station about a kilometre from the headland in this location, and remain submerged until it is fully daylight."

Schneider's acknowledgement was equally brief, but it concealed a growing feeling of resentment against Seebohm's disinclination to discuss, with him at least, what his objective was, even now that they had arrived at what was apparently Seebohm's intended destination. It led him inevitably to renewed speculation about espionage and intelligence. It was the only explanation that might account for Seebohm's strange demeanour. Merely as an explanation, it would not help. What they were doing was undoubtedly dangerous, and foolhardiness was foolhardiness, whatever the explanation.

Schneider would not have been much mollified if Seebohm had been more forthcoming. Seebohm's aloofness over the past several days had been due in part to a case of bad conscience. It was one thing to indulge in an act of personal bravado, however abstruse the act, and the bravado: it was another matter to throw thirty-five other lives into the hazard for the sake of it. It was this, rather than the fact that he was effectively perpetrating a fraud upon the men under his command that had troubled him; although it had not troubled him sufficiently to deter him from his course. On the first night of the voyage, on the evening they had left Wilhelmshaven, some time after midnight they had seen from the bridge the glimmer of the Rottumeroog light on the port horizon - Schneider had pointed it out to him. It had seemed to beckon to him like a Siren, all the more tempting because he knew it was a call that he would answer, on the return voyage: it would be his escape. Would it not have been so much simpler to have responded to the call then, at that moment of passing? That he had not done so also contained an element of sacrifice, to leaven the mixture of pride, revenge, justice,

223

contempt and wrath, that had driven him thus far in a determination to see the matter out to its end. It was a leaven for his conscience, as was the idea that in war, any blow struck at the enemy can be justified at the time, even if it was in reality merely the last blow struck in another, more private war.

But amongst these men, amid their grimy, sweaty presence, his conscience weighed upon him heavily, even when, under their breath, they cursed him for it. He was not now afraid for himself. He had reached a state of mind where all thoughts of the future, all hope, all plans were in abeyance until this business was resolved, because he could imagine no future for himself until it had been. When he had gazed through the periscope into the dawn that painted the sky over the looming darkness of the land with red and gold, and sought for some sign of the trap that he expected the growing light of day to reveal, a trap with jaws of steel and high explosive, it was not primarily on his own account that he felt apprehensive.

The dawn revealed a sea empty of ships. Wispy patches of semi-opaque mist, rolling and churning gently over the surface of a limpid sea were the last remnants of the night to resist the new day. The sea was almost flat calm, the slight swell long and slow, as though the sea's elemental energy slumbered in profound sleep in the tranquillity of a summer dawn. Even in the light, the land was still dark against the sea, dark rock and dark hills lifting into the bright sky, so that its details were hard to distinguish. It was only slowly that the town revealed itself against the background of moorland that rose up behind it: angular rows of terraced cottages spreading up the surrounding slopes, tall chimneys, a church tower, blank, grey buildings along the harbour front, a white lighthouse. A faint industrial haze hung over the place, from furnaces that were never extinguished, and smoking chimney stacks could be seen even at that hour.

To Seebohm, it looked a dreary place; an industrial disfigurement on a landscape that almost invited disfigurement. All along the coast to the north, other industrial scars were visible - a jumble of industrial litter heaped onto an ugly, rocky coast. It was thoroughly unprepossessing; and yet this was Edward Chisam's homeland, his base, the place from where his ships sailed, and from where he had embarked on another, longer and more tortuous voyage. Thither Seebohm had come at last, and he looked upon it for the first time with a certain fascination.

At the same time, he had to prepare himself mentally for what was about to happen. The trap, if it materialised, would be no less effective against a victim who knew what to expect in advance. There might be very little time to carry out his own plan. But there could be no doubts now about what he must do. He had made up his mind about Chisam and whatever he might find when the submarine surfaced, there must be no room in his mind for doubt. It was a crude and shabby denouement to an affair whose sophistication had made it seem the essence of the civilised and the urbane; or perhaps its innate crudity had been well masked by sophistication, a mask that now slipped and fell away - but pride is also a savage thing, as dangerous to the one whose pride is injured as to the one he intends to hurt. It was well, his pride demanded, that he should dwell on what might have been, on the fruits of success and how sweet they had tasted, and on what he had lost. Now, only savagery was left.

U24 hung motionless in the water, everything stopped. Schneider, who had taken over the periscope, turned once again to survey the town, the outer mole of whose harbour was now less than two kilometres away across the water.

"Still nothing?"

"Still nothing, sir," was the soundman's laconic reply. The hydrophones were sensitive enough to pick up the noise of a ship's propellers from over forty kilometres away under ideal conditions: only if the ship was also stopped and listening would the silence be deceptive. But for the tenth time in as many minutes, Schneider had confirmed that nothing was in sight.

"Both motors slow ahead, and come to course zero nine five."

The boat trembled back to life after the long minutes of silence, as it gradually gathered way, its periscope softly rippling the surface of the sea.

"Prepare to surface."

The Control Room crew scrambled to their stations, and the hydroplane operators grasped their controls more firmly.

"Surface."

Wheels were turned and the boat was full of the hiss of compressed air, and the rumble of the tanks being blown. The deck tilted as the hydroplanes raised the bow with the boat's momentum, as it regained positive buoyancy. The watch officer, the navigator, had already climbed up into the conning tower, waiting for the conning tower lights to show clear. He cracked the hatch, and the bridge watch scrambled out onto the platform while the sea still cascaded from the casing below them.

They emerged into the stillness of the dawn. The land slept, apparently oblivious of the danger that now threatened it, and no reaction could be seen to the sudden appearance of the submarine. From a distance of more than a kilometre, the land was still indistinct, too far away for a man to be seen, or for buildings to appear as more than miniature outlines. Perhaps no-one had seen them, or if any had, they had not understood what it was that they saw. From such a distance, U24 would be an insignificant object, even from the top of the three hundred foot cliffs of St Bees Head. At that moment, the menace of

225

the land seemed unreal, unbelievable; despite the evidence of buildings, chimneys industry, nothing moved, no sign of activity or life was visible, and it was as if the emptiness of the sea had overawed the land with its stillness. There was no indication i any eyes watched and understood as, under Seebohm's direction, U24 stood in toward the land at an easy rate, the muffled throbbing of the diesels hardly audible even on th bridge. A scorpion crawled towards a sleeping giant, not knowing if it would strike, or i the giant would awaken.

Slowly, the land became more distinct - buildings took on form and colour, window became visible, even individual blocks of stone could be picked out in the harbour wal as Seebohm took the U24 brazenly right in towards the harbour entrance. Schneider, no also on the bridge, chewed his lip in apprehension. He had not imagined that Seebohr would be as bold and as foolhardy as this. At a distance of a hundred metres from th harbour entrance the submarine swung round and slowed, its engines grinding in revers to take the way off the vessel, so that at last it lay dead in the water, wallowing slightly i the disturbance created by its own wake. The sound of the engines faded to a barel audible mutter, and stillness reigned. The south mole of the harbour now towered abov them, so close that every detail of its gnarled pinkish-grey stone could be seen, ever crevice, every whorled and pitted scar left by the sea over two centuries of storm an frost. The silence was profound, broken only by the soft slap and suck of the gentle swe as it combed the fringe of green weed along the base of the mole. One of a line of gul standing on the top of the mole, watchfully indifferent, mewed mournfully into th morning, its mewing echoing emptily in the silence against the sea and the stor beneath.

The two watch officers whose quadrants faced the land, and Schneider himself, gaze with apprehension at the scene. This weatherbeaten wall of stone, standing high abov them so close were they to it, was England - enemy territory. It seemed almost clo enough to touch, or at least, to throw a line ashore. They had operated close to the enem coast in the past, but never this close, and mostly at night. There was somethin fantastic and bizarre about floating in this echoing silence at the very entrance to a English seaport, while the port, and for all they knew, all England, slept. They stare with bated breath.

Beside them, Seebohm stared also. His gaze searched the top of the mole for any sig that Chisam had kept his word. There was none, and he had not expected any. Indeed, l would have been most surprised if there had been, for he had seen the trap the mome he had read Chisam's letter. He was here because this was the last act in a history th had become a farce, and it was necessary for the sake of history, for the sake of tl

226

record, that he play out his part in it to the very last. Only when he had done that, only when the farce had been played to its conclusion, would the debt be expiated and he would be released from it. Chisam's treachery had brought him here, and he was determined that no part of it, no weasel words of dissimulation or cowardice, should detract from his revenge. He had risked much to come here, and he would omit nothing now.

He raised himself to his full height, and filling his lungs, he shouted into the silence. "Chisam!"

The silence shouted the echo back at him, his voice reflecting from the high concave bulwark of the harbour wall. The gulls, startled by the noise as by a gunshot, rose awkwardly into the air, and one by one skimmed away over the still water of the harbour. The mole, mysterious in the grey shadows of the early morning sun, now took on an aspect of menace: the stone, the flat empty sea, the dark coast, the closed buildings of the town, became charged with an unformed menace. It was as if the hostility of the spirit of the place gathered and concentrated itself in response to this puny challenge.

"Chisam! If you're there, then show yourself!"

Seebohm's voice filled the silence with a great shout; but still only silence reigned over placid water and mute stone.

Schneider, and even the officers of the watch, were staring at Seebohm pop-eyed with astonishment. None of them spoke English, so they did not know what Seebohm was shouting; but they were deeply alarmed, especially Schneider, for whom this was a culminating foolhardiness in a series of foolhardy actions at Seebohm's orders. His first thought was that Seebohm must have succumbed completely to insanity: that he had brought them on this dangerous voyage to within hailing distance of the English coast so that he could shout and bawl at the enemy like some poor latter day Don Quixote.

Schneider turned to face Seebohm, steeling himself to take the appalling step, for a subordinate officer, of ordering Seebohm to be physically restrained and held under arrest below; but as the silence that followed Seebohm's shouted challenge settled over them again, even as the fingers of menace reached out and touched them with renewed alarm, some other sentience awakened in him and stayed his hand. Whether it is a function of the intellect, or of something less rational, less well understood, there are moments of intuition when one suddenly understands what has hitherto been inexplicable: when the behaviour, the motivation, the force of character of another, from being alien and incomprehensible, are suddenly seen in another light, that makes them rational, even if no less distant. It is a sentience of insight, of empathy, and on the rare occasions one is given such sentience, it is a moment of truth. For Schneider, this was

227

such a moment. It was as if the fragments of a kaleidoscope had shifted into a patter that was familiar, and he suddenly understood. Seebohm had been betrayed. Whateve the nature of the business Seebohm had been engaged in, and whether it had been officia or unofficial, Seebohm had been betrayed, evidently by his contact on the other side. The profound revulsion that Schneider had experienced when he first suspected wha Seebohm was about, returned to him now. With it came a sense of detachment, and sense of power. He was suddenly very sure of himself and his position, and of ho matters now stood. If he felt contempt for Seebohm, it was because of his contempt fc the business Seebohm was engaged in. He could at the same time feel pity for the ma and even a certain sympathy, for he understood now that Seebohm was alone, and that i all probability he faced that which most of those who became involved in such busines eventually had to face - the existence which was a non-existence superimposed on th real world; fleeing from a past that cannot be escaped; no longer owning one's name, one's identity.

It took only a few moments for Schneider to adjust to this new perspective. S confident did he become at that moment that he could have carried out the arrest Seebohm without the trepidation he felt when first contemplating it. But in the light this new perspective, he stayed his hand, preferring to maintain the formalities of th situation for as long as they might decently be observed.

Seebohm continued to stare at the harbour wall for a long minute before he turned face Schneider. His face was impassive, giving nothing away. He realised, perhaps eve more than Schneider, how brittle the formalities of the situation had become, and ho near he was to breaking them. He remained formal.

"Herr Schneider, please put the boat about, and resume station about two kilometr offshore."

"Very good, sir."

There was the slightest hesitation in Schneider's reply. He was still trusting to his luc and his intuition. The minutes passed in silence as U24 ploughed out to sea, towards horizon that was emerging from the darkness in the west. Only when the submarine w on station, stopped in the water, broadside on to the shore, was the silence broke Seebohm was gazing back at the land with a glass, and there continued an awkwa pause before he spoke.

"You no longer trust me, Schneider."

His voice was so quiet that Schneider for a moment doubted that Seebohm had spoke He, too, continued to gaze landward without looking at Seebohm. Seebohm's words we a statement rather than a question, but a question was implied.

"I cannot answer to that, sir."

It was an improper question, even if only implied, and they both knew it, and yet it was one that would be asked anyway, sooner or later.

"You cannot answer in the affirmative, so you confirm, by default, that you no longer trust me."

Schneider was surprised that Seebohm seemed to be probing that fragile formality which was all that his authority now rested on. He chose his words carefully.

"I meant, sir, that a subordinate's loyalty should normally be taken for granted."

"This is not a normal occasion. It would be best for both of us if you were to be sure of where you stand, and in particular, how much you intend to become involved in this."

"I already am involved, sir."

"You mean by acting as my skipper on this voyage? No, I didn't mean that, and you must know it. I meant . . . I was talking about taking sides. You cannot be sure which action will be in the ascendant when you reach Wilhelmshaven. Even the wireless telegraph would not help you there because you wouldn't know whose finger was on the key at the other end."

Schneider felt alarm as he saw an abyss opening up before him.

"The officer . . . the Kommodore who was on the quayside when we embarked . . ."

"Yes, yes - the good Kommodore. A powerful man, to be sure - but they didn't like him in Wilhelmshaven. Whether they will be able to close ranks sufficiently to dispose of him remains to be seen. But even if you decide to throw in your lot with the Kommodore, you will not find him very sympathetic, I'm afraid. He's a dangerous man, and if it suited his purpose on the slightest occasion, he would destroy you."

"I fear he may do that anyway."

"Not necessarily - not if there was no occasion. If, up to the time when U24 docks in Wilhelmshaven, you can truthfully say that you were merely carrying out orders, which you are bound to do, then there would be no occasion to believe that you had taken sides."

"You're very, persuasive, sir."

"I'm glad to hear it. Can I take it that the matter is settled, then?"

"I don't seem to have much choice," Schneider observed.

"But it is precisely the point that you do have a choice. It may be that your assessment of me is that I am on the losing side, that I am exposed and isolated. But you won't know for certain until you return to Wilhelmshaven. The choice for you is simply whether or not you wish to become involved."

"I suppose that depends in part on what else you intend to do, sir. We seem to have

229

rather different assessments of how passive my involvement might be."

Seebohm glanced at him speculatively for a moment before gesturing at the land.

"I intend to bombard the port - to destroy the shipping, the harbour, and tl warehouses around it."

Schneider remained silent. For the moment, his doubts about Seebohm's sani remained. He suspected that such a bombardment was essentially part of Seebohm private war, rather than the war between Germany and England, and that it would sure be unacceptable that he should be allowed to go so far, whatever the nature of that war. seemed that it would not, after all, be possible decently to observe the formalities, and prepared to carry out his original intention. For a moment, he temporised.

"That would be sheer murder - the port is undefended - you cannot be serious."

But Seebohm would not give an inch.

"I insist that the choice that faces you is whether or not you wish to become involved this business. If you take matters into your own hands, you will only have yourself blame if you find that you have backed the wrong side when you return Wilhelmshaven. As to the port, it is the harbour I wish to bombard, the shipping and t warehouses, not the town itself. I happen to know that this harbour is used to imp supplies that are strategic to England's war effort, and that makes it a legitimate targ Also, it is not necessarily undefended. You seem to have forgotten that destroyer."

Schneider continued to gaze in silence at the town. He knew he could not push thin any further without taking matters into his own hands, as Seebohm had put it, and he c not wish to become involved. Seebohm was calling his bluff; and yet . . . the convicti remained that this was, for Seebohm, his last throw in a game which he had someh lost, even if Schneider did not yet fully understand what the game had been about. Wl it amounted to in the end was a matter of judgement from moment to moment, fr incident to incident, as to whether Seebohm's intentions were suicidal, or constitu some form of revenge - there was, as Seebohm had pointed out, the matter of the Engl destroyer. And above all, he did not want to become involved. He turned and regard Seebohm for a moment, trying to gauge the man, to judge him. Then, without replyi he stepped over to the voice pipe, and whistled into it.

"Control Room," came the reply.

"Bridge. This is the skipper. Gun crew to clear the gun for action immediately."

Within a minute, the forward casing was a hive of activity. The deck gun was swu out from its recess in the casing and locked into position for firing. Schwarz, the Mas Gunner, swung himself up onto the bridge for his instructions, and studied the harb through a glass. He pulled a wry face.

"It's not going to be easy to hit the ships, sir. If the shells are dropping into the harbour, it won't be easy to mark where they fall."

Schwarz laid the gun himself, then swung back up onto the bridge to observe the fall of shot. He glanced at Schneider, received a nod of assent, and his hand descended in signal. The gun crashed out, causing U24 to heel with the recoil from the 105mm shell, and a billowing cloud of dark smoke rolled slowly away from the gun in the light morning air. Schneider glanced at his watch. It was exactly 4.30 am.

The fall of the shell was not marked even from the bridge, but the sound of the shell burst returned to them as a distant echo of the gun, and Schwarz, through his glass, saw drifting smoke from the explosion.

"Load and fire again."

Again, the visceral bang of the gun, and this time, Schwarz marked the flash of the shell.

"You're firing over. Reduce the elevation."

He swung himself down to re-lay the gun, and back up to the bridge again. This time, Schneider saw the flash of the shell burst, and through his glass he saw that the shells were landing among the buildings of the town immediately behind the harbour. One of the shells had started a fire, and thick black smoke was rising in a mushrooming column. Schwarz glanced at him for approval to fire again, but he held up his hand. Tight-lipped, he turned to face Seebohm.

"I cannot countenance the bombardment of the town, sir. If it is not possible to bombard the harbour without bombarding the town also, then I must order a ceasefire."

"Then damn you for a fool. I repeat, I do not intend to bombard the town. Once we have the range, the town shouldn't suffer much further damage. You had better make up your mind what you're going to do, mister, because if you order a ceasefire, then you'll have to go the whole way. I shall certainly test your authority."

Schneider stared at him. Seebohm had well and truly called his bluff. To intervene now would be more than mere insubordination. This was a military operation against the enemy, however one-sided it appeared to be, and to countermand Seebohm's orders would be a matter of the utmost gravity. Over the other business there was room for doubt and judgement; but over this, there was not. For all the weakness of his position, Seebohm had out-manoeuvred him, and despite himself, Schneider could not help but be impressed. Stiffly, he acknowledged Seebohm's coup.

"Very well, sir." He turned and called to the Master Gunner. "Carry on, Mr Schwarz."

Schwarz had re-laid the gun, and it banged out almost immediately. Schneider, his earlier confidence more than a little dented, had to admit to himself that he had

underestimated Seebohm, or rather, had misjudged the significance of what wa
happening in his moment of confidence. Now, being forced, in effect, to stand and watch
its significance was impressed upon him. Whatever the antecedents of this business, an
these he had made some dark guesses at, this was its climax. This was the reason wh
Seebohm had embarked on this strange voyage, a decision he would pay for, perhap
with his life. This bizarre bombardment was not a whimsical act. It was what he ha
come here to do - it was the purpose of the voyage, and while in one sense it mac
Seebohm easier to understand, in another it made things less clear. What tortuous ar
obscure series of events could have led up to such a denouement? With each bang of th
gun, a little more of Schneider's confidence ebbed away as he became less certain of ho
this business was going to end.

Seebohm's behaviour only confirmed his doubts. Seebohm had clearly dismisse
Schneider from his mind and was concentrating his whole attention on th
bombardment. After the seventh shot, Schwarz was satisfied that he had the range, ar
the bombardment began in earnest. The rate of firing was increased as the gun crew g
into a rhythm, interrupted only when Schwarz adjusted the traverse to cover the whole
the harbour area, or the elevation to compensate for the drift of the vessel in the tid
Even without a glass, the effect of the bombardment was soon only too evident.
warehouse on the quayside was heavily on fire, an enormous column of smoke risir
from its flames, and at least one of the ships in the harbour also appeared to be ablaz
The smoke from the various fires became so dense that it was difficult to distingui
details even through a glass. After a time, the masts of the ship which was on fire we
seen to tilt, and finally to topple, as the ship capsized where it was berthed. Even after
year of war, Schneider had never seen such general destruction in one place, and he w
at once secretly a little proud and also rather appalled at the amount of destruction th
U24, so small and fragile a vessel, had been able to wreak in so short a time. When i
looked at Seebohm, he saw that the man was rapt in the intensity of the momer
Schneider could not decipher all the emotions he read in Seebohm's face as the ma
gazed on the destruction he had ordered, but triumph was undoubtedly there, and, n
pleasure perhaps, but a kind of satisfaction, an intense satisfaction, as if at the rightir
of some private grievance. Perhaps after all, the man was a little mad, and because it w
a madness he could not understand, it made what had happened all the more appalli
for Schneider. One day he might learn the story behind this bizarrely Wagneri
odyssey. Being confronted only with the madness and the fury of it left him doubtful at
appalled.

"Smoke."

He was startled by the cry from one of the watch officers.

"Surface vessel bearing . . . one seven zero."

Schneider swung round, the fear gripping his stomach. They had been extremely foolish to believe that they could sit there bombarding an English town without there being a response. The smudge of funnel smoke was clearly visible to the south, and even before he raised his glass Schneider knew what it would be. The image in the glass materialised into focus and he found himself looking bows on at a sharp stem and two huge plumes of a bow wave. It was undoubtedly the destroyer that had passed them in the night, and there was even less doubt about its objective. Without even glancing at Seebohm, Schneider shouted down to Schwarz.

"Mr Schwarz, cease fire and clear the deck immediately. We are diving at once."

He whistled into the voice pipe.

"Control Room."

"Bridge. This is the skipper. Prepare to dive at once."

The gun was already being swung back into its recess, and the litter of spent shell cases swept from the casing before Schneider glanced at Seebohm again. Incredibly, the man had not moved. He still stared to landward at the great palls of smoke that rose from the shattered port. He was like a man in a trance; but some aura, some presence made Schneider hesitate for a moment from intruding into the spell of that aura. Schneider's assessment of Seebohm's state of mind had been shrewd; but no amount of shrewdness could allow Schneider to be aware of the intensity of the moment - to understand the sweetness of revenge. For the first time since U24 had left Wilhelmshaven, and indeed for the first time since Kommodore Bräuer had arrived in Wilhelmshaven, Seebohm felt at peace. This moment, conceived in the instant when the truth had become known to him, was all that he could hope to distil from the ruin of this enterprise, from the business that had become his whole life; so that if hate and revenge were all that he would have to feed on in the future, then at least there would be a memory of savage sweetness to sustain him. Revenge is a negative emotion, but it can feed a man for a long time, even if he is not given to brooding on it and nurturing it - it is an inner balm, to be resorted to in order to soothe an injured pride. Thus did such a balm bring its own strange peace to Seebohm. Whatever else happened, he knew this - that he was revenged. Whatever physical damage had been done to the port, the bombardment had destroyed its sense of security. The finger of war had reached out and touched even this obscure little backwater, and Chisam would have no haven of refuge here again. It was enough; and yet it could never be enough. Seebohm stared at the picture of destruction he had wrought, trying to imprint every detail of the scene on his memory, to etch it there so that

it could be recalled in opiate fullness moment by moment in all the rest of his days: th
great dark columns of smoke, the flames visible at their bases, the memory of the ship'
masts tilting over, the sound of the gun, the very feel of it in his belly, the smell of th
cordite smoke, the gunners, the morning sunlight in his eyes, sparkling on the water, an
perhaps more than all these, the exercise of power, brutally physical, bloody power. T
exercise power in the abstract was quite different from this, from standing over your ow
gun and hearing it, seeing it, feeling it, smelling it, directing every fall of shot, an
watching the enemy, his enemy, burn. It was as if this unfamiliar place had come t
represent all that had been hostile and inimical, all the vultures who had gathere
waiting for him to fall - Bräuer and all that he represented; Chisam; even Schneider - th
whole lot of them. It was as if they were all there infesting this dingy English seaport i
spirit, if not in fact, and he was able to purge their foul nest with the cleansing fire of th
gun. The gun had spoken his anger, venting its force; and the catharsis had brought hi
peace in triumph: and it was blessed. This was his moment - time might stand still an
yet he might not sate himself enough with it.

He felt a tug at his sleeve.

"Sir!"

Schneider's voice seemed to come from a great distance.

"Sir, we are diving immediately. The enemy destroyer has returned, and we must n
be caught on the surface."

It was over. Schneider seemed to sense something of Seebohm's other-worldly elatio
something of the triumph which he could not share, of the pathos of this rustic victor
and that, like Macbeth's player, his hour was done, his purpose broken, and he wou
trouble him no further thenceforth. It was a respect, not for a superior, but for th
presence of the man's spirit, even as the flame of its wrath was flickering and dying, ar
the respect engendered a new gentleness.

The casing had been cleared and the bows were already dipping beneath the surface
the tanks flooded when Schneider reached up to close the conning tower hatch. Even
he did so, he heard the howl of a shell overhead and the report of its explosion. I
dogged the hatch with a clang, and his ears were filled with the sounds of the boat
compressed air hissed, and the sea roared.

25

It had been the worst Monday morning Superintendent Forbes could remember. The news had reached London before nine o'clock, but the first anyone at Scotland Yard knew about it had been Sergeant Wilson's telegram. The telegram was short, almost curt, and contained the bare facts only. Forbes did not learn until later that Wilson had dictated it from a hospital bed; and although Forbes had been distressed and shocked by its contents, he had, at that point, been sure of what his response should be. Had he been able to see the Chief Superintendent straight away, things might not, even then, have been so bad; but the Chief Superintendent was engaged and could not see him until later in the morning. In the meantime, Forbes had had a visitor. It was an extremely chastened Lieutenant-Commander Maxwell who had been shown up to his office. Maxwell himself was already in very hot water over what had happened, and when Forbes understood the import of what Maxwell had come to tell him, everything had seemed to fall apart.

"You see," Maxwell had said apologetically, "your man Vernier had tipped us off that he was about to make an arrest, and I had assumed that that essentially would be the end of the matter. I had no idea that anything like this would happen. I've really come to find out if Vernier got the man, because my superiors are now yelling for blood, and I'm afraid it's going to be my blood if I can't come up with at least that much to redeem myself with. I hope you understand my position."

Forbes, however, was too preoccupied with the implications of Maxwell's news for himself to have much time for Maxwell's problems. Maxwell, in the end, had to repeat his question.

"Did your man Vernier make the arrest he tipped me off about?"

Forbes was still not very helpful.

"An arrest was made, but apparently the man arrested was not the man we're looking for."

"Where is this man?"

"I'm afraid I don't know."

"But, good God, surely you realise the seriousness of the matter now. What are you going to do about it?"

Forbes didn't answer immediately. He was becoming oppressed by increasingly bleak thoughts about his own future. This was his case, and if things had gone wrong, then he, Forbes, would be made to carry as much of the responsibility for that as could conveniently be heaped on him. He could not expect much sympathy from the Chief Super, but he had little choice left in the matter now.

"I'm afraid it looks as if we will have to disturb the Chief Super's schedule, even if he is engaged. I should like you to come with me if you will."

The Chief Superintendent, apart from his displeasure at being interrupted in the middle of a meeting of some importance by one of his subordinates, had to suffer the further irritation of having the case, which he was not familiar with in detail, explained to him stage by painful stage. It was Maxwell's news which made the case so bad; but as Maxwell was an outsider who therefore didn't count, Forbes made the most of the opportunity that this presented. Maxwell, remaining silent for the moment, seethed inwardly with rage.

"Inspector Vernier had actually identified the man from his investigations in Carlisle gone to this place Whitehaven, obtained a search warrant, and searched the man's house only to find that the man had already gone, sir," Forbes explained to the Chief Superintendent. "His orders had been firstly to identify the man, and then if possible find him and arrest him, and he had made creditable progress in carrying out those orders. However, I feel we were not kept up to date with information about this man's links with the enemy." He directed a meaning glance at Maxwell, who turned pink with indignation.

"What do you mean, up to date with the man's links with the enemy?" asked the Chief Superintendent irritably.

"Lieutenant-Commander Maxwell has only just told me that this man - Chisam, that's his name - tipped them off about the German submarine that bombarded Whitehaven this morning. In other words, sir, the submarine's appearance was not coincidence; but neither I nor Inspector Vernier knew that."

"If I can perhaps explain, sir," Maxwell broke in, coldly. "We received this information at Naval Intelligence only on Friday, by which time we had already been informed by Inspector Vernier that he was going up to Cumberland to make an arrest, by which we understood that he was expecting to close the case. We had no indication from the information we received that the submarine might bombard Whitehaven. We assumed that the intention was to attempt to trap another British warship, in the way that the 'Wrathful' was trapped. I admit that what has happened seems to have made this man Chisam more dangerous than we had allowed for, but it's easy to say that with hindsight. We acted in good faith on the information we had at the time." Maxwell was rehearsing his arguments for another, more difficult interview which he still faced.

The Chief Superintendent's brow furrowed still further.

"Do we know where this man Chisam is?"

Forbes sweated a little more freely.

"No, sir. Inspector Vernier established that he had already left Whitehaven, but he had not followed up beyond that before the bombardment."

"What orders have you given him?"

Forbes stared at him uncomprehending for a moment, before it dawned on him that, in his confusion, he had still not told the Chief the full truth. He became aware of Sergeant Wilson's telegram still clutched in his hand, and he gave it to the Chief.

"Inspector Vernier is dead, sir. He was killed in the bombardment."

The Chief Superintendent was visibly moved as he read the telegram, and when he looked up, he was unmistakeably angry.

"I ought to have seen this as soon as it came in," he said, looking at Forbes. Forbes sensed the inadvisability of pusillanimous excuses and remained silent; but the Chief Superintendent continued to stare at him with a hard unwinking gaze under which Forbes squirmed inwardly, and which finally wrung from him a chastened "Yes, sir."

He expected the worst; but the Chief Superintendent's gaze shifted to Maxwell.

"You say you received the tip off about the submarine on Friday. Was any attempt made to communicate this information either to Inspector Vernier or to Scotland Yard?"

"No, sir. As I've already explained, we assumed that Inspector Vernier was about to close the case with an arrest. The presence of the submarine could hardly be a police matter."

The words slipped out in his exasperation, and he could have bitten his tongue off; but it was too late. The Chief Superintendent repeated his question with an ominous persistence.

"No attempt was made to communicate the information about the submarine either to Inspector Vernier or to ourselves," he said, continuing to gaze at Maxwell.

So the bloody police were going to close ranks, and he was to be the scapegoat. Maxwell's reply was barely more than a whisper.

"No, sir." His face was very white.

"I must tell you that I shall make my displeasure known in the appropriate quarters. I must also insist that from now on, any information relating to this case is to be passed on to us immediately."

"Yes, sir." The bastard.

The Chief Superintendent's gaze shifted back to Forbes.

"Whom do you have up in Cumberland now?"

"Only the officers who were with Inspector Vernier, sir - Sergeant Wilson and two constables.   But all of them were injured in the bombardment. I've been in communication with the local police there. Apparently a shell exploded next to the house

237

where they were lodging. It seems that Inspector Vernier suffered some sort of stroke or heart failure with the concussion. The others were not fatally injured, but they're all in a local hospital, sir."

"Very well, Superintendent Forbes. You will go up to Cumberland immediately, and you will sort out this mess. Take as many of your own men as you feel you can spare. You are to bring this business back under control; and above all, above all else, I want this man Chisam. I want him in custody, and you will not come back without him. I will expect to be kept informed. I am sure you can count on the fullest cooperation from Lieutenant-Commander Maxwell in this matter." He treated the Lieutenant-Commander to a wintry stare as he stood up to dismiss them.

Outside, Maxwell was indignant.

"You bastards. You're as thick as pea soup, the lot of you. As if it would have made any difference if you'd known about the submarine. Well, I'm not taking this lying down. You aren't getting away with this if I can help it."

"Look, Maxwell, it's no use shouting at me. It's a risk we all have to live with, and it's just bad luck it's happened the way it has. The Chief Super's doing what anyone in his position would do. What else do you expect? We have to cover ourselves just as much as you do. You wouldn't be saying this if the boot was on the other foot."

"Well, you certainly made the most of the opportunity. From where I was standing, it felt like a knife in the back."

"Spare me the melodrama. It wasn't exactly going to be sweetness and light for me either. If I don't catch this bloody character, I'm going to be as much in the brown stuff as you."

Maxwell became thoughtful for a moment.

"You'll be going up to Cumberland straight away, I suppose."

"You heard what the Chief Super said."

"But from what you were saying, it looks unlikely that this man, Chisam, is still in Cumberland."

"That may well be, but that's where the trail starts, and that's where I shall have to go."

"What about trying to outguess the man, if he's now a fugitive. Do you suppose he'll try and leave the country?"

"I can't be sure of what he might do at this stage. Look, if you're trying to cause trouble, then forget it. I'm not rising to the bait; and besides, I have my orders. You heard them yourself."

"Cause trouble! You're a suspicious bastard! All that I ever heard about policemen . . .

238

Look, Forbes, you're going to have to trust me if you want my cooperation, at least to the extent of our common interest. Doing you down isn't going to help me with my superiors - and it's just possible that we might both be lined up for the chopping block."

"I don't need reminding of that." Forbes looked worried. "Alright, what do you want?"

"I'm coming up to Cumberland with you. I'm damned if I'm going to sit in Whitehall waiting for my fate to be decided by you lot. If I'm lined up for the chop, then at least it won't be without my having done something in my defence."

Forbes was sceptical.

"This is police work. You're not a policeman. Really, you'd be wasting your time." He nearly added "And ours as well." He was irritated by the idea of Maxwell joining them. He would be an encumbrance, and simply there to serve his own interests. Maxwell, being an outsider, wouldn't feel bound by Forbes' authority, and therein lay the scope for a deal of trouble. On the other hand, he couldn't prevent Maxwell from coming with them if he was determined to do so. They were supposed to be cooperating.

"Very well," he said heavily. "Have it your own way. But I can't help feeling you'll be wasting your time."

Forbes remembered that his wife had planned an engagement that evening. He would have to let her know that he would be away, and she would not be pleased. Perhaps it was as well that Cumberland was a long way off.

The last light of the day was dying in the west. The odd pane of glass still reflected the leaden glare from the horizon, while the surrounding buildings and streets had already merged into the gloom of evening, as Forbes and Maxwell cautiously picked their way along Whitehaven's harbour front. There was still just enough light to see by, otherwise they should not have attempted to venture into the harbour area. The ground was pitted with shell craters and littered with piles of rubble. At one point the way was barred by a tangle of smashed railway trucks and twisted rails, and they had to stumble across huge mounds of spilled coal to reach the far side of the harbour. On the north side, a large warehouse still burned: parts of its walls had collapsed with the heat, and through the gaping windows in the remaining walls, the fire glowed orange with a satanic malevolence. Most dramatic was the sight of the hulk of the ship that had capsized in the harbour after being struck by shells. Its hull had been torn open in several places by shells that had struck it after it had capsized, and the tangled remains of a steam crane lay across it, having been blown off the dockside by another shell. Broken masts and spars protruded from the still, black water of the dock. The stillness of the scene, the tranquillity after the violence was emphasised by the sound of voices and the flickering of lights among figures standing on the upturned hull of the ship. Men were still trapped alive inside the hull and an attempt was being made to rescue them. The air had the wine-like clarity of a summer evening and lay like a balm over the wound of so much destruction and wanton human violence.

For Forbes, there could be no more fitting end to a day such as this. The scale of the catastrophe made little impression on him. For one thing, he was so tired that he was finding it difficult to stay awake, and the deadly fatigue that was overtaking him anaesthetised the horror of what he saw. In any event, it was too large and too impersonal a tragedy to touch him deeply at that moment. Seeing only the aftermath, it had, for him, the impression almost of a natural disaster, for which no individual is responsible; where the majority caught up in it are only touched superficially, and there is an element of public spectacle as well as tragedy involved.

It was a witness of personal tragedy that would remain with Forbes as a memory of that day, rather than the half-seen devastation of the harbour that was the cause of it all. Vernier was his man, his responsibility, and it was in the nature of the Service that there could be no dividing line between a man's official existence and his personal life however much the latter might be either a refuge from the former, or hell on earth. It was incumbent on Forbes to ensure that his men did not keep secrets from him - men had lost their careers, and even their lives, for doing so. To be indiscreet or to have bad judgement was not necessarily in itself an offence: but a man who bound himself into trap of secrecy through guilt and fear was likely to prove a rotten apple, and a danger to everyone around him. In his ordinary failings, Vernier had not been such a man. Indeed it was precisely because Vernier had not cared what either Forbes or anyone else had thought of his domestic arrangements, however reprehensible they might have seemed that Forbes' duty had been doubly unpleasant that day. On the long train journey from London, his thoughts had returned repeatedly to the two women he had visited that morning with the news of Vernier's death. Officially, to perform this duty in respect of man's mistress would be considered an unacceptable breach of conventional decencies but Forbes knew that it was what Vernier would have wanted, indeed expected him to do as a kind of *quid pro quo* for the privilege of his confidence. Vernier had not gone into details about the matter - he was reserved to that extent at least - but he had made sure that Forbes understood the nature of the relationships, even implicitly challenging Forbes to criticise him, a breach of manners which Forbes had not allowed himself to be offended by. They had met on equal terms; and now this small debt was left to be paid.

Of the two women, it had been Vernier's mistress who had made the most impression on Forbes. She was much younger than Vernier - twenty two or twenty three perhaps

240

attractive rather than beautiful in an Irish sort of way: fair, slightly freckled skin, a slender face which gave her a deceptive slightness, almost transparent blue eyes, and a mass of unruly red hair which did not look as if it saw a comb often. Whether she was Irish, Forbes did not know. Her accent was that of south London, not quite respectable. She was a teacher at a local art college, one of the breed of independent young women with money of their own which gave them a greater freedom to choose the terms on which they treated with society than their mothers or grandmothers had ever had. From what Forbes had heard about her, Marie Fleming was a disturbingly unconventional young woman, always ready to challenge any aspect of a society which she felt was challenging her right to an equal place in it. It was surprising therefore, that she should have chosen to have a serious affair with Vernier - a very different personality, one of the conventional majority, and a representative of the authority she asserted herself against. But for Marie, this too had been a challenge. Vernier had had a strong personality in his own, more orthodox way, which made him attractive to women, and Marie loved him simply as a man. His rank and place in officialdom she found pompous and vaguely ridiculous, and she would have scoffed at any attempt by him to make anything of them in her presence. And yet Forbes had been in no doubt that theirs had been a serious affair. Had he believed otherwise, he would not have come, whatever he thought Vernier might have wanted.

Marie Fleming lived in a rather tatty area of Wandsworth, in a street where most of the houses were turned over to rented apartments and rooms. It was not yet a seedy area, however. Most of the people who lived there were young - people making a start in life: teachers like Marie, students, apprentice lawyers, office workers at the bottom of the promotion ladder. Their presence lent a certain air of optimism to the place, charged it with the painful sweetness of youth, its energy and its gauch idealism. If there was tattiness that spoke of poverty, it was a bright poverty, tinged with the optimism of having a lifetime of endeavour and opportunity to look forward to. It was to this street that Forbes had gone that morning, already tired with the burden of the day's events. He had expected to find Marie Fleming at home, as the schools and colleges were still closed for the long summer break, but there was no reply when he knocked. He was about to turn away after knocking for the third time when he heard the gate clang behind him, and a young woman's voice.

"Was it me you were wanting?"

He turned and faced her.

"Miss Marie Fleming?"

"I am Marie Fleming, yes."

241

"Superintendent Forbes, Scotland Yard. I wonder if I might speak to you in private Miss Fleming?"

"Forbes, Scotland Yard - you must be John's boss. Yes, you'd better come in suppose."

She had evidently been shopping and was slightly flushed from her walk from the loca market. She was not wearing a coat, the day being very warm, and her long red hair wa loose in all its unruly glory. He followed her along the passage into the kitchen.

"You'll have to excuse the mess, but I'm afraid I always live like this. I've never bee very domesticated, and I'm afraid I'm not inclined to be apologetic about it."

She turned suddenly to face him, the sunlight streaming through the rather ding kitchen window, catching her hair and making an aurora of it. Her eyes searched hi face, and he found their uncompromising stare disconcerting. He felt that his presenc was resented as an intrusion. Her having an affair with a policeman did not mean tha she was any the less suspicious of the police as an institution, as an arm of officialdom Her extraordinary eyes, their pale transparency almost luminous, were hard and tense a she stared at him. Her mouth was set firm, and a slight flush still coloured her cheek Forbes could easily understand why she had fascinated and enraptured Vernier.

"Why do you want to speak to me?" Her voice sounded suddenly unfriendly, but ther was a suggestion of fear in it which betrayed her vulnerability. "Has something happene to John? You wouldn't come here for any other reason. John says that you know about u - about John and me - because it's necessary for security or something; but it's none o your business otherwise. Even he agrees with that. What's happened to him?"

"Please sit down Miss Fleming. I'm afraid I have some bad news for you."

His attempt to make a refuge of formality was no refuge at all. The form of words wa enough, and she already knew.

"What's happened to him?" She almost shouted the words, and there was a note o hysteria in her voice. "He's . . .he's not dead?"

"Yes. I'm very sorry." He could hardly bring himself to say the words.

"He's dead?" Her face was twisting with the distortion of grief.

"He was on a job which had taken him to a coastal town in the north of England. Th place was bombarded by a German raider early this morning, and he was one of tho killed."

She was shaking her head as if she did not believe him, and her body was tremblin Forbes felt afraid of the power of her grief, which was almost un-English in its intensity

"John is dead? You are telling the truth?"

"Yes. I'm sorry. I'm very sorry."

She started to cry. The string bag full of vegetables from the market which she had been clutching, slipped from her fingers to the floor with a thump, and an onion rolled across the floor, its brown skin glistening in the dusty sunlight. At first her sobs were silent, but when she suddenly sat down as if she no longer had the strength to stand, and buried her face in her hands, her sobs became pathetic little cries that made her shoulders shake gently. Forbes was more affected than he thought he could be: it was not just because of Vernier, but because of the girl herself. Her grief was so intense that he felt that his presence there was somehow improper, and that he should go; and yet the very intensity of her grief prevented him from doing so. She was for the moment so completely overwhelmed by it that she was oblivious to all else; even to his presence. She cried out, her eyes blind with tears.

"Why did it have to be John? Why did he have to die like that? What a stupid, pointless waste. Oh, God help me, God help me that I should be alive when he is dead. Oh, John, John!"

Forbes, moved by he knew not what impulse suddenly sat down beside her and took one of her hands in his own. He was amazed at himself, but the girl's grief had called forth a response in him which overcame the veneer of reserve that normally isolates one human being from another; and even if she had withdrawn her hand in rejection, he would still have felt that his instinct had been sound. But he had done the right thing. She did not withdraw her hand - indeed, at first she seemed unaware that he had taken it - and at length she put her other hand on his, and they sat thus while she continued to cry softly. How long they sat there he could not have said. As in a dream, there was no sense of time; and to think of time at all had no place there at that moment. The doubt he had felt on first taking her hand melted away as he understood what he had done: that there are moments when to have no defences at all is the only defence that humanity may have. When at last she did withdraw her hands, she withdrew them gently, and it was not a rebuff. She looked up at him, her face drawn and white, and wet with tears.

"You must go now. Please go."

He stood up and picked up his hat. Again, it was not a rebuff, as each of them understood. He had done the right thing.

"If you need to contact me, you know where I am."

"Mr Forbes."

He turned back from the doorway. She seemed to be struggling for the right words. "You . . . didn't have to come here to tell me . . . about John. After all, I'm only . . . I'm not even his wife. I . . . I want you to know that I appreciate . . . that you came."

Forbes smiled wanly.

"John would have expected nothing less."

As Forbes walked up the street in the bright morning sunlight, he reflected on th contrast between the two women. Marie Fleming's grief had been transparent and naïve Vernier was probably her first serious love, and her grief was the grief of young love i bereavement. For a time, she would be mad with grief, and whether she got over it in th end or succumbed, she would bear the marks of her grief for the rest of her days. Whe one is young, love has a dimension of eternity, in which the loss of the loved one is th most appalling desolation imaginable; and however precious such feelings, they are th necessary obverse of the sweetness of such love fulfilled, even, and perhaps especiall; when the sweetness is more than a little selfish.

It was easy to see how Marie Fleming would suffer at the news of Vernier's death. had been much less easy for Forbes to make up his mind about Mrs Vernier. He ha made the journey to Wandsworth from the much more genteel street in Fulham whe Vernier lived, and where he had gone on an official errand with the news to Vernier wife. Charlotte Vernier was in her late thirties, and had been married to Vernier for son fifteen years. Forbes had known her for about ten years, and although they had met o many occasions, she was still essentially a stranger to him, and what he knew about h he had gleaned mostly from Vernier. Charlotte Vernier's natural reserve wa compounded by a lack of confidence in herself which made her appear subdued and eve submissive to those who did not know her. This dark and reserved exterior concealed a intelligent, if somewhat unstable mind and personality. Her background was low middle class. She had gone to a girls' grammar school of high repute, and wou probably have gone on to university - not Oxford or Cambridge, but London o Birmingham perhaps - if she had had the opportunity. But her parents had not been ab to afford to pay for a university education, and she had remained at home. This inevitab led to pressure on her to marry. However, when she had married, she had marrie beneath her, much to her parents' disapproval. John Vernier had been a constable whe Charlotte had married him, and this had not been good enough for her parents. But h judgement had been sound. Despite his class origins, she had sensed that he was winner, and so it had proved. Within three years he was a Sergeant, and in another seve he had been promoted to Inspector, and he looked set to go higher still. In compensati for having to suffer the snobbery of relatives and former peers, she was now more th comfortably off, and had more money to spend than many of them. But she had also ha to pay the price of uncertainty about her identity. Marrying out of her class had n meant that she could become something other than what she was, and the realisation this had led her to assume a reserved and unassertive outward face. She felt a dissatisfaction with what her life had become, and this had communicated itself to Vernier. Vernier had done what he could to respond in his own way, but there remained a gap between them which neither fully understood. However difficult it is to define class, and differences between one class and another, it remains the case that there are such differences, even between individuals who are otherwise close. Vernier was not estranged from his wife - having shared fifteen years of marriage they had adjusted to each other, so that they were, on one level, comfortable with each other in a way they could be with no-one else. But there was a part of her that Vernier could never enter, because he could neither understand nor sympathise with it, and this had at last left a gap between them.

Forbes, as an outsider, had been unaware of the matter in detail, but had sensed that something was amiss, even before he had known about Marie Fleming. Marie was about the same age as Charlotte had been when Vernier had married her, and despite the fact that there were differences between Marie and Vernier almost as profound as those between Vernier and Charlotte, Marie had been able to fill that gap of sympathy that Charlotte had been unable to bridge. The additional attraction of a willing and lusty young body meant that Vernier had been unable to resist her, and she had become as important a part of his life as Charlotte. Whether he would ever have abandoned Charlotte in favour of Marie, Forbes did not know - he had the impression that Vernier had become comfortable with his dual relationship and was content with it as a permanent arrangement. The tragedy of Charlotte Vernier was that she not only knew of the illicit relationship, but accepted it as a consequence of what she saw as her failings as a wife. She had long since ceased to have any self-sufficiency of spirit. She was what life had made her and she was no longer able to rise above it - such things were wistful memories of youth, of a time when she would have reacted with indignation to the knowledge of such a betrayal.

She was very formal when she opened the door to Forbes. Her reserve was due in part to the knowledge that others knew of her position, and she could not bring herself to an open show of friendliness towards people who might privately regard her with contempt. Forbes had always been her husband's boss, and no more than that - no personal contact had ever been established. This did not help Forbes as he might have expected, because of the sympathy he felt for her at that moment. Her background was similar to his own, and that of his wife, and he understood her more than she gave him credit for. But she needed neither his charity nor his sympathy, and she gave him no opportunity for either. She must have known that something was wrong even before he spoke, since he was not

245

in the habit of making social calls on her. But she made no concessions to him, and ⬛ had to go through the standard routine as if she were a complete stranger. She sat dow⬛ as he requested, and received the news in complete silence. She remained quite still, t⬛ only betrayal of any emotion being the nervous clasping and unclasping of her hands ⬛ her lap.

"Is there anything you would like me to do to help, Mrs Vernier?"

He was embarrassed, and even a little hurt that she did not acknowledge him, and th⬛ had to remain on the level of formalities: but it was her defence, as he too had defences.

"What will happen about his body?" Her voice was slightly shaky.

"I will make arrangements for his body to be brought back to London. I cannot imagi⬛ that there will be any delay in releasing it. Do you wish for any assistance in arrangi⬛ the funeral and burial? I can make the arrangements if you don't feel you are able to fa⬛ it."

"I should like your advice about the matter, but I shall make the arrangements myse⬛ There will be his family to consider, of course, but," - she turned to look at him - "⬛ was my husband, Superintendent, and he will be buried as my husband, by me and n⬛ one else, and the world shall be a witness to that." Her voice was shaking, but s⬛ remained composed without any other sign of emotion. So hurt had she been that alm⬛ her first resposne on hearing the news was that widowhood brought her a dignity th⬛ had been denied her as a wife. The pain of her loss would come, but at that moment s⬛ had actually gained something in Vernier's death that she had lost in his life, and th⬛ would help her to meet the pain when it came. Dimly, Forbes understood.

"Was . . . was he very much disfigured or mutilated by . . . what killed him?"

"I don't know for sure, but I don't think so. I'm told it was concussion from t⬛ explosion, not blast."

"I don't know if you can understand, but it would be somehow worse if he had be⬛ disfigured. Even if I didn't see him, it would taint all the memories I have of hi⬛ However I remembered him, there would always be the knowledge, or even the mem⬛ of . . . of . . ."

"Mrs Vernier, you must not distress yourself with such thoughts. As far as I know th⬛ are without foundation. It's not right that you should dwell on the manner of his death ⬛ such a way. It cannot help you, and whatever happened to him, it cannot hurt him now⬛

"No. But I don't think you do understand. I did not ask simply for myself. And I w⬛ see his body. I am not afraid of that. I am his wife, and I will bury him."

On the long train journey up from London, Forbes had found his thoughts returni⬛ from among the turbulence of his memories of the day, to those words of Charl⬛

Vernier. He had at first felt that it was inappropriate, even a little cold blooded of her to temper her grief, if grief she felt, with such thoughts. But the more he mused on it, the more he came to understand her instincts, and thus the tragedy of her situation. One of the things he had learned during his years in the Force was the inadvisability of becoming personally involved in cases. But this case had now resulted in the death of one of his own men; and the private misgivings he had had about Vernier's personal life had only been confirmed in the aftermath of Vernier's death.

They reached Whitehaven shortly before sunset. The last stage of the journey had been by motor car from Workington, as the railway north of Whitehaven was closed by landslides caused by the shellfire. They sought out and found a very weary Superintendent Hogg, and made their introductions. Hogg had been involved all day in the direction of the relief and rescue operations, and his horizons had narrowed to the administrative problems he had had to face as a result. The heavy cranes that had been promised from Carlisle had still not arrived; and several unexploded shells were causing severe disruption to rescue operations. Army engineers who had been promised to deal with these had also not yet arrived. Hogg was not, however, so engrossed in his problems that the significance of his visitors was lost on him.

"I hope, gentlemen, that your visit doesn't herald any further trouble, given the consequences attendant on my last visitors from London." He was not speaking entirely in jest, a point which was not lost on Forbes. As briefly as he could, Hogg recounted the events of the previous night, from the arrival of Vernier from Carlisle, the entering and searching of Chisam's house, to the bombardment at dawn that morning. His narrative was at times halting, as if he was recalling incidents from the distant past which he was no longer sure about, or which no longer mattered. This had been the longest day in his life, and the events of the previous day were already a matter of insignificance. Forbes asked him to describe again Vernier's discovery of the burned notepaper in Chisam's bedroom fireplace.

"You would say that Inspector Vernier was convinced as a result that Edward Chisam was the man he was looking for?"

"Most certainly. It was the neatest bit of forensic work I've seen in a while. When he showed me the paper samples, they were unmistakably the same."

"I see. Has . . . any follow-up action been taken?" He asked the question almost apologetically; and in answer, Hogg gave a gesture as if to take in the whole town.

"Hardly, under the circumstances. Anything of that sort naturally became of secondary importance."

"I understand. But no-one knows where Edward Chisam is now?"

"No, I'm afraid not." Hogg's curiosity was now aroused. "Do I understand that it is o account of this Edward Chisam that you've come to Whitehaven?"

Forbes noted the irritation which Hogg had been unable to keep out of his voice. H hesitated, and then said heavily: "It seems that there may be a connection between th morning's events and this man Chisam, which is why we're so anxious to find him." H sensed rather than saw Maxwell bristling beside him. "I should say that this information that we have only just received, and of course, it's for your own ears only."

Hogg digested this information slowly.

"In that case gentlemen, you can count on my fullest cooperation."

From the police station, Forbes and Maxwell went to the Infirmary to intervie Sergeant Wilson and the two constables who had accompanied Vernier. All of them we suffering the after effects of concussion and were not fit for duty - one of the constabl was still under sedation and only semi conscious. The ward was full of people who h been wounded in the bombardment, some of them groaning from the pain of the injuries, and this, together with the to-ing and fro-ing of nurses resplendent in lon starched white uniforms, and relatives of the injured drifting in and out, meant that t place was noisy and allowed for little or no privacy.

Wilson, though still shaken, was lucid, and keen to get out at the earliest opportunit and Forbes agreed to see what he could do. Wilson could add little of fact to what Forb already knew, but in his account of the previous three or four days, he communicate something of the sense of urgency that had driven Vernier in his pursuit of the case, t restless energy of the man, which had at times been hard for the others to keep up wit Wilson himself had become infected with it, and what had been hardest for him to be during that long Monday had been the fact that there was no-one he could talk to abo the case; and that no-one was pursuing it now that he was out of action. The local poli had enough on their hands and were not interested, and he was confined to a hospit bed. The telegram he had sent to Scotland Yard had been as much a cry for help as a act of duty, and when Forbes had walked into the ward, Wilson's cry of "Thank Go you've come, sir!" was so obviously heartfelt that Forbes was genuinely moved. Even could see that Wilson was still not fit for duty, and Wilson could not conceal h disappointment at being told this; but Forbes would at least get him sent home recuperate.

From the noise and confusion of the general ward, where people were apparently al to come and go without let or hindrance, it took Forbes some minutes to find someone authority. Passing nurses were unhelpful; but eventually he located the matron in char She was not in the least impressed by his name and rank, and when he raised the matt of sending Wilson and the constable who had not been seriously injured home, she would not hear of it at first. He had to use all his tact and skill to talk her round. In the end, it was the the prospect of empty beds rather than any compassion for the luckless pair that moved her. When Forbes mentioned the other matter he had come to see her about, she more or less took this as a cue for his dismissal, and handed him over to a junior nurse.

The nurse, a frail looking girl, little more than a child, took Forbes and Maxwell along several long, dingy corridors and down some stone steps to the basement, which was used as the mortuary.

"You'll not have to mind about the smell," she warned them with the cheerful insouciance of youth, which belied her frail appearance. "We've been that busy, we simply haven't had a chance to attend to things down here."

There were far more bodies in the small mortuary than it had been designed to cope with, and they had simply been laid out in a line on the floor, each one covered in an old sheet. They had evidently been left thus in the state in which they had been brought in - the living upstairs were more important than the dead. The nurse consulted a paper, then, after checking the tags which were attached to the corners of each sheet, she finally drew back one of the sheets.

To see the body of someone one knows well is one of the most disturbing experiences possible, and Forbes was spared none of the shock of that moment by knowing what he was about to see. The reality was more awful than all his imaginings; for here were the features he knew so well, of a man whom he had last seen only a few days earlier alive and full of life, with whom he had exchanged a casual farewell in the easy familiarity of a long working relationship, knowing that they would meet again early the following week: and now he looked upon his face for the last time, and death was hard to comprehend. Life was still so close that the manifest marks of death were strange and unreal. Vernier's body was still clothed in the crumpled suit in which he had died, and which he had been wearing since early on Sunday morning. This, together with his hair and face, were covered in a film of whitish deposit, which was evidently wall plaster from the collapsed building. The dust partly concealed a wound in his right cheek, and a flow of dried blood which ran down to his collar. Apart from this, his face was unmarked - his eyes were closed, his lips slightly parted, revealing a gleam of teeth. The thin growth of beard stubble under the film of dust, which enhanced the cold paleness of his skin in death made him look exhausted and weary, as though death had come as a natural relief of a burden no longer to be withstood, rather than as a trauma unlooked for and unwanted by a man of immense zest for life, which Forbes knew him to have been. The stillness of death on the face of one he knew so well was oppressive; but Forbes was

249

also held by the memories of Charlotte Vernier, and of Marie Fleming, almost as if the stood beside him as he knelt by Vernier's body. It was only slowly that he returned to th present. He looked up from his reverie, and turned to the nurse who had stood bac respectfully waiting for him.

"Has anything been removed from the body?" he asked her.

"No sir, not as far as I know. None of them's been touched."

After a moment's hesitation he reached into Vernier's inside breast pocket. The che: under the soiled shirt felt cold, but rather than revulsion at the touch, which he expecter Forbes experienced a sudden feeling of pity - pity for this poor dead thing that was once man; for the closed eyes that would no longer see, nor the ears hear; the heart that we stilled in the cold chest; the the mouth that would never again speak with the voice h knew so well, or smile, or kiss the lips of the two women who grieved; for the uselessne: of death.

Such thoughts would never have occurred to him had Vernier been alive; but deat touches a fear of one's own mortality, which releases in turn a charity which is felt onl for the dead, or those close to death, whatever they may have been in life. This spasm grief held Forbes for a moment only, and he gave no outward sign of his emotions. H hand, stilled also for a moment, now found what it sought, as his fingers closed aroun the familiar shape of an official pocketbook. He withdrew it, and slowly flipped throug the worn pages. Vernier had written copious notes on the case, but what Forbes was ab to read in a first cursory glance meant little to him - he would need to find the time read them properly. As he turned the pages, some small object slipped out and flutter to the ground. He bent and picked it up. It was a fragment of paper, irregular in shap and charred around the edge. At the back of the pocketbook he found a full sheet of th same kind of paper. It was folded in half and slightly dog-eared, but it was unmistakab the same paper as the fragment - a distinctive, light pearly grey bond notepaper.

It had not been possible for Forbes to do anything further on Monday night, and Tuesday, when he began his pursuit, it had been difficult at first to fit together the piec of evidence Vernier had left him. Vernier's notebook was not as helpful as he could ha hoped for, as most of the notes were about the investigation of Robert Harrison, t original suspect, who was now recovering from the effects of concussion in the san hospital ward as Sergeant Wilson, and who had yet to appreciate just how lucky a m he was that day. There were only a few references to Chisam in the notebook: most of t evidence about Chisam was verbal, from Wilson, and from Hogg. And, of course, the were the fragments of notepaper. It was the standard, routine procedures that had, in t end, produced results; but Forbes, in his present state of mind, found the delays almost unbearably frustrating. He began to appreciate more fully the urgency that had driven Vernier during his last hours alive, and which lent to the case a peculiar air of desperation, of a lonely unreality and darkness, which even a man of Forbes' experience found unsettling.

The frustrations were real. The first journey they made was to Seascale, because the booking clerk on duty at Whitehaven station when they went there remembered Chisam buying a ticket for Seascale on the Saturday. A long interview with Joseph Chisam and his wife also proved frustrating, in that they could give him no information about Chisam's movements; but they did provide a good deal of incidental information which enabled him to form an idea of the kind of man he was pursuing. Chisam was transformed from an anonymous name, a mere cipher, into an individual with interests and motives which he could begin to make sense of. There was also, of course, a photograph, which among other things, disposed of Vernier's remaining reason for detaining the unfortunate Harrison.

Joseph Chisam's account of his nephew was strongly coloured, and Joseph made no secret of his views. Edward Chisam was no good, and he made the most of the opportunity to go into details. But a picture also emerged of a man who was in many ways on the margins of life: a man with few if any friends, who was isolated because of his temperament; a man who did not fit in with the conventions of the majority, thus making him an object of suspicion and dislike; a man who would not accept society's judgement on him, or - and here Joseph became most emphatic - the consequences of his own situation. Conventions had been broken, and this could not be countenanced. Now, it seemed, the law had also been broken, and Joseph felt that he had been justified in his views.

This image of the man enabled Forbes to do what he instinctively did as a policeman - to categorise him. Categories were pre-ordained and they acted to type; and however unfair or unjustified categories might be, for his purposes, Forbes found them useful and was quite happy with them. He had an image, and a category, and for the time being, it was enough. Whatever kind of man the real Chisam might be, Forbes was confident that, for what he required, his image, and his category, were a true hypothesis of him.

At Seascale, the trail went cold. The booking clerk at the railway station had no memory of seeing Chisam during the weekend, and Forbes concluded that Chisam must have had a return ticket. They returned to Whitehaven, and further frustrating delays. At Chisam's house in Victoria Road, the police guard had been withdrawn and the place sealed up. When Forbes gained entrance, the house proved to be full of material of tantalising interest, but of no immediate value, as it gave no clue as to Chisam's whereabouts. A cursory examination of the contents of Chisam's bookcase told Forbes nothing; and yet it was not without interest. Like Vernier, Forbes concluded that Chisam had pretensions of being an intellectual; but unlike Vernier, whose reaction had largely been one of contempt, Forbes found that it added to his image of the man. He detailed his most intelligent constable to start going through all this material, and left. His next call was on the Whitehaven Cocoa and Coffee House Company, where at first he was refused an interview with the manager, despite presenting his credentials. The place was in turmoil, as the events of the previous day had been disastrous for the company. Forbes gathered that the warehouse he had seen burning the previous day had been one of the main bonded warehouses in the port. Among the cargo held there belonging to the company which had been destroyed in the fire, were five hundred tons of cocoa, and nearly a thousand tons of sugar, which was partly why it had burned so well.

It was the mention of Chisam's name that eventually got Forbes an audience. It was Chisam's department that was the most badly affected by the disaster, and Chisam's absence was the cause of general irritation and ill will. A rumour was circulating that Chisam had been arrested in the middle of the night and was being held by the police. The manager had at length contacted the Whitehaven police and asked if they knew of Chisam's whereabouts, and had been told rather curtly that they knew nothing of anyone of that name. The rumours persisted, however.

The manager, when he agreed to see Forbes, had no doubt about what he wanted.

"Right, Superintendent, I presume you've come to tell me that you're holding Edward Chisam. I don't know what you've charged him with, but I've got a charge sheet of my own, I can tell you. If it was just dereliction of duty, that would be bad enough - the one time, the one time in his life when he was needed here, where is he? Well, I suppose you've been holding him, that's another matter. But now there's a question of financial irregularity. On that score I would say I've already enough evidence to add another item to your charge sheet. What's come to light as a result of this catastrophe you would hardly believe."

Forbes managed to break into the manager's catalogue of complaint to say that regretfully, they were not holding Edward Chisam.

"As a matter of fact, the reason I've come here is to see if you have any information which might help us to trace him."

The manager became thoughtful.

"Well, as I've already said, if we were able to trace him ourselves, we would already have done so. May I ask why you are looking for him?"

"I'm afraid I can't go into details, other than to say that it's a serious matter relating to national security. You mentioned financial irregularity - what's that all about?"

"Well - and this is for your own ears only, Superintendent - it seems that Mr Chisam has been selling unauthorised futures stock in this company on a massive scale. I was contacted this morning by a man called Earl who has demanded early redemption of stock worth, at face value, almost as much as the total assets of the company; stock which I had no idea existed until this morning. You will understand, Superintendent, that quite apart from the loss we suffered yesterday, if we have to meet this claim against us, the company will be driven into bankruptcy. We are taking legal advice of course, but at the moment, we are in very great uncertainty."

"Tell me a little about Edward Chisam's part in the company. His official part I mean, rather than his extra curricular activities."

Again, the information was nothing to the purpose, only background; but again, it added to Forbes' understanding of his quarry.

"Chisam was in charge of the import business," the manager was saying. "He dealt with the shippers and the agents, and arranged the contracts, although he was not empowered to sign them on his own authority. He dealt with the customs and the port officers, and supervised the unloading of cargoes, and storage in the bonded warehouses. It was an important part of the business, and we've been badly let down. Betrayed is not too strong a word for it."

"How much freedom did Chisam have to act on his own authority in these matters? You say he wasn't empowered to sign contracts on his own authority."

"I supervised all aspects of his work, either directly or indirectly. I like to feel that I'm in charge as manager."

"And that would include the financial aspects of Chisam's work?"

"Er, indeed, through the accounts department. I wouldn't necessarily personally supervise every detail of the financial transactions." There was a hint of embarrassment in the manager's voice. Forbes did not press the matter.

"What goods was Chisam responsible for importing?"

"Mostly cocoa, coffee, sugar and tea. We deal in tobacco and rubber in a small way, but they're not very important. Cocoa, sugar and coffee are the largest items by volume, I would say, and cocoa is by far the largest of those."

"Cocoa and sugar. I see. And these agencies and shippers he dealt with - would any of them be foreign?"

"How do you mean, foreign? If they weren't British, they would be Empire - Accra on the Gold Coast for the cocoa, Jamaica for the sugar, Nairobi for the coffee, Calcutta or

Ceylon for the tea - all reputable companies."

"None of them were German?"

"German?" The manager stared at him.

"I suppose I meant before the war. You didn't deal with any German companies, or with any of the German colonies?"

"Most certainly not. We are a patriotic company, Superintendent, I'll have you know We certainly would not have used German companies, even before the war."

"You can speak for Edward Chisam on that point also?"

"As far as his official duties are concerned, I can. What he got up to unofficially we're only now beginning to discover."

"Indeed. Tell me what kind of a man Edward Chisam is. What do you make of him?"

"I should say, to begin with, that Chisam owed his position in the company partly to his family connections. His uncle was manager before me, and during his time, of course it was expected that Edward Chisam would benefit from this. - you know how it is Nothing wrong with that, of course - it's the way the world works - so long as it isn' used to push a candidate beyond what he's capable of. That can cause trouble - but think that old Mr Chisam was aware of that in Edward Chisam's case.

"You see, in this business, as I suppose in other businesses, a man will do well, or he won't do well, and that's especially true of managers, and those who aspire to b managers. Those who get on without the benefit of personal connections are those who are dedicated to the job, who can put energy and drive into the work consistently and with an ordinary determination, and not allow their minds to become cluttered with air fairy ideas or an overheated imagination. That was Edward Chisam's problem - he was too good for us. He considered both the work and the company to be beneath him, and h didn't have the determination or the dedication that a good manager must have. I don' believe he would ever have amounted to anything in the end - he was a dreamer. His head was full of fancy ambitions, and he had no means of getting anywhere near them."

"What kind of ambitions?"

"Social ambitions I suppose you'd call them. He felt he was too good for us, and b rights he ought to move in higher society. He would get himself invited to places quit outside the normal calling of people of his social standing. I understand he was a Lowther castle the last time the Kaiser came to visit Lord Lonsdale. He subsequently go involved in owning and running racehorses, and I suspect he got into debt over i although he wouldn't admit as much to me. Mind you, had I had firm evidence of it, of any financial impropriety, it would have cost him his job. We don't tolerate suc things in this company, and he's certainly done for himself with this little lot, I can te

254

you."

Forbes was tantalised by the number of leads that seemed to be opening up. None of them, however, seemed likely to help him in his immediate task.

"Where is Lowther castle?"

The manager explained where and what Lowther castle was, in the tone one uses to explain the obvious to ignorant foreigners. No, he couldn't tell Forbes much more about Chisam's presence during the Kaiser's visit. Chisam had not deigned to divulge much about it at the time, and that was four years ago now.

"You can't give me any names - names of people he met there - particularly Germans?" Forbes pressed him.

"Not Germans, certainly. I didn't know anything about that, and I don't remember him speaking about Germans at the time. One name I do remember, though - he was associated with a Lord Hemswell in the racehorse business from about that time. I don't know what became of that association - I haven't heard anything about it in the last couple of years or so."

Forbes smiled gently.

"Lord Hemswell - now that's a name I do know. Most interesting that it should occur in this connection."

He stood up.

"Well, sir, I shall not detain you further. You've been most helpful, and I'm grateful for your time. Oh, one last thing before I go - if you will let me have the name and address of the man who has been demanding redemption of the stock Chisam sold him."

"Yes, I have it here. Earl was the name - William James Earl."

"I will need to speak to Mr Earl. If it turns out that he doesn't press his claim, that may be because he will have other things on his mind."

From the Whitehaven Cocoa and Coffee House Company in the town's market place, Forbes returned to Chisam's house in Victoria Road to see how Constable Lyttleton was progressing in his search of Chisam's papers. Constable Lyttleton had had little success in his search. He had not found it an unpleasant task, however, as the variety of the material he was sifting through was a source of continual interest, to the extent that he had had on occasion to remind himself of his original task. It was a variety which, now that he had a little more time to peruse it, caused Forbes to experience renewed misgivings about the case. Constable Lyttleton's most notable find had been a copy of the 'Communist Manifesto', which had convinced him that they were dealing with some sort of revolutionary. For Forbes, it was the fact that the 'Manifesto' shared the same shelf with copies of the Bible, the Koran, Plato's 'Republic', Machiavelli's 'The Prince', and

255

the 'Anglo-Saxon Chronicle', among others, that was the cause of his sense of misgiving. It was unusual for someone of Chisam's rank, someone relatively uneducated to have such eclecticism of interest. Stereotypes are easy to predict in their actions; but Chisam was no longer entirely understandable. This, together with the fact that, from the state of the house, Chisam's flight, if hastily arranged, had nevertheless been premeditated, increased Forbes' sense of uncertainty and irritation. There was nothing further to be learned there that would give a clue as to Chisam's whereabouts, and so Constable Lyttleton accompanied him back into the town when he left Victoria Road They returned to the Infirmary.

The Infirmary general ward where Wilson and the two constables were being treated was, if anything, even worse than on the previous day. Some of the more seriously injured had been removed to other wards or were undergoing surgery in the operating theatre, and there was an atmosphere of reduced constraint for those who were left. There was a large number of visitors in the ward, and Forbes was dismayed by conditions that were to his eyes, scarcely tolerable. Wilson in particular was desperate to be gone, and Forbes, his immediate problem temporarily forgotten, spent an hour or more in the business of formally taking Wilson and the less seriously injured constable into his charge. It was a good hour before he was able to complete the formalities, having to contend with the indifference and downright obstructive -ness of some of the hospital authorities, who clearly resented Forbes' intervention as an intrusion into their domain On the ward, Wilson and the constable, both now dressed, had returned for their belongings. Wilson in particular could still only walk with difficulty, but declared that he would crawl on his hands and knees if necessary, in order to get out of the place. The constable was in little better shape, and together they hobbled out of the ward. Before following, Forbes had walked over to the bed of the constable they were leaving behind to give him a few words of encouragement; but mercifully perhaps, the man was still asleep Forbes felt it was hard to leave him thus, but the man was still too ill to be sensible of such things, and Forbes did not disturb him.

When he turned to go, he found himself confronted by a woman who stood in his path and he was momentarily taken aback. She was perhaps in her mid forties and she was dressed; and although her face was strained with stress or exhaustion, her gaze was steady and unwavering. She spoke first, and came straight to the point.

"I am Mrs Robert Harrison. My husband is being treated here for injuries he received while he was being held in the custody of an officer from Scotland Yard. He was injured in the German bombardment yesterday. I believe you are the officer now responsible for the case."

"I am, yes. I am Superintendent Forbes, Scotland Yard. You may not know that Inspector Vernier, whose case this was, and whom I presume you were referring to, was killed in the bombardment yesterday."

"I do know that," she said grimly. "God forbid that I should ever rejoice at the death of any man, but I shall shed no tears for his passing. He almost destroyed my life and that of my husband, and it was evidently a matter of complete indifference to him what became of us. His behaviour was not only high handed, it was also completely unjustified. My husband has been treated like a criminal, and yet I understand that no charge has been brought against him. Is this true?"

Forbes was instinctively defensive in the face of such a challenge.

"I'm afraid it is true, yes. But in mitigation of Inspector Vernier, the case was an extremely serious one, and at the time, Robert Harrison was the principal suspect. In such circumstances, Inspector Vernier was justified in continuing to detain his main suspect. Unfortunately, in the disorder following the bombardment, and due to the fact that Inspector Vernier himself was killed, normal procedures have not yet been restored, and it is possible that some legal processes may have been, ah, abridged."

"I will not accept that as an excuse. Almost two further days have passed, and still my husband has been neither charged nor released ."

"Mrs Harrison, I understand fully why you are so angry, and I'm sorry if you've been caused any distress . . ."

"I doubt very much if you're in the least sorry, Superintendent. It's just another case to you, and I suppose I'm just another victim. Well, I assure you that I've not detained you simply in order to plead for your sympathy."

"Mrs Harrison, you may choose to disbelieve me if you wish, but I am genuinely sorry for what has happened. Your husband was detained because he was the main suspect at the time. It seems now, however, that we were deceived by the real culprit into thinking that your husband was the guilty party. I am now prepared to admit our error, with apologies."

She stared at him for a moment before replying.

"And that man is Edward Chisam." It was more of a statement than a question, a statement almost to herself as she took in the implications of what Forbes had just said. "Are you saying that Chisam deliberately implicated my husband in this?"

"Yes, it seems that he did. What do you know of Edward Chisam?"

"I know a good deal about him. But what I know which will interest you most, I can at least now tell you with a clear conscience." She smiled suddenly as she spoke these words, but there was no humour in her face: it was a bitter smile. "What fools we

257

women are to doubt our instincts. For a few honeyed words and histrionic protestations c
sincerity, how many poor fools of women throw over their God-given reason for som
man who is not worth the dirt under their feet if only they would have eyes to see it. An
the shame of it when your eyes are opened. Oh, it hurts; God, how it hurts. To think tha
I begged the man. Yes, I know a good deal about Edward Chisam. In particular, I kno
where he was on Sunday night, because I saw and spoke to him. But," she held up he
hand as she saw Forbes' start of interest, "not a word do I tell until I have my husban
back. I will make a bargain with you. I will tell you what I know if you will release m
husband immediately and without condition."

"I'm afraid there can be no bargain, Mrs Harrison. If you have information which i
material to a police investigation, it is your duty to tell it without conditions."

"Then you may arrest me and lock me up; but no word shall pass my lips until m
husband is released."

"That won't be necessary. I can only apologise that your husband was not release
earlier, and I release him now, without condition as you put it. I discharge him into you
care, or rather, the care of this Infirmary, for what that may be worth."

"Thank God." She closed her eyes, and all the energy seemed to drain out of her in tha
moment, as though the almost superhuman spirit which she had called upon to carry he
through the past several days had fled her body in the instant when its task was finishe
leaving her like an empty shell in the moment of victory. She leaned wearily against th
bed for support for a moment. She took a few seconds to recover herself before turnin
again to look at Forbes.

"Then, Superintendent Forbes, I will tell you that I saw and spoke with Edwar
Chisam on Carlisle station on Sunday night. I was in great distress, my husband havin
been arrested and taken to Whitehaven by your Inspector Vernier, who refused to allo
me to go any further than the station. I had not seen Chisam for some time, and
suppose he was as surprised to see me as I was to see him; but despite my distress h
refused to help me. I begged him to help, and he refused. The humiliation of it rankl
even now that I should have allowed myself to be treated thus by one such as he; but
was *in extremis*, and we do foolish things when we are weak.

"He told me two things which I could not understand at the time, and so I discount
them and they slipped from my mind. All I could grasp was that he had refused n
appeal for help, and that there was no-one I could turn to. What he said sounded li
mere excuses and rambling at the time, but I understand now what he meant. He sa
that the arrest of my husband had been a mistake, an error by the authorities, and that
would be released as soon as the authorities realised it was a mistake. At the time, I cou

258

not imagine how he could know such a thing, and in my naivety, I did not believe that the authorities would make such a mistake. I dismissed what he said as wild talk, or an attempt to comfort me which could have no foundation in reality, even though the second thing he told me was that he could not stay and help me because he was fleeing for his life. He did not explain what he meant by that. He merely repeated, as far as I remember, that if he was caught, his life would be forfeit, and that it was imperative that he should catch a train which was departing shortly. Again, I dismissed this as excuses and meaningless rambling, and I did not connect the two statements, even though, with hindsight, the connection is only too clear.

"And so he left me. I remember that I called after him as he hurried off down the platform. That was the worst moment. The fear of such humiliation haunts every woman, and in my case it was worse than most because of what had happened to my husband. I suppose he may have taken a certain pleasure in a rather sordid little triumph over me after . . . well." She suddenly felt it wise to say no more, and lapsed into silence. The unwitting hint of further embarrassment was not lost on Forbes, but he was no longer interested.

"Can you tell me what time this was?" he asked her.

"I'm afraid not. I had lost all sense of time. All I can say is that it was late, and it was some time after Inspector Vernier had departed for Whitehaven with my husband."

"And Chisam had arrived in the station by train?"

"I assumed so. I didn't see him until he was almost past me. It was the platform for trains to Whitehaven."

It was a strange irony indeed, Forbes reflected, that Vernier and Chisam must have passed each other somewhere along the railway line between Whitehaven and Carlisle. For a few seconds, Vernier would have been within a matter of feet from his quarry, and yet they might as well have been at opposite ends of the country.

When he looked at her again, Mrs Harrison seemed to have lost the air of forlornness which she had had when he first perceived her. She had regained her natural serenity.

"Mrs Harrison, I am indeed most grateful to you for what you have told me. I hope also that you will accept my sincere regrets for the distress you have been caused in this matter."

She stood aside to let him pass, but called to him as he walked away.

"Superintendent Forbes."

He faced her again.

"There is one thing you can do for me. I should like Chisam to know that it was me."

He waited for her to explain, even though he guessed what she meant.

259

"If what I have told you leads you to catch Edward Chisam, I should like him to kno' that it was I who gave you the information. That would please me very greatly."

Forbes said nothing, but nodded slowly before he turned to go.

An hour or so later, Forbes was ready to depart. From the police station, he had ser telegrams to London, and also to the police in Carlisle, advising of his intende movements and the current situation of the case. He had made arrangements f(Vernier's body to be moved to London. Wilson and the constable would accompany hin at least as far as Carlisle. He wasn't sure what Maxwell would do, and he wasn particularly interested. He had seen little of Maxwell that day - Maxwell had apparentl spent most of the day assessing the damage to the port and gathering what informatio he could about the details of the attack. When he turned up at the police station short before Forbes was due to depart, evidently intending to come with them, Forbes fe vaguely irritated, but there was nothing much he could do.

Superintendent Hogg appeared briefly to see them off - Forbes had acquired a goc deal of respect for Hogg during the short time he had been in Whitehaven. Hogg w; having to cope with a disaster, and Forbes had been impressed by his competence in th face of it.

"I hope you'll be able to let me know if you run your man to earth," Hogg had sai "As you can see, I have a very personal interest in the matter."

The railway line north of Whitehaven was still blocked, so they travelled by motor c; to Workington, from where they took the train. At Carlisle, preparations for their arriv were already under way. All the station booking clerks, including those who were c duty, had been assembled at the station by the time Forbes arrived. It was at Carlisle th the pursuit began in earnest.

Two or three of the booking clerks seemed to know Chisam by sight when they wei shown a photograph of him - he was evidently a fairly frequent visitor to Carlisl However, it was the clerk who had been on duty on the Sunday evening, two da previously, who would have the information Forbes was looking for. It was not, howeve what he was expecting.

"Southampton? Are you sure?"

"I clearly remember this gentleman buying a ticket for Southampton, sir. It w because it was so late, and there weren't many people about at that hour."

"Can you remember what time this was?"

"It would have been about half past ten, sir. The gentleman only bought the ticket aft he had found out what trains were running."

"And was there a train?"

"Yes, sir - the overnight express from Glasgow stops at Carlisle at ten to eleven on a Sunday evening. On a weekday, it comes through at eleven o'clock."

"What time does it reach Southampton?"

"Well, this is a sleeper service, so although it reaches Southampton about five in the morning, the coaches are left on a siding for a couple of hours, before being moved into Southampton station for seven thirty. That's the normal schedule; but that's not what happened to that particular train on Sunday night."

"Please explain."

"On the Sunday night - well, it would have been early hours of Monday morning, about one o'clock, there was a derailment just south of Warrington which blocked the line. A northbound coal train came off the rails, and I understand that quite a number of wagons overturned, and the line was closed in both directions. In fact it's still closed - services to London are being re-routed through Settle and Leeds to the main east coast line at Doncaster. However, that particular train was already past Preston when the derailment happened, so it was stopped at Warrington. We've heard that the people on the train were put up for the night at a local hotel, but what arrangements have been made since, I don't know."

Forbes was reflective for a moment before asking: "Let me see a map."

The station master produced a railway map and spread it out on the table.

"The derailment happened here, sir, just a few miles south of Warrington. As Elliot has just said, the passengers on the express were put up for the night in Warrington. On Monday, yesterday, the train was taken to Liverpool, and from there, through the Mersey tunnel and via Birkenhead and Chester to Crewe, where it re-joined the main line south. Most of the passengers travelled with it, although I understand a few made their own alternative arrangements. The train would have reached Southampton in the early afternoon on Monday. I can telegraph to Southampton to find the exact time it arrived."

"The general alert for Chisam was sent out to all the ports yesterday morning, so there should have been a police watch at Southampton docks by then." This was from Maxwell, who had joined them uninvited.

Forbes didn't answer. He was staring intently at the map.

"This doesn't make sense," he said, more to himself than to the others. "Even without the derailment, it doesn't make sense. But with the derailment - it doesn't make any sense at all. I don't think he went to Southampton, or even intended to go there. That's where he went." He reached forward and tapped the map. "He went to Liverpool."

"That's a bold guess," observed Maxwell.

261

"It's a bold guess, yes, but I'm pretty sure I'm right. Use your eyes, man, and look the map. The train actually went through Liverpool. Why would he even think of goin to Southampton when he was already in Liverpool. I think Southampton was a blind, an he never intended to go there. He went to Liverpool."

Maxwell was still sceptical. "You don't have any specific evidence that he went Liverpool," he objected.

"No, but that's where I shall be going. I shall telegraph the police in Southampton, an in Warrington. I shall send two of my men to Southampton as a precaution, just in ca he did go there; but I now think that's highly unlikely." He looked at Maxwell. "Do this mean that you will be going to Southampton?"

Maxwell pulled a wry face, and then shook his head.

"No. Liverpool it is."

26

Forbes and Maxwell arrived in Liverpool on Wednesday morning 18th August. Forbes' first business on arrival was to make himself known to the Liverpool police and the port authorities. From the latter he received a list of all the vessels that were due in to, and out of, the port that week, and all the vessels currently berthed at the port. Styles, the port authority's chief officer, was taken into Forbes' confidence about the purpose of their visit, but was pessimistic about their chances.

"Can I take it," Styles asked "that you're looking to trace this man on board a vessel that has already sailed?"

Forbes admitted that he was.

"The train we believe Chisam travelled on arrived in Liverpool on Monday morning. We have every reason to believe that he knew he was being pursued, and would therefore seek to make his escape at the earliest opportunity. I would be surprised if he is still in Liverpool, although I'm afraid we must conduct searches of all departing vessels until his whereabouts are known."

"But presumably you are only really interested in certain kinds of vessel. You wouldn't, I suppose, expect him to have boarded a coaster, or one of the ferries to Ireland. If he was fleeing the country, he would have boarded either a transatlantic liner or a merchantman bound for a foreign port. That should narrow it down a bit. Nine merchantmen have left here since Monday, only two of them for foreign ports - one for Lisbon, and one for Buenos Aires. But most merchantmen don't carry wireless, so they will be quite out of reach."

"How would he be able to find out a merchantman's destination, other than by hanging around the quaysides asking questions?"

"I'm afraid that's what he would have to do, for a merchantman."

"So we should be able to establish if he went that way. People will remember a suspicious character asking questions of that sort."

Styles was doubtful. "You get all kinds along the harbour front who might be in a similar way - unemployed seamen looking for a ship; the poorer class of would-be emigrant; drifters and hoboes, stowaways - all sorts. Your man wouldn't stand out in the way you're thinking. Mind you," he said after a moment's thought, "it was reported by one of the trading companies that a man had been found trespassing in one of the warehouses on Monday morning. It sticks in my mind because the warehouse is used for storage of sensitive goods, by which I mean, you will understand, ah, war material which is shipped from the United States aboard the transatlantic liners. You will

263

understand without my explaining further why it would be most undesirable f
knowledge of this trade to get into the public domain."

"Indeed not. But are you saying that you attach particular significance to this inciden
You must have problems with tramps and vagrants here, as anywhere else."

"No, this man was not a tramp. The official from the trading company was quite su
on that point. The man was well dressed, as if he were a gentleman - not the sort y
would expect to find sneaking about like that. The official thought that he might ha
been a German spy, given that a consignment of, er, sensitive goods, had just be
unloaded from the 'Arabic', which had docked the previous evening from New York."

"Has this been reported to the Liverpool police?"

"The Liverpool police are dealing with the matter. They've mounted guards on t
relevant warehouses, and on the landing stages, but the man hasn't been sighted again.'

Forbes was apprehensive about the risk of being saddled with other jobs which wou
divert him from his purpose. The words of the Chief Superintendent were still painfu
clear in his memory. If the Liverpool police were dealing with this matter, then he w
happy to leave it with them. A short interview with the company official should
enough to establish whether it was of any interest to him.

"The 'Arabic' is a White Star liner, I presume?"

"That's right. Not a liner of the first rank, but a regular on the New York run. You
see her when you go down to the Pierhead. She's due to sail tonight."

"And other liners that have sailed since Sunday night?"

"Only the Cunard ship 'Orduña', on Monday night."

"On Monday night." Forbes was reflective for a moment. "Monday night. If I was
Chisam's position, I would have made it my business to be on that ship. It would be
far the best, as well as the earliest opportunity, would you agree?"

"I would, sir. But I should also tell you that the ship was checked by the police befo
she sailed. They were as sure as they could be that the man they were looking for was n
among the First or Second Class passengers."

"I shall check with Cunard, and get a wireless message off to the ship. What about t
Third Class passengers?"

"They were checked, but not as thoroughly as the First and Second Class. But i
unlikely that your man Chisam, whether or not he was the same man as this other, wou
have gone steerage class."

"Why not?"

"Well, almost all steerage passengers are emigrants, and they are all held in t
quarantine station in New York for three weeks before they are allowed properly to en

264

the country. Time enough to identify not only those carrying infectious diseases, but also those with a criminal past. If you telegraph the New York authorities, he will not escape them if he is among the steerage passengers. But I imagine he will have thought of that. It would be too great a risk."

"I trust you are right. It would close off one line of inquiry very neatly."

"And the 'Arabic'?"

"I shall supervise the checking of the 'Arabic' myself. He shall not escape on that ship."

The 'Arabic' sailed half an hour after sunset. The city was already a landscape of silhouettes and shadows punctured by the first lights of evening, the Mersey a great streak of pale luminosity flanked by the angular urban skylines of Liverpool and Birkenhead, facing each other across the wide water like armies drawn up in battle array on some ancient field of combat. So it must have looked from the ship. Forbes, standing on the quayside watching as the 'Arabic' swung slowly out into the stream, was oblivious to the splendour of the scene. The 'Arabic' seemed to be sailing away with the last of his hopes of finding Edward Chisam. With the assistance of the Liverpool police, the ship had been searched from top to bottom, and every passenger and crew member checked, a proceeding that had caused much inconvenience and not a little irritation on the part of both the passengers, and the representatives of the White Star Line, who had agreed to the search. Forbes had been conscious of hostile glances as he left the ship, having found nothing, but having used up much of the store of goodwill from people already inconvenienced by the restrictions of wartime travel, and facing a voyage through hostile waters.

He ground his heel into the worn stone of the quayside. To have come so close, only to find that his quarry had slipped through the net. Shortly before the 'Arabic' had sailed, he had received a reply by wireless to the message he had sent to the 'Orduña'. The First and Second Class passengers had been checked again, and there was no-one who answered to Edward Chisam's description among them. The steerage passengers would be checked at New York, assuming he could secure the cooperation of the American authorities. The rather snooty isolationism of much of American officialdom had been considerably less in evidence since the sinking of the 'Lusitania'; but Forbes was prepared to go to New York himself if necessary to check the steerage passengers. He had never travelled abroad, and the prospect of such a voyage would previously have seemed exotic, exciting, even daunting: now, in the urgency of the chase, it was no more to be thought of than a journey to a remote part of the north of England, and an obscure seaport in Cumberland he had never heard of before.

There was now no doubt left that Chisam had come to Liverpool. Forbes had forgotten about the incident of the intruder in the warehouse until later in the day, and he had called at the warehouse office only just before the official concerned was due to leave for home. The man had stabbed with his finger at the photograph of Chisam that Forbes had shown him, as if to confirm that this was a moment of retribution for the humiliation he had suffered on the Pierhead when Chisam had given him the slip.

"That's the bastard," he had exclaimed with grim emphasis. "That's him!"

Lieutenant-Commander Maxwell had his little triumph in the end. Maxwell's position since he had accompanied Forbes to Liverpool had seemed increasingly unenviable. His avowed intention of being in on whatever was going on, rather than waiting in London for the police to decide his fate, now looked increasingly pointless, as he had been able to contribute little or nothing to Forbes' investigation. He was, in the end, a mere bystander after all. But during the course of that day, Maxwell's mood gradually changed, if only because, for much of the day, he had time on his hands to reflect on the situation. Maxwell was now certain that the matter would be resolved in Liverpool, whether they caught Chisam or not. If Chisam were not caught, then that would, in the first instance, be a failure by Forbes and the police; and apart from any personal satisfaction he might derive from that, Maxwell could justifiably claim that if the police had failed in what was essentially a police matter (and had not Forbes himself made a point of emphasising that?) then he could hardly be expected to do any better. However, he had followed the progress of Forbes' investigations during the day, and was as aware as Forbes of the nature of the problems the policeman faced. Gradually, Maxwell overcame his sense of detachment from the problem, and he set himself to considering the business seriously once more. The solution, when he saw it, was like a flash of inspiration, and for a time left him elated. It was unremarkable and obvious, as the truth often is once it understood; but in the moment of revelation it was pure brilliance, and he was buoyed up by conceit at his own perspicacity. So much was this so, that, given everything that had gone before, his first and primary consideration was that this was his idea. If it led to the apprehension of Chisam, then Maxwell wanted the credit for it - he would not simply hand the idea over to Forbes and allow Forbes to claim it as his own. If he could hand Forbes a *fait accompli* which proved to be the solution to the problem, then not only would he thereby save his own skin, but to have scored over Forbes would be more than adequate compensation for the present unsatisfactory state of affairs. But first, he must have something positive, something that would transform the idea into the *fait accompli*

After a little reflection, he came to a decision and proceeded to the nearest telegraph office.

It wasn't until the following morning that Maxwell received any reply to his enquiries. The reply was not as much as he had hoped for, not proof, not yet a *fait accompli*; but it was enough to satisfy his vanity. When he located Forbes, he found the Superintendent deeply pessimistic over the lack of progress. But if Maxwell expected Forbes to be churlish and uncharitable because the solution had occurred to Maxwell and not to him, he was disappointed. With an almost wolfish hunger, Forbes seized on the idea as soon as Maxwell explained it to him. Maxwell could not get through it fast enough.

"You have to remember," Maxwell explained, "that when Chisam was in Liverpool on Monday, the two ships would have both been alongside together, up until Monday night, when the 'Orduña' sailed. We assume also that the liklihood of his being apprehended at sea by means of wireless had also occurred to him. The 'Orduña' was due to sail on Monday night, and the 'Arabic' on Wednesday night. Perhaps there was some way he could throw the pursuit off the scent by making use of both ships. The opportunity to do this arose from the fact that both ships would call at Queenstown before proceeding to New York. What could be simpler? Travel as far as Queenstown on the 'Orduña', jump ship, and wait for the 'Arabic' to arrive two days later - although in fact the 'Orduña' was delayed at sea because of a submarine warning, and didn't reach Queenstown until the Wednesday morning. But the plan was basically sound. Moreover, I suspect that he travelled steerage class on the 'Orduña' as far as Queenstown, which is why he went undetected. Look at this!"

He flourished a telegram. Forbes took it and scanned it impatiently. As he did so, his brows furrowed in anger, and at last he pointed accusingly at the telegram.

"You thought of this last night. Here - reply to your telegram of 16.30 hours 18th August - you had this idea last night, and yet you wait until now to tell me of it."

"But it confirms what I just said. This is from the Queenstown harbour office. A male steerage passenger of about Chisam's age and description left the 'Orduña' on the Queenstown tender. Without this, it would have been mere speculation, which, coming from me, you might not have taken too kindly to. This is not so easily dismissed."

Forbes admitted that that was so, although he did not say that the other's assumption of mistrust was not entirely justified. Forbes had nothing in particular against Maxwell, other than a general desire that he should keep out of his way. Nor was he particularly put out by the fact that it was Maxwell who had apparently hit on the solution to the problem. They would get little enough praise as it was for having come so near to failure.

"What about the 'Arabic'?" he asked.

But Maxwell had no more information to give. It was by no means yet a *fait accompli* as Forbes was about to discover.

The White Star Line offices had no more information to give him either. They could not tell him about passengers embarking at Queenstown unless a prior booking had been made. Nor could they say exactly when the 'Arabic' would arrive and depart. The best they could give was an estimate that the ship would arrive at Queenstown between nine and ten that morning, and would stay for about an hour and a half while the Queenstown tender came alongside. It was already ten o'clock. Would White Star assist him by telegraphing the 'Arabic' in order to try and identify the man Chisam and detain him should he try to board the ship?

The answer, not surprisingly, was 'no'. The White Star officials had finally had enough of Superintendent Forbes. The delays and inconvenience caused by the search of the 'Arabic' before she sailed from Liverpool had already tried a lot of frayed tempers and now Forbes met with solid resistance. If the ship was to be stopped again and further searches made, it would have to be on the authority of a much bigger cheese than a mere superintendent.

Seething, Forbes left the White Star offices and made his way to the main telegraph office, where he got off three telegrams in quick succession. The first was to the Queenstown harbour office, which had already proved to be so helpful to Maxwell. The second, which was the longest, was to the Cork police. The third, which was short and very terse, was to Scotland Yard, and concerned the Liverpool offices of the White Star Line. After a minute's thought, he got a fourth telegram away, this time to the master of the 'Arabic'. It was more than a possibility that White Star had already telegraphed the 'Arabic' on their own account; but there was no harm in his trying.

Maxwell's prediction that they would see the affair brought to its conclusion from Liverpool was therefore borne out. The replies, as they came in to the telegraph office, marked the unfolding of events which Forbes was now powerless to influence further. He was a spectator, reading the messages brought to him by the telegraph operator, and sometimes sending back a response. At ten twenty-five, there was a reply from the Queenstown harbour office, to say that the 'Arabic' had already anchored in the harbour and the Queenstown tender had been alongside since before ten. A few minutes later came the reply from the Cork police, to say that they were on their way to Queenstown. They had telegraphed ahead to Queenstown, and also to the 'Arabic'. No response from the 'Arabic'.

At eleven o'clock, the police from Cork arrived at Queenstown in a motor car with a badly overheated engine, just in time to see the Queenstown tender swinging away from the angular bulk of the 'Arabic', at anchor a mile out in the roads. At the same moment, a telegram was received at the Queenstown harbour office, and in Liverpool, where it was passed to the impatient Forbes. It was from the 'Arabic', stating that no-one of the name of Chisam was among the First or Second Class passengers, including those who had come aboard from the Queenstown tender. The master of the 'Arabic' regretted that under the circumstances, he could not delay his departure. Warnings had been received about enemy submarines, and both he and his passengers were anxious to clear the submarine infested southern Irish waters as soon as possible and get well out into the Atlantic and safety.

From the harbour at Queenstown, the police from Cork watched helplessly as smoke started to plume from the liner's tall funnel. She was starting to move - her anchor was already aweigh, and as they watched, her long profile shortened as her bows swung southward towards the sea. Muted by distance, the dull boom of her siren echoed back flatly from the low hills surrounding Cork Harbour. If any of those who watched had been superstitious, they would have seen the intervention of Fortune in such an escape; that if their quarry was indeed aboard the 'Arabic', Fortune, almost as an act of mercy, had reserved for him a fate with greater dignity than such a comic opera ending. As the momentous news of greater events filtered down to their world, the justice, even the compassion of it, seemed to have the resonance of a natural propriety, as inevitable as the laws of nature are to the physical world. Later, they would nod to each other sagely over such things, as if the awareness of the larger order was ever within their purview of life. As it was, they merely shrugged their shoulders. They had done their best: doubtless the unknown English policeman would pursue his enquiries through the usual channels. The matter was off their patch, and there was nothing more they could do.

When the Queenstown tender berthed shortly afterwards, it was the harbourmaster who asked the question of the pilot when he came ashore.

The pilot was philosophical. "Well, you know, I was in half a mind to mention it to you, seeing as how you asked the question before. It was only a smallish party I was taking out this time, so I was able to observe them each and every one, if you follow me. And it was because of you asking before, that I couldn't help noticing this feller. He was one of the Second Class passengers, travelling on his own, but well dressed, like a gentleman. It was the clothes that put me off at first, but if it wasn't for that, and the fact that he was clean shaven and generally presentable and all, he was the image, the very image, of the man who left the 'Orduña' as a steerage passenger yesterday. I'd swear it on the holy book, so I would. Now, have I said the wrong thing?"

But they were not looking at him. Far to the south, on the narrow line that marked the

269

distant entrance of Cork Harbour, and the sea, the 'Arabic' was barely more than a smudge of smoke.

27

For more than twenty-four hours, there had been a blessed relief from the ceaseless grinding of engines, from the smells, the noise, the cheek-by-jowl humiliation of steerage; from the sea itself and its pitiless vastness which, even in the darkest night was a presence in the darkness, a ghostly glitter of a half-imagined horizon, a menacing heave of black water streaked with luminescent foam seen momentarily in the night. For a space of time, the ship had been a universe. Its lonliness was distinct even from that of the sea, for it was unnatural and transitory, and from it, on its crowded lower decks, there was no refuge. It was a world of noise, of doors and hatches slamming, of boots on planking and steel decks, of voices raised against wind and sea, words half heard, of booming sirens and venting steam, of rattling fittings; and underlying all, the pulse of the engines that gave the ship life - the tremble of power that seemed to be part of life itself. Seven hundred souls were held thus in thrall in this steel cocktail of noise, their lives in suspense; no longer what they had left, but not yet what they were to become.

For all, or all but one, the voyage had barely begun. Most scarcely noticed Queenstown, a last glimpse of the land again - Ireland, a country of refugees. Some of them were on the tender that came out to the ship - peasant women in shawls and heavy, voluminous skirts, men in the battered black fustian of Irish countrymen. Most were steerage - yet more steerage; a few were hucksters who spent a brief and lucrative hour working the First Class cabin with Waterford Crystal, Irish lace, Belfast linen. To a stranger's eyes, Queenstown was an oddly familiar place that had a habit of being suddenly unfamiliar. The moles and quays were those of a big port - but where were the ships? A glimpse of masts and funnels, grey superstructures - but they were warships - destroyers. Only one funnel smoking - a merest glimpse. Further in there were fishing boats, a jungle of masts, dirty brown sails, seagulls. To the left, some much taller masts, and below them, the long, low hulls of ocean racing yachts: poverty and work, wealth and idleness.

A last look back and up at the high, rusty black sides of the ship, fixing its image in the mind - portholes surrounded by countless rusty rivet heads; the high blunt stem, the ship's name in white letters that were almost unreadable; a few loafers hanging over the rail in the Third Class area in the forward well deck - steerage passengers. It had been thirty-six hours of purgatory, every minute of which had been spent in suppressed desperation looking forward to this moment. And now that it was come, was there perhaps a suggestion of pride, of something achieved, a *coup de main*, a cleverness to chuckle over on quiet evenings in that almost unimaginable life to come, that had suddenly and inevitably become the future, a future that there had been no time to contemplate in the panic of escape? What was America, more than an exotic rumour, place whose sordidness had no more reality than that of the world through the lookin glass, and which might be laughed at as being just as childish? In the solidity of a fixe existence, it was safe to laugh, to marvel that such things could be, to belittle the exot because it was small and remote. Now, when it loomed with the apparent inevitability the dawn, there was no more laughter, only the business of escape. It was enough   have escaped, and yes, yes, there was pride in what had been achieved in those wear restless hours, and perhaps also something approaching affection for the rusty hulk o whose noisome lower decks the achievement had been won. It was just another ship, second rater or not even that, as far away from Blue Ribbands and glamour as a dra horse is from the Derby: but this was the ship that had made escape possible. It was i the past now, and the past was safe: there could be different feelings about the wor experience when it held no more terror, and time and distance made it safer. Half a mi of the soft greyness of Cork Harbour shifted the focus of the world: now the sea wa much closer, a long, smooth, almost imperceptible swell, silver-grey in the vastness of i expanse, green with depth overside; and the 'Orduña' was reduced to a smoking toy.

The release from the sea was onto a wide quay of worn stone studded with bollar and puddles of water, herring gulls perched boldly in the breeze, fat and watchful; ar Irish soil was underfoot. This was a seaside holiday - beyond the quays and t warehouses there was a seafront promenade with railings and park benches, ornament palm trees, a pavilion, a bandstand, and beyond, a solid frontage of respectable sm hotels and boarding houses. Morecambe? Scarborough? Grange? The Irish didn't call Queenstown. That was only because of Queen Victoria, and she was only there for a da or so it was said. Queenstown was British. Cove was Irish. Cove of Cork. And she w only there for a day. Or so it was said.

And now here was another day. Just one more day - twenty four hours before the ne ship.

"Just the one night is it? And will you be wanting it just for yourself? Well, now, i right at the top, up three flights of stairs I'm afraid, but it's all we have at the minute. I the holiday season, and you'll be lucky to get even this much at such short notice. never ceases to amaze me how many people just turn up and expect to get exactly wh they want at a moment's notice. And half of them behave like pigs, with habits you scarcely believe if you hadn't seen it yourself. The front door's locked at half past ni sharp every night, and if you're not in by then, well, it's hard luck. Breakfast is at h past seven, and you've to be out of the room by nine o'clock. No visitors allowed in t rooms, and especially no women. Payment is in advance."

272

She was about fifty, and hard; not, one felt, with a natural hardness, but with the hardness of cynicism, of experience, and of the necessity of being dependent on a clientele for whom she had nothing but contempt, and with whom the only relationship possible was one of distrust. And yet, none of it would be necessary if she had not set herself standards which, while they might be nothing more than those of conventional respectability, engendered a certain grudging admiration. Above all, she had the air of one who lived on the very margin of what was possible; one for whom a single day could mean the difference between being able to carry on, and insolvency.

The atmosphere of respectable poverty pervaded the streets of the place - something Italian or Spanish about the squalor behind bright facades: barefoot children in side alleys where lines of washing billowed like the ragged sails of a ragged ship, and piles of rubbish lay on a deck not scrubbed from one year's end to another; potato peelings and cooking smells, fat women in men's cloth caps, with loud voices and foul mouths, pools of bright sunshine reflecting on white walls, a black cat curled up on warm stone; and in another breath, a vision of heaven, of a long street climbing the hill to a great steeple, pinnacle upon pinnacle, white stone blazing in the light, celestial perfection standing over temporal darkness; and sweetly, sweetly on the uncertain air came the sound of bells, many, many bells, a joyous carillon voluptuous in their splendour, as un-English in their sharp tones as this tall steeple, where in England there would be an iron tower decked in coloured lights. What a strange place to build a cathedral, here, where the calls of whelk stallholders mingled with the mewing of seagulls, the squeals of children splashing in the shallows, Punch and Judy, donkey rides, the pungency of dried seaweed, and the smack of a toy spade on firm wet sand. But there was no blasphemy, only a bold innocence, a bright face on the world, a façade turned in the direction of America as surely as the tall steeple pointed straight to heaven.

"A single cabin, sir? Port or starboard? Starboard is recommended for New York - the weather is mostly from the south. Will you be requiring accommodation for servants, sir? You will be travelling alone. Very good, sir. If you will sign here."

Travelling alone . . . Was there something desperate, something manic in the lightheartedness of such aloneness, of slipping between the legs of Brobdingnagian giants who crushed with blind malice, knowing that the malice will not be blind forever? And beyond all this, was there not also excitement, the blissful excitement of irresponsibility, of rushing headlong towards a predetermined goal, the details of which were as exact as they were unknown? In another twenty-four hours . . . in another week . . . In New York, there was a great railway station, from where the lines stretched across the length and breadth of America, to Chicago, to Texas, to California; and in moments

273

when the mind was stronger than the senses, then stronger than the reality of this soft Irish evening with the sun touching the heights around Cork Harbour, releasing the brilliant green of distant meadows, setting the tall, fretted spire of St Colman's aglow with soft, pink fire, and turning the leaden water of the harbour into the most delicate translucent jade; stronger still was the yet unseen reality of Grand Central, a subterranean dimness filled with the smell of steam and iron and oil, the whiff of furnaces, a hissing presence of hot metal, a transitoriness, an immanence of distant places; of great plains filled with a narrow infinity of small towns; of mile wide rivers on which steamboats slipped slowly down to the steamy heat of New Orleans where Spanish trumpets sang, and dogs and alligators danced the Mardi Gras; of buttes and mesas immense in the clear air, where the ghost of Cochise walks with his warriors, and a skull whitens in Pleistocene stillness in the desert dust; of an occidental Canaan wherein flowed rivers of milk forever fresh, rivers of delectable wine, pools of clearest honey, and harems of dark-eyed houris in the houses of the faithful; of a wilderness of virgin mountains sheathed in eternal ice; of a gold rush of empty shacks, rootless as tumbleweed; of poor, broken San Fransisco; and at last, the sea: and in every place, there pulsed the same rhythm, from Grand Central to Golden Gate, of American wheels on American rails. What might not be possible when those wheels were audible in reality?

"Spare a penny, mister?" An urchin of about seven, no shoes, a dirty face, both hands firmly in the pockets of a pair of filthy shorts, as though the proposal had been more in the way of a speculation than a demand for money. In England, the urchins would try to sell you something, even if it was only a stone wrapped in a bit of paper. Perhaps here such a deception was too implausible. Would a penny make him go away, or bring a score more urchins demanding pennies? At least a stone in a bit of paper would only fool you once.

Grey stone walls and bay windows, dimly lit rooms, a steep staircase, an attic room with a steeply sloping ceiling, and sleep. But sleep would not come. The broad bed was softer than any bale of wool, and the bare room with its big brass washstand and wicker chair, and a dormer window looking out over the roofs of the town which fell away below down the hill to the water's edge, and over the wide waters of the harbour, was safer than any warehouse in the Liverpool docks; but there was no safety here, only a tossing and turning wakefulness, counting away the hours to the dawn, to the new day, to the ship. A loose slate beside the dormer window rattled with maddening irregularity in the gusting south-west wind - click, clack, click . . . clack: counting nothing, but measuring out in periods of silence the precious hours of darkness, filled only with idle, useless thought that drove out sleep. Was this the only way? Was there no other way? Must it be? If only

274

things had been different, if chance had ordained another way. What if . . .? If only. Click. Clack. At last, a 'clack' disturbed a doze, a memory of a dream lingered, and there was satisfaction that sleep had won, even if its domain was at an end. Dawn was come, and below the window the grey slate roofs were warmed with the new light, the hills were glowing with pink fire, the mirror-still water of the harbour was a great cold furnace of molten pink steel. It was overwhelming, enormous, and in another age perhaps, it would have been the object of reverence, of worship - it jarred with some remnant of an atavistic paganism that something so vast and terrible should be set at nought; that in each and every little Lilliput, what was given freely and with such munificence should be held scarcely worth a glance away from the business of pilfering a little money from one's neighbour.

Sleep returned in earnest now that there was no longer time for it, and was ended finally by all the noises of the new day. Downstairs at breakfast, the fellow guests eyed each other furtively while attempting to mind their own business. A commercial traveller sat alone in a coarse tweed suit which informed the world that he was not well off. Two businessmen sat and talked in low tones, quite oblivious to everything outside their own well-dressed prosperity, their conversation caught in snatches over the apologetic clinking of cutlery that intruded into the church-like quiet: " . . . initialling of contracts . . broad enough range of samples to impress . . . New York agent . . ." They also were waiting for the ship. A little man in rough working clothes and a weather-brown face sat by himself in another corner. He did not belong in such a place. If he had had long hair done in a pigtail, he would have been a gipsy; but when he was drawn into conversation by the landlady, it was revealed that he was a ship's engineer, and that he, too, was waiting for the ship. A last climb up three flights of stairs to the bare room with its wide bed and rattling slate. The wind had died with the dawn and the slate no longer rattled - another guest had had a sleepless night and its job was done.

To be alone in the aloneness of the world, waiting for the world's end on a quiet Irish morning, watching a bold sunbeam slip slyly through a disapproving frown of cloud and touch the grey water with a sparkle of diamonds. There was yellowness in the grey, a streak of bottom clay swirled up by the turning tide in a muddy deepness cloudy with menace. Water was movement; it was life in death, a beginning and an endlessness, the infinity of the world. The land was death in life, thin and still, as respectable as hododendron bushes in municipal gardens where clumsy bees worked the waxy meretricious blooms; it was an accounts ledger where each man was measured and graded and all things had their place, and those who did not fit, who would not fit, were discarded, displaced to the margin; it was a heedless casino, where the future was the next throw of the dice; it was the thief of Pompeii snatching a handful of sestertii at th end of the world and being baked thus into eternity; it was a travelling circus whe bright lights and tinsel covered over what lay beneath; it was an abattoir where generation was scattered like chaff, seedless, on the dead earth.

It was a place where a woman pushed a perambulator on a grey Thursday mornin; where a builder's cart and a doctor's carriage clopped and jingled down the esplanad where old men whose time was done stood and stared with all the time in the worl where urchins begged for pennies; where a man stood at the margin of life, waiting for ship, and in that moment, from land to sea, his vision reached beyond light from th darkness of a high place, gazing with sightless eyes over the black horizon of infini while his boots scraped on a stone quay, and he saw only a mirage of the Ambrose lig winking in the mist, while the universe wheeled in burning splendour; and a hundr thousand worlds burned out in the mud of a Flanders field; a submarine slipp southward unknowing; and old gamblers waited in spittled silence for the wheel turning, and the truth which will burn the fabrication of deceit to ash at the world ending.

A shout went up and the hills danced to a distant siren, boots shuffled, horses shift and fertilised the earth, cockroaches moved towards the shore, and a ghost crept in view, half seen in a dark memory, a scatter of lights against the Pierhead, shimmering the blackness of the river, suggesting by imagination rather than by sight, a power steel, a massive presence in the night, a menace of tall sides seamed with sightless riv heads, a pride of masts grasping the stars with winking red and green; and Fortu smiled as the wheel turned, and the ghost returned at last, a white toy on grey wate nearly still and slowly growing, wide stem creamy with movement, sliding into the roa serene with excitement, challenging the hills, tall masts and tall town, whaleback Haulbowline, and a roar of hawsers rolling softly over the water. A lap of an oily tide the sea's margin, stained faintly with the blood of an ancient pantomime: it was time quit old Europe where laughter tinkled merrily in bright salons and the four horsemen the apocalypse met in shield-jarring wrath on fields littered with accounts ledgers. Gu mewed and skittered, wide-eyed children waved with vacant sweetness and the la moment on European soil was surrendered into the embrace of the tender 'Americ Lass', broad and squat. Great trunks were jumbled lustily by grizzled sea dogs who sail the length and breadth of Cork Harbour in waistcoats and braces and touched the world gossip with a thrown cable. The world swayed gently in the morning breeze and t smooth water rippled like a great grey mackintosh and the tall street that led to the gat of heaven was marked only by a sombre steeple dancing a slow sarabande, and the la vas grey. Was this the sharp-etched wraith that had glittered in the night? This great black tun with rusty white top works, pumps spewing out the bilges like an incontinent cow - was this the ghost returned? Bonnets and skirts fluttered, smoke belched, and sea dogs roused out cables and a gangplank thumped on an iron coaming. Oh, but could here be sleep! Beyond the coaming, Ireland, all Europe, was a memory. The world was a long, dim passage, a door marked B59, and a little box the size of a cupboard, with a bunk, a chair, a washstand, a chamber pot, a big brass porthole, and a door that closed and locked, for this was Second Class. The porthole had brightly coloured chintz curtains tied neatly back, and beyond the distorting glass, far over the grey water, was a low, strange coast, never seen before. The bunk had a raised coaming to secure the sleeper in heavy weather, and its mattress was hard. Above, a plain deckhead was painted cream, and was supported by a heavy steel flange that projected from the bulkhead. The flange was studded with rivets, and the rivets, and the flange, and the bulkhead and deckhead, and the bunk and the little box with its washstand and chamber pot and big brass porthole trembled with life, with restless impatience, with the inanimate power that gave life, and made of steel and brass, oak and pine, coal and fire, a ship, a living ship. This little box, this cockpit of suspended hope was her womb, turbulent in placental stillness is a mother who moves her baby in her waking body and in her restless dreams, in her eating and breathing, and in the very pulse of her heart, and as she sings to her child, and he feels the power of her voice, and the force of her life. In the dewy stillness of early morning the sun caught the tops of the elder trees in glowing fire, and the soft grass and dark earth were hushed with the expectancy of a new beginning, and a thrush hopped and gnats danced in a sunbeam and the air was sweet with an inarticulate joy that shouted across forty summers from the dust of a secret garden. Somewhere a door slammed and boots thumped on the deck. Voices murmured briefly in the passage outside and then faded. In the flange overhead there were exactly twenty rivets, in two rows of ten, and in several the rust was staining through the cream paint. In the darkness, it was no longer possible to see the great vaulted roof, and even the hardiest spirit was stilled in the bitter cold, as a lone treble soared upwards in the lovliest of Christmas carols, an ethereal voice, ghostly with echo in mediaeval shadow, cold as the cold candles reflected in seried splendour in the tall, stained glass windows blank and dead with the blackness of a December night. Faintly, a muffled bumping noise was heard from somewhere for'ard, and the trembling gradually grew in power as the engines beat to a quicker pulse to give the ship headway. There was no sense of motion, but seen dimly through the distorting glass, the land moved. The sun cast a uniform orange glare, and at first it was hard to see anything at all, but as the light moderated, it could be seen streaming softly

277

through the high rectangular windows of the great hall, touching the heavy oak lecte
on its raised dais. The hall was full - the whole year was there, but there was alrea
something in the air that touched the familiar camaraderie of five years, for this was t
harbinger of the parting of the ways, the sorting of those who would succeed from tho
who would not, and already a little distance had separated one from the other as each w
isolated by the oppressiveness of the future. The hall stilled as the headmaster took h
place at the lectern and began to speak, and one by one the names were read out. But h
words were indistinct and the names were blurred by long years of memory as famili
faces, frozen in childhood, became players in a thousand plays as a life turned and ran
course and the future was darkened in a brightly sunlit room. There was no money, th
said. Not enough money. "It's marvellous that you've got the scholarship, but there j
isn't the money to send you to university. There just isn't the money." Isn't the mon
The money. Money. Money. Ledgers thumped on tall lecterns and dingy offices bustl
with people who were there and were not, and who whispered in disapproving voic
From the dusty hollow, the lane ran between hedgerows wet with the unkempt lushn
of early June, prickly with coppiced hawthorn through a rough meadow to a high pl
warm in the sun where a skylark sang to still the shimmering air and flyblown co
drooled with curiosity and breathed a sweetness of grass and milk and countl
butterflies caressed the lazy air in terpsichorean delight and a distant steeple bell w
faint in a sleepy afternoon and all were with God save one, and there in a steep vall
guarded by dark familiar hills, beneath a long wood echoing with a stillness of primro
and the rustling leaves of all the autumns of childhood was the roof beneath which s
lay and shielded her days, was the house whose air she breathed, which heard her voi
was the bed that held the warmth of her body and would not hold his, for that half m
was an eternity in which every leaf and every blade of grass was cold and dead and
buds bursting with the green of spring and the red fruit shining with the urgency of s
and the pollen in the still air taunting with the scent of smooth skin and round flesh, s
cheeks and soft hair, and the wet sap which oozed with life and all the fruitfulness of
earth mocked his barrenness with its joyful plenty and the long lane was empty save
dusty footprints and the trees were wrathful in the anger of the wind and spirits fled
spindling in a storm that roared across their nakedness and froze the fruitful seed in
wet earth and a sift of autumn ebbed and flowed like the sea grinding the night in
mill of time and the leaves of a ledger rustled with quiet satisfaction and blood pulsed
with shame as ravens cawed and seagulls mewed and a spade shifted the spoil from
open grave and an empty house echoed with mocking laughter and the eyes of the ch
in the stillness of the soul were wet from savage weeping and he cried out for forgiven

278

from the pity of remorse and no answer was given but the shaking of a thousand bones in the terror of eternity and black rain ran off black hills and filled the pools of life with salt tears: and the voice of life called from the garden and the garden was empty and the voice called again and the dusty lane was empty and again the voice called and then, oh, then she was there and she ran from him and they ran to the high place and her dress was green with the green of life and he caught her and her arms were soft and she laughed in his face and her mouth was wet with joy and her softness taunted him and the sweet pollen of her skin and the scent of her and in the heat of her enveloping she was mother and daughter and lover and goddess, Stella, oh, Stella was a child in his arms and her womanhood was the Earth that held him as the earth holds a grave; she was cold and still as the shadow that took away the sun and turned greenness all to dust and turned love to ice, to hate, to shame, to death as Harrison leered his triumph in thrusting maleness and in all the sacred chalices of love were filled the sewage of his greed and love was a stinking corpse that rolled and bounced as the world rocked and crashed and Harrison reached out a taloned claw to tear out his eyes and he knew in his terror that he would be blind but the world rolled and roared and as he looked up he saw the porthole covered in foam and the bunk he lay on was now vertical as the ship lay on her beam ends and the sea found the torpedo's mortal wound and the sea burst through the fragile glass and filled the little cockpit of his dreams with a savage cold that choked and froze and shocked all his dreams into oblivion and blinded his eyes with a blinding light and filled his ears with roaring pressure as the ship plunged deeper and his mouth was filled with salt water and vomit and his lungs were an agony of fire and his limbs were numbed and useless in the bitter cold and great catherine wheels of pain seared his eyes and brain, yet still he was conscious and thought to live, and when his flailing hand found the shattered porthole he grasped the jagged glass with bleeding hands and fought and kicked to batter a way through; but his strength was almost finished and the implacable sea bit by bit squeezed the breath from his body and began to fill his eyes with a colder blindness and cover his mind with darkness as he drifted up towards the light.

POSTSCRIPT

The White Star liner 'Arabic' was torpedoed and sunk by the submarine U24 off the Fastnet Rock, Co. Cork, on 19th August 1915. Of the 429 passengers and crew, 42 were known to have died when the ship went down.